On the Pleasure Planet

Cyrille was a world of illusions, and no one knew that better than Juille. For she herself was an illusion—her role of sensation-seeking tourist masking her identity as the warrior Princess of Ericon, heir to the throne of the Empire.

And Egide, the handsome, lighthearted, shallow man who had sought her out on Cyrille . . . was he what he seemed, or an illusion as well?

Was he courting her as a lover—or stalking her, waiting for the perfect moment for the kill?

Judgment Night

C. L. Moore

A Dell Book

Published by
Dell Publishing Co., Inc.
1 Dag Hammarskjold Plaza
New York, New York 10017

ISBN: 0-440-14442-6

Printed in the United States of America
Reprinted by arrangement with the author
First Dell printing—August 1979

Contents

Judgment Night

Judgment Night

Here in the flickering darkness of the temple, a questioner stood silent before the Ancients, waiting an answer he knew he could not trust.

Outside were the soft green hills and the misty skies of Ericon, but not even a breath of that sweet rainy air blew through the portals of the House of the Ancients. Nothing temporal ever touched them now. They were beyond all time and change. They had lived here since the first silver ships came swarming through the Galaxy; they would never die.

From this world of Ericon the pulse of empire beat out through interstellar space, tides waxing and ebbing and breaking in distant thunder upon the shores of the planets. For the race that held Ericon held the Galaxy.

Kings and emperors beyond counting had stood as this questioner stood now, silent before the Ancients in their star-shot dark. And the questioners were always answered—but only the Ancients knew if the answer meant its hearer's doom.

For the Ancients were stern in their own strange code. No human minds could fathom it. No human ever knew if his race had met their rigid tests and passed them, or if the oracle he received was a mercy-blow that led by the quickest road to destruction.

Voiceless, unseen behind their high altar, the Ancients answered a question now. And small in the tremendous shaking darkness of the temple, he who had come to satisfy a doubt stood listening.

"Let them fight," the unspeaking oracle said. "Be patient a little longer. Your hour is almost here. They must have their chance in the final conflict that is nearly upon them now—but you know how blind they are. Be patient. Be silent. Watch all they say and do, but keep your secret—"

The hundred emperors of Ericon looked down gravely out of their hundred pasts upon Juille, striding with a ring of spurs through the colored twilight of their sanctum.

"If I were a man," said Juille, not turning her head, "maybe you'd listen to me."

No answer.

"You used to want a son," reminded Juille, and heard her own voice echo and re-echo high up among the arches where sunlight came pouring through plastics the color of jewels.

"I know, I know," the old emperor said from the platform behind her. "When I was your age, I was a fool, too."

Juille flashed him a sudden grin over her shoulder. Once in a while even now, she thought, you could catch a glimpse of the great and terrible man her father had once been.

Out of their crystal-walled niches his predecessors and hers looked down as she strode past them. Here were men who had conquered the Galaxy world by reluctant world, great warriors who had led their armies like devouring flame over alien planets and alien seas and the passionless seas of space. Here were emperors who knew the dangerous ways of peace and politics, who had watched civilization mount tier upon shining tier throughout the Galaxy.

She turned at the end and came back slowly along

the rows of later rulers, to whom peace and the Galaxy and a rich heritage of luxury had been an old story. Pride of race was strong upon all these faces. People on outworld planets had worshiped them as gods. All of them had been godlike in the scope of their tremendous powers, and the knowledge of it was vivid upon their faces. Not many men have looked up by night with a whole planet for a throne, to watch the stars that are their empire parading in slow review across the heavens. Such knowledge would give even a weak face an appalling pride and dignity, and none of the emperors of Ericon had been weak. Men like that would not live very long upon the throne of the Galaxy of Lyonese.

The last three faces in the row had known humiliation almost as vast in its scope as the great scope of their pride. For now there were rebellious stars in the nightly array across the sky. And that fierce trouble showed in the eyes and the grimly lined faces of the emperors who had been defied.

The last portrait of all was the portrait of Juille's father.

She stood in silence, looking up at the young emperor in the niche, and the old emperor, arms folded on the platform rail, leaned and looked down across a gulf of many years and much hard-won experience, into the face of a stranger.

"Yes," the emperor said gravely, "I was a fool too, then."

"It was a fool's work to let them live," Juille told him hotly. "You were a great warrior in those days, father. Maybe the greatest the Galaxy ever had. I wish I'd known you then. But you weren't great enough. It takes a great man to be ruthless."

The emperor looked at her under the shadow of his brows. "I had a hard problem then," he said, "—the same problm you're facing now. If I'd chosen the solution you're choosing, you probably wouldn't be here today. As a matter of fact, you might be sitting in a cave somewhere, gnawing a half-cooked bone."

Juille gave him a bright violet glare. "I'd have wiped them out," she declared furiously, "if it meant the end of the empire. I'd have killed every creature with a drop of H'vani blood, and razed every building on every world they had, and sown the rocks with radium! I'd have left their whole dead system hanging in the sky as a warning for all time to come. I'll do it yet—by the Hundred Emperors, I will!"

"The Ancients permitting, maybe you will, child." The old emperor stared down into his own young face in the niche. "And maybe you won't. The time may come when you're old enough to realize what warfare on that scale would mean, even to the victors. And there'd be no victors after a fight like that."

"But father, we'll have to fight. Any day—any hour—"

"Not yet awhile, I think. The balance is still too even. They have the outer fringes with all their resources, but we . . . well, we have Ericon and that counts for a lot. More than the men and machines we have. More than all the loyal worlds. Nobody knows how many dynasties there were before ours, but everyone knows that the race on Ericon rules the Galaxy."

"As long as they hold Ericon. But sooner or later the balance is going to tip and they'll attack us. We'll have to fight."

"We'll have to compromise."

"We could cut our throats and be done with it."

"That's what I'm trying to prevent. How much of civilization do you think would survive any such holocaust as that? It would mean our ruin even if we won. Come up here, child."

Juille gave him a searching, sidewise glance and then turned slowly, hooking her thumbs into her sword belt, and mounted the shallow steps to the dais. Here in orderly array were the worlds of her father's empire, stretching in a long row left and right along the platform. She watched a little sulkily as the emperor laid a possessive hand upon the great green globe of Ericon in the center of the row and set it whirling beneath his fingers. The jewels that marked its cities flashed and blurred.

"This is the empire, Juille," he said. "This one world. And the empire means a great deal more than—well, a row of conquered planets. It means mercy and justice and peace." He shook his head unhappily. "I can't administer all that any more to every world in the Galaxy. But I won't throw the loyal worlds after the ones we've lost if any word of mine can prevent it." He let his hand fall from the spinning globe. Its turning slowed, and the jeweled cities flashed and faded and twinkled over the curved surface. "After all," the old man said, "isn't peace as we've known it worth—"

"No," said Juille flatly. Her father looked at her in heavy silence. "I can do *that* to Ericon," she told him, and with a slap of her hand set the big globe spinning again, until all the glittering cities blurred upon its sides. "As long as I can, the empire is ours. I won't share it with those hairy savages!"

The emperor was silent, looking at her from under his brows.

After a slightly uncomfortable pause, the girl turned away.

"I'm leaving," she said briefly.

"Where?"

"Off-world."

"Juille—"

"Nothing rash, father, I promise. I'll be back in time for the council. And I'll have a majority vote, too. You'll see the worlds agree with me." Her voice softened. "We've got to fight, father. Everyone says so but you. Nothing anyone can do will prevent it now."

Looking down, her father saw on the girl's face a look he knew very well—the terrible pride of a human who has tasted the attributes of divinity, who rules the turning worlds and the very stars in their courses. He knew she would not relent. He knew she could not. There were dark days ahead that he could not alter.

And he wondered with sudden self-doubt if after all, in her frightening certainty, she might be right.

Juille strode down the hallway that led to her living quarters, her spurs ringing with faint rhythmic music and the scabbard of her fire sword slapping against her thigh.

There had been many tremendous changes in the Lyonese culture even in her own lifetime, but perhaps none greater than the one which made it possible for her to take the part a son might have taken, had the emperor produced a son. Women for the past several generations had been turning more and more to men's professions, but Juille did not think of herself as filling a prince's shoes, playing a substitute role because no man of the proper heritage was available. In her the cool, unswerving principles of the amazon had fallen upon fertile ground, and she knew herself better fitted and better trained for the part she played than any man was likely to be.

Juille had earned her military dress as a man might have earned it, through lifelong training in warfare. To her mind, indeed, a woman was much more suited to uniform than a man, so easily can she throw off all hampering civilian ideas once she gives her full loyalty to a cause. She can discard virtues as well as vices and live faithfully by a new set of laws in which ruthless devotion to duty leads all the rest.

For those women who still clung to the old standards, Juille felt a sort of tolerant contempt. But they made her uneasy, too. They lived their own lives, full of subtle nuances she had never let herself recognize until lately. Particularly, their relationship with men. More and more often of late, she had been wondering about certain aspects of life that her training had made her miss. The sureness and the subtlety with which other women behaved in matters not associated with war or politics both annoyed and fascinated Juille. She was, after all, a woman, and the uniform can be discarded as well as donned. Whether the state of mind can be discarded, too—what lay beneath that—was a matter that had been goading her for a long while. And now it had goaded her to action.

In her own rooms she gave an abstracted glance to the several women who hurried forward at her entrance, said briefly, "Out. And send me Helia," and then leaned to the mirror and stood there peering with solemn intentness at her own face under the shining helmet. It was a sexless face, arrogant and intolerant, handsome as her fluted helmet was handsome, with the same delicately fine details and well-turned curves. The face and the helmet belonged together.

She saw a figure move shadowily in the doorway reflected beyond her shoulder, and said without moving, "Helia—how will I look in dresses? Would you say I'm pretty?"

"You certainly aren't ugly, highness," Helia told her gruffly. It was as much of a compliment as she had ever extracted from the amazon ex-warrior who had been Juille's childhood nurse and girlhood tutor in the arts of war. She had a seamed face, scarred from combat in the revolution zones, and the twinkling narrow eyes of a race so old that Juille's by comparison seemed to lack a history. Helia was an Andarean. The tide of conquest had swept over the Galaxy and ebbed again since the day of Helia's race and its forgotten glory. Perhaps somewhere under the foundations of the Lyonese cities today lay rubble-filled courses the Andareans had once built upon the ruins of cities yet older. No one remembered now, except perhaps the Ancients.

Juille sighed.

"I'll never find out from you," she said.

"You'll get an answer on Cyrille, highness, and you may not like it."

Juille squared her shoulders. "I hope you've kept your mouth shut about all this. Is the ship ready?"

"It is. And I haven't told a soul. But what your father

would say, highness, if he knew you were going to a notorious resort like Cyrille—"

"Perfectly respectable people go there, and you know it. Anyhow, I'm going incognito. And if I hear another word about it I'll have you whipped."

Helia's lipless mouth compressed in disapproval.

"Incognitos don't always work, highness. You should know how secrets leak out around a palace." She caught a dangerous violet glance and subsided, muttering. She knew that stubborn look upon Juille's fine, hard features. But she knew the dangers upon Cyrille, too. She said, "You're taking me with you, I hope?"

"One more word and I won't," Juille warned her. "One more word!" She straightened from the mirror, after one last curiously appraising glance. "Come along, if you want to. I'm leaving."

At the door a small, smoothly furred creature rippled past Juille's ankles with an ingratiating murmur and looked up out of enormous eyes. Juille stooped to let it climb upon her shoulder, where it sat balancing easily and staring about it with the grave animal dignity and the look of completely spurious benignity and wisdom that distinguishes all *llar*. Very few on Ericon own such pets. They were perhaps the true aborigines of Ericon themselves, for they had lived here, and upon no other world, from time immemorial, reserved little creatures of fastidious habits and touchy, aloof ways.

"I'll take both of you," Juille said. "And I expect you'll be just about equally in the way. Come on."

Their ship spiraled up through the rainy gray air of Ericon, leaving the green mountains farther and farther below with each wide circle, until the surface of the planet looked like undulating green fur, soft with Ericon's eternal summer. Presently they were above the high clouds, and rain ceased to beat softly against the glass.

The little ship was riding a strictly prescribed course. The sternest of the Ancients' few restrictions upon human life on Ericon was the restriction on air traffic. All passage was forbidden over the great forests in which the living gods dwelt. The Galaxy's vast space liners had of their own weight to establish an orbit and transact all direct business through tenders, but tenders and private ships plying Ericon's forbidden airways complied with rigid rules about height and course. Because of them, Ericon was a world of surface traffic except in the rarest instances.

Juille sent her vessel flying along an invisible airway of strict boundaries. Presently they overtook twilight and plunged into the evening air that was darkening over the night side of the world. A great luminous bubble floated in the dark ahead, too large for a star, too small for a moon, rolling along its course around Ericon. Helia scowled at it.

This little pleasure world swinging opalescent upon its orbit housed the tangible distillation of all pleasure which a hundred emperors had made possible in the Galaxy. No human desire, however fantastic, went unfulfilled upon Cyrille so long as the client paid for his fantasy. It is an unhappy commentary upon human desires that the reputation of such a place must inevitably be bad.

Juille's ship hovered up below the shining curve of the bubble and a dark square opened in the curve. Then luxury reached out in the form of a tractor beam to take all navigation out of her hands. They rose with smooth speed through a shaft of darkness.

Because privacy and anonymity were prerequisites of many patrons here, they saw no one and were seen by none. The ship came to a velvety stop; Juille opened its door and stepped out straight into a cubicle of a room whose walls glowed in a rosy bath of indirect sunlight. Low couches made a deeply upholstered ledge all around the room. There was a luminous panel beside a closed door. Otherwise—nothing.

Helia climbed out disapprovingly. "I hope you know what you're doing, highness," she said. For answer,

Juille stepped to the luminous panel and let her shadow fall across it. Instantly a voice of inhuman sweetness said dulcetly:

"Your pleasure?"

"I will have," Juille said in a musing tone, "a lounge with sunlight and an ocean view—no particular planet—and a bedroom that— Oh, something restful and ingenious. Use your own ideas on that. A water bath with the emphasis on coolness and refreshment. Now let me see the public rooms for today."

"Immediately," the dulcet voice cooed. "The suite will be ready in five minutes. Refreshment?"

"No food yet. What have you?"

A breath as soft and cool as a mountain breeze at dawn sighed instantly through the room. It smelled faintly of pine. Gravity lessened almost imperceptibly underfoot, so that they seemed to be blowing with the breeze, though they did not move.

"Very nice," Juille told the panel. "Now, the public rooms?"

"The central hall will be a spring twilight on Egillir for the next twelve hours," the inhuman voice announced, and in the panel, in miniature, appeared a vast sphere of a room, the inside of a luminous bubble whose walls were the green translucence of an evening in spring, just dim enough to cloud the vision. Up through the center of the bubble sprang an enormous tree, its great trunk gnarled and twisted. Around the trunk wound a crystal staircase entwined with flowers. Men and women moved leisurely up and down the steps around the vast trunk.

Spraying out exquisitely through the hollow of the sphere were the tree's branches, feathery with leaves of pastel confetti. And floating here and there through the green twilight of the bubble, or nested among the limbs, or drifting idly about through the flowers and the leaves of the vast tree, were crystal platforms upon which diners sat embowered in little arbors of confetti leaves like the tree's.

A soft breeze blew delicately through the twilight, stirring the leaves, and the softest possible music swelled and sank upon the air.

"There is also," the disembodied voice went on as the vision faded, "dancing upon the royal lake of the Dullai satellite—" And in the panel Juille saw couples gliding to stronger music across what appeared to be the mirror-smooth waters of a lake that reflected a moving array of stars. She recognized the lake and the lighted tiers of a city around it, which she had visited on a political mission once several years ago, on a world far away across the Galaxy. The panel blurred again.

"We have also," continued the sugary voice, "several interesting variations of motion available for public use just now. A new swimming medium—" Pause. "An adaptation of musical riding—" Pause. "A concert in color and motion which is highly recommended as—"

"Never mind just now," Juille interrupted. "Send me your best dresser, and let me have some of the Dullai mountain music. I'll try your flower scents, too—something delicate. Keep it just subsensual. I don't want to be conscious of the separate odors."

Helia gave her mistress a piercing look as the panel went blank. Juille laughed.

"I did it well, didn't I? For one who never visited the place before, anyhow. I've been reading everything I could find about it for a month. There—nice music, isn't it?"

The distinctive plaintive vibration of Dullai music sheets began to shiver softly through the room. On a world far away in space, from a period three generations ago, the sad, wailing echoes rang. No living musicians could play the flexible metal sheets now, but upon Cyrille all things were available, at a price.

"The rooms seem to be ready, highness," Helia remarked dryly.

Juille turned. A broad doorway had opened in the wall, and beyond it was a long, low room through which sunlight poured softly. The floor gave underfoot, firm and resilient. Furniture held out upholstered arms in invitation to its series of upholstered laps. Beyond a row of circular windows which filled one wall an ocean of incredible greenness broke in foam upon colored rocks.

The bedroom was a limbo of dim, mysterious blue twilight beyond a circular doorway veiled in what looked like floating gauze. When Juille stepped through she found it was a sort of captive fog instead, offering no resistance to the touch.

The nameless designers of Cyrille had outdone themselves upon the bedroom. For one thing, it appeared to have no floor. A film of very faintly dim-blue sparkles overlying a black void seemed to be all that upheld the tread. A bed like a cloud confined in ebony palings floated apparently clear of the nonexistent floor. Overhead in a night sky other clouds moved slowly and soporifically over the faces of dim stars. A few exquisitely soft and firm chairs and a chaise longue or two had a curious tendency to drift slowly about the room unless captured and sat upon.

There was a fog-veiled alcove that glittered with mirrors, and beyond it a bathroom through which a fountain of perfumed water played musically and continuously.

Helia's astringent expression was eloquent of distaste as she followed her mistress through the rooms. The pet *llar*, clinging to her shoulder, turned wide eyes about the apartment and murmured now and then in meaningless whispered syllables.

"Just what are your plans, highness?" Helia demanded when they had finished the tour. Juille glanced at her crossly.

"Very simple. I'm going to spend a few days enjoying myself. Is there anything wrong with that? I'll have some new clothes and visit the public rooms and see what it's like to be an ordinary woman meeting ordinary people."

"If you were an ordinary woman, there might still be

something very wrong with it, highness. But you aren't. You have enemies—"

"No one knows I'm here. And don't look so grim. I didn't come to experiment with exotic drugs! Besides, I can take care of myself. And it's none of your business, anyhow."

"Everything you do is my business, highness," Helia said gruffly. "I have no other."

Elsewhere in Cyrille a young man in a startling cloak sat at breakfast beside broad windows that opened upon a fairyland of falling snow. The hushed, whispering rush of it sounded through opened casements, and now and then a breath of chilly wind blew like a stimulant through the warm room. The young man was rubbing the curls of the short, yellow beard that just clouded the outlines of his jaw, and grinning rather maliciously at his companion.

"I work too hard," he said. "It may be Juille of Ericon, and again, it may not. All the same, I'm going to have my vacation."

"It's time to stop playing, Egide," said the man across the table. He had a tremendous voice, so deep and strong that it boomed through the hush of the falling snow and the glasses vibrated on the table to its pitch. It was a voice that seemed always held in check; if he were to let it out to full volume the walls might come down, shaken to ruins by those deep vibrations.

The man matched his voice. He wore plain mail forged to turn a fire-sword's flame, and his hair and his short beard, his brows and the angry eyes beneath were all a ruddy bright color on the very verge of red. Red hair grew like a heat haze over the rolling interlace of muscles along his heavy forearms folded upon the table, and like a heat haze vitality seemed to radiate from his bull bulk and blaze from his scarred, belligerent face.

"I didn't . . . acquire . . . you to be my conscience, Jair," the young man said coldly. He hesitated a little over the verb. Then, "Oh, well—maybe I did." He pushed back his chair and stood up, the outrageous cloak swirling about him. "I don't really like this job."

"You don't?" The big red man sounded puzzled. Egide gave him an odd glance.

"Stop worrying about it. I'll go. What will she be like? Hatchet face, nose like a sword— Will I have to kiss her feet?"

Jair said seriously, "No, she's incognito." The glasses rang again to the depth in his voice.

Egide paused before the mirror, admiring the sweep of cloak from his fine breadth of shoulder. Alone he would have seemed a big man himself; beside Jair he looked like a stripling. But no one, seeing them together here, could fail to sense a coldness and a curious lack of assurance behind all Jair's dominant, deep-voiced masculinity. He watched Egide with expressionless eyes.

The younger man hunched his shoulders together. *"Br-r-r!* What a man will go through to change the fate of the Galaxy. Well, if I live through it I'll be back. Wait for me."

"Will you kill her?"

"If I can."

"It must be done. Would you rather I did, later?"

Egide gave him a dispassionate glance. For a moment he said nothing. Then—

"No . . . no, she doesn't deserve that. We'll see what she's like. Unless it's very bad, I'll spare her that and kill her myself—gently."

He turned to the door, his amazing cloak swinging wide behind him. Jair sat perfectly motionless, watching him go.

Helia said, "This will be the dresser." A sustained musical note from the entry preceded the amplified sweetness of the familiar inhuman voice, and Juille turned to the door with considerable interest to see what came next.

The best dress designer upon Cyrille seemed to be a soft-voiced, willowy woman with the pink skin and narrow, bright eyes of a race that occupied three planets circling a sun far across the outskirts of the Galaxy. She exuded impersonal deftness. One felt that she saw no faces here, was aware of no personalities. She came into the room with smooth, silent aloofness, her eyes lowered.

But she was not servile. In her own way the woman was a great artist, and commanded her due of respect.

The composition of the new gown took place before the mirrored alcove that opened from the bedroom. Helia, her jaw set like a rock, stripped off the smart military uniform which her mistress was wearing, the spurred boots, the weapons, the shining helmet. From beneath it a shower of dark-gold hair descended. Juille stood impassive under the measuring eyes of the newcomer, her hair clouding upon her shoulders.

Now she was no longer the sexless princeling of Lyonese. The steely delicacy was about her still, and the arrogance. But the long, fine limbs and the disciplined curves of her body had a look of waxen lifelessness as she stood waiting between the new personality and the old. She was aware of a certain embarrassed resentment, suddenly, at the step she was about to take. It was humiliating to admit by that very step that the despised femininity she had repudiated all her life should be important enough to capture now.

The quality of impassivity seemed to puzzle the artist, who stood looking at her thoughtfully.

"Is there any definite effect to be achieved?" she asked after a moment, speaking in the faintly awkward third person through which all employees upon Cyrille address all patrons.

Juille swallowed a desire to answer angrily that there was not. Her state of mind confused even herself. This was her first excursion into incognito, her first conscious attempt to be—not feminine; she disdained that term. She had embraced the amazon cult too wholeheartedly to admit even to herself just what she wanted or hoped from this experience. She could not answer the dresser's questions. She turned a smoothly muscular shoulder to the woman and said with resentfulness she tried to conceal even from herself:

"Nothing . . . nothing. Use your own ingenuity."

The dresser mentally shot a keen glance upward. She was far too well-trained actually to look a patron in the face, but she had seen the uniform this one had discarded, she saw the hard, smooth symmetry of her body and from it understood enough of the unknown's background to guess what she wanted and would not request. She would not have worked her way up a long and difficult career from an outlying planet to the position of head designer on Cyrille if she had lacked extremely sensitive perception. She narrowed her already narrow eyes and pursed speculative lips. This patron would need careful handling to persuade her to accept what she really wanted.

"A thought came to me yesterday," she murmured in her soft, drawling voice—she cultivated the slurred accent of her native land—"while I watched the dancers on the Dullai Lake. A dark gown, full of shadows and stars. I need a perfect body to compose it on, for even the elastic paint of undergarments might spoil my effect." This was not strictly true, but it served the purpose. Juille could accept the gown now not as romance personified, but as a tribute to her own fine body.

"With permission, I shall compose that gown," the soft voice drawled, and Juille nodded coldly.

The dresser laid both hands on a section of wall near the alcove and slid back a long panel to disclose her working apparatus. Juille stared in frank enchantment and even Helia's feminine instincts, smothered behind a military lifetime, made her eyes gleam as she looked. The dresser's equipment had evidently been moved into place behind the sliding panel just before her entrance, for the tall rack at one end of the opening still presented what must have been the color-section of the last patron. Through a series of level slits the ends of almost countless fabrics in every conceivable shade of pink showed untidily. Shelves and drawers spilled more untidiness. Obviously this artist was great enough to indulge her whims even at the expense of neatness.

She pressed a button now and the pink rainbow slid sidewise and vanished. Into its place snapped a panel exuding ends of blackness in level parallels—satin that gleamed like dark water, the black smoke of gauzes, velvet so soft it looked charred, like black ash.

The dresser moved so swiftly and deftly that her work looked like child's play, or magic. She chose an end of dull silk and reeled out yard after billowing yard through the slot, slashed it off recklessly with a razor-sharp blade, and like a sculptor modeling in clay, molded the soft, thick stuff directly upon Juille's body, fitting it with quick, nervous snips of her scissors and sealing the edges into one another. In less than a minute Juille was sheathed from shoulder to ankle in a gown that fitted perfectly and elastically as her skin, outlining every curve of her body and falling in soft, rich folds about her feet.

The dresser kicked away the fragments of discarded silk and was pulling out now such clouds and billows of pure shadow as seemed to engulf her in fog. Juille almost gasped as the cloud descended upon herself. It was something too sheer for cloth, certainly not a woven fabric. The dresser's deft hands touched lightly here and there, sealing the folds of cloud in place. In a moment or two she stepped back and gestured toward the mirror.

Juille turned. This tall unknown was certainly not herself. The hard, impersonal, perfect body had suddenly taken on soft, velvety curves beneath the thick soft fabric. All about her, floating out when she moved, the shadowy billows of dimness smoked away in drapery so adroitly composed that it seemed an arrogance in itself.

"And now, one thing more," smiled the dresser, pulling open an untidy drawer. "This—" She brought out a double handful of sequins like flashing silver dust and strewed them lavishly in the folds of floating gauze. "Turn," she said, and Juille was enchanted to see the tiny star points cling magnetically to the cloth except for a thin, fine film of them that floated out behind her and twinkled away to nothing in midair whenever she moved.

Juille turned back to the mirror. For a moment more this was a stranger whose face looked back at her out of shining violet eyes, a face with the strength and delicacy of something finely made of steel. It was arrogant, intolerant, handsome as before, but the arrogance seemed to spring now from the knowledge of beauty.

And then she knew herself in the mirror. Only the gown was strange, and her familiar features looked incongruous above it. For the first time in her life Juille felt supremely unsure of herself. Not even the knowledge that the very stars in the Galaxy were subject to her whim could help that feeling now. She drew a long breath and faced herself in the glass resolutely.

The tiny elevator's door slid back and Juille stepped out alone upon a curve of the crystal stairs which wound upward around that enormous tree trunk in the central room. For a moment she stood still, clutching at the old arrogance to sustain her here in this green spring twilight through which perfume and music and soft breezes blew in twisting currents. In that moment all her unsureness came back with a rush—she had no business here in these despised feminine garments; she belonged in helmet and uniform. If she walked, she would stride as if in boots and rip these delicate skirts. Everyone would look up presently and recognize her standing here, the warrior leader of the Lyonese masquerading like a fool.

But no one seemed to be looking at all, and that in itself was a humiliation. Perhaps it was true that she was not really pretty. That she did not belong in soft silken gowns. That no man would ever look at her except as a warrior and an heiress.

Juille squared her shoulders under the cloud of mist and turned toward her waiter, who had snapped the switch of a cylinder fastened to the back of his wrist and focused the invisible beam of it upon an empty floating platform across the great hollow. It drifted toward them slowly, circling on repellor rays around intervening objects. Then it was brushing through the leaves of a mighty bough above them, and Juille took the waiter's arm and stepped out over green twilit space into the tiny leafy arbor of the platform. She had expected it to tilt a little underfoot, but it held as steady as if based upon a rock.

She sank into the elastic firmness of a crystal chair, leaned both elbows upon the crystal table and moodily ordered a strong and treacherous drink. It came almost instantly, sealed in an apricot tinted sphere of glass on a slender pedestal, a glass drinking tube rising in a curve from the upper surface. The whole sphere was lightly silvered with frost.

"Shove me off," she told the waiter, and sipped the first heady draft of her drink in mild defiance as the arbored platform went drifting off among the leaves. A vagrant current caught it there and carried her slowly along in a wide circle in and out of the branches, past other platforms where couples sat with heads close together with exotic drinks. Juille felt very lonely and very self-conscious.

On the curving stairs a young man in a startling cloak looked after her thoughtfully.

There were times, he told himself, when even the most trustworthy of secret informants made mistakes. He thought this must be one of the times. He had been waiting here for some while, watching the crystal stairs patiently. But now—the amazonian princess of Ericon was a familiar figure to him from her newsscreen appearances, and it was impossible to identify that striding military creature with this woman swathed in shadows, her garments breathing out stardust that drifted and twinkled and faded behind her like wafts of faint perfume as she moved.

The young man knew very well what magic the dress designers of Cyrille could work, but he could not believe their magic wholly responsible for this. He grinned a little and lifted his shoulders imperceptibly under the remarkable cloak. It would be amusing to find out.

He kept an eye upon the drifting platform and mounted the stairway slowly, keeping level with it.

Juille watched her drink go down in the frosted sphere and was somewhat ironically aware that her spirits were rising to match it. The rigid self-consciousness of her first few minutes had relaxed; the drink made her mind at once cloudy and sparkling, a little like the shadowy draperies she wore. This was a delicious sensation, floating free upon drifts of perfumed breeze while music breathed and ebbed around her in the green twilight.

She watched the other patrons drifting by, half-seen among the confettilike leaves of their bowers. Many of the faces she thought she recognized. Cyrille was not a world for the rank and file of the Galaxy to enjoy. One had to present stiff credentials to make reservations here, and by no means all of the patrons came incognito. It was a place to enjoy forbidden pleasures secretly, of course, but equally a place to see and be seen in. The wealthy and the noble of all the Galaxy's worlds took considerable pride in showing off their elaborate costumes and the beauty of their companions here, for the very fact of their presence was as good as a published statement of wealth and ancestry.

Presently a flash of scarlet seen through the leaves of a passing platform caught her eye. She remembered then that she had noticed that same shocking cloak upon a young man on the stairs. It was a garment so startling that she felt more than a passing wonder about the personality of the man who would wear it. The garment had been deliberately designed to look like a waterfall of gushing blood, bright arterial scarlet that rippled from the shoulders in a cascading deluge, its colors constantly moving and changing so that one instinctively looked downward to see the scarlet stream go pouring away behind its wearer down the stairs.

Now the blood-red deluge moved fitfully between the branches of a passing arbor. The platform turned so that she could see through the arch of the entrance, and for a long moment as they moved lazily by one another she looked into the interested face of a young man with yellow curls and a short blond beard. His eyes followed her all during the leisurely passing of their platforms, and Juille suddenly sparkled behind the delicious languorous spell her drink had laid upon her. This was it! This was what she had hoped for, and not quite admitted even to herself.

A panel glowed into opaque life in the center of the table she leaned upon. The ubiquitous, inhumanly sweet voice of Cyrille murmured:

"A young man in a red cloak has just asked the privilege of speaking to the occupant of this platform. His identity is not revealed, but the occupant is assured from our records that he is of noble family and good reputation except for a casual tendency toward philandering of which the occupant is warned. He is skilled in the military arts, knows most forms of music well, enjoys athletic games, has done some composing of considerable merit. If the occupant wishes further acquaintance, press the left chair arm which will cut front repellors."

Juille almost giggled at the curious blend of chaperonage, social report and conversational guide with which the honeyed voice prefaced an informal meeting. She wondered if her own anonymous record had been presented to the man, and then decided that it would not be, without her permission.

She wondered, too, just how another woman in her place, with the background she had usurped, would probably act. After a moment of almost panicky hesitation she laid a hand upon the chair arm and leaned on it.

The other platform had evidently made a wide circle around her while the introduction was in progress. Now it swung about in front of her arbor and she could see that the red-cloaked man was leaning on his own chair in a similar position. Across the clear green gulf he called in a pleasant voice:

"May I?"

Juille inclined her dark-gold head, carefully coifed under the hooding veil. The platforms drifted closer, touched with the slightest possible jar. The young man ducked under the arbor, darkening the entrance with the swoop of his bloody cloak. It billowed out behind him extravagantly in the little wind upon which the platforms drifted.

Juille was glowing with sudden confidence. Now she had achieved part of what she had set out to do. Surely this proved her capable of competing with other women on their own unstable, mysterious ground. The magic of the shadowy gown she wore had a part in it, and the drink she had almost finished added its dangerous warmth.

After all, humanity was a strange role to Juille, not one to maintain long. The subservient planets had wheeled across the heavens for her imperial family too long. That look of intolerable pride was coming back subtly into her delicate, steely face beneath the veil that drew its shadow across her eyes.

She nodded the newcomer to a crystal chair across from her, studying him coolly from under the cobwebby veil. He was smiling at her out of very blue eyes, his teeth flashing in the short curly beard. He looked foppish, but he was a big young man, and she noticed that the cloak of running blood swung from very fine shoulders indeed. She felt a faint contempt for him—music, composing, when the man had shoulders like that! Lolling here in that outrageous cape, his beard combed to the last careful curl, oblivious to the holocaust that was rising all through the Galaxy.

She had a moment's vision of that holocaust breaking upon Cyrille, as it was sure to break very soon even this close to the sacred world of Ericon. She thought of H'vani bombs crashing through this twilight sphere in which she floated. She saw the vast tree trunk crumbling on its foundation, crashing down in ruins, its great arms combing all these drifting crystal bowers out of the green perfumed air. She thought of the power failing, the lights going out, the cries of the suddenly stricken echoing among the shattered Edens. She saw the darkness of outer space with cold stars twinkling, and the vast luminous bulk of Ericon looming up outside through the riven walls of Cyrille.

The young man did not appear to share any such premonitions of disaster. He sank into the chair she had indicated and stretched his long legs out comfortably. He had set down on the table a crystal inhaler shaped like a long flattened pitcher with its lip closed except for a tiny slit. Blue-green liquid inside swung gently to the motion of the platform.

He smiled at Juille very charmingly. In spite of herself she warmed to him a little. The charm was potent; though she disparaged it, she could not wholly resist returning the smile.

"This is Cyrille at its best," he said, and gestured toward the twilit hush through which their transparent islet was floating in a long, ascending spiral. The gesture came back to include the bower's intimacy. "Maybe," he said reflectively, "the best I've ever known."

Juille gave him a remote glance under the veil.

"The best dream," he explained seriously. "That's what we come for, isn't it? Except that what we get here is much nicer than most dreams. You, for instance." The charming smile again, both repelling and attracting her. "If this were a dream, I might wake up any moment. But as it is—"

He stared at her for an instant in silence, while a little

breeze rustled the leaves about them and green space swam underfoot below the transparent floor.

"You might be a princess," he went on in a voice of deliberate musing. "Or something made up out of synthetics by some magic or other—I've heard of such things on Cyrille. Maybe you have no voice. Maybe you're just made to sit there and smile and look beautiful. Is it too much to hope you're alive, too—not an android?"

Juille said to herself, "This young man is much too glib, and he certainly enjoys the sound of his own voice. But then, I enjoy it, too—"

Aloud she said nothing, but she smiled and inclined her head a little, so that from the disturbed veil a mist of frosty lights floated out and twinkled into nothingness in the bowery gloom.

The young man stared at her, half enchanted by his own fancy, half convinced in spite of himself that she might after all be one of the fabulous androids of Cyrille, endowed with a compelling charm stronger than the charm of humans.

"If you were," he went on, "if you were born yesterday out of a matrix just to sit there and be beautiful, I wonder what we'd talk about?"

Juille decided it was time to speak. She made her voice remote and low, and said through the sparkling shadows of her veil:

"We'd talk about the worlds you know . . . you would tell me what it's like outside Cyrille."

He smiled at her delightedly. "They gave you a beautiful voice! But I'd rather show you the worlds than talk about them. What would you like to see?"

"Which do you like best?"

Egide lifted his crystal inhaler and put its slitted lip to his mouth, tilting out a few drops of the blue-green liquid within. Then he closed his eyes and let the liquor volatize upon his tongue and go expanding and rising all through his head in dizzying sweetness. He was wondering if he would have to kill this beautiful, low-voiced creature, and if so, whether he would strangle her or use a knife, or whether the little gun tucked inside his belt would be safest. He said:

"I've never been sure of that. You'll have to help me decide. If we find one beautiful enough, I'll take you there tonight." He leaned forward above the panel in the table top and spoke into it briefly. "Now watch," he said.

Juille leaned across the table, folding her arms upon its cool surface. The veil settled about her in slow, cloudy shadows, little lights sparkling among them. With their heads close together they watched pictures form and hover briefly and fade in the panel.

Their islet floated out in a long arc over the abysses of spring evening, and followed a vagrant air current back through the branches again, while they reviewed world after changing world.

"Do you know," said Egide, "that we're doing what only the emperor of Ericon could do?" He watched Juille's dim reflection in the table top, and saw her expression change sharply. He smiled. Yes, she was probably—herself. He went on. "We're making the worlds parade for our amusement. I'll be emperor and give you the one you choose. Which shall it be?"

Juille was hesitating between laughter and outraged divinity. Did the lesser races really talk like this among themselves, with disrespect even for the emperor of the Galaxy? She did not know. She had no way of guessing. She could only swallow the unintended sacrilege and pretend to play his impious little game.

"There," she said in a moment, pointing a tapered forefinger, "give me that city."

"Yorgana is yours," he told her, with a regal gesture that made his cloak sweep out in a sudden gush of blood. And he spoke again into the panel. The great swinging branches began to drift more swiftly by them as their platform picked up motion toward the giant tree trunk and the stairs.

Juille was accustomed to a certain amount of informality from her officers and advisers. She had never insisted upon the full rendition of her imperial rights, which in some cases bordered almost upon semidivinity. But she knew now for the first time that no one had ever been really at ease in her presence before.

Half a dozen times as they went up the stairs and entered a fancifully drop-shaped elevator she was on the verge of laughter or outraged dignity, or both together, at the young man's attitude toward her. No one before had ever pretended even in jest to bestow largesse upon her; no one had ever assumed the initiative as a matter of course and told her what she was expected to do next. For the moment Juille was amused, but only, she thought, for the moment.

The real Yorgana had been in ruins a thousand years. Here in Cyrille, under the light of its three moons, it lay magically restored once more, a lovely city of canals and glimmering waterways in a night made bright as some strange-colored day by its circling moons.

They walked along the sand-paved streets, strolled over the bridges, dropped pebbles into the rippling reflections of the canals. And they talked with a certain stiffness of reserve which began to wear off imperceptibly after a while. Their range of subject matter was limited, for her companion appeared as determined to preserve his incognito as Juille was herself. So they talked of Cyrille instead, and of the many strange things it housed. They talked of the libraries of Cyrille, where the music of all recorded times lay stored, and of the strange pastime of musical levitation which was currently popular here. They speculated about the nationalities, the world origins, the rank of their fellow strollers through the oddly ghostlike city of Yorgana. They talked of the dark places of Cyrille, where beauty and terror were blended for the delectation of those who loved nightmares. But they did not talk of one another except guardedly, and any speculation on either side was never spoken aloud.

Juille was surprised at her own rather breathless enjoyment of this evening. They shared a little table on a terrace that overhung the spangled heights of the city, and they drank pungent deep-red wine, and Juille sat silently, watching the three moons of Yorgana reflecting in tiny focus in her glass while Egide said outrageously flattering things to her.

They drifted in a boat shaped like a new moon along the winding canals under balconies hung with dark flowers, and Egide sang cloyingly sweet ballads, and the night was theatrically lovely. Once he leaned toward her, making the boat rock a little, and hesitated for what seemed a very long moment, while Juille tensed herself to repel whatever advances he was about to make. She knew so little of matters like this, but she knew by instinct that this was too soon. She was both relieved and sorry when he sank back with a deep sigh, saying nothing.

Except for that one incident, insignificant as it was, Juille had no reason at all to distrust the man. But as the evening went on she found that she did distrust him. There was no logic about it. His ingratiating charm struck responsive chords in her against her own desire, but the distrust went deeper still. It was not any telepathic awareness of his surface thoughts, but an awareness of the man himself as his casual opinions revealed him. He was, she thought, too soft. His height and his easy muscular poise had nothing to do with it. She had felt gun callouses on his palm when he helped her into the boat, and she knew he was not wholly the careless fop he pretended, but too many of his casual words tonight had betrayed him. He reminded her more than once of all she disliked most in her father's attitude. She thought, before the evening ended, that she knew this young man better than he suspected, and she did not trust him. But she found his facile charm curiously disturbing.

The disturbance reached its height at the end of the evening, when they danced upon the starry black mirror of the Dullai Lake, where lessened gravity let them move with lovely long gliding steps to the strains of music which seemed to swoon extravagantly from chord to lingering chord. Juille was delightfully conscious of her gown's effect here, in the very scene that had inspired the designer to create it. She was part of the dark, drifting shadows; the clouds of dim gauze billowed out behind her, astream with vanishing stars. And the dance itself was perfection. They were both surprised at the intoxicating rhythm with which their bodies moved together; it was like dancing in a dream of weightless flight, buoyed up on the rise and flow of music.

In this one thing they lost themselves. Neither was on guard against the other while the music carried them along, swirling them around and around in slow, lovely spirals over the starry floor. They said nothing. They did not even think. Time had suspended itself, and space was a starry void through which they moved in perfect, responsive rhythm to music that was an intoxicant more potent than wine. They had known one another forever. In this light embrace a single mind controlled them and they moved to a single rhythm. Apart, their thoughts were antagonists, but in this moment all thoughts had ceased and their bodies seemed one flesh. When the music circled intricately to its close, they danced out the last lingering echoes and came reluctantly to a halt, looking at one another in a stilled, mindless enchantment, all barriers let down, like people awakening from a dream and drenched still with the dream's impossible sweetness.

They stood in a little tree-shadowed cove on the lake shore, dark water rippling in illusion beneath their feet. They were quite alone here. The music seemed to have lifted from the surface of the lake and breathed above their heads through the stirring leaves. And Juille was suddenly aware that Egide had tensed all over and was looking down at her with a queer intentness. Light through the trees caught in his eyes and gave them an alarming brightness. He reached for her in the darkness, and there was something so grimly purposeful about the gesture that she took a step backward, wary and poised. If he had intended a kiss, there was still something frightening in his face and the brilliance of his eyes.

Perhaps even Egide had not been sure just what he intended. But after a moment of intense silence while they stood in arrested motion, staring at one another, he let his arms fall and stepped back, sighing again with a deep, exhaling breath as he had sighed in the boat.

Juille knew then that it was time to leave.

When she came out into her own quiet apartments, sunlight still gleamed changelessly upon the sea beyond her windows. It was not really night, of course. Arbitrary day and night are not observed upon Cyrille, so that though individuals come and go the crowd remains fairly constant in the public rooms. Helia looked up and gave Juille a quick, keen stare as she went through the sunny room without a word.

She stepped through blue mist into the shadowy bedroom, walking upon a mist of twinkling lights through its dimness. A delicious weariness was expanding along her limbs, and her mind felt cloudy like the cloudy, inviting bed. Deep under the lassitude a reasonless unease about that last moment on the lake stirred in her mind, but she would not follow the thought through.

She was looking back with lazy amusement upon the incredible romance of their hours together, and seeing now, without annoyance, how deftly her companion had induced the mood which drowned her now, against her own will and judgment, submerging even the strange, chilly remembrance of the moment after the dance.

Deliberately he had led her through scene after scene of the most forthright and outrageous romanticism, moonlight and starlight, flowers and rippling streams, songs of incredibly honeyed import. She felt vaguely that if the romance had been stressed a little less blatantly it might have been laughable, but the sheer cumulative weight of it had bludgeoned her senses into accepting at its full, false value all the cloying sweetness of the scenes. Toward the end, she thought, he had overreached himself. Whatever his original intention had been, whatever hers, in that one timeless, intoxicating dance they had been caught in the same honeyed trap.

And afterward, when he reached for her with that frightening purpose and the frightening brilliance in his eyes—well, what was so alarming about a kiss? Surely it had been foolish to read anything more menacing into the gesture. She would see him again, and she would know then.

Juille realized suddenly that she had been standing quite still in the middle of the room for a long while, staring blindly at the slowly drifting chairs, reviewing the dance over and over, and the dissolving sweetness of the music and the rhythms of their motion.

She said, "Damn the man!" in a clear voice, and yawned extravagantly, and stepped through another veil of fog into the showering bath. The shadowy gown she had worn all evening melted upon her and went sluicing away under the flashing water. She was both glad and sorry to see it go.

Her dreams in the cloudy bed were lovely and disturbing.

"We've known one another three days," Juille said, "and I may as well tell you I don't like you. Wouldn't trust you out of my sight, either. Why I stay on here—"

"It's my entertainment value," Egide told her, and then rubbed the cropped curls of his beard in a thoughtful way. "Trust I don't expect. But liking, now—you surprise me. Is it the short time we've known each other?"

"Hand me a sandwich," Juille said. He pushed the picnic basket toward her over a billowing surface of clouds—curious, she thought, how the cloud motif had haunted her days here—and remarked:

"I can manage the time angle if that's all that bothers you. Wait." He took up a luminous disk lying beside him and murmured into it. After a moment the clear sunlight that bathed them began to mellow to an afternoon richness.

They were lunching in shameless, childlike fantasy upon a cloud that drifted across the face of a nameless planet. Any pleasure that the mind can devise the body may enjoy in Cyrille. Its arts can expand the walls of a room so that sunlit space seems to reach out toward infinity all around. From the cumulus billows they rode upon today they could lean to watch the shadow of their cloud moving over the soft-green contours of the turning world below, very far down. For the present all gravity and all logic had released them, and in this simple fulfillment of the dream every child knows, Juille let all her past float away. And she had sensed in her companion a similar release. He had been almost irresistibly charming in these careless days, as if, like her, he had deliberately shed all responsibilities and all remembrance of past duties, and had interests now only in being charming and being with her. The three days had affected them both. Juille found she could sit here now and listen to her companion's nonsense with very little recollection that she had been and must be again the princess of Ericon. There was no shadow over the present. She would not look beyond it.

She could even accept without much disbelief the fantastic thing Egide was accomplishing now, and when he said, "Look—not even the emperor could do this!" no shadow crossed her face. He was not watching for such signals now. He had no need to.

Over the world below them evening had begun to move. The air dimmed, and the great soft billows of their cloud flushed pink above the darkening land below. A star broke out in the sky, and another. It was night, full of flaming constellations in the velvet dark. And then dawn began to glow beyond a distant mountain range. The air sparkled; dew was bright upon the face of the turning world.

"See?" said Egide. "Tomorrow!"

Juille smiled at him indulgently, watching the morning move swiftly across the planet. He made no move to halt its progress and the shadows lengthened fast below them as the day declined once more. A fabulous sunset enveloped them in purple and pink and gold, and the sky was green, and violet, and then velvet black. The cycle repeated itself, faster and faster. Evening and night and dawn, noon, evening again.

When a week of evanescent days had flashed over them, Egide spoke into the disk and the circling progress slowed down to normal. He grinned at her.

"Now you've known me about ten days," he said. "Don't I improve with acquaintance? Do you feel you know me any better?"

"I've aged too fast to tell." She smiled. "What fun it is, being a god." She rose on an elbow and looked down over the edge of the cloud. "Let there be cities down there," she said, and waved a careless arm along which bright blue water appeared to ripple, breaking into a foam of bubbles about the wrist.

"Cities there are." Egide snapped his fingers and over the horizon a twinkle of lights began to lift. "Shall we have evening, to watch them shine?" Juille nodded, and the air dimmed about them once more. She held up a blue-sheathed arm to watch the light fading along the liquid surfaces of her sleeve.

They had sailed yesterday under leaning white canvas over a windy sea, and Egide had sent the dress designer to Juille this morning with a new idea. So today she wore a gown of changing blues and greens that flowed like sea water as his cloak had once flowed like blood. An immaculate foam of bubbles rippled about her feet.

Almost every waking hour of the past three days they had spent together. And Juille had almost forgotten that once, on their first meeting, some look about him had frightened her. In her sight the look was not repeated. Behind her back—perhaps. But the three days had been unshadowed, full of laughter and light talk and the entertainment Cyrille alone knew how to provide. They still had no names for one another, but restraint had long gone from their conversation. Juille had even let her first mistrust of him sink into temporary abeyance, so that only occasionally some passing word of his evoked it again.

Just now something else evoked it. At any other place and time there would probably have been real annoyance in her voice, but she spoke today with gentle lassitude.

"You have a decadent mind," she told him. "I've often noticed that. Look—even your clothes show it."

Egide glanced down with a certain complacence. To all appearance he was cloaked today in long blond hair that rippled rather horribly from his shoulders. Beneath it his fine muscular body was sheathed in wetly shining blue satin the exact color of his eyes, and of the same translucent texture.

"Oh, there's a lot I haven't tried yet," he assured her. "Rain, fire— By the way, how would you like a rainstorm over your cities?"

Juille dismissed her shadow of distaste and leaned upon one elbow, peering down.

"Not now. Look. How pretty they are!"

Dusk was purpling over the world below, and the cities twinkled in great spangled clusters of light that shook enchantingly all over the face of the darkening planet as the air quivered and danced between them.

"Look up," murmured Egide, his voice hushed a little in the growing hush of their synthetic night. "I wonder if the stars really look like that, anywhere in the Galaxy."

There were great shining rosettes of light, shimmering from red to blue to white again in patternless rhythms against a sky of thick black velvet. And as they leaned back upon the cloud to watch, a very distant music began to breathe above them among the stars.

It made Juille think of the music upon the lake to which they had danced so beautifully, and in a moment she knew she must sit up and say something to break the gathering magic in the air. She did not trust that magic. She had been careful not to let another moment like the moment of the dance engulf them. She mistrusted it both for its own sake and for the sake of what barriers it might let down in her. The thought of Egide's embrace was frightening, in some obscure, illogical way she did not try to fathom. In just a moment she would break the gathering spell.

The music sank slowly toward them in intangible festoons of sweetness. The stars blazed like great fiery roses against the dark. They were floating through space upon that most lulling and deeply remembered of all motions—the gentle swing of the cradle. Their cloud rocked them above the turning world and the stars poured down enchantment. And now it was too late to speak.

The same dissolving magic was upon them as their cloud went drifting slowly among the stars. All reality was draining away. Juille heard the long breath her companion drew, and saw the stars blotted out by the silhouette of his curly head and broad cloaked shoulders leaning above her. And suddenly something about their tensed outline roused Juille from her lovely lassitude. She sat up abruptly, terror flashing over her. In this swimming darkness his face and the brilliance of his eyes was veiled, but she could see his arms reach out for her and all the latent fear came back with a rush.

But before she could move he had her. His strength was surprising. He held her struggles quiet in one arm, and she felt the calloused palm of the other hand fitting itself gently around her throat. For one unreasoning moment, in the face of all logic, she knew what he intended. In her mind she could already feel that hand tightening with its terrible gentleness until the night swam red around her as she strangled. If this was murder, she must forestall it, and her body knew the way. What she did was pure instinct, unguided by reason. She relaxed in his arms with a little sigh, letting her eyes close softly. When she felt his grip begin to loosen just a bit she got one arm free and laid it about his neck.

What happened then must have amazed them both if their minds had been capable of surprise. But their minds were not functioning now. As in the moment of the dance, all antagonisms of thought had ceased without warning, and it was the flesh instead that governed and responded. Juille felt one dim warning stir far back in her brain, drowned beneath the immediate and urgent delight of his expert kisses, but she would not think of it now. She could not. Later, perhaps, she would remember. Much later. Not now.

The burning stars had paled a little when she noticed them again. Some warm, light fabric covered her—that cloak of rippling yellow hair. Her head was pillowed upon the cumulous couch and dawn was beginning to freshen the air, though no light yet glowed above the horizon. She could see her companion darkly silhouetted against the stars as he sat upon a billow of cloud a little distance away, resting his chin on his fist and staring downward.

Juille pushed the clouds into a support behind her and leaned upon it, watching him, formless thoughts swirling in her mind. Presently his head turned toward her. In this warm darkness his face was barely visible, lighted by the dimming stars. She could see starlight reflecting in the mirrory surfaces of his tunic and glancing down, she caught the same reflections broken among the water ripples of her own skirt.

They looked at one another in silence, for a long while.

Juille woke in the dimness of her apartment, upon her bed of cloud, and lay for a few moments letting the fog of her dreams clear slowly away, like mist dispelling. Then she sat up abruptly, knowing that after all it had been no dream. But when she looked back upon the bewildering complexity of what had happened on the cloud, she saw no rhyme or reason to it. The dimness was suddenly smothering about her.

"Light, light!" she called pettishly, brushing at the room's darkness with both hands, as if she could clear it away like a curtain. And someone waiting beyond the call panel of the bed must have heard—it was strange to wonder how much those listeners heard and watched and knew—for the darkness paled and a rosy glow of morning flooded the room.

Helia stood in the doorway, the little *llar* preening itself upon her shoulder. Her weathered face showed no emotion, but there was a certain gentleness in the look she bent upon her mistress.

"Did I sleep long?" Juille asked.

Helia nodded. The *llar* unclasped its flexible pads and plucked at her dark hair, beginning very swiftly and deftly to braid it between quick, multiple fingers like the fingers of sea-anemones. Helia stroked the little animal and it snapped sidewise with razory teeth and sprang to the floor with one fluid motion of grace like flight.

"Any calls?"

"Not yet, highness." Helia's grave stare was almost disconcerting.

Juille said, "Go away," and then sat clasping her knees and frowning. In the mirrors of the dressing alcove she could see herself, the fine, hard delicacy of her face looking chill even in this rosy light. She felt chill.

What had happened last night was too complex to understand. Would his hand have tightened about her throat if she had not taken the one way to prevent it? Or was the heavy touch a caress? What possible reason, she wondered, could the man have for wanting to strangle her? But if he had meant to, and if he had let her seduce him from his purpose—why, that was no more than she might have expected from him. The old mistrust, the old dislike, came back in a flood. His decadent clothes betrayed him, she thought, and his sensitive, sensuous mouth betrayed him, and the careless opinions he had expressed too often. He was a man who would always make exceptions; he would always be pulled two ways between sentiment and duty. If it had not really happened last night, then it would happen when the first test came. No, she did not respect him at all—but a dangerous weakness loosened all her muscles as she leaned here remembering that stunning of the sense which Cyrille's false glamour could work upon her.

Everything about her was an illusion, she realized with sudden cold insight that no Cyrillian art could dispell. But it was an illusion so dangerous that the very integrity of the mind could be enchanted by it, the keen edge of reason dulled. And she felt frightened as no possible physical threat could frighten her. When the amazon discards a woman's gentleness of body and mind she is almost certain to make the discard complete. Juille thought she was not asking too much of an intellectual equal when she expected from him the same cold, unswerving devotion to a principle that was the foundation of her own life. Egide would never have it.

But she knew she had better not see that disarming face of his any more. Not even to solve for herself the perplexing question of his intention last night. Better to let it slide. Better to go now and forget everything that had happened upon the drifting cloud, beneath those burning stars. Now she knew the shifting, unstable ground upon which women walk; she would not tread it again. She sat up.

"Helia," she called through the fog-veiled doorway. "Helia, send for our ship. We're starting back to Ericon—now."

Egide sat clasping one knee, leaning his head back on the window frame and looking out over a field of pale flowers that nodded in the rays of tricolored suns. He did not look at Jair. His cloak today was a mantle of licking flame.

"Well?" said Jair, the boom in his voice under close control. No answer. Jair looked down reflectively at his own clasped hands. He tightened them, watching the great muscles writhe along his forearms under the red-heat haze of hair. "Has she recognized you?" he asked.

Egide picked up the glass beside him and spun it thoughtfully. Rainbows flickered across the floor as sunlight struck it. He did not answer for a moment. Then he said in a detached voice, "That. It's a false alarm, Jair."

"A false alarm!" Jair's voice made the glass shiver in Egide's hand. The muscles crawled spectacularly along his arms as his great fists clenched. "She *isn't* the emperor's daughter?"

Egide flashed him a clear, blue glance, and grinned. "Never mind," he said. "You don't have to impress me."

There was a certain blankness in Jair's reddish gaze that Egide recognized with an odd, illogical shiver. He said, "Sometimes I forget how good you are at your job, Jair. And sometimes it surprises me—"

"You mean," Jair said, and even in restraint his voice made the glass vibrate, "we've wasted all this time and money—"

"Well, no, I wouldn't call it wasted. I've had a very pleasant time. But we'd better leave today. It wasn't the emperor's daughter."

Rain danced from the high curve of the crystal wall and went streaming in long, irregular freshets down the sides of the glass room, veiling Ericon's soft-green hills outside. Within, firelight wavered beneath a great white mantelpiece carved with the mythological loves of gods and goddesses worshiped a long time ago by another race.

The rain and the firelight and the silence of the people in the room should have made it a peaceful hour here under the high glass curve of the walls. But over the mantelpiece was a communicator panel that was like an open window upon death and disaster. Every man in the room leaned forward tensely in his chair, eyes upon the haggard, blood-streaked face that spoke to them hoarsely through the panel.

The voice carried over long-lapsed time and the unfathomable dark distances that stretch between worlds. The man who called was probably dead now; he spoke from another planet that circled far outside the orbit of Ericon.

"Dunnar has just surrendered to the H'vani," he was telling them in a tired, emotionless voice that sounded as if it had been shouting a little while ago, though it was not shouting now. "We hadn't a chance. They came down in one wave after another all around the planet, bombing everything that moved. They landed troops on the night side and kept raining them down all around the world as the dark belt moved on. The day side got the bombing heaviest, beginning in the dawn belt and moving on around with the planet. They had their own men planted everywhere, ready to rise. Smothered our antiaircraft from the ground. Much of it must have been manned by their spies. Some of our interceptor craft were shot down deliberately from below. Watch out for H'vani men planted—"

Behind the speaker a flaming rafter fell into the range of the communicator screen and crashed somewhere near, out of sight. The man glanced back at it, then leaned to the screen and spoke on in a voice of quickened urgency. Above the crackling of the flames, other voices shouted in the background, coming nearer. There was the noise of what might be gunfire, and another sliding crash as more beams fell. The speaker was shouting now, his voice almost drowned out in the rising uproar of Dunnar's destruction.

"The weapon—" he called above the crashing. "No chance for us . . . came too fast— We've smuggled out one man . . . fast ship . . . bringing a model to you. Watch for him. They'll follow—" A blazing beam came down between his face and the screen. Through a thin curtain of fire he mouthed at them some last urgent message of which only a word or two came through. "Weapon . . . might save the Galaxy . . . give them a blast for Dunnar—" And then the fire blazed up to blot out face and voice alike, and Dunnar's ruined image faded from the screen.

For a moment after it was gone, the warm firelight flickering through the room seemed horrible, a parody of the flames that had engulfed the spokesman in the panel. The crash of burning Dunnar still echoed through the quiet, and the hoarse, despairing voice of the last man. Then the emperor said in a flattened tone:

"I wanted you all to hear it a second time, before we go out to meet the ship."

Juille uncrossed her long bare legs and leaned forward, scowling under the crown of dark-gold braids.

"We're ready for them," she said grimly. "That weapon wasn't quite finished, though."

"That's why they struck when they did," murmured an amazon officer beside her. "Beautiful timing—beautiful! Almost a split-second attack, between the finish of the weapon and the mounting of it."

There was silence in the room. The opening blow had been struck of a battle that must engulf every world in the Galaxy before it ended. No one spoke for a while, but the air was heavy with unvoiced thoughts and most of them were grim.

The emperor put out a hand to the game set up on a table before him and moved a bead along a curve of colored wire. It was a game of interplanetary warfare, played like chess, though the men moved both vertically and horizontally on wires like an abacus. Firelight glinted on the colored beads carved like ships and worlds.

"You'll lose your master planet unless you bring up the blues," Juille told him absently.

"This is a solitaire game," said the emperor. "Mind your own business."

The rain blew pattering against the glass and the fire crackled softly. Juille's *llar* came out from beneath her chair, stretching elaborately, yawning to show a curved pink tongue. The crackling of the logs was a whisper of the terrible roaring crackle they had heard across the void from Dunnar's collapsing cities. They would hear it again from other worlds before the holocaust ended that had begun almost before their eyes here. Perhaps they might listen to it in this very room, on the sacred soil of Ericon itself. Other dynasties had crumbled upon Ericon before theirs.

"Why don't they report again on that ship?" the emperor said irritably, flipping a carved bead around a curve with too much force, Juille, seeing its course, automatically opened her mouth to object, and closed it again without saying anything. The *llar* swung itself up on the emperor's table with soundless ease and put out its webby-fingered paw to move two beads precisely along the notched wire.

"Ah, so you know Thori's Gambit, little friend?" The emperor's tired face creased in a smile as the *llar's* round-eyed stare met his through the maze of painted wires. He moved a translucent red bead between the two the *llar* had shifted. "I wish I could be sure that was an accident. How much does a *llar* really know?"

The little animal put its head down, rolled up its strange, shining eyes and wriggled all over, like a playful kitten. But when the emperor stretched out a hand to stroke it, the *llar* turned deftly away and flowed down over the table edge onto the floor with a grace that was almost frightening in its boneless ease.

The screen glowed above the fireplace. Everyone looked up, even the *llar*. An expressionless face announced in expressionless tones:

"Escaping Dunnar ship approaching landing field from space. Three enemy pursuit ships have succeeded in passing the Ericon space guard and still survive."

The emperor got up stiffly. "Come along," he said. "We'll watch."

They came out in a window-walled room above the landing field. A fine mist blew in through the openings, sweet with the fragrance of the wet green hills beyond. The clean smell of wet concrete rose from the broad, brown expanse below, where the small figures of attendants dashed about excitedly in preparation for the landing.

One inner wall of the room was a screen upon which they could all see now what had been taking place overhead, above the layers of rain cloud. The emperor sat down without taking his eyes from the screen. Juille crossed her arms on the high back of his chair and watched, too, ringing one spur in a half-unconscious, continuing jingle. Everyone else was silent, standing respectfully back, and the sound of breathing was loud in the quiet.

On the screen they could see how the tiny black ship from Dunnar had cut its rockets and hurled itself headlong into the gravitational embrace of Ericon, swinging around the planet to subdue the speed it had not dared slacken in space. Behind it, still in suicidal pursuit, the three H'vani ships flamed on. They had escaped the space guard only because of their smallness and mobility, which meant that the range of their weapons was too limited to do much damage at a distance. But they were cutting down the space between them and their quarry, and the race was close.

"They'll have to turn back now," breathed Juille, gripping the chair-back. "They won't dare . . . look, there go our interceptors."

The screen divided itself in half with an oddly amoebalike motion, one section showing the swift rise of Ericon's interceptors while the other mirrored the orbit of the newcomer as it swung around the Control Planet still at dangerous speed. It was curious to think of the plunge into circumscribed space-time which that ship was just now making as it emerged from deep space where neither time nor distance have real meaning. The fugitive had flashed through morning and noon and night, and come around the world into dawn again, and so into the misty forenoon above the watchers.

Now they saw it put out wings upon the thin upper air, like a diver suddenly stretching out his arms, and come coasting down upon their sustaining surfaces in a great sweeping spiral above the field.

"There goes one of 'em," the emperor said in a satisfied voice. Juille glanced back at the upper screen and saw one of the pursuers from space twisting downward, its black sides beginning to glow already from the friction of that thin high air. It dropped incandescently out of the picture, which was following the other two ships in their headlong flight. Their own sheer speed gave them an advantage. They were drawing away from the interceptors, taking full and suicidal advantage of the fact that upon Ericon immutable law forbids any aircraft to fly at will over the surface of the sacred planet.

"They won't dare—" Juille told herself under her breath, leaning forward. Behind her a rustle and an indrawn breath all through the room spoke the same thought. For the enemy ships, winged now and swinging down through the heavier air in pursuit of their escaping prey, were being driven farther and farther off the prescribed course beyond which all air traffic is forbidden.

The interceptor ships were sheering away. Juille could picture the frantic indecision of their commanders, torn between the necessity to destroy the invaders and the still more urgent necessity not to transgress an immemorial law laid down by powers even higher than the Galactic emperor's.

In the lower half of the screen, the single-winged ship had leveled off for a landing. Someone outside shouted, and for a moment all eyes turned to the windows and the broad concrete field outside.

Down out of the misty clouds came a duplicate of the

shape upon the screen. In silence, the black-winged ship came swooping through the rain, lower and lower over the heads of running attendants. It hovered to a halt and sank down gently upon its own reflection in the wet concrete. And upon the screen behind them, the same scene took place in faithful duplicate.

Indeed, the image was more faithful than the reality, for at this distance the naked eye could see only a swarming of tiny figures around the newly arrived ship. The emperor called, "Closer," and turned back to the screen.

The scene below rushed into a close-up upon the wall, swooping toward them with dizzy speed. Now they could watch the opening slide into view upon the ship's side, and the man who ducked out and stepped down upon the brown concrete in the drizzle of misting rain. It beaded his shoulders with moisture in the first few moments. He blinked the rain out of his eyes and looked about calmly, not in the least hurried or alarmed.

The envoy from Dunnar was an astonishing figure, so tall and so very thin that at first glance he looked like a scarecrow shape beside his vessel. But when he turned to face the crowding attendants and the screen, he moved with a grace and sureness that had something unmistakably regal about it. He wore his plain black overall with a remarkable sort of elegance, and his own quiet sureness seemed to throw everyone else on the field out of focus. The muscular attendants looked squat and brutish by contrast with his scarecrow height; the well-dressed officials moving forward to receive him were vulgar beside his overalled simplicity.

He looked up into the featureless clouds where his pursuers and his defenders still waged an invisible battle. All around him the crowding men looked up, too, futilely. Only in the control room, where the emperor and his staff sat, did the eyes that followed that lifted gaze see what was happening overhead.

And now, as their gaze went back to the neglected drama above, a horrified fascination seized upon every watcher in the room. Even Juille's unconsciously jingling spur was silent. She felt the sudden clutch of small fingery paws, but she did not glance down as the *llar* came swarming up her leg to a vantage point upon her shoulder. She felt its tiny, quick breathing against her cheek as it, too, stared.

Not within the memory of any living man had the law of the Ancients been violated which forbade air traffic over Ericon. Obedience to those laws had been rooted as deeply as obedience to the law of gravity. There were violations, of course; tradition said all such violators died instantly.

Juille watched the first such episode in modern times with a catch in her breath and her throat closed from tremendous excitement. She wondered if everyone else in the room felt the same half-guilty anticipation, the impious wonder.

For there was a wide gap now between the enemy ships and the Ericon interceptors. It had been a suicide pursuit anyhow, for the H'vani. They were certainly doomed. And they were taking one last headlong chance in the hope of destroying their quarry before they were themselves destroyed. The interceptors had forced them by now far out of the narrow traffic lane whose invisible boundaries should have been so rigid. For the first time in living memory, ships spread their wings upon the forbidden air of Ericon.

They were swooping down in a long dive now, coming fast through the clouds toward the landing field where the newcomer stood unconcernedly staring up into the mists that hid them.

"They're going to make it—they are!" Juille whispered to herself, gripping the chair-back with aching fingers.

Out of the landing field, crews were manning the antiaircraft guns in frantic haste, sheer incredulity numbing their fingers as they worked. No one had ever quite believed that these guns could be needed. They were meant for defense against ships attacking from directly overhead, in the prescribed landing lane from space. Even that possibility had seemed absurd. But now—

"Get that fool off the field!" the emperor roared suddenly, making everyone jump. "Get him off! They'll be here in a minute. Look at them come!"

Down through the mist the two surviving ships came driving through air that shrieked away from their wings. Men were scattering wildly from the field. Loudspeakers roared at the Dunnarian to take shelter. He stood imperturbably, tall and thin and quiet, looking up into the clouds.

And for a timeless moment a faith rooted millenniums deep in human minds shook terribly as the Ancients were defied—and stayed their hand. No peril to the defenseless envoy on the field—though he carried a secret that might save their race—moved the watchers half so deeply as what they were seeing now. The ships dived on through the screaming air, and behind them clouds boiled furiously in the vortex of their passage.

Did the Ancients really exist at all? Or had all those legends been legends only? The breath of every watcher paused in his throat as he waited the answer.

But no one saw the vengeance the Ancients took. All over the planet shaken watchers followed the action upon their screens—but no human eye saw the blow fall.

One moment, the black ships were screaming down through grayness; the next instant, without warning, there came a soundless flash like the flash of sunlight glancing from some colossal mirror, blinding every eye that watched.

There was no sound. The riven air screamed itself quiet. When those who stared could see again out of dazzled eyes, nothing remained but the vortex of clouds split by the plunging ships. And even the vortex was quieting now. Of the ships, nothing remained. For the first time in living memory, the Ancients had struck, invisibly, before a world of watchers, in the deadly dignity of silence.

And all over Ericon, a world-wide sigh of relief went up wordlessly.

In the utter quiet, the envoy moved forward at last across the wet concrete. Overhead, that vast boiling of clouds had cleared a space for the rare blue sky to shine. The reflecting pavement turned suddenly blue and glorious as he stalked across it with his long scarecrow stride. Awed eyes watched him come, a black figure moving with strange, smooth elegance over the blinding blueness of the sky's reflection.

"Stop that jingling and come along, Juille," the emperor said at last in the silence, rising as stiffly as he had sat down. "We'll see him in my library, alone. Wake up, girl! Come along."

"—And the weapon?" said the emperor eagerly, leaning forward between the arms of a great carved chair before his library fire.

No one could have guessed from the look of the man before him that he had come straight from a desperate flight and an awesome rescue, or that he carried a cargo so precious a whole Galaxy's fate might depend on it. He was the last Dunnarian left to speak for his ruined world, but no emotion at all showed upon his cool, impassive face.

"I'll want my men to look over the weapon at once," the emperor went on. "It's in your ship?"

"Highness, I brought no weapon."

"No weapon!"

Juille watched a familiar thunderous look gather upon her father's face, but the storm did not quite break and Juille smiled to herself, understanding why. It was difficult to treat this man like an ordinary person. His appearance was extraordinary enough, without that recollection of an hour ago which had struck a whole world into reverent silence.

This was the man who had stood unafraid beneath the plunge of the enemy ships, unprotected, so confident in the power of the Ancients that he had not wavered even when death seemed certain. This was the man above whom the Ancients had for the first time in living memory put out their hands and wrought a miracle. He had, of course, been only the occasion, certainly not the cause. But he was haloed still in the reflected glory of that moment which was already taking its place in legend.

"I have no weapon," he said again, meeting the emperor's glare with an imperturbable gaze from his great, luminous eyes that never winked. "We dared not risk letting a model fall into H'vani hands, highness. I will have to make one for you."

Juille saw her father settle back, mollified, perhaps a bit relieved that he need not thunder at this remarkable and disconcerting man. Perhaps it had occurred to the emperor, as it had to Juille, that immortality which might outlast their own had already descended upon the envoy's smooth, narrow-skulled head. Unborn generations would repeat in awe the story of his experience today.

She stared frankly at the man, wondering very much from what ancient line he sprang and what knowledge lay behind the strange, thin face with its falcon nose and its large, transparent gray eyes and the mouth that looked at once cruel and oversensitive. Seen this near, he seemed even taller and thinner and more oddly scarecrowlike than on the screen, yet the extraordinary fastidious precision of his motion made every other man alive seem crude and clumsy. He had an ageless face, and a poise that seemed bred into the very genes of his ancestors. Juille had a glancing, vivid recollection of Cyrille—for a moment she was drifting on a cloud again, and a young man cloaked in flowing yellow curls bending above her—and she thought wryly how much he would have envied this Dunnarian's unstudied elegance. Even the stained overall, thus worn, looked like some fashion a Galactic prince had just set for the capitals of the worlds to copy.

"You'll have to get to work immediately," the emperor's voice recalled her to the urgent present. "We must have a model of the weapon at once. Too bad the H'vani timed their attack so well. In a few days more you might have fought them off with it, eh?"

The Dunnarian shook his narrow, bird-shaped head gravely.

"Our men never succeeded in expanding the scope of the weapon that much, highness. It remains a weapon for the individual, against the individual, but within that scope I believe it's the most effective thing ever made."

"A delayed-action killing, isn't it?" Juille said.

The luminous eyes turned to her. There was an infinite quietness in their stare, curiously at odds with the man's words.

"It is, highness. That gives it a strong psychological threat value, as well as a physical one. With every other comparable weapon, its operator has to sight and fire while the enemy is exposed to view. With the new one, a man may be killed not only at any distance, but at any time, once its sight has been fixed upon him. A quasi-photograph of the victim's brain pattern is snapped, and he is doomed from that moment, though you may not choose to pull the trigger for many days. Then, irrevocably, the weapon remains focused upon him, figuratively speaking, until it is discharged. He will be unable to travel far enough to escape it, and no hiding place can save him."

"Like a fuse," Juille murmured. "An invisible fuse, long enough to follow him wherever he goes, and you can light it when you wish. Oh, very nice! It's easily portable, I suppose?"

"The weapon itself is a bulky machine which must be set up in some impregnable position, perhaps sealed in against possible bombardment. But the focusing instrument is a small double lens in a frame. It has a slightly telescopic property. Once a man is centered in the cross hairs and a trigger sprung, he's your victim whenever you spring the second trigger on the lens and thus touch off his particular pattern in the central machine."

The emperor put his fingertips together and stared at them, shaking his head.

"It's a treacherous thing," he said. "The ultimate refinement of a stab in the back, eh? I suppose the victim can't tell if he's been spotted?"

"Probably the victim never does know, highness. Death is almost instantaneous."

The emperor shook his head again. "Personally," he said, "I don't like it. But I can see why the H'vani wiped out a world trying to get it away from us. As you say, the psychological value of the thing is tremendous, once they know what they're up against."

Juille laughed, a short, triumphant sound. "*I* like it," she said. "I'm not squeamish. Think of it, father! We can send armed spies into their bases to snap their leaders, and wait until the height of battle to pick them off. Imagine the effect during some complicated maneuver if all the leaders fell dead simultaneously! And that's saying nothing of how the leaders themselves will feel, knowing they're walking dead men, doomed the moment they step into a responsible position and start giving orders. Oh, I do like it!"

Her father nodded, frowning. "Once it's known," he said, "once it's actually proved in combat, I should think every H'vani officer with any responsibility would become either a reckless fatalist or a nervous wreck. It isn't so bad to be killed outright—every soldier knows that can happen, and there's an end of it. But to know the assassin will strike inevitably at the high point of your responsibility, when thousands of lives depend on yours and the whole outcome of a battle may hinge on what you do—This ought to cause the most profound psychological reactions all along the line in any army the weapon's used against."

* * *

Juille took a short turn about the room, spurs tinkling, and came back with shining violet eyes.

"Do you know what we've got here?" she demanded. "It's something so new it almost frightens me. Not just the weapon—but the principle behind it. It's the only new thing, really, since cavemen led off the procession of warfare with the bow and arrow. From that time forward, weapons have been increasing in range and scope and volume. The whole story of military warfare's been a seesaw between defense and offense—new method of attack, new defense against it, stalemate, then a newer weapon that kills more people quicker. But now—" She laughed exultantly. "Don't you see? This is a complete rightabout-face. Ever since the beginning of time, all martial invention's been forging ahead in one direction only, toward bigger and bigger weapons with greater range and scope. Men's minds are trained to think in those terms only. But with this new thing, we're flashing back in the other direction entirely, turning their flank, smashing them in a vulnerable spot left absolutely unprotected all this while. Their minds won't even be able to cope with it or devise a defense. People just don't think in terms like that."

The emperor looked at her thoughtfully, stroking his beard. The envoy's great, translucent eyes dwelt upon her animated face with an impersonal remoteness.

"See it?" Juille demanded. "Now we can strike them where they least expect it. We're back at the very beginning, even before the sword or the club. It's the individual we attack now. This is a weapon as terrible as anything that wipes out cities, but aimed at the other end of the scale of offense—the individual himself. Each man alone, in personal danger of a doom that's picked him out from all the rest and will follow him wherever he goes. This attacks the mind as well as the body. It's like a germ of terror that can eat a man's morale out and leave his body intact. He won't trust himself or his leader. And do you know the only possible defense?"

She struck her hands together and her voice almost crowed with triumph.

"Individual responsibility. The breakup of an integrated war machine. No one can depend on anyone else for anything, once our weapon's in action. They'll have to throw out all their elaborate maneuvers and all their training and start again from scratch. Each man for himself. An army of guerrillas. Utterly reckless, of course, fatalistic to the last degree. But I don't see how they can hope to conduct space warfare with every man in the army independent of every other man. It'll win the war for us, father!"

The emperor drummed his fingers on the table. "You may be right," he conceded. "If we can keep it for ourselves, that is. But if anyone stole it—"

"Who else knows how to build the machine?" Juille demanded of the Dunnarian.

"No one, highness. There were few of us at the beginning, and I saw all my co-workers die. The knowledge is quite safe so far, with us."

Juille bent upon him a curiously cold, violet stare. The grave, gray eyes met it without a flicker, though he must have known what passed through her mind. Artisans who create the unique for jealous emperors are notoriously shortlived, and in this case the need for uniqueness went far beyond petty jealousy.

"You'll want a constant guard," Juille told the man thoughtfully. "And you'll have to work fast."

The Dunnarian bowed silently as the emperor waved a dismissing hand. He looked more than ever falconlike for a moment, and as he turned his head and Juille saw the narrow skull and the beaked nose outlined, she wondered how he could seem so birdlike and yet so smoothly poised, for birds are creatures of small, nervous motions.

Then she remembered that before the bird came the snake. It was the snake behind the falcon that epitomized this man's smooth gestures, his elegance, his quiet, lidless stare.

* * *

In another part of the palace a figure slipped quietly and unseen out of a curtained window. He dropped to the dark grass of a garden and, moving with the sureness of one who has come this way many times before, went out through an unguarded postern and through a band of trees dripping with rain that flashed in the lights behind him.

Quickly and silently through the rustling silence of the night he moved away, leaving the turmoil of the palace behind him, where the news of the ruin of world after world flamed across the luminous screens that pictured their destruction.

He went disdainfully through the dark, picking his way with delicate steps. He knew the path so well that no one challenged him, no one saw the dark figure slipping from shadow to shadow. He had a long way to go, but he knew every step of it, even in the dark.

He was tired when he came to the far end of the journey, for it had been a long way to come on foot. In the end it was intricate, too, because he had to enter by a hidden way.

But the end was reward enough for all his weariness and secrecy, as he had known it would be. Indeed, he knew and loved each step of the path because it brought him nearer this goal. He stood in a dark archway at the end of the journey, and looked out over the low rooftops of the city of his people, glittering with warm, soft lights through curtained windows. No two curtains were of quite the same shade, nor were the windows shaped alike at all, so that the city glowed with myraid flowery shapes, like a lighted garden. His heart swelled with the knowledge that he was at home again, that the city was his and he the city's. He no longer moved stealthily as he went down the slope of sand toward the sandy streets before him.

There were few abroad at this hour, but those he passed knew him and exchanged with him the reserved formula of greeting behind which lay a deep, sure affection between individuals for the sake of the group itself—a feeling almost indescribable to anyone unfamiliar with such a community as this.

He went along the sand-padded street silently, straight for the house where his friends awaited him. Reserve was strongly rooted in them all, and their meeting betrayed no emotional unbalance, but common purpose and common danger had welded them into a group so close and strong that words were scarcely necessary among them.

Still, when he was refreshed and relaxed, he could not help voicing the dominant emotion which had harried him all the way here.

"I wish it were over!" he sighed. "I left them listening to the news of their own destruction, and making noises about it. Ericon will be a better world when the last of them dies."

"A better place for us, I hope," one of the others said. "Will it be soon?"

"I think so, don't you? I think they're finished now, if they only knew it."

"They stand at a very definite crisis," said someone else, and glanced around the group with grave, affectionate eyes. "They can still save themselves—perhaps. There's time for it, if they only knew the way. Such a simple way, too. Some of them see it, but I don't think they'll have the chance to try."

"They're doomed," the newcomer declared in his soft voice. "I know them too well. Poor ignorant, blundering creatures." He hesitated. "I almost feel pity sometimes, watching them. But they've had their turn, and the sooner they finish the better. We've waited so long—"

"Would you help them if you could?" asked someone.

"If it weren't for us—perhaps. At heart they mean well. But they're muddled beyond all hope now, and I can't believe anything could straighten them out. Think how long we've waited—"

"Think of *Their* promise," murmured a voice.

"It wasn't a flat promise, remember," someone else warned cautiously. "It was contingent, you know. They haven't failed yet. If this war turns in the right direction, they still have their chance, and we may have to begin our waiting all over again."

"They'll miss the chance," the newcomer said, half exultantly and half in reluctant pity. "I know them too well."

The officers' lounge in one of the tower tops was roofed and walled in glass, against which gusts of storming rain beat fitfully now, out of a purple sky. Ericon is so much a world of rain that all its architecture is designed to take advantage of rain's beauty, much like solariums on other worlds.

Today the lounge was crowded, and there was a murmur of grave undertones beneath the voice of the news screen that filled one wall. It rolled out the toll of ruined cities and silenced worlds. All over the Galaxy, insurrection was spreading inward toward Ericon like a plague from the rotting fringes of the empire. The imperial cities were going down like ninepins on world after crashing world.

"They're slowing up a bit, though," Juille said thoughtfully. "You know, I believe they had to strike sooner than they meant to, because of that weapon from Dunnar." She nodded at the envoy from that now voiceless planet, who sat in a deep chair beside her, long legs crossed, long fingertips interlaced, his lidless stare upon the screen that covered one wall of the room. Unobtrusively his bodyguard leaned upon the wall behind him.

Around them sat Juille's staff of officers, most of them young, many of them women, who among them divided most of the power of the empire today. Helia leaned across the back of her chair, the *llar* on her shoulder preening its sleek sides with hands like fingery starfish.

"You're right about that, highness," remarked a

grim-faced woman in a plumed helmet. "They're definitely slowing down. But the best we can hope for now, I think, is the striking of some balance. We can fall into a deadlock—beyond that we can't hope to pass just now."

"There are worse things than deadlocks," Juille told her. "Wait till the weapon's finished! But if my father's conference this afternoon comes to anything—" She slapped the chair arms angrily. "If it should, I think the whole Galaxy's lost."

"The emperor, highness, would call it lost if the conference fails." The man from Dunnar turned his grave, luminous eyes upon her.

"I won't sit down to a peace conference with those bloody savages," Juille declared fiercely. "Why they ever agreed to a conference I can't understand, but there's something behind it we won't like. As for me, I wouldn't offer them peace if they held a knife at my throat, and now—when we really hold a knife to theirs, if they only knew it—" She gave an angry shrug and did not finish.

"Do you feel there's any hope of their accepting the emperor's terms?"

Juille scowled. "It depends on how intelligent they are. I'd have called them utter savages, unable to see beyond the next battle, if they hadn't planned this invasion of the inner systems so well. And just now, of course, they do have the upper hand. They took us by surprise. But we're finding our balance and beginning to strike back. They may realize they've struck a little too soon. Maybe they can see ahead to the time when we'll reach that deadlock—and then the new weapon may very well turn the balance to our side." She shook her head fretfully, so that the windows gleamed in reflection upon her shining helmet. "I don't know. It worries me that they came at all. Since they did, it's just possible they might agree to a treaty. Yes, I might almost say I think there's some danger of their agreeing to peace."

"You consider it a danger, highness?"

"The greatest the empire has to face. I say crush them utterly, whatever it costs us. I'd rather inherit a bankrupt empire, when my turn comes, than live on side by side with those murderous savages, giving them our arts and sciences, letting them think themselves our equals. No. No, I feel so strongly about this that I've had to discard a luxury no empire can afford to keep when it threatens the common good." Juille glanced around the room, gathering the eyes of her staff. She nodded.

"We've all agreed to this," she went on. "We make no secret of it. I'm so afraid of even the remote chance of peace at this stage that I've given orders to prevent it." She paused a moment. "I've given orders that the H'vani ambassadors be assassinated before they reach the conference table."

There was silence for a moment. The Dunnarian regarded Juille with expressionless eyes. "They're under truce," he said at last, matter-of-factly. Juille's lips thinned.

"I know. But I intend to be merciless in victory, and I may as well start now. In this case I believe that the end more than justifies any means necessary to achieve it."

"You feel there is that much danger that the H'vani will agree to peace at this stage, when they're winning on all fronts?"

"Why else would they consent to come?" Juille shrugged. "I don't mean to waste any more thought on the matter. If they don't agree now, my father will offer it again and again, to prevent a long war. Sooner or later, as we gain more of the balance of power, they'll accept if they have the chance. If we kill their envoys under a flag of truce now—well, there'll be no more conferences."

The Dunnarian nodded quietly. "A very interesting decision, highness. I assure you I wouldn't interfere even if"—he glanced up at the clock—"even if you'd given me time to."

Juille followed his gaze, "Ah," she said. "You're right—they should be landing. Helia, get us the scene."

Helia, moving with the forthright clumping tread of an old soldier, crossed to the screen where an animated map of an embattled world was tracing the course of insurrection. As she passed the Dunnarian the *llar* on her shoulder gave itself a last preening stroke, gathered its sleek limbs and leaped without a jar onto the envoy's shoulder. He put up a hand to stroke it, and the little creature bent its head to the caress, rolling up its great round eyes with solemn pleasure.

Juille stared. "I've never"—she stammered with surprise—"never in my life . . . why, he'll hardly let me touch him! I'll swear I haven't stroked him like that twice in my life. And he never even saw you before!"

The envoy's delicate, lean features creased in the first smile she had seen upon them. "I feel the honor keenly," he said to the *llar*. It butted its round forehead against his palm like a cat.

A blast of music from the screen interrupted them. Swimming into focus as Helia turned the controls, the scene of the H'vani envoy's landing sharpened into colorful view. Juille curled her lip at it.

"All that ceremony," she murmured, "when we ought to be cutting their throats! Well, they'll soon see what the empire really thinks of them. My men ought to show up very soon now."

She took off her helmet and leaned forward to watch, chin on fist, her dark-gold braids catching the red reflections of banners from the screen and shining as if in firelight. The braids were pinned like a coronet across her head to cushion the heavy helmet which she held now upon her knee. In its surface the red reflections moved too, blurrily, as if—in obvious simile—she cradled the momentous event in her very lap.

The H'vani newcomers were small, brightly clothed figures moving in a press of soldiers. Because the emperor had insisted that their representatives be the highest officials of the enemy race—its hereditary leader and its commander in chief—there had been tremendous haggling over the terms of safe conduct. In the end, they had been assigned a camp outside the city, near enough the boundaries of the Ancients' forbidden territory to remind them of the fate their ships had suffered. And now in the midst of a bodyguard of imperial soldiers they rode toward the city on horseback, amid much flurry of trumpets and streaming of red imperial banners.

Juille was not much interested in the dignitaries as individuals. Her eyes were sweeping the crowd in quick, impatient glances, picturing the flash of her assassins' guns. And the same thought, the same picture, was in every mind in the room with her. No one moved, waiting for that instant. If the power of thought had tangibility, their common concentration of purpose should have been enough in itself to strike the H'vani down.

With intolerable slowness, on the backs of tall, mincing horses, the procession drew near the city. It was a long, colorful ride. The people of Ericon, at the heart of the Galaxy's culture, paradoxically ride horseback when they travel. Except for the straight, paved roads which link city to city, there is little power-driven traffic, and that chiefly the transportation of supplies. Radio-television is so superlatively developed that almost no occasion ever arises for travel upon Ericon itself. Sightseeing is not encouraged upon the sacred control planet, and so much of its surface is forbidden by the Ancients for their own mysterious ends, and by the emperor for his imperial prerogatives, that as a rule only legitimate business traffic, with its prescribed roadways, moves upon the face of Ericon.

As a result, horseback riding is highly fashionable, pleasant enough and sufficiently picturesque to satisfy those of that world who go abroad for amusement. Actually, the terrene of other planets is much more familiar, and more easily reached, because of these restrictions, than the surface of Ericon itself.

The party had been riding a long time, and the tension in the room where the watchers sat was growing unbearable, when a nagging familiarity about one of the mounted figures she watched struggled up past the level of awareness into Juille's conscious mind.

"Focus it down, Helia," she said sharply. "I want to see those men."

The picture swooped dizzily as the vision seemed to hover downward above the slowly moving procession. Then the two H'vani were large upon the screen in bright, three-dimensional life, the rustle of their cloaks audible in the room, the creak of harness, the clink of fire sword against belt.

Juille struggled against a moment of sheer suffocation. She was horrified to feel a tide of prickling warmth sweep up within her, clear to the roots of the dark-gold braids. Too many emotions were striving for dominance in her mind—the effect made her reel. For she knew this blond and bearded young man with a harp slung across his shoulder, riding a tall horse toward the city. She knew him very well, indeed.

Then their meeting on Cyrille had been no accident. And—that half-forgotten grip upon her throat had been no caress. For a moment, her mind and her gaze turned inward, calling back the brief, puzzling idyl which the urgency of recent events had so nearly eclipsed even from memory now. It came back vividly enough, with that picture moving on the screen to remind her.

She sat quite still, sorting out the memories of those three careless, oddly disturbing days on Cyrille. Egide—that was his name, then, Egide the H'vani—must surely have come there because of certain knowledge of her presence. And he must have come with a purpose that was not hard to guess. Especially not hard now, when she looked back to those few strange, tense interludes when she had been frightened without understanding why.

But he had never fulfilled his mission. He had come to kill her and he had let her live. She felt a sudden triumphant flush of vindication—she had guessed his weakness even before she knew his name. It was all there to see in that sensitive and sensuous mouth of his, and she had forestalled him through sheer instinct in the moment of his greatest resolution. A wave of scorn for him washed over her. A man like that was no fit leader for revolutionaries to follow. She had forestalled him in his most urgent duty—but how had she done it? Juille felt the deep blush returning, and bent her head futilely to hide it as her mind went back to that strange, frightening, delightful interlude upon the cloud.

Whatever her motive, she knew it had been herself, not he, who made that first inviting gesture. He had meant to kill her. Every calculating compliment he paid, every scene of elaborate romance he lead her through, had been meant only to lull her to unguarded ease. He must have had no other purpose. But she . . . she took it all at face value and had seemed in the end to beg for his kisses. The deepest depths of humiliation closed over her head as she sat there motionless, burning to the hairline with a red blush of rage.

When her swimming gaze focused again, she met Helia's warning eyes and fought for self-control. And because Helia had bred discipline into her from infancy, after a moment she gained it. But the turmoil of her thoughts went on. No wonder, she thought bitterly, he had agreed to this conference. He had every right to think that she knew him now—had recognized him in some portrait or news screen if she did not recognize him on Cyrille—and he must believe that she herself had insisted upon the meeting, that the terms of peace were hers. He might preen himself now with the thought that his amorous work upon Cyrille had borne fruit already in her betrayal of her own people into compromise with the enemy. She thought hotly that he would judge her by himself and think her as ready as he to toss principles away for the weakness of a personal desire. She had to fight down another surge of blinding humiliation that she had made herself vulnerable to the patronizing scorn of such a man as this. And for an instant she hated, too, the amazonian upbringing that had left her unarmed against him.

Well, there was one good thing in the ugly situation. She would never have to face him again. Her assassins had delayed unpardonably already, but they surely would not delay much longer. He would die without seeing her, without knowing—without knowing she was not deceived! Still thinking the peace plans were hers, because of love for him! No, if he died now she thought she would die, too, of sheer anger and shame.

She sat forward in her chair, watching the two H'vani, reading insolent swagger into every motion they made. To her eyes they rode like conquerors already, coming to accept the peace they thought her ready to hand them on a platter. And she knew she must kill Egide herself or never know self-respect again.

They were at the city gates now. She watched feverishly, on a sword-edge of impatience for the assassins to fail after all. Trumpets echoed from the high white walls and the procession wound along broad streets toward the palace. Juille, waiting on tenterhooks for the flash of the gun that would rob her of her last hope for self-respect, began to realize as the procession moved on, that somehow her hope was to be granted. Somehow the assassins had failed. It was too late already for any efficient job of killing to be done, here in the crowded streets. She leaned to the screen, breathless, seeing nothing else.

She did not know that Helia was watching her anxiously, or that the Dunnarian's great luminous eyes dwelt upon her face with a fathomless sort of speculation.

She puased outside the arch of the conference hall, balancing the *llar* upon her shoulder, drawing a deep breath. Behind her Helia whispered, "All right, all right. Come along now." The familiar voice was marvelously bracing. Juille smiled a grim smile, tossed her cloak back over one shoulder and strode in under the archway, hearing the trumpets blare for her coming.

They rose from their chairs around the white table in the center of the room. She would not look at individual faces as she swung down the room with a clank of empty scabbards—externally she must keep the truce. She felt very sure of herself now. She held her bright-helmed head arrogantly, making the cloak ripple with every long stride, hearing her spurs jingle as she came. The trumpet notes shivered and echoed among the arches of the ceiling.

Above them rose the soaring transept of a vast hall. Its purple walls paled to violet and then to white as they rose toward an intricate interlacing of arches through whose translucent heights pale sunlight came pouring. It was a very old hall. The emperors of Ericon had reared it upon the ruins of the race they had displaced. And that race had built here upon the ruins of other emperors, ages before.

The present emperor stood white and tall at the head of the table. Juille bowed to him formally, but she flicked over and past the other two men a glance so icy that it barely acknowledged their presence.

In one glance, though, she saw all that she needed to see. It was Egide. The same handsome, rash, blue-eyed young face with the curly short beard, the curly hair. He had hung his harp over the chair arm where he sat, and Juille thought it the ultimate touch of decadent foppishness, incongruous in a barbarian prince. He wore today not an extravagantly designed cloak of blood or hair, but black velvet that looked spectacular against the silvery gleam of his mesh mail. There was a fire-sword scar half-healed across his cheek and temple, and he looked a little more tired and wary than the careless lover of Cyrille. But the blue eyes were as confident as ever on her face.

All this in one cold, flashing glance that ignored him. She folded her fingers lovingly over a tiny palm gun hidden in her hand, its metal warm from that close hiding place. Her glance flicked over the other man and went on.

Big, bull-chested, with reddish hair and beard and eyes. Huge forearms crossed over his chest. A barbarian, typical of the savage H'vani. And yet so openly savage, with such a direct, fighting glare on his scarred face, that she felt a reluctant flash of kinship with him. Such a man, she thought, her own remote forefathers must have been who conquered the Galaxy by brute force and left it for her heritage. Beside him Egide looked the fop he was, and her father the senile idealist.

She nodded distantly as the emperor introduced the two. Egide, hereditary leader of the H'vani, Jair, his commander in chief. Her only thought was a murderous one. "If I can kill them both, what a blow to the H'vani! And what fools they were to come!"

Her father was speaking. She scarcely listened to the sonorous voice whose echoes went whispering among the arches in confused murmurs high overhead.

"We sit today," the old man declared, "over the graves of a score of races who made the same mistake we are on the verge of making here, and who died because they did."

She could feel Egide's blue stare upon her face. It was intolerable. All the ages of imperial pride rose behind her, the pride of a hundred generations that had commanded the stars in their courses. This one bearded barbarian sitting here staring at her unashamedly, as if he were her equal, as if he thought she, too, must be remembering a fantastic night-time ride upon a cloud, under stars like burning roses in constellations without a name.

She turned full upon him one bright, furious glare that flashed like a violet fire sword beneath the helmet brim. "You ought to be dead," the burning glance implied. "When I find who failed me, and why they failed, they'll be dead, too. You're living on borrowed time. You ought to be dead and you will be soon—you will be soon!" She made a chant of it in her throat, letting her eyes half-close to slits of bright fire-blade violet.

The emperor talked on. "We are too evenly matched. Neither can win without such destruction as will cast the whole Galaxy back a thousand years. On all the worlds of that Galaxy—many new worlds that have not yet known war—our forces stand poised in armed, precarious truce, watching what happens here today. If we join in battle—"

Juille made an impatient gesture and recrossed her legs. The little palm gun was warm in her hand. She wished passionately that the platitudes were over. And then a treacherous spasm of pity went over her as she listened to the deep old voice roll on. He had been a great warrior once, her father. This meant so much to him, and it was so hopelessly futile— But there was no room for pity in the new Galaxy of today. Her lips thinned as she fondled the trigger of her gun. Soon, now.

"The H'vani are a young race," the old man went on. "A crude race, unlettered in any science but warfare. Let us give you the incalculable wealth we have to spare, that you could never take by force. We can teach you all our science has learned in the rich millenniums of our history. In one stride you can advance a thousand years.

"If you refuse—there is no hope for you. At the very best, we can and will destroy you, if only after such struggles as will cost us all we have. At worst—well, other races have met in deadly conflict on Ericon. Where are they now?" He pointed toward the marble floor. "Down there, in the dark. Under the foundations of this hall lie the building stones of all who fought here before us. Have you ever been down there in the catacombs, any of you? Do you know the old kings who once ruled Ericon? Does anyone alive? And will anyone remember us, if we fail to learn by their example?"

Juille's hand came down roughly on the sleek-furred

little animal that had slid down upon her knee, and then all her scornful inattention vanished as the small body twisted snake-like under her hand. She snatched it back with lightning quickness, just in time to avoid the slash of her pet's teeth. It stared up at her, nervously poised, clutching her knee with flexible fingery pads, a look of completely spurious benignity and wisdom in its round eyes even now.

A new voice, so deeply resonant that the air shuddered in response to it, was saying powerfully, "When peace terms are proposed, it'll be the H'vani who dictate them!"

Juille looked up sharply. The emperor had paused. He stood beside her now with his head sunk a little, watching the two envoys from under his bristling brows. She felt a fresh spasm of pity. But the new voice was making strong echoes rumble among the arches of the ceiling, and she knew it was time to pay attention.

Jair was on his feet, his great fists planted like mallets upon the table edge. "We'll talk peace with the Lyonese," he boomed triumphantly, "but we'll talk it from the throne. Time enough for—"

Juille shoved back her chair with a sudden furious motion and leaped to her feet, her eyes blazing across the table. The *llar* had sprung sidewise and caught the emperor's arm, where it hung staring over its shoulder at her with enormous benignant eyes.

But before she could speak, Egide's chair scraped leisurely across the floor, the harp strings ringing faintly with the motion. He stood up almost lazily, but his words preceded hers.

"We ask the emperor's pardon," he said in a calm voice. "Jair, let me talk."

Jair gave him a strangely blank look and sat down. Egide went on:

"What my general means to say is that peace terms must come from us if they're to come at all. What the emperor says is true and we realize it, but we believe it to be only part of the truth. A divided victory isn't enough for the H'vani, no matter how many secrets you offer as a bribe. My people are not to be bought with promises for the future." He smiled whitely in the impeccable flaxen curls of his beard. "My people, I am afraid, are a very literal race. Not too ready to trust an enemy's promises. Now if you had some specific benefit to offer us here and now—something that might reassure the H'vani about your sincerity"—he glanced from Juille to the emperor and went on with an impulsive persuasion in his voice that Juille remembered well—"I think we might have a better chance of convincing my people that you mean what you say."

Juille met his guileless blue gaze with a steely look. She knew quite well what he was hinting. So that was why they'd come, was it? To wheedle the Dunnarian weapon out of the emperor's senile, peace-bemused hands, and taking full advantage of their supposed immunity because of what had happened upon Cyrille, because they must think that she herself was equally bemused at the memory of it. Obvious strategy, and yet—Juille glanced at her father. No expression showed upon his thoughtful face, but she felt a sudden cold uncertainty about what he might decide to do. Surely he could not believe that the H'vani meant what they said. Surely he must see that once they had a share in the new and subtle weapon from Dunnar there'd be no stopping them this side of the imperial throne. No, he was certainly not yet mad.

But this was only the beginning. Talk would go on and on, endless circlings around the proposal Egide had just voiced. Endless counterproposals from the emperor. Days and days of it, while Egide still went on believing that she was the reason why he had been invited here, still exchanged with her these sudden blue glances that recalled their days upon Cyrille—the crystal platform drifting through flowery branches and the green evening light of spring. The starry lake beneath their feet as they danced, and the long smooth rhythms when they moved together to enchanting music. The landscapes unreeling beneath their couch of cloud, the great stars blazing overhead.

No, she would not endure it. She would end it here and now.

"Egide—" she said in a clear, high voice.

He turned to her with a quick eagerness she had not seen before. This was the first word she had addressed to him upon Ericon, the first time she had ever spoken his name. He was searching her face with a look of eagerness she did not understand. She didn't want to.

She walked slowly around the table toward him. They were all on their feet now, looking at her in surprise. All speech had ceased and the hall was very still. The emperor said, "Jullie?" in a voice not yet very much alarmed, but she did not glance at him. She rounded the end of the table and saw Egide push his chair out of the way with a careless thrust that knocked the harp from its back. In the silence, the jarred strings wailed a thin, shrill, plaintive discord through the hall, and Egide caught the falling instrument and smiled uneasily at her.

She came toward him without a flicker of returning smile. "Egide—" she said again. She was quite near him now. Near enough to see the crinkling edges of the scar that furrowed his cheek, the separate curling hairs of his shining beard, his thick golden lashes. Behind him she was aware that Jair had drawn an uneasy step or two nearer. She was looking straight into Egide's blue eyes, large and unfathomable at this nearness. She came forward one last step, bringing her gun hand up.

"I want you to know," she said distinctly, "that I had no part in asking you here. I hate your race and all it stands for. I mean to do everything I can to prevent any truce between us. Everything. Do you understand me?"

The emperor did. He knew his child. He took one long stride toward her around the table, crying, "Juille, Juille! Remember the truce—"

But he was too far away. Juille fixed Egide's fascinated stare with a hot, exultant stare of her own, and her lips drew back in a tight grin over her teeth. With her face very near his, and her gaze plumbing his gaze, she smiled and pulled the trigger.

Then time stopped. A dozen things happening at once, jumbled themselves together bewilderingly, prefaced and veiled by a great fan of violet heat that sprang up terribly between her face and Egide's. Juille heard Jair's roar and her father's cry, and the crash of overturning chairs. But her brain was numbed by the shock of that violet heat where there should have been no heat—only a thin needle beam of force boring through Egide's corselet.

She and Egide reeled apart with singed lashes and cheeks burning from that sudden glare as the instantaneous fan of light died away. Her dazzled eyes saw dimly that he was gasping like a man who had taken a sudden sharp blow in the stomach, but he was not dead. He should be dead, and he only stood there gasping at her, blinking singed golden lashes.

For a split second her mind could not grasp it. She saw the silver mail burned away across his chest where that fierce needle beam should have bored through flesh and bone. She saw beneath it not charred white skin and spurting blood, but a smooth shining surface which the beam had not even blackened. Everything was ringed with rainbows, and when she closed her smarting eyes she saw the outline of burned mail and gleaming surface beneath in reversed colors bright against the darkness of her lids.

Then time caught up with her. Things began to happen again with furious speed. The explanation flashed into her mind as she saw Egide reaching for her. He wore some sort of protection even under his mail, then—some substance that deflected the needle beam into a blast of thin, scorching heat diffused into harmlessness. And she had an instant of foolish and incongruous rage that he had come thus protected, doubting the validity of their truce.

Then Egide's arm slammed her hard against the unyielding surface of whatever armor he wore beneath his mail. She felt a small, reluctant admiration of the strength in that arm—an unexpected strength, remembered from Cyrille—and of his almost instantaneous action even when she knew he must be sick and breathless from a severe blow in the pit of the stomach. The gun's beam would have bruised him heavily even through the armor, before its force fanned out into sheer heat.

It all happened too quickly to rationalize. She did not even have time to wonder why he seized her, or why Jair, bellowing with a sound of exultation, was dragging them both across the floor toward the far wall. She had a confused glimpse of her father's bewildered and outraged face. She saw the guards leaning out of their hidden stations in the wall across from her, guns leveled. But she knew she herself was a shield for the two H'vani, though what they planned, she could not even guess.

Other guards were tumbling from their posts, running toward them across the hall. Juille suddenly began to fight hard against the restraining clasp that held her. She bruised her fists upon the armor beneath Egide's mail. Jair roared inexplicably:

"Open up! You hear me? Open!"

Egide crushed her ribs painfully against his corselet and swung her feet off the ground. For a dizzy instant the violet walls and the sunlit white arches of the ceiling spun in reverse around her. She was hanging head-down over Egide's shoulder, seething with intolerable rage at this first rough handling she had ever known in her life. But she was bewildered, too, and off-balance and incredulous that such things could happen. She was briefly aware of cries from the hall, her father's voice shouting commands, the guards yelling. And then came sudden darkness and a smooth, swishing noise that cut off all sounds behind them.

The dark smelled of dust and age-old decay. Juille's mind told her what her reason refused to accept—that somehow, incredibly, these barbarians had come forearmed with knowledge about some panel in the walls of the imperial council hall which a hundred generations of ruling emperors had never guessed.

She was still upside down over Egide's shoulder, acutely uncomfortable, her cheek pressed against something cold and hard, her eyes stinging from the heat of her own gun. Voices whispered around them. Someone said, "Hurry!" and there was the muffled sound of feet through dust that rose in stifling clouds. And then a long, sliding crash that filled the darkness deafeningly and made the eardrums ache from its sudden pressure in this confined space. Someone said after a stunned moment, "There, that does it." Someone else—Jair?—said, "How?" and the first voice, familiar but unplaceable:

"When they break through the wall, they'll find this rock-fall, and a false tunnel that leads outside the city walls. They'll think you went that way. We laid a trail of footprints through it yesterday. Safe now."

But who . . . who was it?

"Put me down!" Juille demanded in a fierce, muffled voice. That someone whose tones sounded very familiar indeed, said:

"Better not yet. Come along. Can you manage her?"

And the nightmare went on. Someone ahead carried a light that cast great wavering shadows along the rough walls. Juille was joggling up and down across Egide's shoulder through the musty dark, sick with fury and outrage and bewilderment. Her eyes streamed with involuntary tears as an aftermath of that heat flash; her burning cheek was pressed hard against the corner of something cold and unyielding—Egide's harp?—and the dust rose chokingly all around.

After smothered ages, the familiar voice said: "You can put her down now."

There came one last upheaval and Juille was on her feet again, automatically smoothing down her tunic, glaring through the dimness in a speechless seizure of rage. She saw Egide looking down at her with expressionless eyes, saw Jair's savage face dark in the torchlight, his eyes gleaming. Between them she saw the familiar, comforting, tough-featured face of Helia.

For an instant her relief was greater than she would have thought possible. All her life that face had meant comfort, protection, gruff encouragement against disappointment. In the midst of this bewilderment and indignity, the one familiar sight made everything all right again. Even in the face of reason—

Egide still held her arms.

"Turn her around," Helia told him, in the familiar voice, with the familiar homely gesture of command Juille had known all her life, from nursery days. She found herself spun around, her arms held behind her, while Helia reached under the mail tunic and took away the little dagger that no one else knew about, the dagger that Helia herself had taught Juille to hide there and use unexpectedly as a last resort.

Juille closed her eyes.

"The others will be waiting," Helia's capable voice remarked calmly. "First, though—highness, I had better tie your hands."

Juille wondered madly whether that violet flash of heat had really killed her. Perhaps it had only stunned her—that must be it—and all this was an irrational dream.

Helia's familiar hands that had bathed her from babyhood, dressed her hurts, taught her sword play and target practice—were binding her wrists behind her now with sure, gentle swiftness. The well-known voice said as the binding went on:

"You must understand, highness, before you meet the rest. I don't want you to face them without understanding." She drew the soft cords tighter. "I am an Andarean, highness. Your race conquered ours a hundred generations ago. But we never forget. Here under the city, in the catacombs that were once our own imperial halls, we've met to pass along from father to son the tradition of our heritage. We've planned all these centuries for a day like this. There." She gave the cords a final pat. "Now, keep your head up and don't let them see it if you're confused. Wait a minute." She came around in front of Juille, clucked disapprovingly, and took out a handkerchief to wipe the dust from Juille's hot face where the tears had streaked it. Then she straightened the helmet that had fallen by its chin strap over one ear.

"Keep your head up," she said again. "Remember what I've taught you. We may have to kill you later, my dear—but while you live, you're still my girl and I want to be proud of you. Now—march!"

And so, bewildered to the point of madness, still choked by the dust in her nostrils, her eyes burning and her hands tied behind her, but with her head up because Helia, insanely, wanted to be proud of her, Juille let herself be marched forward, up shallow steps and into a big low cavern lighted by square windows through which light streamed from some outside source.

There were people here, sitting along the walls on benches. Not many. Juille knew some of the faces—servants and small courtiers about the palace. A few of them held responsible positions with the defense forces.

From among them a man stepped forward. Juille did not know him, except that his features were Andarean. He wore a purple tunic and cloak, and he bowed to the two H'vani.

"We are making history here," he said in a soft, low-pitched voice. "This is the turning point in the war for Galactic domination. We of Andarea welcome you and the future you will control."

Jair drew a deep breath and started to say something. Juille was aware that Egide's elbow jammed into his ribs. Egide, still breathing a little unevenly from the gun bolt in the stomach, spoke instead in his most courtly voice:

"We H'vani will owe you a great deal. You've managed things perfectly so far. But we haven't much time now. The weapons—"

The Andarean's long eyes slid around to Juille. It was at once a query and a murderous suggestion, without words. Juille felt a sudden shudder of goose flesh. New experiences had crowded one another in these last few minutes until she was dizzy with trying to adjust to them—she had never been man-handled before, she had never been treated like an object instead of a person, and she hotly resented the fact that Egide had not directly addressed a word to her since the moment in the hall when she had tried to kill him.

Behind her dimly she saw Helia step forward to lay a hand on Egide's arm. Suddenly she knew how Egide had learned of her presence on Cyrille—perhaps, too, why her assassins had failed to reach the H'vani during their ride into the city. But when Egide spoke his voice was firm, as if he had not needed prompting.

"Juille is our hostage," he told the Andarean. "There, I think, we've improved on your plan. If anything goes wrong, we still have something to bargain with."

The Andarean nodded dubiously, his narrow, impassive eyes lingering on her face as if in reluctance. "Perhaps. Well, we'd better get started. We—"

"Wait." Egide glanced around the cavern, dim in the light that so oddly came through from outside. "Are these all of you?"

"Almost all." The Andarean said it carelessly. "Our numbers have dwindled very much in the last few generations."

Juille narrowed her eyes at him. That was a lie. The Andareans were few, but certainly not this few. Grateful for some problem she could take a real hold upon, she cast her mind back searchingly over the past history of this race, making a mental note to have the heads off certain of her espionage officials if she ever got out of this alive.

Long ago the earlier emperors had kept close spies

upon their overthrown predecessors, but the watch had relaxed as generations passed and the Andarean numbers grew less. They were too few, really, to matter except in some such accident as this, when chance assembled just the right factors to make their treachery dangerous.

So the two H'vani had come—why? Exactly why? Groping back among the tangled skeins of plot and counterplot Juille lost her grip again upon clear thinking. They were here because they thought in her weakness she had asked them to talk peace terms—because they hoped to trick possession of the Dunnarian weapon out of the Lyonese hands—because of some treacherous promises from these skulkers in the underground. And those skulkers themselves were lying out of the depths of further schemes of their own.

She got a cold sort of comfort out of that. If the H'vani had deceived her and her father, they in turn were being deceived. For there were far more Andareans upon Ericon than she saw here. Their leader would not have lied just now if he were not playing some desperate game with his new allies.

Weapons. Egide had asked about weapons. Were the Andareans offering him some new offensive measure to use against the Lyonese? And why? The Andareans were a subtle race; surely they had cherished the memories of their great lost heritage too long, if Helia told the truth, to give up their future to H'vani rule, supposing the H'vani won. And surely they were too wise in the ways of deceit to trust H'vani promises even should they win.

Juille gave up the problem as Helia took her arm again and drew her after the others. They were moving out of the low cavern with its strange outside lighting. Helia padded along softly at Juille's side, her eyes downcast. Juille looked at her in the dim light, finding no words with which to reproach her. She was still too stunned by this sudden failure of the solidest assurance in her life to look at it with any rational clarity.

Nor was Helia a woman to offer apologies.

"Look around you," she said brusquely as they filed out of the cavern. "You may never see a sight like this again."

The cavern, seen from outside in clearer light, was obviously the collapsed remnants of a much higher room. What might once have been a hallway ran around it outside, the walls patterned with luminous blocks that shed a glow which must be three thousand years old.

The walls showed scars of age-old battle. Juille's first imperial ancestors might very well have commanded the guns that made them. For this uppermost level of the tunnels which lay beneath the city must once have comprised the lower stories of the palace the Andareans had built in the days of their glory.

The ruins had been leveled off and sealed when the modern palace was built. Everyone knew of the honeycombing layers which went down and down in unknown depths of level under level. Some of them had been explored, cursorily. But they were much too unsafe for any systematic examination, and far too deep to be cleared out or filled up to give the city a firm foundation.

The confusion of interlacing passages, level blending with level, was so complex that explorers had been known to vanish here and never reappear. And immemorial traps, laid down millenniums ago by retreating defenders in forgotten wars, sometimes caught the innocent blundering along dusty tunnels. Walls and floors collapsed from time to time under the weight of exploring footsteps. No, it was not a safe place for the casual adventurer to visit.

But perhaps in each dynasty the survivors of the defeated race had lurked here in the cellars of their lost and ruined city, remembering their heritage and plotting to regain it. Perhaps—Juille thought of it grimly—her own people one day might creep in darkness through the shattered remnants of her purple plastic halls and jeweled arches, buried beneath the mounting stories of a new city, whispering the traditions of the Lyonese and plotting the downfall of triumphant H'vani. And perhaps they, too, might explore downward, as the Andareans had obviously done, searching the dangerous lower levels for some weapon to turn against the victors.

From the murmurs that drifted back to her along the tunnels she knew that something valuable lay hidden here, unless the Andareans were lying again. It was hard to believe that any such weapon actually existed, unknown after so many generations of curious explorers. And yet the Andareans sounded very sure. Egide and Jair would certainly not have risked their necks on such a mission unless the promise had been soundly based on evidence.

Indeed, it seemed incredible that these two foremost leaders of the revolt would have dared to endanger their lives and their whole campaign on such a gamble as this, had they not been very sure of escape.

Someone ahead was carrying a radiant globe of translucent plastic on the end of a tall handle. She could see Egide's confident yellow head haloed with light from it, and Jair's great bulk outlined against the glow. The light sliding along the walls showed scenes of forgotten Andarean legends, winged animals and eagle-headed men in low relief upon which dust had gathered like drifts of snow. They passed windows of colored glass that no longer opened upon anything but darkness. They passed rooms which the soft light briefly revealed in amorphous detail under mounds of smothering dust.

And once they came out on a balcony over a scene that took Juille's breath away. The vast hall below them was built on a scale so tremendous that it seemed incredible that human minds had conceived it. Its vast oval was proportioned so perfectly that only the giddy depths below them made the room seem as large as it was. A muted blue radiance lighted it from incredible heights of windows lifting columns of blue unbroken glass from floor to ceiling, all around the walls.

Helia said with a sort of gruff pride, "This was one of our temples once, highness. No one's ever built such a temple since. See that glass? The secret of it's lost now. The light's in the glass itself, not from outside." She was silent for a moment, looking down. Then she said in a softer voice, "Andarea was a great nation, highness. You feel the same about yours. Remember what you said today, about breaking the truce? The end justifies any means you have to take. I think so, too."

It was as near as she could come to apology or explanation. And Juille, after a moment of blinking dismay at this application of her own theories turned against her, was conscious of sudden respect for this inflexible woman at her side. Here was the true amazon, she thought, more ruthless than any man in the naked simplicity of her cast-off femininity. This was the one quality Juille could respect above all others. She glanced ahead at Egide's broad back, despising him for the lack of it. Unswerving faithfulness to a principle, whatever that principle might be.

Juille wondered what Egide was thinking, how he interpreted to himself her attempt at murder. Well, if she had failed it was not for weakness like his. And there might come another chance. Her mind had begun to awaken again after the stunning shocks of the past half hour. Already she was making plans. Helia she thought she understood. Helia would protect her while she could. She would see to her comfort and save her face whenever possible, but when the time came, Helia might kill her with a steady hand. And Juille would have despised her if the hand shook.

They went down a sweep of tremendous stairs and filed, a pigmy row, across the floor of that vast hall under the shining blue columns of the windows. And from there they went down sharply, and down again.

There was tension in the air of these lower levels. Once an Andarean went ahead to a curtain of spider webs that veiled the passage and lifted it aside on the point of a staff, with exaggerated care, while the party passed beneath. And once they balanced carefully in single file along a bridge of planks laid upon perfectly solid flooring.

They had come so far now, by such devious ways, that she had no idea where she was, or at what level. She was sure the H'vani were equally at a loss. And it occurred to her briefly that they were at the mercy of their guides now—that the Andareans could come very close to putting an end to the Galaxy-wide warfare here and now in the dusty dark. For robbed of their leaders, the armies would certainly falter. But Juille felt quite sure that whatever the Andareans wanted, it was not peace.

They had, perhaps, taken steps even surer than her own to make certain that the emperor's peace conference came to nothing. The H'vani, primed with promises of mysterious weapons, would be in no mood to make a truce with any idea of keeping it.

She demanded suddenly of Helia, still walking at her elbow in the old accustomed place, "Why haven't the Andareans used these weapons themselves?" And she saw Egide's broad back tense a little, the harp slung across his shoulder—where she had hung ignobly a little while before—shifting place at the motion of muscles beneath. She knew that he must have been wondering the same thing. And she knew he was listening.

"As we told the H'vani," Helia said, "we aren't a nation of fighters any more, highness. And there are too few of us. We couldn't risk losing the weapons in any tentative uprising."

So they'd told the H'vani that already, had they? And it hadn't satisfied Egide any more than it did herself. Helia was a magnificent fighter. She had taught Juille all she knew. A determined, secret band of men and women armed with an unexpected weapon could have seized key positions on planets enough to swing the balance of power to themselves if they chose, and if they were gifted with the subtle minds the Andareans had already shown themselves to possess. Juille would not have hesitated, in such a case. And she didn't think Helia would either, if there were no alternative.

Obviously, there was an alternative. They were using the H'vani against the imperial forces—why?

Suddenly, Juille saw the answer. It was the simplest strategy in the world, and the safest. You could risk an uprising, your own neck and ultimate failure by acting yourself, or you could pit the two forces of greatest power against one another, preventing any truce between them by devious methods, arming one against the other to maintain a perfect balance—until they had wiped each other out. When both sides had struggled to exhaustion, then let the Andareans step in and take over the control they had been prepared to take for so many centuries. It was so easy.

"Here it is," the Andarean in the purple tunic said.

They all crowded forward to stare. And it was a sight worth staring at. The shadows hid most of the long room, shadows heavy as velvet curtains, as if their own age had thickened them into tangible things. But they could not wholly hide the weapons racked shining upon the walls, shining and defiant of dust and rust and the æons. Cobwebs had formed upon them like festoons, gathering dust until their own weight tore them. There were many layers of such cobwebs, woven and thickened and torn anew over these untarnished swords and pistols and nameless things. Wherever the velvety dust of the webs revealed them, they were brilliant in the light. Some other lost race had known and buried with itself the secret of such metal.

The Andarean dismissed that array with a gesture.

"Unimportant things there, on the walls. Only variations of weapons already in use. Out of all this arsenal there are only three important weapons that haven't been paralleled in later ages. We want to give you those three."

He padded silently forward through the dust, lifting his feet like a man who walks in snow, and took up from a clean-swept stand a little pistol not much bigger than the palm gun Juille had dropped in the council hall.

"This," he said, hefting its shining smallness on his hand, "discharges a miniature lightning bolt that feeds on metal. It leaps from armed man to armed man, or from girder to girder, feeding and growing as it goes, until the gap becomes too wide to jump."

Juille stared at the little gun, a confused realization taking shape in her mind that this war was to be unlike any war before in Lyonese history—unless she could escape somehow in time to prevent the use of these weapons. It would be as if the gods took part, so strange and new would the weapons be on both sides.

The Andarean leader was looking at her uneasily. "Is it wise to let the princess hear about all this?" he asked Egide.

The H'vani turned and for the first time since that moment in the council hall, looked straight into Juille's eyes. She met the look almost happily, with a defiance he could not mistake. She was eager to bring into the open all her hatred of him, all her scorn. She wanted it put it into words, but before she could have spoken, he said in his faintly malicious drawl that she remembered very well, "You'd better stay here. Helia will keep you company." It was a patronizing tone. Half turned away, he added over one shoulder, "I'll be back—" and gave her a long look.

Speechless with fury, Juille watched him plowing away through the dust with the others. Everything he had said might have been deliberately calculated to enrage her. She twisted her wrists futilely against the cords.

Helia was looking at her with narrow, speculative eyes. Juille gave her a quelling glance and turned her back, looking up at the dust-swathed weapons with an angry, unseeing stare. Voices receded down the room. And as Juille's anger ebbed a little, she found that the rack of weapons made a very interesting sight. Just possibly some of those guns might still be loaded. If their look of shining, immortal efficiency could be trusted, she might, with luck, find one that had been left in working order.

And there had, she thought, been something a little false about the Andarean's casual dismissal of the guns. She would have been willing to bet that six months from now, if the H'vani, with their gift of weapons, were gaining the upper hand too quickly over the imperial forces, there would be Andarean patriots from the tunnels to make a gift of other weapons to the Lyonese. These Andareans were much too subtle to give away their whole stock to the first comer. And if they were really holding back weapons to offer the Lyonese should the H'vani seem to win too easily, might not some of these devices on the wall be worth taking? If she could—if she only could—

This rack before her presented a display of curiously shaped weapons half shrouded in velvet-thick webs of dust. Some of them looked vaguely familiar. She didn't want those. Probably the Andarean had told at least a half-truth when he said many of them were simply variations of known things. But this odd, slim, flexible pistol, with a bell-shaped mouth and a coil of silver tubing twined about its length—

Juille turned her back on the wall and glanced down the room. Helia was watching the group at the far end, where men appeared to be handling what looked like a big folded net of loose meshes with nodes that sparkled opalescent in the light. She could not hear what they said.

Juille took three steps backward, soundless in the deep dust, hitched her cloak painstakingly out of the way and groped blindly with her bound hands through layers of velvety dust. She thought shudderingly of the spiders that had spun these webs, and it occurred to her that she would probably never like the touch of velvet again as she tore the clinging, thick softness from the gun she wanted. It was not easy, with her hands bound. She prayed for Helia to watch the other end of the room a moment longer—

There. Cool and slick against her palms, enigmatic, potentially very dangerous—the slender gun was hers. What might happen when she pulled its trigger no one could guess. Probably nothing at all. But the feel of it was heartening. She thrust it down inside the back of her belt and let her cloak swing over it. And when Helia turned again to glance at her, she was looking up at a rack of daggers with bored, aloof eyes.

"Those won't help you, highness," Helia said. "That cord I used on you is a woven plastic. Knives can't touch it."

"I know," Juille told her, not turning.

Voices drew nearer along the big, dim hall. Juille glanced around. She could see that Egide wore the lightning gun thrust through his belt, and Jair's bull-bulk was padded even further by the heavy net folded and looped through his own belt. She could see no third weapon. She could not even guess what the net was for. But she had her own secret now, and her feeling of utter helplessness was mitigated a little.

She watched them come slogging back through the dust, their voices rumbling between the walls. Now and then, curiously, a weapon's delicate blade rang with a thin sound when some chance note of the voices struck it to response, as if the immeasurable past protested in futile, tongueless, inhuman speech against this violation.

There was a new and triumphant assurance in the very carriage of the two H'vani as they neared her. Jair's eyes and teeth gleamed from his ruddy dark face, and Egide glowed with a sort of shining exhilaration.

At the door of the room he paused to look back along the shadowy depths, and his bright, carelsss face lighted. Then he grinned and unslung his harp. The others stared. Egide's calloused fingers swept the strings into a sudden, wild, wailing chord, and another, and then a third. The underground room rang with it, and on the wall a quiver of life leaped into shining motion as here and there a thin blade shrilled response. Egide laughed, a deep, full-throated sound, and shouted out what must have been a line or two of some old H'vani battle song. His voice was startlingly sweet and strong and true.

The arsenal boomed with the deep, rolling echoes of it. Somewhere hidden under tons of dust, a forgotten drum boomed back, distant and softly muffled. Some metal cylinder of forgotten purpose took up the echo and replied with a clear, metallic reverberation, and down the hall an æons-dead warrior's helmet rang with its hollow mouth like a clapperless bell, and fell clanging to the floor and the silencing dust.

Egide laughed again, with a timbre of sudden intoxication, and smote his harp to a last wild, shrilling wail, sent one more phrase of the song booming down the room. And all the room replied. The muffled drum boomed back, and the clear ringing twang of the hidden cylinder, and the little blades shrilled like tongues upon the wall, shivering and twinkling with tiny motion.

Echoes rolled and rolled again. Egide's voice sang on for a moment or two without him, diminishing against the walls. And this was no longer a thin, hopeless protest of the voiceless past against intrusion as the arsenal replied. Egide's was a warrior's voice, promising battle again, strong and savage with the savagery of a barbarous young race. These weapons had rung before, in the unfathomable past, to the voices of such men. Arsenal and weapons roared an answer to that promise of blood again, and the echoes died slowly among the blades and the drums and the hollow, hanging shields that might never echo any more to the sounds they were made to echo.

Juille, meeting the unashamed melodrama of his blue eyes and his laughter as he turned away, was appalled by a surge of genuine warmth and feeling. This was naked sentiment again, like the deliberate romance of Cyrille, but to her amazement she found herself responding, and with an unexpected, overwhelming response she did not understand. Egide, laughing, had reslung his harp. He said:

"Come on—now the danger starts. You have a ship for us, Andarean?"

"Ready and waiting. You'd better not try to leave, though, until dark."

"The real danger comes then," Jair rumbled.

Egide bent a shining smile upon Juille. "That's where you come in, my dear. We couldn't have a better hostage."

Juille gave him her stoniest glance and looked away. She was profoundly troubled by that moment of sympathy with his unashamed romanticism. It made her think of the warm, resistless mood which had engulfed them both on the dance floor, and that hour on the starry cloud—swift, irresistible, and vanishing to leave nothing but humiliation behind, and a stronger dislike and distrust of the man who could evoke such weakness.

They went back along winding, upward tunnels, past the carving of forgotten history upon the walls, past level above level of successive cultures whose dust mingled now under the feet of new rival cultures, one of which must pass so soon. Several times they edged past danger points again, and the leading Andarean twice closed and locked metal grilles after them across their path. The implication was ominous, though no one referred to it aloud.

Egide's intoxicated assurance began to ebb perceptibly and he grew more thoughtful as they neared the upper levels. Juille, watching his broad back and thinking with a sort of detached passion how pleasant it would be to set the bell-muzzle of her new weapon against it, began to wonder presently at his preoccupation.

She saw him murmur to Jair, and saw the big red

beard turn in the lamplit dimness to stare almost incredulously at his leader. Then Egide went ahead to murmur further with the purple-robed Andarean. Juille began to feel a bit cold. Were they talking about herself? Had the time come already to dispose of her? Surely not yet, before they were safely away—

When they came out onto a lighted level that showed signs of Andarean traffic, Egide halted. Helia and Juille exchanged an involuntary glance of mutual query. Egide came back through the column to them. There was a strange, stilled look upon his face, as if he had come to some momentous decision in the grip of which he seemed to want human nearness, for he put out both hands and laid them upon Juille's shoulders. Automatic reaction against the lese majesty made her tense to shake him off, but something about the look in his eyes halted her.

"I'm going—out," he said, in a quiet voice not at all like the melodious roar that had shaken the arsenal below.

"They'll catch you." She had meant it for a threat, but his look subdued her and the words came out a warning.

He shook his yellow head. "I think not. They tell me there's a tunnel into the forest from here."

"But the forest—" Julie broke off and stared up at him, a sinking in the pit of her stomach. For the forest marked the edge of that forbidden ground surrounding the temple of the Ancients. They looked at one another briefly, antagonisms forgotten for a moment. Egide was nodding.

"I think I need advice. None of us ever had this chance before. Now I'm here—well, I'm going to take it."

Juille stared up at him with real awe. Even the emperors of the Galaxy, with the stars of heaven for an empire, dared not think too deeply or too often of the living gods of Ericon. Long ago, she knew, there had been emperors who went to consult the Ancients in their temple. So far as she knew, none had done so for a long while now. Upon this one world of all the Galaxy, men lived side by side with the gods, and they had learned not to presume upon their nearness. The very aloofness of the Ancients, striking only to punish, never to reward, did not encourage familiarity. She looked up at Egide with eyes emptied of all thought but reluctant awe.

His own eyes were very still. He had not quite her feeling of the god's remoteness because, paradoxically, he had not lived so near them. But everyone tended to fall silent at the thought of the Ancients.

He looked down at her thoughtfully, and for a moment Juille knew, with a sort of angry certainty, that he was about to kiss her. Her pride and her scorn of him made that thought intolerable, but a dissolving warmth was running through her treacherous body as she met his look, and the most humiliating gladness that her arms were tied so that she could not resist. Then the humiliation drowned everything else as he let his hands fall and turned away.

"Tie her up somewhere until I get back," he said briefly to Helia. "Jair, come with me as far as the tunnel—"

Juille sat angrily on a floor deeply cushioned with dust, leaning upon a dusty wall. Profound dimness all around her was feebly diluted by the light of a distant lamp. Helia had left it, after a short disagreement with her companions. Juille realized that the Andareans probably distrusted the depths of Helia's loyalty to themselves where Juille was concerned, and oddly, she rather resented their distrust. The cult of the amazon was still too new not to resent man's misunderstanding of its principles. Juille was conscious of a sort of fierce pride in Helia's betrayal of her lifelong trust, for the bleak ideal of Andarean loyalty. The Andareans' doubt of it was a slap in the face to all amazons.

But she was not thinking of that now. She was mentally following Egide through the dripping green forest toward the temple which she had never seen. She knew it would be dark and broad and tall among the trees. She pictured Egide in his black velvet and charred silver mail, striding up to the portal and— But her mind balked at following him farther.

And that, too, humiliated her. It seemed to her that she had been wallowing in enforced humilities for the past several hours, each of them more irritating than the last. This was particularly so, because it involved the moral courage she prided herself on possessing. She did not like to think of Egide walking boldly up to a doorway so awesome that she herself scarcely dared visit it in thoughts. Even the knowledge that he was a barbarian and an outworlder, with the courage of ignorance, was not too comforting. And presently, in the dimness, she began to wonder whether she could do as he was doing, supposing herself free again. Step in under that great shadowy, unimaginable portal and ask for guidance? Intrude her small human presence upon the living gods, whose millenniums of aloofness showed so clearly that they did not welcome human interference?

Even if she were free, would she dare?

Suddenly, hideously, there were tiny cold hands fumbling at hers.

The darkness reeled about her. Mad thoughts went racing through her mind—denizens of the lower levels, creeping up in the dark to seize her? Unseen things against which the Andareans locked their great grilles in vain? Tiny, clammy-fingered demons from some lost race's hell— Clammy-fingered—many-fingered—

Juille sank back against the wall and laughed hysterically in the dark, weak with relief, feeling a sleek, furry side brushing her wrist as the little hands tugged at her bonds. The *llar*, of course, but how . . . how could it possibly have followed or found her here? No *llar* had ever done such a thing before. They had none of the canine's fawning faithfulness. No, there must be rescuers close behind it, though how anyone could have followed her here unseen by the Andareans, she could not imagine.

She called softly into the dimness. No answer, but the *llar* hissed at her gently, rather like a man whistling in preoccupation as he works. A moment later, she was amazed to feel the cord slackening at her wrists. Knowing how efficiently Helia had tied it, she could not believe the little animal could have loosened the knots. Nor could its teeth have parted the strands no knife could touch. But her hands were free, and already prickling with the pins and needles of returning circulation.

She rubbed them together, luxuriating in the pleasure of relaxed arm muscles again, and then felt the *llar*'s lithe, boneless weight on her knees. Something was thrust into her hands. Her fingers closed stiffly on a packet—a little leather bag. With fingers clumsy as thumbs, she expored it.

A tiny cylinder fell out, and something like a mirror on a chain, and what felt like a card. She knew the shape of the cylinder. It was a needle-beam flashlight that was weapon and torch in one. Cautiously, awkwardly, she switched on the flash to its weakest power. In the little blue-white circle of its light she could make out writing on the card.

It was a message of almost incredible impersonality:

> I am sending you the first completed focusing agent for our weapon. Center your target in the cross-hairs, then press the white stud. Target will register in the machine here; can be destroyed at will by pressing the black stud. Sorry this is a model, good for one shot only. Choose well.
>
> DUNNAR.

Juille reread the note slowly, puzzled by its laconic detachment. This might be a problem in ethics instead of the desperate reality it was. She saw in her mind's eye the strange, avian face of the envoy as it had so often regarded her with an impersonal, lidless gaze. She could not imagine emotion showing in it. Not even his own danger, she remembered now, had moved him at all when he came in from space with the weapon. Certainly no peril of hers moved him. She sensed some unfathomable purpose of his own working out, calmly and unhurried, behind all that had just been happening. Was he an Andarean? Certainly there was something behind those great, unwinking eyes, something locked secretly in the narrow skull, that evoked awe and distrust together.

Well, at any rate, now she had a weapon. Two weapons, for the flashlight would serve, too. She turned the thing like a mirror over in her hand. A double lens on a chain, she saw now, each lens threaded with a cross-hair and manipulated by studs in the tiny frame. A white stud, a black one. Such a simple thing to carry that deadly power. She tossed it up and caught it in her palm, grinning with sudden, fierce confidence. The tables were turning a little. Egide had left her bound and helpless; he would come back to her free and armed with a weapon of such surpassing treachery as no race had owned before, a weapon that struck out of empty air, in solitude, at the striker's will. But since this was a model, it would strike only once. She cursed that restriction in a whisper. Would it be Egide, then? Her feeling for him was too much a jumble of passionate contradictions now, to be sure. Although—

The *llar* squeaked impatiently at her knee. She glanced down in the faint blue light. "Well, little friend?"

It was hard sometimes to know just where to place the limitations of that tiny animal brain. The *llars* were like cats in their fastidious withdrawal from any human attempt to probe their small minds or catalogue them according to human standards. She thought her own pet understood a limited vocabulary very well. She said, "What is it now? Where *did* you come from? Is there danger?"

The great benign eyes stared up at her; the furry

body twisted away and then back as if in an urgent plea to follow. Juille said, "All right," and stood up, brushing off the thick dry dust. The *llar* scuttled to the door and peered out. Then it scuttled back and looked up expectantly. "Run along," Juille told it. "I'll follow."

She slipped the lens chains over her head and dropped the circular instrument down inside her tunic. It would look like some innocent ornament if anyone caught her now. But she felt, without knowing why, a curious faith in the *llar*'s ability to guide her out of this place in safety. She even experienced an illogical flicker of gratification that the impersonal little beast had troubled itself so much in her behalf. The entire performance was one no naturalist would have believed possible, certainly no owner of the proud, fastidious animals.

She went swiftly along the tunnel, over the cushioning dust, lighting her way with the dimmest blue radiance of her torch. It could be changed to a weapon of needle-beam force by a twist of the handle if anyone came out to intercept her, but her unreasoning faith in the *llar* was justified more deeply with every passing moment, for it led her along tunnels that seemed to have been uninhabited since the last Andarean emperor died at the hands of the first Lyonese.

Watching the sleek, lithe body flowing through the dimness, Juille wondered at its unerring certainty of the path. Some homing instinct, or actual knowledge of these passages? No one knew enough about the *llar* species to answer that.

The chain of small, flower-shaped footprints in the dust led her on and on. Up level, down level. Over crumbled ruins, through chambers of resounding echoes and caverns muffled in age-old dust.

They must be nearing the end of the journey now. She could smell fresh air blowing along the tunnels and smiled as she pictured the excitement in the palace when she came out. Her deep uneasiness about the unknown weapons of the Andareans would be appeased soon; those weapons would never now be turned against her. And she thanked her imperial ancestors that Egide had thought he must consult the Ancients, for it gave her the time she needed. The H'vani and their smuggled weapons would never leave Ericon now.

Her own emotional reactions to the immediate past and the immediate future were too tangled to sort out. She didn't want to. That would come later. At any moment she would be coming out into the bustling exhilaration of the palace, and her long inactivity and helplessness would be ended. She smiled into the dark.

At her feet the *llar* scurried, rippling, on ahead.

The end came suddenly. They turned a corner and an unbarred door hung half open before them. The *llar* gave one small, whispering cry and then drew aside into the shadows of the tunnel. Cautiously, but with a beating pulse of triumph in her throat, Juille pushed the door open. Words were on her lips—urgent commands, reassurances, all the details of the plans she had been working out to put into practice the moment she reached her destination.

But she stood open-mouthed in the doorway and said nothing. There was no one to say it to. A gust of sweet, rainy air blew past her, the smell of green things and fragrant wet earth. The freshness was delightful after so long underground, but this was no palace scene. It was not even a city garden, but an empty, dripping forest stretched out as far as the eye could see. Nothing stirred anywhere but the patter of rain on leaves.

Juille glanced wildly around for her little guide. It had vanished. She shot a blue beam around the corridor behind her, finding only a confusing array of fingery footprints that vanished into the dark. She cursed the evasive little beast in a voice that was close to tears. To come so near victory and then find only this!

For she knew what this forest must be. Indeed, when she cast her blue light down she saw what must be the footprints Egide had left when he came out this very tunnel into the woods where the Ancients lived. Forbidden woods, uncharted, unknown, kept sacrosanct by countless generations of human life on Ericon.

She glanced about uneasily. Jair and the Andareans could not be far away. But what she could do next she had no idea. Where or how far the city lay was impossible to guess. Certainly she could not return through the pathless honeycomb of the caverns, and if she tried the forbidden woods she might wander for days in the wrong directions. If the *llar* had been visible now, she might have blasted it with a needle beam for bringing her so far astray. But there was no help for it. She would have to get back to the city, hit or miss, perhaps too late to do anything but warn them of impending blows from nameless weapons.

The memory of Egide's glowing confidence when he came back to her armed with the Andarean gifts gave her a feeling of sinking dismay. The impending conflict had taken on too many prospects of unguessable proportions. The effect of the new weapons might be overwhelming, unless she could find some way to prevent it.

Unless—Juille stared out speculatively through the trees. If she could delay Egide—but how could she, short of killing him? And did she want that? Her mind flashed off on a tangent—he had stayed his hand, too, when killing her might have meant a great deal in the outcome of the revolt. Her scorn for that weakness had gone deep. Yet she was hesitating now in the face of the same problem. She set her chin.

This was the way he had come, down this narrow glade into the forest. For all the woods seemed to slope downward as if toward a sunken path that wound between the hills. She could trace his tracks, perhaps, in the sodden ground.

If she hunted a way out of the forest, she might wander for days, while Egide and Jair escaped unhindered with their loot. But if she followed Egide now, if she used her needle beam upon him, or the lens of the Dunnarian weapon—would Jair leave Ericon without him?

Could she gain time enough to find her way back to the city, leaving Egide dead here in the rainy forest?

It was too confusing—she did not know what she wanted. But this alternative seemed best of all the impossible choices she had. Follow Egide—let the rest take care of itself.

It was very quiet here in the woods. Juille could not remember ever having been quite so alone before. She walked through a drowned green gloom beneath the dripping trees, making no sound. Egide had gone this way before her; she found his prints now and then in bare places along the valley. She strained her ears and eyes for him returning, but nothing moved except the leaves, nothing made any sound except the drip-drip of rain and the occasional liquid bubbling voice of a tree frog enjoying the wet.

And presently, in spite of herself, the silence and the solitude began to lull her senses. This was the holy place, and the old awe began to oppress her as she walked. Through this quivering gloom the gods had moved upon their own unfathomable errands; perhaps they were moving now. She looked about uneasily. She had seen the power of the Ancients manifested tangibly, terribly, overhead in the open sky so brief a time ago that the memory was still appalling.

And then sudden anger washed over her. Egide had come this way. He was a fool, blundering in ignorance through the sacred woods, but wherever he dared to go surely she dared follow. Even into the temple itself.

Her mind went back to those troubled thoughts in the solitary caverns, before the *llar* had come. Could she go? Could she not, when Egide had ventured there and perhaps learned celestial wisdom that might turn the tide of battle? For the Ancients *did* give advice, so legend said. If human supplicants dared make the pilgrimage, they sometimes brought back knowledge that could make them great.

Well, it would be humiliating to come second into their presence, but if Egide had come and gone, Juille began to realize that she must, too. Indeed, in this rainy solitude she realized even more. Her mind was clarifying itself of shock and confusion, and now as she walked alone, it began to grope back toward that firm bedrock of principle and duty upon which she had prided herself so long. In her mind she had faltered at the thought of killing him. Far back, deep down, the roots of weakness were there when she thought of Egide. Even to herself, she could not admit that yet. But subconsciously, perhaps, she knew herself as weak as he in this one thing, and subconsciously she sought to justify herself by surpassing him. It took less courage from Egide than from her to face the Ancients in their temple, because he knew less about them. She knew this much clearly—that she would never be at peace again with herself if she let him outface her here. Impatiently, she shrugged the tangled thoughts away. Time enough for introspection if she lived through the next hour.

Before she left the tunnel, Juille had taken the belated precaution of removing her bell-mouthed pistol from its uncomfortable hiding place and pushing it up into the lining of her helmet, where its flexible barrel adjusted to the curve. Should Egide by any mischance see her first here in the woods, he might not think of searching there for this last reserve, unpredictable as the weapon was. But she did not mean him to surprise her. She was better prepared than he for the meeting before them, and she knew very well that if they met unexpectedly only one was likely to return.

All the strange undertones of their relationship, confused, twisting together, not clear to either, were unimportant in the basic motive behind their final reckoning. She must not forget that. She must let nothing swerve her. If she died before Egide, the H'vani would most likely sit next upon the throne of Ericon. Egide knew that as well as she, and she thought that this time he would not forget it.

How did a traveler through this trackless wood know the way to the temple? Juille could not guess, but she did know the way. It was a part of the magic of the Ancients which she could feel thickening about her in the fragrant green silence as she went on. And how did one know what the temple would look like, when no human creature had ever brought back word of it? She could not guess that, either—but she knew.

She knew without surprise how the great black walls would lean inward above the trees that hid their foundations. She stood almost without breathing, gazing up between the branches at that towering, massive darkness which housed the living gods.

It was a little while before she could bring herself to come nearer. Only the thought of Egide made her do it. He must still be in there, in the unthinkable sanctum of the Ancients, hearing the voices that no living man had ever told of. At the back of her mind, a craven alternative stirred briefly—why not wait until he came out, and do then whatever impulse moved her to do? With a mental squaring of the shoulders she dismissed that idea. No, if he were in there still, she would confront him before the very altar of the gods.

Her heart was beating heavily as she went up the slope toward those great dark leaning walls that breathed out silence. She saw no door. The grassy furrow she had been following led up between the trees to a clear space against the solid black wall, and ended there. She was not breathing as she took the last step forward and put out hesitant hands toward that blackness.

She could tell then, of course, that it was not there at all. The walls were black and the dark inside was black, and the entrance made no difference between them to the eye. Light from outside did not penetrate over the threshold. Juille took a long, deliberate breath and stepped forward.

She walked three paces through utter darkness. Then light began to show faintly underfoot. Glancing back now, she could see the outlines of the portal, and the woods beyond looking indescribably changed and enchanted, like the woods of another dimension. Beneath her feet the light grew slowly stronger as she went on.

Above rose only the fathomless heights of the dark. And there was no one here but herself. She felt that with unreasoning certainty. The terrible, oppressive presences of the gods, which she had expected must paralyze her with their very awesomeness, she did not feel at all. And she thought Egide was not here, either. The dark around her had that vast, impersonal emptiness she had known before only during flights through the emptiness of space—cold, measureless, still beyond all human compass.

The light from below was strengthening, with an oddly vertiginous effect. She could see nothing down there, not even the substance of the floor. If she walked on pavement, it was pavement of the clearest crystal without flaws or jointure. She was like one walking above a void on invisible supports that might vanish before the next step. When she thought of that she slowed automatically, unable to control the fear that each next step would overreach the edge of the flooring and plunge her into the lighted infinities below. By contrast, the dark overhead was almost a solid, unrelieved in the least by any reflection of light. The impression grew so strong that she began to imagine the blood was pounding in her ears and temples from reversed gravity, as she walked upside down like a fly across a ceiling of glass.

She took a few more dizzy steps and then halted, too confused and frightened to go on. She had forgotten Egide. For the moment, she had even ceased to expect the Ancients. There was nothing anywhere but herself standing upon a crystal ceiling looking down into the sky, frozen with awe and terror.

Nothing happened for what seemed a very long time. No sound, no motion. Juille stood alone in the darkness upon the light, not conscious of any presence but her own. She was never conscious of any other presence, from first to last. But after a long interval, something began to happen.

Far, far away through the crystal on which she stood, a lazy motion stirred. Too far to make out clearly. It moved like smoke, but she did not think it was smoke. In a leisurely, expanding column it moved toward her, whether swiftly or slowly she did not even think, for awareness of time had ceased. And she could not tell if it were rising from fathoms underfoot or coiling down out of the sky toward her as she stood upside down on a crystal ceiling.

Nearer and nearer it came twisting, intangible as smoke and moving with the beautiful, lazy billowing of smoke—but it was not smoke at all.

When it had come almost to her feet it expanded into a great, slow ring and came drifting toward her and around her and up past her through the solid substance on which she stood. And as the ring like a wide, hazy, yawning mouth swept upward a voice that she thought she knew, said quietly in her ears:

"You may speak."

The shock of that voice, when she had felt no presence near, was nothing compared with the deeper shock of the voice's familiarity. "I can't stand it!" Juille told herself in sudden hysteria. "I can't!" Was there no one at all to be trusted? Did everyone she knew have a second self waiting behind veils of intrigue to speak enigmatically when she least expected it? First Helia—now— Whose was the voice? It might be her father's. It might be her own. It might not be familiar at all until this terrible enchantment made it seem so.

A second intangible yawning ring swallowed her and passed by.

"You may speak," it said with infinite patience, in exactly the same inflection as before. And this time she decided wildly that it must indeed be her own voice.

"I . . . I—" What did she want to say? Was she really standing here upon a ceiling of glass, speaking in the gods' voices and answering herself with her own? It could not be the gods who spoke. They were not here. No one was here but herself. She knew that. She had an unalterable conviction of aloneness, and it must be herself who spoke with the yawning smoke-mouths and answering herself in the same stifled voice.

"You may speak," the third mouth said, and drifted on past her into the solid darkness above. (Or was it really below?)

"I . . . my name is—" She paused. It was ridiculous to stand here telling her own voice who she was. She tried again.

"I came for guidance about the . . . about what to do next. So many lives depend on me—tell me how to save my people from the H'vani."

The smoke shifted lazily as if in a little breeze. Then a series of widening rings floated up—or down—around her in quick succession, and as each went by, a voice spoke in her ears. One of them was familiar. It might still be hers. The others she had not heard before, and this multiplicity of voices coming just in time to shatter her theory that she had been talking to herself, was intolerably bewildering. The voices spoke to one another impersonally, as if she were not there.

"She says she came for guidance."

"She came out of jealousy."

"She cares very little for her people. It was for herself she came."

"Is her race worth saving?"

"They must have their chance, remember." (This was the voice she knew.) "The game is almost played, but not quite finished yet. Give her the guidance she asks, and then—watch."

"But this is so wearying. We have seen it all before. Is there any good in her at all?"

"Little. Little enough. But let the game play out."

And with that last ring the dizzying swirl of them past her face came to a pause. Juille's head was reeling. For a while, nothing happened except that the column which was not smoke swayed gracefully like a hazy snake. Then it widened to another mouth that came gaping up through the floor to swallow her.

"You will have your chance to save the race that bred you," the voice she knew so well said leisurely. "Think well before you take it, for your instinct will be wrong. Upon you and the next few hours the fate of your race depends. What you are yourself will decide it."

The lazy cloud floated past and faded into the darkness beyond her.

And then a vertigo came upon Juille, so terrible that every cell in her body seemed struggling against every other cell to right itself—to separate and right itself even at the expense of partition from the rest. Up was down, and down was up. In the dreadful, wrenching confusion, she thought she had one glimpse below her of rolling clouds and rain that came lancing straight upward toward her feet, while she saw despairingly that treetops, head downward, were blowing in a strong breeze above her. For an instant she stood reversed in space, like an image which the retina reverses upon the brain.

And then she was stumbling through darkness again, with the universe right side up.

She was stumbling through a darkness all clouded with swimming colors. Would the gods appear at all? Was the audience over without a glimpse of them? Or would they rise presently through this swimming dark, vast, inscrutable, wearing no human shapes?

Grass was slippery beneath her feet.

Someone seized her by the shoulders and a man's voice said, "Open your eyes! Open your eyes! You're all right now."

"Egide!"

Her eyes flew open. There was no darkness. The temple—She looked around wildly. Egide's hard grip bruised her shoulders. Automatically she felt for the needle flash that was her only immediate weapon. Nothing. Her relaxing fingers must have let it fall somewhere in that bewildering darkness. She was still too dazed to understand what had happened, but reflexive animal reactions made her whip into motion, squirming away from his grip.

"No you don't." Egide's hands slid down her arms to clench like iron about her wrists. Memory of Helia's training came back now and she arched all her whipcord strength to pivot him off balance. But he knew that maneuver as well as she, and it resolved after a moment into a blind, furious hand-to-hand struggle. And since he was much stronger than she, with the sheer, solid bulk of muscular weight, in a short while she hung gasping with rage against his chest, both arms twisted agonizingly behind her.

"This," said Egide with a breathless grin, "is luck!"

"Luck!" Juille's blind and frantic brain cleared a little at the word. Luck? Perhaps it was. At any rate, now she had found him. What she would do next she had no idea. Somehow she had to gain the upper hand, keep him from Jair, delay the H'vani flight until she had power enough to stop it. And the Ancients had promised her a chance—

She made herself relax. "Well?" she said coolly.

Egide frowned down at her, taken aback. "Not angry?"

No, she could not afford to be angry. Somehow she must find some lever to control him, and she must control herself until she had. She must control more than her temper— It was infuriating that this nearness to him made her heart quicken and sent a treacherous weakness sliding through her limbs. Hanging helpless against his shoulder, her wrists fixed immovably in his grasp, Juille looked up at him with forced detachment. She was an amazon. She must remember it. Her heart and mind were trained to a discipline as stringent as her body's, and they must not falter.

She made herself study his face with critical calm,

looking for the flaws of character she had marked there before. Coolly she regarded him. The fine-grained texture of his weathered skin. The sweat upon his forehead from their sharp struggle, and the drops of blowing rain. Rain beading his hair and the fair curls of his short, careful beard, and his curling yellow lashes. The blue eyes narrowed as he returned her scrutiny.

Yes, it was a weak face. Too sensitive a mouth. She knew she would never trust an amazon with that look about the mouth and eyes. Sentiment and self-indulgence showed there plainly. And other qualities that might pass as virtues in a peacetime world. But she remembered the code of the amazon that demanded a sacrifice of virtues as well as vices to serve the common good. Pity, mercy, compassion—she saw them all here and she despised them all as they looked down out of Egide's face.

But by the simple, unfair advantage of weight and muscle, he had the upper hand. She must alter that before she could afford to despise him. She made her voice impersonal and asked quietly, "How did you catch me?" And between the question and his answer, she knew suddenly what she must do. One sure weapon remained to her. Somehow she must trick him into freeing her long enough to use that lens the *llar* had brought. Afterward—well, then she would have him on a leash, with death at the far end of it. The threat would be a whip to make him obey whatever commands she chose to give. After that, there would be time enough to consider these tangled personal feelings that were undermining all her amazonian resolve. First of all, she must get away.

"Catch you?" he was saying. "Don't you know? You came out of the temple with your eyes shut and walked down the slope. I was sitting by the . . . the door there, under the trees. I was—thinking."

Juille glanced around. Trees everywhere. No great walls leaning inward above their swaying tops. She said: "Where are we? The temple—it's gone."

"Yes. I followed you away from the door. Not very far—but it's gone now."

They looked up together, searching for those leaning walls. But the gods had withdrawn with a finality that seemed to deny they had ever been. Juille had a sudden, desperate feeling of loneliness and rebuff. The human mind needs so ardently to lean upon its gods. Even upon terrifying gods, cold and impersonal and aloof as these. But the Ancients had heard their pleas, tolerated their uninvited presence, sent them forth with comfortless, enigmatic words, careless whether humanity lived or died. As if they had tired of human doings altogether. The forest seemed very remote about them just now. It, too, would go on unchanging, whether man lived or vanished from the face of Ericon.

Well—Juille squared her shoulders mentally again—she was far better prepared to face such a universe than Egide would ever be. As to what the gods had told him, it wouldn't matter once she centered him in her lens. What *had* they told him? Overpowering curiosity suddenly filled her.

"What . . . what happened in the temple?" she asked him a little diffidently. He looked down at her, his eyes going unfocused as he remembered. She was pleased to notice that his grip on her wrists had slackened perceptibly, too. A little more conversation and perhaps—"Tell me what happened," she persisted. "Did they speak to you? Egide, was it really upside down?"

He glanced at her briefly. "You must be crazy," he said.

Juille stiffened. Another count against him. But curiosity was still strong. She tested his loosening grip very subtly and said again:

"Do tell me about it. You saw the light, and the . . . the smoke rings—"

"I saw a light, yes." His eyes came into focus again and he scowled at her. "Smoke rings? You're out of your head. There was a high altar like a wall, with the . . . the figures . . . above it. What did they tell you?"

Juille opened her mouth to protest, and then closed it again, trying to remember what it was they had said. They? Had there really been more voices than one? Voices—voices. For a tantalizing instant, she poised on the very verge of remembering whose that familiar tone had been. But when she reached for the memory, it slipped away.

What was it they had told her? They'd said unpleasant things, certainly. Something about a game that was almost played. Some assurance that she would have her chance—what chance? When? And her instinct would be wrong.

"Never mind," she said. "But I'm not concerned about the H'vani any more. Not now." And she smiled secretly. After all, it was nearly true. For she thought she understood what her chance would be. Egide's grip was slack. In a minute or two she would wrench loose, spin away from him into the forest, hide somewhere just long enough to center his figure in her lens as he blundered after in pursuit.

And then—well, she might not need to kill him. The threat might be enough. With luck, she might even find her way back to the city before Jair gave up waiting and tried for open space. Night was hours away still.

He looked down at her strangely. "You're lying," he said. "Unless—" He hesitated. "You know the legend, don't you? Is there any truth in it?"

"That they'll give you bad advice if they've decided against your side? I don't know." Juille exchanged a grave, long look with him. "I don't know. Do you believe it?"

He hesitated a moment longer, and then his eyes crinkled with laughter.

"No, I don't. Whatever they told you, I know how to win now."

She gave him a speculative glance. "Then they lied to one of us. Because I know, too."

Egide threw back his head and laughed. The confident, full-throated sound of it rang through the forest, silencing the tree frogs' bubbling songs. His grip upon her wrists was the merest touch now. Juille raked the woods for the nearest refuge, set her teeth and wrenched away. And she knew even as she wrenched that she had moved too soon. Sick dismay flooded her as he whipped out a long arm and grazed her shoulder with clutching fingers—grazed—gripped—held.

Her momentum spun them both around and it was touch and go for a moment. Then his big hands locked upon her shoulders and her jerked her toward him so that she smashed breathlessly against the hard armor of his chest and was pinned there in a heavy embrace that had no tenderness in it.

Not then.

They stood together in that close interlocked intimacy which only lovers or struggling enemies ever share.

"They gave you the wrong advice, then," Egide told her, as if the scuffle had never happened. Only his shortened breath testified that it had. "They mean your side to lose."

"How can you be sure?" Juille asked him, straining hard away against his arms.

And he sobered as he met her eyes. He could not be sure. Neither of them could ever be sure, until the last battle ran to its bloody close. There was silence between them for a moment. The dripping forest rustled all around, full of the whisper of fine rain upon leaves, the throaty, dovelike throbbing of tree-frog voices, the murmur of the wet, soft breeze. And there was a feeling of sorcery in the air. Perhaps the vanished temple still lifted its great inward-leaning walls above them, filled with the watching eyes of gods and the gods' humorless, dispassionate patience that waited to see their doomed supplicant take the first step toward his own ruin.

Each of them was suddenly very thankful for human companionship. For an instant they were no longer antagonists, and the struggle in which they were locked resolved itself imperceptibly, with the old treachery their bodies knew, into an embrace neither intended. In the back of their minds, neither of them forgot that they were enemies. Each remembered that only one of the two might leave these woods alive. But for the moment, another memory came back to engulf them both, blotting away the forest and the rain and even the aloof presence of the gods.

They did not speak for a while. They looked at one another with remembering eyes, and Egide's embrace held no more of its savage coercion, and Juille was not straining against it. Presently, he said in a low voice:

"Juille—did you know me on Cyrille?"

She shook her head in silence, not sure that she wanted to recognize this mood with speech. Before, it had been a thing of the senses, to let slip when the senses released it, and with no words to pin the remembrance inescapably in their minds.

But Egide went on. "I knew you," he said. "I meant to kill you. Did you guess that?"

She nodded, her eyes on his face watchfully.

"But no one else ever knew about it," Egide told her. "Not even Jair. No one knows at all but you and me."

Juille stared up at him. She knew the truth when she heard it, and she thought this was the truth. If she accepted it, a great many preconceived ideas would begin to turn themselves over in her mind. So many implications lay behind that simple speech—but just now she could not pause to think. Just now Egide was about to kiss her—

It was a long kiss. Their first since Cyrille, and perhaps their last. While it endured, all sound blanked out around them and a dissolving intoxication loosened all Juille's muscles, and even her mind ceased to be wary and afraid.

Then Egide's unsmiling face was looking down at her from very near, an eagerness and a humility upon it she had never seen there before. And suddenly she knew how treacherous this was. Egide had surrendered without reservation to it. In this moment she knew she could bend him to whatever purpose she chose. Even compromise with the Lyonese. Even peace, if it were peace she wanted.

Abruptly she was frightened. This strong emotion between them was a drug and a drunkenness more dangerous than wine, the most treacherous thing that ever happened to an amazon. Because he might be able to sway her, too—and she desperately feared her own surrender. Like drunkenness, this emotion distorted the focus of reality, dulled reason's keen edge, reduced the mind to a maudlin softness that denied all values but its own. It was no more to be trusted than drunkenness. It was as false as the illusions of Cyrille. As false, and as irresistibly lovely, and as dangerous as death.

If she ever gave up to it, the moment was not now. Later, when she had him under tangible control—He was weak now, but the weakness might not last. She needed the leash of the Dunnarian weapon, and the whip of the threat it held. She lifted her eyes to Egide's.

He was holding her like a lover, waiting with an eagerness he made no attempt to conceal. This was the moment the Ancients must have meant. Now, in his weakness—now!

Juille lowered her head and struck him a heavy blow beneath the chin with her helmet. In the same moment, she leaped backward out of his embrace and whirled toward the nearest trees.

Egide dropped—dropped to hands and knees and thrust one leg out to its full, long length. Juille saw just too late what was coming. Futile rage flared up consumingly in the timeless instant while she struggled to avoid him. She could not let Egide frustrate her again—she could not! But momentum was too much for her. She felt her own foot catch against the outthrust leg, and she felt herself plunging face down into the underbrush beneath the trees.

Hard hands dragged her upright before she could

move. She had a glimpse of blue eyes blazing with anger. She had one flash of a big square fist, startlingly foreshortened, hurtling toward her face.

Then moons and stars exploded between her and the green woods.

With no consciousness whatever of elapsed time, Juille found herself lying on a bank of soft blue grass at the edge of a lapping sea. Her mind was as blank as the mind of Adam first wakening in Eden. It took her a perceptible while to remember who she was. That returned after a little uneasy groping, but where she was—

She sat up with difficulty. Her hands appeared to be tied behind her. And then memory rushed back in a flood. Egide, the sacred forest—her chin felt sore and swollen—That moment of warmth and treachery—and humiliation.

How much time had passed? And where in the Galaxy was she now? Egide must have left her here, securely tied, while he went about some private business—the weapons? Had the Ancients given him some special knowledge? It was painful to think. Too many questions spun through her mind. She looked confusedly around.

Low blue hillock, blue lapping water out to the hazy horizon. Behind her, a high wall of colored stones, with an iron-hinged gate in it. And to left and right, willows that trailed their yellow-green streamers down across the grass.

Blue grass—grass on Ericon was green. She listened. A faint breeze was moving among the willows, and upon the beach scalloping wavelets whispered. No other sound. No craft at sea. No Egide. Nothing even remotely familiar anywhere she looked. She had a moment of serious wonder whether she could possibly have switched personalities with some unknown woman, under the power of the all-powerful Ancients.

With some vague idea of looking beyond the willows, she walked awkwardly across the beach, off-balance because of her bound hands. The yellow-green leaves streamed across her shoulders like extravagantly flowing hair as she pushed through their swaying lengths. A roadway curved down toward the water a little distance away, and she could see people strolling along it, laughing and talking. As she watched, a young couple came toward her, swinging hands, murmuring together. She called.

The strolling lovers did not turn their heads. Juille called again, more loudly. They did not even glance around. Juille shouted in a parade-ground voice that made the willows shiver. No response. The girl looked up to smile at the young man, and her face was turned so that she must see Juille, but she gave no sign.

Not sure whether to be more angry or alarmed—was she invisible?—Juille pushed forward toward them through the leaves. And suddenly something moved in the air before her—someone materialized in her very face, ghostlike, blocking her path. Juille started back. The ghost did, too. It was a ghost in cloak and helmet, with its arms behind it—

Juille stood perfectly still before the faint reflection of herself. Presently she pushed out one knee and felt a transparent wall between her and the road. Shouldering up to it, she traced the unseen barrier from the willow grove up to the stone wall. By the time she reached it, she had an idea where she was.

The strolling lovers went obliviously past, laughing to one another, and vanished around another clump of trees. Along the road a boy with a donkey came whistling, but Juille made no attempt to signal him. He did not, she thought, exist. Or if he ever had lived, most likely he had been dead for some while. There was almost certainly war upon the world he lived on. There was war upon most worlds now.

Juille went up the slope toward the wall, her lips set thinly. She thought she knew what she would find there, and in a moment or two she did—a rectangle of cloudy glass set into the stones. That settled it. Egide, for some unfathomable reason of his own, had brought her back to the pleasure world where their brief idyl had run its course. This was Cyrille.

Why was she here? She had a brief, wild idea that Egide might have imagined the revisiting of old scenes would win her anew to the evanescent mood that had once enchanted them both. But in the urgency of current happenings, she knew not even Egide would attempt anything so fantastic. No, if he were here—and he must be—then Jair and the Andarean weapons would be here, too. Obviously they had come this far at least without interference from the imperial forces. Was this, then, a stopover on their way to the H'vani base, or had they a reason for visiting Cyrille? Or—might they have dropped her here and gone on alone? No—because the real danger from the Lyonese space guards lay beyond Cyrille's orbit, not inside it. If they needed her at all, they needed her as a hostage to pass them by the guards.

Well, they must be here, then. Somewhere on Cyrille, with their nameless weapons, and perhaps armed also with advice from the Ancients that could certainly mean no good for Ericon. She could not even count very much on interference from the skeleton staff of attendants left on Cyrille. The H'vani were armed and ruthless. She could imagine Jair making very short work of anyone who crossed his path. Her very presence, bound and helpless in this room, testified that no staff member had lived long enough to spread an alarm.

She stood before the gate, looking around what must be a moderately small room, though her gaze reached out unhindered toward distant horizons. The grass, the foremost willows, the wall were real. Perhaps some of the lapping water. But the rest was all illusion reflecting upon mirrored walls. Somewhere beyond them, Egide and Jair would be at work—on what? And alone? Probably, unless some of the Andareans had come on with them. Their own ship and men would have been impounded from the very first.

Well—She twisted at her tied hands hopefully. The bonds felt softer, like cloth instead of the knifeproof cord Helia had used. How could she test it? There were no sharp stones; the glass walls would not break, she knew. There was nothing that—

Juille laughed suddenly and fell to her knees. She had her spurs. It seemed interminably long ago that Helia had put them on her heels for a morning ride. In the crowded lifetime since so much had happened that she knew she might never ride a horse again, perhaps might never live to see these spurs removed. But they could do her one last service now, if her cords were made of cloth. She strained backward, sawing precariously.

The rowels bit satisfyingly into her bonds. It was back-breaking and tedious, but it was working. After a long while she felt the cords let go, and for the second time began to rub the prickles of returning circulation from her hands.

And now—what? To all appearances, Juille still sat upon an open beach with blue water breaking at her feet. It was difficult to believe that the walls of a small room were really close about her. The door itself probably lay beyond the gateway in the wall, but she knew it would be locked—It was. Her only contact with the outside was the communication panel, which might be dead. Still, since the illusion of this beach with its strolling ghosts persisted, the communications might be open, too. It was difficult to guess what effect the death of Cyrille's operators would have on the persistence of Cyrille's illusions. Perhaps none at all.

Rubbing her wrists, she walked up the blue grassy slope and pressed the buttons for sight and sound beneath the panel. In the brief moment while it glowed into life, she heard a distant murmur of laughter and saw the young lovers strolling again beyond the trees. The sight of them was oddly dreadful, and somehow oddly pathetic. They were so perfect an illusion of a perfect, idyllic past which might never come again, a peacetime when lovers could walk unheedingly over open beaches. Somewhere, the originals of this living reproduction had once walked hand in hand. They might have grown old many years ago; they might have died yesterday or last week on some other world under the bombardment of H'vani guns. Or they might be cowering at this moment in some underground shelter shaken with the detonation of bombs. But they walked here in an eternal moment of laughter and murmuring, beside a bright blue sea, and they turned indifferent, blind faces to Juille's predicament. Their detachment partook, in a way, almost of the Ancients' divine disinterest, or of the cold, still, passionless reaches of space.

Juille looked away.

The panel was lighting up. She looked through it into a corner of some office, with a black glass desk below a wall board on which lights winked busily. Across the desk, a dead man sprawled. Juille looked at him stonily and pressed the buttons again. She did not know the proper combination, but she thought that eventually she must find a room where the men she sought were working. Probably the control room. Because, until she knew better, she must assume that the H'vani had come to Cyrille for a purpose, and she knew the only purpose in their minds would be destruction. The control room, she had heard, was the only one here with a visual screen that looked down upon the great green world of Ericon. She hunted on and on.

And she found other dead men. She found offices wrecked and charred. She found empty rooms. But she found no living creatures until at last, by a lucky accident, she finally hit upon the combination that opened a little window upon the men she was hunting. And her guess had been right. They were in the control room.

Its vast space was crowded with the machinery that kept Cyrille upon its course and filled with the living illusions of its fantasies. One wall was glass, like a telescopic lens focused upon the world beneath. And though that world was directly below, in the window it stood at right angles to the floor like a looming green wall.

Before it, two men were laboring busily. Juille, watching as if from a small opening high up on the side of the great room, saw Jair's red head and beard, and Egide's yellow curls. No other figures moved in the room. They had come on alone, then. And they worked with utter absorption before the glass wall.

The object of their interest was a great searchlight, far larger than themselves. They had maneuvered it before the window on its rolling frame and were centering its focus now upon something outside, with much reference to a chart engraved upon the wall. Over the face of the light, a metal net with rainbow nodes had been spread.

Juille remembered that net. Watching, she felt a cold sinking in the pit of her stomach. She had no idea how the arrangement would function, but its implication was very plain. The Ancients had betrayed her, then, and Helia's people had betrayed her, and unless she could get out into that room very soon, the Lyonese Empire would be betrayed, too.

For Egide had found a substitute for his invading fleet. Here inside the defenses of Ericon, was a ship so cunningly disguised that it could swing a path of destruction all around the planet. He was making Cyrille itself that ship. And Juille thought to herself that if this were the advice the Ancients had given him, then they must have lied to her and the Lyonese. For, unless she could put a stop to it quickly, the world below them was certainly doomed.

Until now, no weapons had ever existed strong enough to bridge the airless gap between Ericon and its satellite, but the confidence showing in every gesture of the men she watched must mean that such a weapon existed now. This searchlight, netted with shining, colored bulbs. It was hard to believe that the light could be cast so far, or that the simple addition of the net would charge it with destroying violence. But the H'vani worked like men who knew what they were doing. Obviously they meant to let the little pleasure-world circle on around Ericon until it floated above the target they had marked. That target would almost certainly be the Imperial City itself. And before avenging ships could blast Cyrille from its course, the city and half the countryside could be wiped out if this weapon had any real power.

Could she stop the destroyers first? It looked hopeless. From this angle she could see only a great panoramic curve of hill and forest below, partly obscured by a rolling thunderstorm. That dim light might be morning or evening; they could be ten minutes from the city or a full turn of the planet. And she had no idea which way the control room lay from here. Even if she knew, the door that shut her in was locked.

Wait, though. She had one weapon, if Egide had not found it. Hopefully Juille groped in her helmet lining. A hard handle met her fingers, and her spirits rose on a swift curve to something almost like hope. She laughed aloud and pulled out the little gun. There it lay, fitting her hand as it once had fitted the hands of a race whose very name no longer had meaning in the Galaxy they once had ruled. It might yet save the race that ruled today, if luck was with Juille.

Slim, flexible barrel with its spiral of silver tubing, bell-shaped muzzle, trigger curved like a tiny sickle—What would happen when she pulled it? Most likely—nothing, unless just possibly the Andareans had made use of the weapons on that rack within recent years. Lightning might come blasting out when she touched the trigger, or the gun might explode in her hand, on—

Juille set her finger on the trigger, clenched her teeth and turned the bell-muzzle toward the lapping sea. Slowly she tightened her finger.

She pressed it back to the guard, and nothing happened. Nothing? She had time for one wave of sickening disappointment, and then thought she felt life against her palm. The gun was quivering. The quiver ran up the coil of tubing and shook against her fist, and a tiny glow seemed to be forming about the bell-shaped orifice. A glow that spun and spun. Juille stood holding the gun out at arm's length, while the glow grew brighter and faster, and the spinning increased.

Then a globe of luminous fire drifted from the bell-muzzle. It spun brilliantly like a tiny sun, moving away from her at leisurely speed and expanding as it moved. Straight out to sea it went, and the ripples mirrored its broken reflection on their surface. Juille held her breath.

There was a moment more of silence, while the waves lapped softly on the beach and the willows whispered and distant voices laughed. Then the spinning sun in midair flared out in one expanding flash and one tremendous hissing roar, like fire in water. The flash was golden.

When Juille could see again what she saw looked unbelievable even in the face of knowledge. Hanging in what seemed like open air above the still-rippling ocean was a circle of twisted girders, black and peacock blue from the heat of their destruction. Through the wall she could see a stretch of dim corridor. Plaster fell crumbling between the beams. And all around the edge of the opening a strange little dazzle of dancing colored motes faded slowly. The revolving sun had vanished.

Except for that hole in the air, everything remained unchanged about her. And though that hole was the only touch of reality in all this small world, it was fantastic as it hung there over the serene ocean rolling in from illusory distances.

She waded out through the warm blue ripples. Even when the shattered wall was within arm's length and she could see the transparent glimmer of her own reflection swimming above the wavelets in the reflecting wall, she had a feeling of instability as she set one knee upon a girder that hung unsupported on the air.

Beyond the opening lay a narrow corridor running left and right, lighted only by a dim thread of luminous paint down the center of the floor. Which way? What next? She had no idea even of how many charges remained in her weapon. Perhaps none. Perhaps only two or three. What she must do was find Egide as soon as possible and somehow manage to see him first, just long enough to focus him in the cross-hairs of the lenses which still hung about her neck.

She thought she had shut her mind to Egide now. He must remain only an enemy to kill if necessary, to capture if possible on the invisible leash of her strange lensed weapon. Until she held his life a forfeit in the lens all else must wait. And Jair—well, she must deal with him as opportunity arose. Without quite understanding it, she had a feeling that Jair was less of a danger than Egide.

She turned at random to the right, following the luminous line warily. At the end of the corridor she came out into the office with the black glass desk which she had first seen in the communicator panel. The dead man still sprawled across the glass. Juille, struck by a sudden hopeful thought, began jerking open drawers of translucent opal plastic. Papers—files of colored cards—a bottle of green brandy. A manicure kit. And—ah! A little palm gun with an extra clip of charges!

Juille laughed exultantly. This was for Jair! The bell-mouthed pistol might never fire again; the lens at her throat was a one-shot weapon. But this find put her on an equal footing with the two H'vani.

There was a large communicator panel on the wall behind the dead man. One of the labeled buttons below it said, "Control Room." Juille thought to herself, "I'm not afraid of you now," and pushed the button, watching the panel glow and the great central room take shape beyond it.

Egide and Jair had finished their work. The searchlight was like a long-legged bird with its big eye craning downward through the window that opened upon Ericon. The trap was set. The Imperial City somewhere on the face of the globe below was rolling slowly upward toward its doom.

Egide at the moment was talking into a tiny portable communicator which he certainly had not worn when he landed upon Ericon that day. Reporting—success?—to some H'vani base. Perhaps summoning some armada of invading ships to follow the path of destruction he was about to launch upon the Imperial City. Juille wasted no fruitless speculation on that. She put her face close to the communicator and called:

"Egide! Egide, look up!"

She could hear her own voice echoing hollowly from the walls of the huge room beyond the panel. Egide stared about for several seconds before he located the connected panel. At that distance, though she could see his face change, she was not sure what emotions showed there for a moment. He shouted, "Where are you?" and the echoes rolled back from the high walls.

"Come and find me," she called derisively, and waved her unbound hands at the panel to show that she was free. Before he could answer she pressed the disconnector. Then she counted to ten and pushed the same button again, looking down with a grin into the big room. A struggle of sorts was taking place there. Egide, dropping his private communicator, had evidently made a lunge toward the master control panel to locate the screen she had just used. Jair held him by the cloak and they were disputing fiercely. Juille scowled. Evidently the big red man did not trust his prince with this dangerous captive. But it was no part of her plan to have Jair come hunting her. She listened to the indistinguishable deep murmur of their argument. Then Egide gave a savage shrug and turned back to the window. Jair's white grin split the dark-red beard, visible even from here. She saw him give his belt a hitch, draw his gun and lumber purposefully away, his enormous shoulders swaggering a little.

Juille made an insulting noise into the panel. The two men glanced up, startled. She waved again, even more insultingly, and disconnected the panel. Well, no help for it now. She must find the Control Room herself, and do it quickly, and she must play hide and seek with Jair through the strange interior of Cyrille while she hunted it. Luck decidedly was not with her. But she was well armed now, and the element of surprise was in her favor.

The first thing to do was to get as far as possible from this room before Jair arrived. And since he might come by some swift intramural means she did not know of, she had better go quickly. It was eminently satisfying to feel the weight of a gun in each hand as she turned to the opposite wall—even though one gun might be empty, or very nearly empty. The very feel of it sent her spirits soaring. The odds were fairly even after all, for she did not think Jair could know much more about Cyrille's inner workings than she did, nor could he guess that his quarry was as well armed as he. She had no illusions about Jair's purpose. He would certainly shoot on sight. No need any longer to hold her for a hostage, with that deadly mechanism in the Control Room already trained upon Ericon. Jair would shoot without warning, but he would not know that she could, and that gave her a little advantage.

Outside the office a wide, shallow, moving ramp carried Juille down to a hall and an empty foyer with arched doors all around its wall. She glanced about nervously. This was no place for her. Her spurs rang faintly as she ran across the floor and dodged under the nearest arch. Another hallway, curving to the left. For all she knew she might be running straight into Jair's arms. She opened the first door she came to, glanced inside, and then sprinted through a field of waving lilies, knee-high, leaped a chuckling stream, tore open the door of a thatched cottage and found herself in another dim hall lighted by a luminous floorstrip.

The next random door led her into an arcade above a frozen twilight sea, with gusts of snow blowing through the open arches. Her breath went pluming frostily over one shoulder as she ran. Another hallway. An orchard that showered pink-scented blossoms upon her and housed one startled rabbit. It lolloped ahead in a frenzy, dodging off to the side just before she came to a gate in the orchard wall that let out onto the usual hallway.

She lost all sense of direction and ran as haphazardly as the rabbit had done, through a confusion of smallish rooms filled with every conceivable scene and climate. In several that she passed time had stopped. Clouds hung motionless in illusory skies, scenes reflected upon the wall were motionless, too, and lost all power to deceive. No water stirred and the air was windless. But most of the rooms she ran through were functioning still, and she passed a medley of mornings and noons and nights dwelling upon a wide variety of tiny worlds.

So closely is the human mind bound by the revolutions of its planet that after a while she found she had lost her time-sense as well, and could not help feeling that the hours had telescoped together in a dream as she ran, that this should be tomorrow, or even the day after that. Egide's playful device upon the cloud for making the days go by had turned to convincing reality here. She had been through too many nights and mornings for the present to remain today. She had even passed too many winters and blossomy springs for her own mental comfort, and though her reasoning consciousness derided the feeling, it lurked uneasily just below the surface and darkened her subconscious thoughts as she ran on.

But the time came when she tired of running. She must have come far enough by now that Jair would not be likely to trace her from the office where she had called. As a matter of fact, Cyrille was so large and so intricately honeycombed with rooms that it would be quite possible for them to wander about for hours, or even days, without meeting. And Juille was of no mind for such a flight as that. She had little time to waste. Every moment that passed now carried Cyrille closer to its target.

The Control Room, then, was her real goal. Jair might or might not find her soon, but if she failed to find Egide and the controls and the enigmatic weapon angling downward toward Ericon, it would not matter much what came after. And she might wander for hours through these circling rooms without reaching Egide.

Juille scowled thoughtfully and hefted the bell-muzzled pistol in her hand. There might be one more charge in it, or a limitless number, or none at all. But this was no time for indecision, not when the very minutes of life left to the Imperial City might be ticking off to nothing.

She was standing in a corridor at the moment. After a second's hesitation she pointed the bell toward the light-striped floor and pulled the trigger. The gun shivered. A glow gathered again within the bell mouth, gathered and spun and grew. The tiny sun came whirling from its socket, drifted floorward, struck with the hiss of fire in water. When Juille's sight came back after that golden glare, she saw blued girders again, and again the little storm of dancing colored notes which marked the edges of the gap. They flew up in her face this time as she leaned over the hole, stung her briefly and went out.

Below was a dim-green twilight forest of wavering weeds. Not too far below. Juille took a tight grip on both her guns and jumped. She was in midair before she saw the terrible pale face peering up at her through the reeds, its dark mouth squared in a perfectly silent scream.

It was a madman's face.

Juille's throat closed up and her heart contracted to a

cold stop as she met that mindless glare. She was falling as if in a nightmare, with leisurely slowness, through air like green water that darkened as she sank. And the face swam upward toward her among the swaying weeds, its mouth opening and closing with voiceless cries.

The floor was much farther than it had seemed, but her slow fall discounted the height. And the creature came toward her as slowly, undulating with boneless ease among the weeds. Juille sank helpless through wavering green currents, struggling in vain to push against the empty air and lever herself away. The room was a submarine illusion of retarded motion and subdued gravity, and the dweller in it, swimming forward with practiced ease against the leverage of the tangled weeds, had a mad underwater face whose human attributes were curiously overlaid with the attributes of the reptile.

Juille's reason told her that she had stumbled into one of the darker levels of Cyrille, where perversions as exotic as the mind can conceive are bought and practiced to the point of dementia and beyond. This undulating reptilian horror must be one of the hopeless addicts, wealthy enough to indulge his madness even when civilization was crumbling outside the walls of Cyrille.

There was no sound here. Juille's feet came down noiselessly upon the sand, scarcely printing it with her weightless contact. The thing with the mouthing inhuman face came writhing toward her through the blue-green shadows and the swaying of the reeds. She felt her own throat stretching with a scream, but the silence of underwater rippled unbroken around her. For one sickening moment she stood there swaying on tiptoe, scarcely touching the sandy floor, staring at the oncoming madman while her lips opened and closed like his and no sounds came forth. The illusion of fishes in a submarine cavern was complete.

Then she saw a door between two marble pillars that wavered as if behind veils of shifting sea water, and wheeled unsteadily toward it, moving with nightmare slowness over the ripple-patterned sand unmarked by footprints. Behind her the thing came gliding.

As Juille struggled forward she had to force herself against every instinct to draw each breath. The illusion was so perfect that she could not help expecting strangling floods of bitter water to fill her lungs. Her garments wavered up around her and the helmet tugged at its chin strap.

The door was locked. Automatically she burned out the bolt with her palm gun, too sick with utter revulsion to notice, except dimly, that its characteristic thin shriek of riven air was silent here, too. But when the jolt of the gun against her hand responded and the door swung open, reason returned to her. She was armed. She need not fear this hideous writhing thing that swam after her with clutching webby hands outstretched.

She gave one last strong lurch against the weightless gravity of the room and stumbled out into the corridor, where normal gravity for a moment seemed to jerk her down against the floor. Stumbling, she regained her balance and then swung up the gun and sent a thinly screaming bolt back into the green dimness of the submarine room where the creature that mouthed its soundless screams was floating after her. The gun bolt struck him in the chest and its impact sent him wavering backward through the watery air. She saw him double with the strong, convulsive arc of a fighting fish. He began to sink slowly floorward through the reeds, but like the reptile he aped, he was slow to die.

Holding her gun ready for a second shot, Juille backed away. And slowly the madman swam toward her, one clawed hand pressing to its chest where the bolt had gone through. He moved with hideous, inhuman grace until he reached the threshold. Then gravity slammed him flat upon the floor and he lay there gasping and heaving himself up like a fish out of water. The normal pull of Cyrille was more than he could fight against. Juille pressed against the wall and watched him die.

She was badly shaken. Common danger was an old story to her, but the dark, contaminating psychic horrors which she thought she stood among now were a menace she had no armor against. She glanced about the corridor, reluctant to move lest she intrude upon another of the small private hells which, she knew now, fully justified the evil reputation of Cyrille's hidden levels.

And yet she must move. There was no time to waste now. She set her teeth resolutely and leveled her bell-mouthed gun at random toward an angle of the wall and floor. With luck it should open up to avenues of escape, and if one proved untenable, the other might do.

The gun quivered in her hand; its spinning sun gathered and floated free. And she was not sure if her imagination alone made the glow of it look duller than before. Was the precious charge running low? She wondered for one panic-stricken moment if she would have to defend herself now with the little palm gun alone, and then the sun bullet struck with its golden flare and hissing, and she had no more time for wonder.

Low in the wall a broken opening showed when the glare died away. Through it Juille had an incredulous glimpse of a city spread out in sprawling avenues and parks between the ridges of rolling hills. She saw people moving like tiny animated dots through the streets—all of it either in incredibly perfect miniature or incredibly far away. Then a cloud of saffron smoke came rolling through the gap and billowed up into her face. She caught one whiff of its exotic, spicy fragrance and then pulled her short cloak over her face and dived precipitously through the other gap in the flooring, without looking where she dived. For she knew that smoke. She had no desire to go mad in any of the delirious ways its spicy odor offered.

She struck the floor below and rolled for a moment in a bank of pale-pink snow that tingled instead of chilling. More snow drifted from low clouds, blinding her when she looked up. Veils of it, dancing rosily about her, hid the rest of the room. A wind blew, and the veils spun and writhed together in serpentine columns, through which she saw just a glimpse of motion before the wind died again. All the room was pink and dancing with warm snow, and through it a hideous low laughter quietly shook the air.

Juille scrambled to her feet, her heart thudding madly. Snow blinded her, but her ears gave the warning her eyes could not, and she was sure she heard footsteps shuffling nearer through the silence and the blowing veils. The laughter came again, low, satisfied, evil as she had never imagined laughter could be.

Until she felt the quiver of the bell-mouthed gun in her hand she did not know she had pulled its trigger. There was a paralyzing quality about that voice. The whirling sun drifted from the muzzle, vanished briefly through clouds of pink snow, then struck somewhere invisibly with its hiss and its golden flash. The voice chuckled, fell almost silent, then chuckled again, nearer. And Juille plunged wildly away from it, her feet slipping upon the snow.

Light pouring through a gap in the wall made the dancing flakes glitter with all their rainbow facets. But it was a very thin beam. When Juille had groped her way to the source of it, watching across one shoulder and holding her breath as she listened for the laughter in the snow to follow, she found a breach barely large enough to squirm through. The gun was certainly losing its strength.

It took all Juille's courage to force herself through the gap. Only her glimpse of a calm, sunlit meadow beyond made her try; that and the sound of a low, evil chuckle somewhere beyond the swirling veils. For to squeeze through the wall meant rendering herself helpless during the passage, and what might happen while she struggled there she could not and dared not think aloud.

But, somehow, she made the meadow unharmed. And then stood gripping her two guns and looking back sheepishly at the ragged gap through which pink snow whirled now and again. She heard no further echo of the terrible, soft, satisfied mirth. But her self-confidence was very seriously disturbed now. It annoyed her to find her hands shaking and the thumping of her heart refusing to slow even though she stood alone in an empty, static meadow in some little world whose functions had ceased.

Turning over rather panicky thoughts in her mind, she crossed to a gate at the far side, keeping her attention alert for any following thing from the broken wall. She had hoped to blast her way somehow through to the Control Room and destroy the great searchlight there with the aid of the bell-muzzled gun. But she knew now that would be impossible. Each charge might be the last, and each lessened in effectiveness. She wished passionately for the lightning gun Jair might be carrying. She wished even more passionately for human company, even Jair's. And she began rather shakily to fit the two desires together.

Supposing she lured Jair within range of her palm gun. Could she force him to give up the lightning-caster or to guide her back with him to the Control Room? Certainly she could try. Even if the plan failed, she would be no worse off than now, for at very worst she could surely kill him before he killed her. And incongruously she found herself longing for the presence of his impressive human bulk, the vibration of his voice. Even though he meant to kill her, and she him. He was so reassuringly human, after these horrible inhuman travesties in their madhouses.

So she went out the gate and into a corridor, and she followed the corridor to the office at its end. And closed and locked the door after her, between herself and any sound of laughter that might follow from the room of the pink storming snow.

This office was almost a duplicate of the other. A desk of deep-blue glass this time, and with no dead man behind it. But the wall behind the desk had the same array of communicator panels. She went straight across to it and pressed the universal broadcast button.

"Jair," she said clearly. "Jair, do you hear me? I'm in"—she glanced at the board—"Office No. 20 on the Fifth Level. I'll wait here until you come. Please hurry."

The thought of her own voice echoing among all the corridors and the strange myriad worlds of Cyrille made her shiver a little. Even Egide would hear it, where he worked out Ericon's destruction in the Control Room. And somewhere in the homeycomb of apartments and corridors Jair would hear it, too. He might already be very near. He would put his own interpretation on the appeal, for he must think her unarmed.

There was not much hope for an ambush here. Cyrille was not a world that offered materials for building gun-proof barricades. She pulled a screen patterned in And somewhere in the honeycomb of apartments and waited behind it, watching the two doorways that opened in the far wall. She had her guns ready. The whole world was silent about her, and the moments dragged interminably.

She heard Jair approaching before he entered the room. He made no attempt to come quietly, and his heavy boots woke echoes along the corridor. Very obviously he thought her unarmed.

He paused in the doorway, big and red-bearded, his red-brown eyes frankly murderous in a cold, dispassionate sort of way as he glared about the room, gun lifted and ready. Juille saw that it was the lightning gun, and her heart jumped. She had to have it. But she saw in her first glance that he had no intention of speaking a single word before he killed her. She might not have been of the same species as he at all, so matter-of-factly did he scan the room for his quarry.

Juille had not expected quite this workmanlike preparedness. She had imagined some interval in which she could address him from behind her shelter and offer a bargain. But she felt that her first word now would serve only as the target for his shot. Still, it had to be done. Perhaps if he knew she was armed—

She said in a clear, firm voice, "I have a gun—"

Jair's lightning thrower leaped up. His fierce eyes raked the room, not quite sure where the voice had come from. He did not believe what she had said, or he did not care. Obviously he hesitated only long enough to know where to fire.

Sighing, Juille fired at him around the edge of the screen, her needle beam making the air shriek as it passed. She had meant to pierce him through the shoulder, but he was inhumanly quick. He must have jumped even before she pressed the stud, because the screaming beam only seared him across the arm and died away in a thin, high wail and a splatter of blue heat against the wall behind him.

Jair laughed, a cold, satisfied sound that partook a little of the terrible laughter in the snow room, and seemed to throw his gun and a thunderbolt at her in one incredibly quick overhand motion. But the shock of his burn must have confused him, spoiling his judgment if not his aim. The bolt went rocketing over Juille's head where she crouched as nearly flat upon the floor as she could in a poise for flight.

The painted screen disintegrated in a rain of colored flinders around her. Those that touched her burned, but she scarcely felt it. Both she and Jair were stunned by the violence of the bolt as it crashed through the wall in a blinding, blue-white glare, leaving behind it a moderate thunderclap and a smell of ozone.

After a second, Juille's mind cleared and she heard Jair's bull-like roar deep in his throat, saw his finger tighten again on the trigger. She faced him over the ruins of the screen, not daring to wait for another shot at him. He was too quick, and a second thunderbolt might strike her squarely.

She was whirling as the room still shook with thunder. Of its own accord her hand closed on a fragment of weighted plastic from the screen and she flung it at Jair, seeing it splinter against his forehead. Then she had spun away toward the shattered wall, moving more quickly than she had ever moved in her life before.

She cleared the wall with one flying leap, grateful in a flash of remembrance to Helia's relentless training over years and years, that had built muscles and reflexes to hair-trigger response. How very strange it was that Helia had trained her thus, so that she might escape the weapon which Helia herself had put into the hands of her enemies.

The thunderbolt had made havoc through a series of rooms before it came to a gap too wide to leap. If Cyrille's materials had not been almost uniformly fireproof, she might never have lived to run even as far as this. But she knew she must dodge behind some other ambush and shoot Jair from behind where he could not be forewarned by the sight of her motion. His reflexes were even quicker than her own. Luckily the bolt had leaped haphazardly, not in one straight path, or Juille's flight must have been halted before she finished her second stride.

Arch upon shattered, tottering arch opened up before her through rooms of sunlit fields whose light spilled over into rooms of twilight. At the far end she could see an angle of a room full of branches and terrified birds. She ran smoothly, dodging, taking advantage of every broken wall. If Jair was behind her, he came silently. She dared not glance back to see.

When Juille came to the room of branches it seemed to have no floor, only leaves and vines and more branches below at various levels leading down to sunny, bottomless space. But some of the birds lay dead in midair, and she guessed the presence of a glass floor and went skating precariously over nothingness toward the gap in the far wall. Birds beat hysterically about her head, screaming protest and alarm.

In the last room, but one which the bolt had wrecked, she dropped behind a ledge of green ice, on a floor of strange green moss, and waited with steady gun. This time she did not hear Jair coming. He went silently past her a dozen feet away, moving with smooth, deadly speed. Juille took careful aim and her finger tightened upon the stud.

Jair's quickness was inhuman. His senses must have risen to razor-keenness under such stress as this, for something warned him in the instant before Juille fired. Some tension in the air, some awareness of her breathing or sight of the motion she made vaguely reflected in the crystal walls of the room. He flung himself flat upon the moss and the needle beam shrieked over his head and flattened to blue heat in midair upon some invisible wall. He fired from the floor, grinning up at Juille with a singular cold detachment that fascinated her. Then the leaping bolt dazzled her eyes. Fantastic luck was still with her.

Because he fired from such an angle, he missed by a very brief margin. Juille felt the searing heat of its passage and heard it go crashing through walls again, somewhere behind her. The concussion shook them heavily again, and low thunder rolled and echoed through the opened rooms.

Juille spun around. Beyond the broken wall was dimness. Dimness to shoot from—an ambush at last. She reached the opening in three flying strides, a split second before Jair could scramble to his feet. She knew vaguely that he was lunging after her, almost upon her heels, as she vaulted the gap into dimness. But she knew very little else with any degree of clarity for some seconds.

For she landed not upon a level floor, but on a rubbery, cushioned surface that swooped into life as she touched it. Inertia flattened her to the cushions as it rocketed toward the ceiling in a long, smooth glide. Behind her she heard Jair's startled bellow trailing out and away as something unexpected happened to him. For a few moments she could see nothing.

Then violet light dawned slowly about her and she was gliding swiftly down a long mirrored slope between trees like great nodding plumes, white in the purple dimness. The slopes were deep-violet and all the pale trees stood upon their own reflections.

Juille was sitting in a cushioned boat with a harp-shaped prow. And it was sliding faster and faster, down and down, while the plumy trees blurred together and a great crashing chord of music paralleled her flight. Far off through the trees she saw motion—red beard, a streaming cloak. Too dazed to realize what had happened, she was not yet too dazed to recognize Jair, and she sent a random beam screaming at him through the trees. He bellowed a distant, echoing challenge.

By the time its resounding chords had died away a little, and her boat carried her around a wide swinging curve under the trees, she thought she knew what was happening. They had stumbled, somehow, into one of the game rooms of Cyrille. Jair's last lightning bolt must have opened a wall directly above a waiting line of cars, and the two of them were swooping now, very fast, through the opening measures of some one of the elaborate competitive entertainments of Cyrille.

Unexpectedly the familiar despairing wail of a needle beam screamed overhead and spattered blue-violet in the dimness upon an unseen wall behind her. Juille ducked instinctively and heard Jair's diminishing shout as he was carried past along a curve beyond the nodding trees. Obviously he was afraid to use the lightning bolts here. If he wrecked the invisible track, he might come to grief himself before he could escape from his flying boat.

Juille craned about her in the sleepy twilight. The trees nodded with soporific soothing motion; the cushioned boat swept on up a swift incline to the music of an invisible orchestra. Again the screams of a gun beam split the music, searing the cushions before her. Scorched rubber tainted the air. She twisted in time to see the other boat go swooping away through the trees in a long, smooth dive, and hurled a whining beam in pursuit. Jair yelled derisively.

The music swelled and sank. The boats swung gracefully around tree-shadowed curves, under feathery plumes that brushed the cheek. The mirrored slopes reflected everything in violet distances underfoot, like still water. And above and below the music Jair and Juille exchanged random shots that missed in blue-spattering fountains or seared the cushions of one boat or the other, but because of their speed, somehow never quite struck the occupants. Several times severed tree trunks came down in avalanches of white plumes.

But presently the light began to glow with a rosy brightening, and Juille realized that a second phase of the entertainment was about to begin. What it would be she did not know, but since this was very likely a competitive game, it would no doubt involve a clearer light and a more open field for some kind of maneuvers in the gliding boats. She imagined the music that kept pace with the speed of her flight had some connection with the harp on the prow of each boat. Was it some sort of musical competition as well? She remembered Egide in the underground arsenal, shouting until the weapons all replied, and for an unexpected moment she was appalled by a melting warmth at the memory. She had an irresistible vision of the young H'vani riding in a boat like this with his yellow hair streaming, leaning forward to strike music from the harp and shouting out the stanzas of some ballad in reply to the distant, shouting song from other boats, and the wild chords of the harps.

She turned her mind grimly away from that, wondering if anyone who had ridden this track before could have imagined the deadly stakes for which she played today. And she knew she dared not play it through. In the light and the open, Jair would have the advantage.

Those lightning bolts would probably not miss a third time.

But one advantage she did have. She had entered the game first. She remembered enough of the contests to know that they usually involved an elaborate crossing and recrossing of paths, woven in and out like a Maypole dance. It was not impossible that Jair's boat, while not following exactly the path of her own, did cross it now and then in her wake. If she could wreck the track—

Leaning over the back of the swiftly gliding boat, she pointed her bell-mouthed gun at the floor and pulled the trigger. While she waited for the whirling sun to form she speculated as to what would happen if she herself were carried over the resulting chasm first.

Something was wrong. The gun was shivering in her hand like some living creature forced beyond its strength. But no glow gathered. Juille shook it in some faint hope of utilizing the last of whatever charge it used. But the shivering itself began to slacken in a moment or two, and then the little weapon from the nameless past lay dead in her hand. She looked at it regretfully. Well, now she would have to take the lightning gun from Jair or give up all hope of reaching the Control Room even in time to take vengeance. After an instant's hesitation she gripped her palm gun tightly and slipped over the side of the boat.

This was a slow place, mounting the rise of a mirrored hill. She skidded a moment or two on the uncertain flooring and then caught herself and watched the boat go sliding on down a slope to waves of diminishing music. Juille dived into the shelter of a great feathery tree that overhung the path. Violet twilight closed about her. She stood in a bower of shivering white plumes, exquisitively delicate, wavering upon the air so that her very breath stirred them into slight motion all around. She could trace the departure of her boat by the quivering plumes in its wake.

The music sank and swelled again. She spent an interminable five minutes thinking she had guessed wrong, and wondering wildly how she could ever hope to escape now, without her bell gun to blast a way through the floor. And then upon a rising tide of music she saw a boat come gliding by, parting the trailing plumes. Jair leaned forward over the prow, his red-brown eyes raking the twilight with quick, comprehensive glances. He was almost machine-like in the cold efficiency that lay like a hard foundation beneath the warmth and the dominant, overwhelming masculinity of him.

But he did not see Juille. This time she was hidden. This time she could not fail.

She raised her gun, took steady aim, and shot him through the stomach.

The beam's high wail still shook the scorched and plumy branches around her as she leaped for the stern of the sliding boat. It was picking up speed again. Jair had doubled forward without a sound, both big hands clutching at the wound. His lightning gun thudded softly to the car's cushioned floor. The air smelled of burned flesh and burned feathers. He did not move as she leaned over the moving side and snatched up the gun. It was all over in the flash of a moment.

Then she dropped off the padded gunwale as the boat gathered more speed. She stood watching it go, sliding faster and faster to the beat of rising music, swooping away over the violent reflections of the floor while the white trees foamed in its wake.

The gun was still warm from Jair's hand. After a moment of quiet staring as the boat and the dying man vanished, Juille drew a long breath and pointing the lightning gun at random, pulled its trigger.

Thunder and lightning—the crash of the bolt against some hidden wall, then booming echoes that rolled and rolled again. Plumed trees convulsed violently away from that path of destruction, delicate fronds tearing free so that the air was filled with a storm of feathery snow. Through their drifting, Juille could see only confusedly what had happened. In the wake of the thunderclap, and tinkling between its echoes, she heard shattered crystal showering from some ruined wall.

Setting her lips, she turned the gun in the opposite direction and loosed a second bolt. There was a curious intoxication in the feeling of sheer destruction as she heard the lightning smash and another wall come sliding down in musically tinkling fragments. Echo piled upon echo through the boiling snow of feather fronds. Again and again and again, in diminishing distances, she heard the bolt strike and leap and strike again, wall beyond wall, until it found a gap too wide to bridge. The thunder rolled away and rolled again long after the crashes ceased, and the air was heady with ozone. The whole forest was lashing itself to fragments now, and the storm of feathery snow had become almost too thick to breathe.

Holding her cloak over her face, Juille tilted the gun down and loosed a bolt at the floor some distance ahead. Destruction was her only goal now. Jair had fired recklessly, in the hope of killing her, but he had not shared this utter recklessness of Juille's. She knew she could not find the Control Room except by chance, but the lightning bolts she was loosing must sooner or later crash through the floors into the room where Egide stood waiting by the window that looked down upon Ericon.

Whether the Imperial City still stood she could not guess. Perhaps not. She did not know how much time had passed since her escape from the first room, or how near Cyrille had been then to the city. At best she might still save it; at worst she would have revenge. For if she missed the Control Room, she must eventually pierce the outer walls of Cyrille and let free the air that kept them both alive. And she would do it if she had to demolish the whole pleasure world, room by room.

A fan of bright sunlight glowed upward through the wrecked floor. Like the pink snow in that room of terrible laughter, the feathery snow of this one turned and twisted like great motes in its beam. Juille skipped back in alarm as the floor before her collapsed with a great sliding crash into the gap. Dust billowed up into the sun rays.

When the sliding had ceased, Juille saw a network of beams that looked fairly steady, and made a precarious descent to the floor below through the choking dust and the swirls of feathers. The air still shook to thunderous echoes and the distant crashes as her lightning bolt went leaping on, far away.

Here was another jumble of ruined rooms opening upon one another, mingling the components of their worlds into one insane potpourri of incongruities. Strong sunlight from a wrecked daisy field stretched fingers of illumination into the fragments of a spring night sparkling with stars. A burst of feather snow from above blew past on some sudden draft and swirled over the daisies and through the broken wall above them into a stretch of desert that lifted blue peaks against the sky miles upon miles away.

Juille looked about upon the chaos she had wrought and laughed aloud with something of a god's intoxication in the sound. She felt like a god indeed, hurling the thunderbolts, wrecking the helpless worlds about her. She drilled a fresh path of destruction through the nearest wall, reeling a little with the concussion of the blow, and then breathed the ozone deeply and felt her head spin with its stimulation.

Through the wrecked wall in the wake of the lightning and thunder a gust of sudden rain came beating, and the sound of distant surf breaking upon rocks, and a swirl of leaves from some exotic purple tree. Juille climbed through the gap and watched her bolt leaping three rooms away across a jungle glade to crash with redoubled violence into a twilight scene where pink boats drifted. Beyond it some scarcely visible new world opened up, a place of darkness and blazing orange suns whirling in a black sky.

* * *

Something cold lapped about Juille's ankles. She looked down at a stream that appeared to have sprung to sudden existence from empty air between the columns of a golden autumn wood. It gushed harder as she looked, broke away more of the wall upon which the autumn trees were reflected, and became a minor torrent in the course of a few seconds.

Remembering the many water scenes of Cyrille, Juille took alarm. There must be great reservoirs of it somewhere here. She had no wish to release it all at once, to overwhelm her before her work was done. She cast another lightning bolt at the floor in the torrent's path, staggered from the concussions and watched the broadening stream plunge downward in the wake of thunderous echoes to create new havoc beneath.

Then she clambered over ruins and hurled a new bolt before her to blast a path through the worlds. Where was Egide? Which way did the Control Room lie? Echoes piled upon echoes as she blazed her way along. Ozone mingled with the heavy fragrances of tropic flowers and autumn leaves burning, and nameless, unknown odors from the opening rooms.

There was something truly godlike about such destruction as she was wreaking. This was more than human havoc. As she went striding and destroying from room to room she left ruin in her wake that could not have been paralleled since God first created the Galaxy out of similar chaos. All the ingredients of creation were here, tossed together in utter confusion. And if her race was doomed, if it never ruled the stars again, then she was creating here in miniature all the havoc her race would leave behind it when it fell. World by tiny world she returned them to the original anarchy from which God had assembled them, but there would be no gods to come after her and build them up again.

She was glad that she came upon none of the scenes she might have remembered from her few days here with Egide, in the lost times of peace. Subconsciously she kept watch for that vast central room of the floating platforms and the great tree, where they had met. And once she came to an opening that might once have been that room, and stood on the brink of its great space, looking out. Lightning bolts had been here before her, and nothing coherent remained. The whole enormous space had evidently once been veiled with vast swinging curtains of gossamer, but they were in ribbons now and held startling bits of flotsam in their nets, as if some giant had been seining chaos for the relics of ruined worlds.

Methodically she went on with her labor of hurling the thunderbolts.

Cyrille was builded well. The little worlds collapsed into one another and the walls and floors collapsed, but the small planet itself held surprisingly long. But eventually, as Juille paused to look down a long newly-opened vista—like someone gazing godlike from the shore of the river of time, looking across the eras into many parallel worlds—she saw something amazing happen.

Far away, tiny in the distance at the end of the lightning-riven chain, trees and walls and shattered buildings began with stately precision to collapse. An invisible hand seemed to be sweeping toward her along the newly created corridor of the worlds, crushing them to the floor in leisurely successions. Juille had a moment's insane impression that by the hurling of the thunderbolts she had made herself a god—that the world bowed down before her.

She stood amazed, watching the long sets fold slowly to the ground, nearing and nearing, until—A giant palm smashed her to the floor. She was no god now, but a puppet in the grip of a monstrous gravity that was making the very floor sag beneath her incredible weight.

It passed on and she got up shakily, full of a grim exultance even in the face of this terrible threat. Cyrille was breaking up. The gravity machines had been damaged. And that—she laughed aloud—must mean that one of her random bolts had reached the Control Room at last. From now on, anything might happen. She thought with chilly amusement of Egide's surprise. He must think Jair was being very careless indeed with the Andarean lightning. Perhaps he might come to investigate. Perhaps he might! She warmed at the thought. She had no idea along which of the many corridors that her bolts had opened the Control Room lay, but Egide might follow the path that had broken in its wall and so find her. She began to watch for a human figure among the vistas.

But Cyrille was collapsing faster than she had thought. The faraway, hissing howl of air through punctured space walls had not yet begun to drain the planet of life, but some other force of destruction was loose among the worlds now. She felt the roar before she heard it, a thunderous shaking of the air that swelled and swelled into a stunning juggernaut of sound. The floor tilted, sending her reeling against a wall through whose breach bright-scaled branches hung. They clutched at her feebly, with a malignant reptilian life. But she scarcely noticed. The roaring grew so vast that its own weight seemed to turn Cyrille off balance as it neared. She heard a series of tremendous avalanching crashes beyond the walls.

Then a solid stream of green water burst through the wall she leaned on, and crashed against the opposite barrier, brimming the room waist high in a split second. Juille went whirling helplessly into the vortex boiling at its center. But before she had gulped more than a searing lungful of the water a screaming uproar filled the room as it dropped away again around her. She leaned gasping against the wall while the sudden torrent drained away through a hole in the flooring. The last of it vanished with a gurgling, shrieking scream that sounded nearly human.

Gravity shifted madly while the sound still echoed. Juille found herself shooting up diagonally toward a corner of the ceiling which had suddenly become the floor. An utter hodgepodge of her self-created chaos fell with her. Before she could adjust her balance on the angular floor, it tipped anew and amid floating debris she drifted down again. Far off the roaring of the released torrent diminished among the echoing rooms, but the floor still vibrated from its thunder. Obviously the water supplies had burst their reservoirs at last and were crashing through Cyrille, flattening everything in their path.

If she had created chaos before, there was no word to describe this.

Gravity tilted again, to send her reeling down a steep incline of inter-opening rooms. Warm rain beat in her face, snow stung it. Air currents went screaming by, mingling the odors of a dozen ruined worlds. Then the floor retilted, so that the bottom of the slope she stumbled along was suddenly the top of a high hill, and she went scrambling and spinning away sidewise through a cold ice cavern that opened upon a swamp.

When Juille found herself looking up into Egide's face, she was not at all surprised. Creation had flown apart all around her; nothing would be surprising now. Everything in her brain was as hopelessly confused as the external confusion all about, and with the letting go of gravity, all sense of responsibility seemed to have let go, too. Far away, long ago, she knew she had been desperately worried about something. It was all right now. Nothing mattered. Nothing remained intact to matter. When natural laws suspend and reverse themselves, the mind tends to accept suspension as natural in itself.

Egide seemed to be carrying her. Everything bobbed curiously around them. He was carrying her doggedly through a snowstorm that changed to a gust of tiny frightened birds, white and pink and yellow, rushing by them shoulder high in a great beat of wings. And now they were flying, too, twisting over and over around each other in the midst of a twisting tornado of colored debris. Juille laughed weakly at the ludicrous feeling of weightlessness.

"Glad it amuses you," Egide told her savagely, trying in vain to right himself. "If this is your idea of suicide, go ahead. I'm leaving." He shoved her violently away and struck off awkwardly through midair, pushing a way ahead through the floating jetsam of the worlds, and holding on to the ceiling for leverage.

"Wait! Come back!" Juille floundered after him, knowing vaguely in the back of her mind that there had once been some urgent reason why he should not leave her. Nothing mattered now that had mattered before, but there was still that nagging remembrance.

"Stop following me!" Egide barked angrily, pushing a drifting boulder aside.

"Wait! Wait!" Juille wailed, and brushed the boulder from her way.

If they had been tensely staking their lives a few minutes before on the hope of killing each other, all memory of that had relaxed and floated away with the floating worlds. There was nothing ludicrous to either of them now in the futile anger of their voices. And if, in this utter suspension of all they had been thinking and believing, Egide fled from Juille as a danger and a menace, and if Juille struggled after him calling him to return, it may have meant nothing at all.

Juille had little recollection of what happened between that time and the time she found herself helping Egide, who resisted her irritably, to lever open a door in a slanting ceiling. They hoisted themselves through it with difficulty. Then Juille turned suddenly very sick as gravity reversed itself in midair and whirled the floor around underfoot, jerking the door handle from her grasp.

After a moment, everything righted itself. Juille found herself leaning on a cold, smooth wall of plastic, looking over a familiar room. Machinery filled it, and from the walls, hundreds of paneled screens looked down in serried rows. Many of them still functioned, mirroring insane pictures as world tumbled through world. Sounds howled down from their windows, hodgepodging together into a continuous ululating roar. And before her, a vast glass wall opened upon the red glow of fire.

That was Ericon down there.

Remembrance avalanched back upon her. And for a stunned moment, the sight she saw below meant nothing. She had looked too long upon ruin to be shocked by it now. Ericon stood up like a great green wall before her in the telescopic glass, its surface crisscrossed with a path of destruction. The Imperial City, like a toy relief map spread upright on the wall, sent great rolling plumes of smoke upward from its shattered buildings. She could see the wreckage of the Imperial patrol ships lying where they had fallen among the ruins. The futile flashes of gunfire from far below sparkled like fireflies in the dusk of the consuming smoke. But she could not quite force her mind to believe any of it. She had seen too much miniature destruction in the past few hours to accept this destruction, so far away, as real, full-sized, disastrous.

No. What sent a cold flooding of despair through her now was the sight of the great black shapes which were forging silently past the window in perfect formation, silhouettes against the pulsing red glow of Ericon beneath.

The great armada of the H'vani was driving in from space through the breaches of the devastated space defenses. They were coming in now—now, as she stood watching. This was something real. There was no parallel for this in the make-believe destruction she had just wrought. She leaned against the wall and let her wide eyes absorb the sight of Ericon's ultimate ruin, unable to make her mind take hold upon anything but that.

So her futile adventures among the little worlds of Cyrille had been for nothing, then. Sometime while she had gone striding among them dealing thunderbolts, Cyrille had swung at last over the target Egide awaited. And he had loosed a real thunderbolt upon a real world. She could see the ravaged surface of it interlaced with broad molten tracks of ruin. Cyrille's traitorous work was done. Juille thought sickly of what must have happened down there when the unsuspected moon, which had circled Ericon for countless ages, suddenly began to pour death upon the city.

That silent armada could take over now. It would take over, against whatever resistance might be left in the stunned and ruined city below. Her father might be dead already. And without either of them to organize the shattered remnants of the empire, what hope did the Lyonese have? She tried to turn over in her mind the names of those who might succeed her, she tried to think how quickly the forces on the outlying planets of this system might be summoned in, but with the very heart of the empire lying in burning ruins down there, it was hard to think at all.

Then her hand at her throat touched the outlines of that small lensed weapon which had been Dunnar's last gift to the Lyonese, and a faint hope began to struggle in her mind. If the Lyonese had lost their Imperial City and the services of herself as a leader, had not the H'vani lost their leaders, too? Jair, dead somewhere out in the raving chaos of Cyrille, and Egide here—Egide leaning against the window and looking down at the great armada that was pouring in upon Ericon.

Egide had crossed the still-intact floor of the Control Room while Juille stood stricken against the wall, gazing upon the ruin of her empire. Now he lifted his head and watched her without moving as she pulled out her lens upon its chain. She must have seemed to be looking in a mirror as she lifted the lens and tried vainly to steady it enough for her purpose. Certainly there was no overt threat in the action. He stared, not interfering, as she braced her elbows on a projecting bar and centered him in the thin cross-hairs of the weapon.

Then Juille drew a deep breath and pressed the white stud. Nothing happened. Nothing, of course, would happen until the other stud was pressed. But Juille felt oddly disappointed that her supreme purpose had been accomplished in this moment, with so little fanfare. It surprised her a bit that she had no emotional reaction now. Neither triumph nor regret, although Egide's life hung upon the pressure of a stud. No feeling seemed left in her at all.

She looked around vaguely, wondering just what to do next. Egide still stood before the window where the great black shapes of his armada passed in stately formation, silent, limned against the light of the burning city. All around them the howling from the ruined worlds of Cyrille still poured down from their screens upon the wall. Through the one ragged gap where Juille's lightning bolt had crashed came more confused roars and thunderings as the tides of water and the shifting gravities put a last touch of havoc on the work she had done. But here in the Control Room, gravity still prevailed, and so far the ruinous tides had not rolled this way. Very likely they soon would. And then there would be no survivors at all upon Cyrille.

Juille shook herself awake. One last faint hope remained with her, but even that must be fulfilled quickly. She held the lens up, her thumb upon the black stud that meant death.

"Egide," she called. "Egide, look here. Remember the weapon from Dunnar?"

He blinked. He had not recovered quite as quickly as she from that curious relaxing of all human values which the shifting gravities induced. He had not had reason to recover so soon, as Juille did, at the shock of what lay below the window. He said:

"What do you mean? Dunnar?"

She flashed the lens impatiently at him. "This is the weapon. This, here! Do you understand me?" She saw that he did, for he reached abortively toward his holster. "No, don't move!" She cried it sharply above the noise from the walls. "I can press this stud before you shoot, and then—" She made a grim little gesture.

Egide hesitated. "That's not the weapon there."

"It's enough to kill you."

He furrowed his brow at her. "The real weapon—that must be down below, on Ericon." He glanced over his shoulder at the gliding armada and the flames of the burning city, and his hand moved a little nearer his gun.

"Don't do it!" Juille's voice was confident and commanding. "The real weapon's safe, even now. In a bombproof vault outside the city. We thought of everything, you see. Even this. I wouldn't risk it, Egide." She held the lens higher, so the red light from below caught brightly in it, and showed him her thumb already on the lethal stud. He hesitated a little even now.

Juille held her breath. She did not want to kill him yet. She was not sure she wanted to kill him at all, and certainly he would be no use to her dead at this stage. But she might have to press the stud. This harmless-looking adjunct of a distant machine lacked the compelling power of a gun muzzle aimed between a man's eyes. Her own confidence might be a more effective psychological threat than the very real danger of the lens in her hand.

She said in a brisk, decisive voice, "You're coming with me to Ericon, Egide—if we can find a way to get there. The Ancients promised me my chance, too, you know—and mine comes last. You can come back with me to be our hostage—or stay here dead. We haven't lost yet. With Jair gone and you captive, and with this new weapon of ours, I think we've still a good chance. The weapon's going to work its very best under circumstances like . . . don't touch that gun!"

He stood there staring at her, fingers hovering over his holster, decision still tilting in the balance. What would have happened had nothing interrupted them, Juille had no way of guessing. But as they faced one another in tense silence, a voice suddenly boomed from the wall above.

"So that's the Dunnar weapon!" Jair's bull-throated bellow roared above the roar of smashing worlds.

Juille started violently. But even in her amazement,

she kept her thumb upon the stud and her eyes upon Egide's gun, though insane thoughts whirled frantically through her mind. Jair? Jair alive, with a needle beam through his stomach? Jair, talking in that full, confident bellow of his, when she'd left him dead and drifting through the violet twilight? It was some trick. She had seen illusions enough here to know that it *must* be some trick.

She risked one lightning glance away from Egide. The unmistakable figure of Jair himself leaned forward into the communicator screen of some yet undamaged world, grinning a bold white grin through the red beard. His red eyes twinkled with triumph, and the burn of her needle beam still marred his tunic to show that the shot had gone home. It *must* have gone home. There had been no heat flare to prove the presence of armor such as Egide had worn when she turned her gun on him.

She dared not look long at him, but her bewilderment had registered upon the screen as she flashed her gaze back to Egide, and she heard the familiar, rolling vibrations of Jair's laughter ring through the room.

"You shot me straight enough," he announced. "But you'll never kill me with a gun. Tell her, Egide."

Egide was looking up at the laughing giant with a strange expression on his face.

"Jair is an android," he said. "You can't kill him."

Juille gave him a blank stare. She heard herself repeating stupidly, "An android?"

But she did not believe it. That was against all reason. Jair, the very essence of all warm, human masculinity—the frankly barbarous, the laughing Jair, with his voice that shook the walls to its deep timbre. She knew, of course, that androids existed. Cyrille had been making robot humans for a long while now, in such perfect simulacra of reality that only the very closest association could prove the difference. To all intents and purposes, they were real anthroids—manufactured humans with all the external attributes of flesh. But Jair—

"I had him made ten years ago," Egide told her in a

bemused sort of voice, his eyes upon the window where the counterfeit H'vani looked down. "The perfect H'vani type—for a figurehead, you know. I'd got so used to him I seldom think of his not being—human. Sure you're all right, Jair?"

A bellow of mirth shook the walls above the roaring of Cyrille's worlds.

"All right?" Jair doubled a mallet-like fist and struck himself heavily upon the needle char where Juille's shot had gone home. The two humans winced involuntarily. "Just doubled me up for a minute," the android said. "That was enough, though. You did a fine job of wreckage, girl. Now we'll do a better—down below."

Juille got her breath back with a rush.

"Oh, no, you won't," she told him confidently. "Not now." And she caught the red firelight again in her lens.

Jair's laughter was curiously cold. And Juille realized that it had always been cold. The laugh itself should have proved him inhuman. And a flurry of small recollections came back to convince her—his incredible quickness in gun-fighting, his speed, his silence, his machine-smooth efficiency of motion. Even the fact that he had not worn needleproof armor beneath his tunic. Then the bull-voice with its deeply vibrant pitch that should have been warm and human, and was instead cold to her ears now with the chill of machinery beneath the flesh said:

"Go ahead, girl. Kill him."

Egide's face did not change. Juille thought she understood then his oddly bemused look of a few minutes before. He had remembered that Jair was what he was. He had known this moment was coming, and it did not surprise him now. The android could have no human emotions; loyalty was not in him.

And there went Juille's new hope of forcing Jair into captivity, too, with the threat upon Egide. Her shoulders sagged a little. But even in this fresh disappointment she kept her pressure firm upon the lens stud, and her eyes upon Egide.

"I'd save you if I could," the android's deep voice told the man who had ordered his creation. "It can't be done now. You aren't necessary any more. We've got Ericon, or will have. Too bad, Egide."

Egide nodded, no emotion on his face.

"The barons can carry on now," Jair told him carelessly. "Malon can take over, or Edka. They'll need me."

Egide looked up at the grinning, red-bearded face in the screen.

"They don't even know you're an android," he said emotionlessly.

Jair bent down upon them one last brilliantly warm smile. His eyes glinted with a sudden look of the pure machine.

"I know," he said.

Then he swung away and they watched his broad back receding into the depths of the panel. Beyond him Juille could see the shapes of tiny space boats racked as if in hangars, and untouched as yet by the destruction that was raging through Cyrille. That was the room she must get to, then.

Juille turned back to Egide, realizing for the first time that she had forgotten to keep her eyes on him. But he had not moved. He stared up at the screen, and his shoulders had the little sag her own had assumed a few minutes ago. When he met her eyes he grinned a bit.

"Am I still worth killing?" he asked.

Juille jerked her head toward the empty screen. "What do you think he's planning?"

"He wasn't built to plan. I don't know."

"What was he built for?"

Egide looked at her speculatively. "You don't understand the H'vani very well, do you? Savagery isn't always a vice, you know. There's got to be an influx of it every so often or civilization would bog down in its own rut. It always has happened—it probably always will.

Right now my people are on the first rung of the ladder—they're emotional and childish and they need a figurehead. Well"—he nodded toward the wall—"that's Jair."

"Why not you?"

"They don't quite trust me. I'm not typical. Too much veneer for a true H'vani. Maybe too many brains. I had to have some perfectly trustworthy bully who could outfight and outyell the people. Someone with his own brand of charm, too. But anyone with those gifts would be too dangerous to use. He might want to take over, and I couldn't have stopped him. So"—Egide grinned ruefully—"I had the Cyrillians make Jair. It seemed like a wonderful idea. And it worked, too. Jair did a magnificent job. He never had to think, but he certainly could lead. I suppose even now he's done the right thing. From a perfectly cold-blooded viewpoint, the H'vani need a rallying point worse than they need me as a leader. Jair's much better for the job."

"But if none of your men knows he's an android—"

"I'm not so sure it matters now. I kept it a secret because I couldn't trust anyone at all not to let it slip, and my people—well, they wouldn't like that. But Jair's done his job well up to now. No reason why anyone needs to know."

"He certainly doesn't mean to tell them."

"I wonder. Hard to understand what was in his mind. No android ever had an opportunity just like this before. He never showed any more ambition, until now, than you'd expect from a machine. He may never show any."

"He won't." Juille said it confidently. Egide gave her an inquiring look. "The H'vani are going to find out their leader's not human. You're going to tell them." Her voice took on warmth as the new idea grew. "I haven't lost yet! You're still a hostage. You're going to broadcast to your people just what Jair is. Maybe we'll suggest that some of the other leaders are androids, too. If Jair's what they've been worshiping and following, that ought to shake all their confidence—or else nothing would!"

Egide stared at her almost with a reluctant admiration. She gave him no time to speak. "Drop your guns," she said. "And then go over there and try to get Ericon on the communicators. I don't think you can, but it's worth trying."

Egide gave her one long, searching look, as if not yet quite convinced of the validity of her weapon. But a change in the timbre of the noise that still poured in distantly through the breached wall reminded them both of the imminent danger, and after a moment, he obeyed.

Juille watched the guns clatter to the floor. Her mind was spinning with wary plans now—how to reach the room of the ships, how to keep Egide from overpowering her on the tumultuous way there, what to do first if they ever reached Ericon alive.

Egide turned from the unresponsive screens after ten minutes of futile effort.

"Cyrille's dead," he shrugged. "Now what?"

Juille looked down at the lens in her hand. "We'll have to suspend hostilities for a while," she told him. "I can't keep my thumb on this stud forever. And I don't want to kill you now. I'll have to, though, unless you promise to keep a truce until we get back to Ericon. I'll even have to trust your word—"

He looked down at her with a smile. "I seem to fall somewhere between H'vani and Lyonese," he said dryly. "I'm civilized enough to make a promise and—well, savage enough to keep it. You can trust my word, Juille."

Juille's lips thinned; she dropped the lens back on its chain inside her tunic. All she said was, "We'll have to trace the hangar room from the screen up there. Do you know how?"

Egide pointed to a chart engraved on the wall beneath the panels. "If anything like halls are left outside here, we'll find it," he declared.

There were halls. Not many and not much of them, but enough to help materially. They opened the door and stood staring out at a crazily angled ceiling on which a tangle of debris clung as if to a floor. And Juille glanced up to find Egide looking at her gravely, without words. It was not difficult to guess his thoughts. Perhaps anger was the dominant emotion that made her flush so hotly. She could not be sure herself. After a moment, she said in a voice that sounded a little unsteady, "Let's go."

The fragments of hallways that remained were small, lucid stretches between lengths of howling chaos. Nothing in those lengths had any resemblance now to any normally balanced world. Juille found time to be thankful anew that most of Cyrille's materials were fireproof. Earth and air and water were churning insanely through the broken walls; if the fourth and most ravenous element were loose here too, not she or Egide or Jair would ever have left alive.

As it was, they were nearly swept away time and again as they made frantic dashes from shelter to shelter through the hurricane. Curiously, only the very small and delicate relics remained intact now. Trees, buildings, furniture that had made up the illusions were battered almost unrecognizably, but a swarm of gorgeously colored autumn leaves, for instance, had ridden with the storm and brushed stinging past.

Gravity shifted imponderably. They ran slowly, like people in a leaden-footed nightmare; they changed with unexpected suddenness to long, swooping strides that covered ten feet at a step. They sailed through the clogged air; they were smashed crushingly to the ground amid a rain of fragments made suddenly heavy.

The air was in strong motion now, and twice as they staggered along they heard the distant shriek of it rushing furiously through punctured space walls, dragging great winds behind it. But each time the tortured pleasure-world healed itself and they heard the suck and slam of locks automatically closing off the broken rooms. It might be a matter of minutes or hours before some stray lightning bolt, still ravening through the walls, pierced some bulkhead with broken locks, and Cyrille was sucked empty in one vast, sudden gust.

The avalanching water thundered somewhere not far off as they came at last to the hangar room, buffeted, breathless, very sore from the bounding of the tornado. But they had no time to rest. This apartment, like the Control Room, seemed to have a gravity machine of its own and the ships remained intact in their cradles, waiting to be launched each through its separate door. But a bolt might come smashing through the walls at any moment. The two refugees never remembered afterward just how they managed their escape. Neither of them had really expected to leave Cyrille alive.

The emperor looked up from his map. The cluster of officers looked up, too, but no one said anything as Juille came quickly into the room, saying, "Father—"

"Glad you got back," the emperor told her in a voice she did not know. She found she scarcely knew the man himself—this helmeted warrior with the fierce blue blaze in his eyes and the look of stunned bewilderment still a shadow upon his lined face. They all had that stunned look. Ericon had been invincible so long— Only the emperor seemed to know exactly what he was about. Even with this disaster upon him, even with the bewilderment still in his eyes, he knew what he was doing now, what he must do next. This was the man who had been so great and terrible a leader in the days of his youth; he was great and terrible again. No trace remained of the patriarch in white robes, pleading for peace. No trace remained either, Juille thought, of the indulgent father she had left.

He said again, "Glad you're back—" and for a moment stared at her with eyes that really saw what they looked at. But it was a curiously blind stare still. He knew vaguely that something more than that phrase might be expected of him, that in normal times, his only child's return from death would have been a signal for tremendous emotional release. Not any more. He was no longer a father or a man, but an emperor with the weight of imminent disaster on his shoulders. His mind was not functioning now except in terms of empire. He was a machine at this moment as Jair was a machine, all his faculties bent toward one consuming purpose.

"We're evacuating the city," he told Juille without preamble, and a cold, bright intensity burned in his voice and his lined face. It was not his daughter he spoke to, but a tried officer whose advice might be helpful. He was not questioning her presence or her past experiences, only her usefulness at this terribly urgent moment. "Through this pass here—" His steady finger traced a course across the map. "Up into the mountains where the forbidden woods make a pocket, the H'vani can't attack by air. Enough troops are left to make a stand until reinforcements start coming in from the planets. That Dunnar weapon ought to prove useful, too. Now—"

"It's still working?" Juille had seen too much of the city and the surrounding countryside ravaged by those dreadful broad swathes of molten ruin to have much confidence in anything material now.

"It's working. With any luck, it always will work." The emperor gave a ghost of a chuckle. "The H'vani sealed it in so tightly I don't believe anyone could ever dig it up again. That's once they've overreached themselves."

Juille received that and dismissed it with a nod. "Good luck for us. Father—so much has happened. You've got to listen to me. Haven't you even a minute to spare alone?"

The emperor gave her a keen look under his brows, then nodded to the little group of men and women around the table. "All right—one minute." Juille waited while they fell back out of earshot, down the length of the big shattered room through whose walls the smoke of the burning palace blew now and then in pungent, strangling gusts. She spoke fast.

"The Andareans—you don't know about that yet? They've been holding revolutionist meetings in the tunnels. And there's Egide—they told you I've brought him in as a hostage? I—"

"Hostage be damned," the emperor said abstractedly. "Only one thing matters right now—getting my troops out. You can't bargain with madmen like the H'vani when they're looting a city. Later—maybe. A wonder you ever got through their fleet—"

"I didn't come through. I thought I'd better circle—"

The emperor wasn't listening. "We have half an hour to clear the city. If you have anything important to say, say it and let me get back to work." He gave her a sudden cold glance across the map. "I haven't forgotten what you did in the council hall, Juille. That was treason. You'll have to stand trial for it later. You may be responsible for the loss of the city."

"Your peace wouldn't have gone through, father. The H'vani came in conspiracy with Helia and her people. They got their new weapons from them. They never meant to keep the truce themselves."

The emperor's fierce blue eyes fixed her sharply. "You're not lying about that, are you? It's true?" His voice deepened with a note of anger she knew well. "All of you were playing me for a fool, eh? Using my truce to work your own lying schemes in. All of you! By the Ancients—" There was a thunder as vibrant as Jair's in the old man's voice. "By the Ancients, you all deserve to die together! I ought to let you! I had the possibility of peace in my very hands, and I let you destroy it among you—" But the brief anger passed, and the deep old voice diminished to a rumbling echo. "No, it wasn't your fault or mine. I saw the way out, but I couldn't show it to you. The race isn't worth saving." His big shoulders slumped. Then he saw the map and his head came up with a familiar blue glare in the eyes. "But I will save it! By the gods, I will. Get out of here and let us work, will you?"

"But father—" Juille groped in bewilderment for the reins of government that seemed so abruptly to have dropped from her hands. "I want to broadcast to the H'vani. If they find out we have Egide—and about Jair being an android, they—"

He scowled at her, his face bright with alert intensity. "Android?"

Juille explained it in a few jumbled phrases, and saw a shadow dim the brilliance of his eyes as he followed that knowledge to its conclusion.

"Stop babbling," the emperor snapped. "You can't broadcast, you little fool. Didn't you see what's happened to the city? About that android—"

Juille gaped at him, not listening. She had seen ruin indeed, all the way here. Whole city blocks melted into slag, fire pouring from the public buildings, half the palace itself battered into a shambles. But the thought of a blinded and silenced communicator system had somehow never occurred to her.

"None . . . none of it works any more?" she stammered.

"None." The emperor's voice was definite. "About the android—I don't like it. I don't like it at all." He brooded a moment. "Well—we'll climb that wall when we come to it. Now by the gods, will you get out and let me work?"

Juille looked up at the shattered walls of the room, with rain blowing through them, pungent with the smoke of nearing fires. She could see a stretch of purple thunderclouds, and her mind seized almost eagerly upon the sight—was it the same storm she had glimpsed from Cyrille, moving majestically over the face of Ericon? She knew she was grasping at straws, anything to avoid facing the truth. She had not yet realized the full extent of what had happened here, she did not really want to.

Ericon was lost, but her mind would not face that yet. Automatically she looked about for the nearest communicator screen, so that she might convince herself with the grimness of the actual sight.

And there were no communicators. She could see no farther now than her unaided eyes could look. The knowledge was suddenly smothering. All her life she had had the wonderful windows of those screens to open at a touch upon any view she wanted, anywhere in the Galaxy. No walls had ever really shut her in before. No limits of eye or voice seemed narrow, for the sight and sound of worlds light-millenniums away had always been available at the touch of a stud. But now—

Juille looked frantically about the broken room, feeling for the first time in her life the full, crushing weight of a claustrophobia such as no race could ever have felt before now. Not a fear of confining walls, but of confining worlds—of solar systems too small to be endured. This was a blindness and a deafness beyond all previous experience—a god's scope cut abruptly down to the scope of a human. For a moment she fought an insane desire to batter against the intangible prisoning limits of her own senses. Their terrible pigmy boundaries struck her dumb. For the first time she knew what it was to be one small human creature in a galaxy of worlds, unaided by all her race had achieved on its way to the powers of godhood.

This was what the loss of civilization really meant. For the first time the full import of the Galaxy's great loss overwhelmed her. So long as she could see those lost worlds she might hope to win them back, but to be struck blind like this was to lose them forever. She knew a sudden agony of homesickness for all the planets she might never see again, a sudden terrible nostalgia for the lost, familiar worlds, for the fathomless seas of space between them. Ericon's eternal greenness was hateful, strangling in its tiny limitations.

And this was what her father had so desperately feared to lose that he had been willing to compromise even with the H'vani, so long as both races might maintain it. In this shattering revelation of what barbarism might really mean, she knew that her father had been right, indeed, and herself terribly wrong. But it was far too late to do anything at all about it now.

Through the green folds of the hills veiled by slanting rain, the emperor watched the remnants of his army wind slowly upward. He sat his fretting horse easily, looking down from this hilltop with much the same look upon his face that his portrait had worn in the Hall of the Hundred Emperors. Eager and fierce and proud. Around his neck over the armor he wore a chain and the small lens of the Dunnarian weapon. It was ironically pleasant to know that the heart of that weapon lay safe forever beneath the very halls the H'vani were tramping now.

Juille knew he was thinking of that by the shadow of a grim smile that crossed his bearded face as he glanced back toward the tower of smoke above the city. Once, it seemed very long ago, she had wished aloud that she might have known the young warrior her father used to be. She knew him now. The emperor was magnificently that man again, with all the years of his experience added to give a depth the young man never knew. Age seemed not to have touched him today. He sat at the front of a little group of officers, watching the armies that were to avenge the Lyonese go streaming up the pass.

From this elevation they all could see the distant, undulating mass far down the valley that was the pursuing H'vani. Juille smiled a tight, triumphant smile. They were fighting on their home planet now, under conditions they knew by heart. They would beat the H'vani yet. On any other planet, planes could have bombed their infantry out of existence in a few minutes. But here, in this long arm of mountain land that lay between two forbidden territories, the Ancients permitted no aircraft to fly. The H'vani—Juille's smile deepened—had learned that to their awe-struck cost a little while before. They would send up no more ships over the lightning-guarded territory of the Ancients.

She looked sidewise at Egide. He sat with bound hands before him, his two guards near, his eyes on the following H'vani horde. They had spoken very little to one another since that long, silent flight through the H'vani fleet, with Ericon turning on its axis far below. Juille was a little startled to hear Egide speak now.

"Jair'll be leading them," he said, nodding down the valley. She gave him a keen glance, not at all sure even yet just how she felt about the H'vani's captive leader. She said in a noncommittal voice:

"He won't be leading long. We'll get our broadcasters in order again—"

"Maybe," said Egide, and was silent.

Juille glanced down at the small animal balancing on her knee. The *llar* had a curious way of turning up at most of the crises in her life. It was here now at one of the highest. She put out a tentative hand to caress it, and to her surprise, the little creature permitted the gesture. She wondered if its recollection of that episode in the tunnels had reconciled it to her touch at last. The great eyes stared up into hers with owlish intentness as it pushed its smooth head against her hand.

Someone said, "I see we have something in common, highness," and she looked up into the gray gaze of the man from Dunnar. He was smiling and nodding toward the *llar* as it bent its head to her caress. Juille smiled.

"It's my turn to be flattered now. The two of you did me a great service. I may not have thanked you properly yet."

The envoy shook his head. "Your pet deserves the thanks, highness."

"It was amazing," Juille began eagerly. "How did you manage it? I'd never have believed such a thing could happen."

The man smiled his remote, enigmatic smile. "I will tell you that soon, highness," he said. "Not quite yet, but soon." He flung one corner of his dark cloak over his shoulder and turned away. Juille watched him thoughtfully, a tall thin figure of regal elegance in that cloak.

Egide's voice recalled her.

"I think I can see Jair from here," he said, leaning forward over his bound hands on the saddlehorn. "They've got that third weapon, Juille. See it—the glint of light there at the front?"

Juille caught her breath sharply. The third gift of the Andareans! She had forgotten that. She had let her father plan his campaign without considering it.

"What is it?" she asked Egide fearfully, wondering if he would tell. He looked at her with an expression difficult to analyze.

"A paralyzer," he said simply.

"But we've got those. That's nothing new."

"This works on a bigger scale than anything we've ever had. You've got small hand-paralyzers. This is an attachment that transforms a standard heat-beam caster into a machine to throw a long cone of force. It can whittle your army down by battalions. Once that goes into operation—" He shook his head, lips tightened.

Juille gave Egide a curious glance. Then, without speaking, she shook her reins and rode forward to her father's side. They spoke briefly. In a few minutes, several men with lenses hanging at their necks, slipped down the hillside and vanished into the underbrush bordering the valley. Juille rode back looking confident.

"All right," she said. "They won't find it so easy now. We have our weapons, too, you know. You might have guessed I'd stop that cannon if I could."

"Of course I guessed."

Juille looked at him in bewilderment. He was smiling.

"I'd like to talk to you alone," he said. She hesitated. Then she nodded to his guards and turned her horse aside, leading the way a little distance off toward the brow of the hill. They sat there side by side, watching the two armies winding up the valley. Rain had almost ceased now. A cold wind blew in their faces, and overhead the purple thunderclouds came rolling up faster than the H'vani hordes.

Egide said, "Juille—" and stopped. After a moment, he tried again. "Juille—do you think the H'vani will defeat you?"

"They have a chance," she admitted. "But no, they won't."

"You're sure?"

"How can anyone be sure? I don't believe they will."

"But they have the edge now."

"What of it?" She twisted to face him angrily. "You don't have to boast about your people."

He smiled at her. "They aren't my people now." Juille looked at him with bewildered eyes. He went on, "I'm through with the H'vani. I couldn't say so before—you'd have thought I was afraid and trying to join the winning side. But you can't think that now."

Juille struggled for words. "But—why? *Why?* You organized the attack! You—"

"Oh, I had a great many plans," he said, smiling rather wryly. "I liked working out ideas and watching them succeed. But lately—I've changed." He looked at her as if uncertain whether to follow that idea any further just now. She was still staring at him in puzzled confusion. He said, "Don't look at me like that. I've been thinking this over for quite a while. It isn't as if I were deserting them when they need me. And I've never had much in common with them. Remember, it took Jair to win their hearts."

"But you can't change over like that, without any reason," Juille insisted uncomprehendingly. "You don't—"

"I have my reasons. You're thinking it's a trick, aren't you? Well, it isn't. Why should I trick you now, when it's your side that's losing? When you've got my life there around your neck on a chain?"

Juille's hand went up automatically to her breast where the lenses hung. She thought she was beginning to understand what Egide meant. Her mind went back over the confusion of disastrous things that had happened so swiftly, and paused at the episode in the forbidden woods of the Ancients, when she had stood in Egide's arms and tentatively made herself a promise. When she had him where she wanted him, she remembered now, she had told herself she might not fear the treacherous weakness of emotion. She had thought then that even love might be safe—later. And it was—later—now.

Egide was watching her, a smile beginning to quirk his mouth. She watched his face warm and soften, finding that she knew just how each line and plane would alter with the changing mood. He was very attractive when he smiled. The rain had made his yellow curls darken and tighten to almost sculptured flatness, and the rain on his lashes and his beard twinkled as he shook his head, still smiling.

"You'll never trust me, will you?" he said. "You'll never trust anyone. Even yourself. Least of all yourself—"

"I might," Juille told him softly, hardly knowing her own voice. Her fingers were on the chain about her neck, and almost unconsciously she found herself pulling out the deadly little ornament that held Egide's life. When she realized what she was doing she glanced down, and then sat perfectly still for a long moment, her eyes growing wider and wider. Very slowly she pulled the chain all the way out of her tunic. The color had drained from her face; and as Egide looked, his own color faded. They sat in silence, looking at the broken chain.

The lens was gone.

Juille stared down at the break, too stunned for thought. Somewhere, somehow, in the turmoil of evacuation, she had lost it. Anywhere. In the city. Along the road. In these pathless hills. Somewhere—anywhere. At this moment some curious person might be stooping to pick it up and toy with the black stud. It might lie lost forever, untouched, here in the woods. Or at this moment, or any moment hereafter, Egide might slump over dead in his saddle.

There were many disastrous implications behind the loss, but her thoughts had room for only one just now. All the emotions that had churned in her mind so long about him—all the distrust, the contempt, the reluctant warmth—suddenly crystallized. Her defenses went down with a rush and she knew that of all things in life, what she wanted least was Egide's death.

They sat looking at one another in the midst of a tremendous silence. For this small interval, there was nothing at all to stand between them, neither H'vani nor Lyonese, nor could ideals nor mistrust, nor any of the hours of their enmity. During all the time they had known one another, only a few moments had validity. The interval on the cloud beneath the stars; the interval of their dance, the moment of their kiss in the green, forbidden woods. All other meetings had been meetings of strangers, not themselves.

For Juille it was a moment of almost intolerable poignancy. And perhaps her barriers were down so utterly in this one destroying moment because she knew in her heart that the hours of this surrender were numbered. Traitor she might be to all her amazon principles—but she could not be traitor long.

Wordlessly Juille leaned forward and untied the cords that held Egide's hands together. While she touched him, for an instant longer, the stars and the shadows of the wood still hung about them. But before either could speak, or wanted to, the emperor's voice broke in.

"Juille, I'm going down," he called. "Wait here, child. I'll signal when I want you. The H'vani are catching up with our rear guard."

She came out of the bemusing quiet slowly, too distracted to realize how completely now the reins of control had been taken from her hands. The emperor and most of his men were riding down the hillside before the import of his words came to her clearly. She watched them hurrying down, cloaks billowing, and the rain slanting in long gusts between.

Farther down, half hidden by the hills, she could see that the vanguard of the H'vani was almost upon the last of the escaping Lyonese. There was a turmoil about the length of the shining cannon whose secret the Andareans had betrayed, and Juille knew the new weapon of the Lyonese had taken its first toll among the enemy. There would be more.

She turned to Egide. He was watching her gravely, hands clasped on his saddlehorn. There seemed very little to say just now. Perhaps the time had not yet come for speech. Juille urged her horse nearer his and they sat side by side, knees touching, and watched the emperor riding down the hill.

In the valley the two forces had begun their meeting. From here they could see a big figure at the H'vani's front, red beard and red head a beacon for the invaders to follow. Now and again an echo of Jair's tremendous resonant roar floated up to them above the rising clamor of battle, but for the most part, they heard little. The wind was strengthening; it screamed in their ears and carried the shouts of the fighters away up the valley.

They could see turmoil growing among the H'vani. Far back in the ranks where no men should yet be falling, men fell. The Dunnarian weapon was reaping its first casualties. But Jair's great voice and his irresistible, compelling presence were keeping order among the frightened men.

And suddenly Juille knew that the Dunnarian weapon must fail. Its intrinsic purpose was the slaughter of the leaders at their peak of importance. And Jair would never die by that weapon. He was immortal, not heir to any weakness of human flesh. So long as he remained on his feet the H'vani would not break even in the face of this mysterious silent death that had begun to strike among them.

Jair would become a legend. He might even become a god for his awestruck followers. And the last hope of demoralizing the barbarians was gone now. If Juille could have proclaimed Jair's origin before this battle, the H'vani might have been shaken. But now nothing could shake them. Even if they believed her story, the very belief might deify Jair still further.

A familiar voice at Juille's side echoed the thought. "How strange," said the man from Dunnar, "that they found no human creature to personify for them half the courage and warmth and power they see in this man of metal!"

Something about the pitch of his voice made Juille turn sharply, almost unseating the *llar* that still clung to her knee. The Envoy was looking down the valley, his strange, narrow-skulled head in outline against the piling storm clouds. The cold wind whipped his cloak backward, but his great translucent eyes did not narrow to the blast. Juille was searching his face with a new fascination. The beaked nose, the controlled, cruel mouth. The air of intolerable elegance and fastidious, aloof poise. Juille swallowed hard. For she had heard his voice before, under strange circumstances. She groped after the memory, almost caught it. That calm, clear, familiar tone, saying—

Suddenly she knew. She had heard it in the temple of the Ancients.

He turned his head slowly, and the enormous, clear eyes met hers. He smiled.

"Yes," he said.

Afterward, looking back, the interlude seemed like a hallucination, an unconvincing stage-set painted upon gauze, drawn briefly between Juille and the woods, while the thunderstorm rolled above them in the purple sky. But in the first moment after she had recognized that voice, realities stood out sharp and clear all around her, intensified because she could not speak or think coherently. Everything else was drowned in the overwhelming knowledge of who this man must be. And that he was no man at all. And what unimaginable shape he must really wear behind that illusion of humanity. And—

"Yes," said the Envoy, smiling his thin smile across her at Egide. "You, too."

Juille never knew how long they sat there in silence, while the cold wind whistled about them and in the strange yellow light of storm, the two armies locked in battle down below. She thought she would never speak again. She could not even turn her head to face Egide for comfort in this bleak and overwhelming moment.

The Envoy said, "Each of you came to us for help. And each of you was answered. But you and your people had gone too far already along the road all humans go. There was still one brief moment when you could have saved yourselves. But your instincts were wrong. That time is gone now.

"Every race has come to this end, since the first men conquered the Galaxy. Each of them sows the seed of its own destruction. Always a few see the way toward salvation, and always the many shout them down. But each race has its chance—"

He looked down sternly over the struggling masses in the valley. Mists were beginning to drift between them now. The Envoy was a tall silhouette against the purple clouds of the storm. As he spoke again, the thunder rolled in his voice and in the darkening sky.

"Every nation digs its own grave," he said. "And we are weary of mankind, forever thwarting his highest dreams and trapping himself in the end to a ruin like"—he nodded—"that down there."

Silence for a long moment, while the noises of battle came up faintly, Jair's great rich, carrying shout above all the rest, bellowed from his throat of brass. Juille sat very still on her horse, glad of the pressure of Egide's warm knee, all thought and speech frozen in her as she saw the Envoy's head turning her way. He looked thoughtfully into her face.

"You have set in motion already the forces that must destroy the Lyonese. You were the spokesman for your race, chosen fairly, typical of your kind. And of your own free choice you did it. Nothing can change that now." Then the narrow skull turned farther and he looked across her at Egide. His great eyes were the color of the spattering rain, as cool and translucent and inhuman. "You," he went on, "gave your people a man of iron to worship, and nothing you can do now would swerve them from following it. It will lead them to destruction. How very strange—" The Envoy paused a moment and looked at the two with a sort of puzzled wonder. "How very strange you humans are! How unerringly you unleash upon yourselves the instruments of your own destruction. How long ago the two of you here took the turnings that led you to this hilltop, and your people to their ruin down there. Perhaps the turnings were taken long before your births." He smiled impersonally in the vivid yellowish light. "I know they were. Your first forefathers took them, and you had no choice but to follow, being of human flesh." He sighed. "But the end comes just the same. It's very near now.

"You wonder which will win down there." He glanced toward the struggling armies, almost hidden in the mist. "Neither.

"Neither will win," he told them. "Man has run his last course in our Galaxy. There were those before him who ran theirs, too, and failed to profit from it, and died. Now we weary of man. Oh, he may live out his failing days on the other worlds. We plan no pogrom against mankind." His voice quivered for an instant with aloof amusement. "Man himself attends to that.

But here on Ericon, our own peculiar world, we are weary of man and we want no more of him."

He sent one cool downward glance toward the sounds of battle in the fog, the shouts, the muffled roar of guns, the flashes of fire-sword and pistol and artillery. Then he shook his reins gently and his horse turned toward the woods, where rain was beginning to rustle again among the leaves.

"We have great hopes," he said, "for our new race to come." And he held out his hand.

Something stirred upon Juille's knee. She looked down dumbly. The *llar* flashed up at her one fathomless glance, all the sadness and wisdom and benignity of its race luminous in the great grave eyes so startlingly like the Envoy's. Then it flowed down from her lap to the ground with its alarming, boneless ease, and went rippling over the wet grass toward the Envoy.

Juille looked up. She had no idea why. But she was not surprised to see again the heights of great inward-leaning walls looming dark above the trees. When she lowered her eyes the Envoy and the *llar* had gone.

"I suppose we'd better go down now," Juille said, and put out her hand. Egide turned a quiet blue gaze upon her. The faintest flicker of a smile touched his face and his warm, gun-calloused fingers closed about the hand.

"Yes, I suppose so," he said.

Juille had an extraordinary conviction of hiatus in her life for the past ten minutes. She knew quite well what had been happening while she sat there stricken voiceless and all but mindless in the presence of the gods. She knew she would never quite forget it—or ever speak of it to Egide. But it seemed singularly unreal. The human mind is not constructed to accept defeat even in the the face of finality. She could not now bring hers to accept that memory. What had happened seemed of a different time and texture from the period before or since—an interval of flimsy unreality, a gauze incident, to be dismissed and forgotten.

And yet, she thought, if it were true—if she herself had set into motion the juggernaut that would destroy all her hopes—a part of it was still good. Egide's life was forfeit to pure chance now, through her doing alone. But if she had not imperiled it, she might never have valued the life or the man. Meeting that faint softening of a smile that touched his face, she knew he was sharing a thought like hers. Thanks to that one terrible error, they would at least live each measured moment that remained to them with a vividness that should pack a lifetime's awareness into every hour.

Still clasping hands, they rode down the hill slowly. Mists were thick now, and they could see almost nothing of the turmoil below, but Jair's great brazen voice, rich with the vibrating warmth of his spurious humanity, came rolling up to them in brief snatches. A juggernaut of brass. Egide's juggernaut. Perhaps mankind's last and coldest and most ardently worshiped god.

In the temple of the Ancients a small figure stood before the high, dark altar like a wall, too high for it to see the gods. It clasped and unclasped the facile, fingery paws, like a sea-anemone's tendrils—so many-fingered, so dexterous, so nervously eager to be about the great task of testing the limits of their skill.

Its mind was not here in the temple. It was seeing the warm, sand-floored caverns of its people, lit by a garden of colored windows, multi-shaped in the twilight of the cave. It was not alone, though it sat here nervously twisting those eager, impatient fingers. No llar is ever alone. The warm awareness of its unity with its city lies behind that poise and quiet pride. It looks out of the strange round eyes with a wisdom and benignity which is of the race, not the individual. This race alone, of all thinking species, finds deity in itself, in the warm closed circle of its own unity. Once it gains the little foothold it needs on which to found its soaring possibilities, this race alone need not depend upon the gods.

Serene in its own confidence, in its own warm knowledge of identity with its race, the llar sat clasping and unclasping those eager fingers and listening to the oracle it knew it could not trust.

Paradise Street

Loki planet rolled its wild ranges and untrodden valleys up out of darkness toward morning under Morgan's thundering ship. Morgan was in a hurry. His jets roared out ice-plumes in the thin, high air, writing the scroll of his passage enormously in vapor across half Loki's pale sky. There was no other visible trace of man anywhere in the world.

Behind Morgan in the cargo bin there were three kegs with *sehft* washing about oilily inside them. They made the tiny cabin smell of cinnamon, and Morgan liked the smell. He liked it for itself, and for the pleasant memories it evoked of valley canebrakes and hillside forests where he had gathered his cargo in discomfort, danger and perfect freedom. He also liked it because it was going to be worth fifty thousand credits at Ancibel Key.

Either fifty thousand, or nothing.

That depended on how soon he reached Ancibel Key. He had caught a microwave message back there in the predawn over Great Swamp, and he had been pushing his ship to top speed ever since. He had been muttering angrily, kicking the ship along her course, cursing her and Loki planet and mankind in general, after the fashion of men who are much alone and talk to themselves for company.

Radar patterns pulsed noiselessly across the screen before him, and ahead under a blanket of morning fog he knew Ancibel Key lay sprawled. Around the edges of the fog he could see the telltale marks of civilization spread out upon the soil of Loki—carbon-blacked fields with neat straight roads between them, racks of orchards checkering the sides of the valleys he remembered wild and lonely. He thought of old days not very long ago when he had hunted the bearded Harvester bulls across these meadows and trapped *sehft*-rats where the orchards grew.

The sky was a little soiled already, above Ancibel Settlement. Morgan wrinkled his lean, leather face and spat.

"People!" he said with fierce contempt to the pulse of the radar pattern. "Settlers! Scum!"

Behind him in the clear morning the vapor-trail of his journey swept in one enormous plume clear back to the horizon, back over Wild Valley, over Lookout Peak and Nancy Lake and the Harvester Range. He decelerated above the invisible landing field, and the soft gray fog closed over him. The plume of the passage he had scrawled over half a planet dissipated slowly above the peaks and the lakes that had been his alone for a long time now, grew dim and broad, and vanished.

Morgan stamped into the assay office with a carboy of *sehft* swashing on his shoulder. He moved in a haze of cinnamon. The assay office was also general store now. Morgan scowled around the too-neat shelves, the laden bins and labeled barrels. Toward the back a red-headed youngster with the dark tan of Mars on his freckled face was waiting on—yes, Morgan looked twice to make sure—a parson. A parson on Loki!

The Mars-tanned boy was belted into a slick silver apron. So was the storekeeper himself. Suppressing a snort of contempt, Morgan gazed past the heavy, bent shoulders of a settler in brown knitted orlon and met the keen and faded blue eyes of Warburg, assay agent turned storekeep.

Morgan's eyes flicked the silver apron. And then he grinned thinly. The settler straightened his heavy shoulders and glanced from the list in his hand up along the shelves. He was a youngster in his twenties, thick-muscled, tall, fair as a Ganymedan, with flat, red-flushed cheeks.

"Need some more of that hormone spray, Warburg," he said. "Same as last time. And what about this new fungus? My potatoes aren't doing so good. Think actidione might do the trick?"

"It did with Laany'i," Warburg said, evading Morgan's gaze. "And his fields are right next to yours. Actidione's a good antibiotic. O.K., Eddie. Had any trouble with rats lately?"

"Just a little. Not enough to mention."

"Stop it right there," Warburg advised. "I got some compound forty-two just in—the dicoumarol stuff. It fixes rats better than squill. Those critters breed too fast to take chances."

"Not as fast as settlers," Morgan said.

The young settler looked up sharply. He had mild brown eyes under sunbleached brows that drew together with suspicion as he regarded the lean newcomer. Morgan ignored him. Shouldering forward, he thumped the carboy on the counter.

"Forty gallons, Joe," he said.

"In a minute," Warburg said.

"I haven't got a minute. I'm in a hurry."

"It's late for that, Jaime," Warburg said, looking at him.

Morgan's hand tightened on the neck of the carboy. His eyes drew up narrowly. He swung his gaze to the young settler and jerked his head doorward.

"Take a walk," he said.

The settler straightened to his full height and looked

down on the slighter man. The red deepened in his flat cheeks.

"Who's this, Warburg?" he demanded. "One of the fast-money boys?"

"Easy," Warburg said. "Easy, now." His hand moved toward the gun on the counter. It was a Barker ultra-sonic—it barked before it bit, uttering loud threats before its frequency slid up into the killing range. Morgan sneered at it.

"Up till lately, before the rats moved in," he said, "when a man pulled a gun he used it. I guess people scare easy around here these days."

"Who is he?" the settler demanded again. "Gunman?"

"I carry one," Morgan said.

Warburg came to a decision. Smoothing down his silver apron, he said, "I'll send Tim over with your stuff, Eddie. Do me a favor and—" He nodded toward the door. "Here," he added, shoving a cellobag into the settler's big hand. "For the kids. Go on now, git."

But the settler, scowling at Morgan, didn't move.

"You're wrong," he said. "The rats didn't come till the settlers were here already. Your kind isn't wanted in Ancibel, mister. We don't need any more hoodlums or gambling houses or—"

Morgan's whole lean body, moving very slightly, tightened forward in a barely perceptible crouch. Perhaps the settler didn't know what that meant, but Warburg was an old Loki frontiersman himself. He knew. His hand closed on the butt of the Barker gun.

Feet grated on the dusty black floor. From the back of the store the parson came forward, nodding casually at Morgan, moving equally casually between the two men. Behind old-fashioned lenses his mild eyes regarded them. He took the cellobag out of the settler's hand.

"What's this?" he asked. "Candy? Well, we'd better make sure your kids get it, Eddie. Be a pity if a bullet went through the bag. Might mash the candy."

Warburg said quickly, "I've got some news for you, Jaime. The—"

"Shut up," Morgan said. He looked from the parson to the settler, shrugged, spat on the black floor and turned away. He was ready to let the quarrel drop. He knew he'd have to talk to Warburg alone. Behind him he heard retreating footsteps and a door thudded shut.

Warburg bent and lifted a roped carton from under the counter. Lettering on its side in three languages said, "Micrografting Kits."

"Tim," Warburg called. "Get this over to Eddie's. And don't hurry back, either."

The boy came forward, unbelting his slick apron. His eyes regarded Morgan with a sort of grave wariness. His freckles scarcely showed under the deep Martian tan. Morgan grinned at him a little and said in hissing Middle-Martian, "What do you hear from the cockeyed giant, young one?"

The boy's sudden smile dazzled in the dark face, showing missing teeth. He was about eighteen, but he made a child's gesture, holding up both hands, making a wide circle in front of one eye and a narrow one in front of the other. It was the old, childhood legend of the watching giant with Deimos and Phobos for eyes.

"All right, Tim," Warburg said. "Get at it."

The boy hoisted the carton to his shoulders and staggered out with it. Morgan's grin faded. The store was silent when the door had closed.

Morgan slapped the carboy on the counter.

"Forty gallons of *sehft,*" he said. "Fifty thousand credits. Right?"

Warburg shook his head.

Morgan snarled soundlessly to himself. So he was too late, after all. Well, that just made it harder. Not impossible, he thought, but harder. Surely Warburg couldn't refuse him. Not even the Warburg who faced him now, plump and soft in a storekeeper's apron. Warburg had been here almost as long as Morgan himself, from the days when Loki was as wild as the men who trapped and hunted here. And it was wild still, of course. He told himself that fiercely. Most of Loki was still untrodden. Only here at Ancibel Key the spreading disease called civilization fouled the planet. So long as Morgan could find a market for *sehft,* so long as he could buy the few things he needed from that disease-source, it wouldn't matter how many settlers swarmed like flies around Ancibel.

"How much?" he asked grimly.

Warburg snapped open a transparent sack, set it on the little scale at his side, and began weighing sugar with a rustling noise. He pinched the top of the first sack tight to seal it before he spoke.

"Five hundred for the lot, Jaime," he said, not looking up.

Morgan didn't move a muscle. The store was very still except for the hiss of sugar into the cellobag. Softly Morgan said:

"Sure your authorization on the price-cut came in before I did, Joe?"

"It came in," Warburg said, "a couple of hours ago. Sorry, Jaime."

"Don't be," Morgan said. *"I* came in four hours ago. Remember? It's four hours ago now. That means you can still pay me fifty thousand."

"Sorry, Jaime. I had to turn in a spot-check inventory."

"All right! You overlooked this—"

"Nobody overlooks forty gallons of *sehft,"* Warburg said, shaking his head regretfully. "I've got a license to worry about, Jaime. I can't do a thing. You should have got here faster."

"Look, Joe—I need the money. I owe Sun-Atomic nearly ten thousand on my last fuel grubstake. I can't get more until I—"

"Jaime, I can't do it. I don't dare. I guess you caught the broadcast about the price-cut, but you didn't go on listening or you'd know who's here to enforce it."

"Who?"

"Old friend of yours. Major Dodd."

"Rufus Dodd?" Morgan asked incredulously. "Here?"

"That's right." Warburg snapped open a fresh sack noisily and shoved it under the sugar spout. The glittering white torrent hissed into the bag, expanding it to plump solidity. The two men regarded it in silence.

Morgan was thinking fast. Coincidence has a long, long arm. Dodd and he had grown up together in a little town on Mars. Dodd went into the Jetborne Patrol and Morgan had hit for the empty places as soon as he was big enough to work his way aboard a freighter, but the two ran into each other now and then in spite of the vastnesses of space. It wasn't too unlikely. Space is wide and deep, but men tend to congregate in big centers of civilization on central worlds, and those with like interests inevitably seek out like spots.

"Funny thing, isn't it?" Morgan said reminiscently. "Last time I saw Rufus I was running furs on Llap over in the Sirius range. A bunch of Redfeet ganged up on the Jetborne and I helped Rufus hold 'em off till relief came. A long time ago, that was. So now he's here on Loki. What for, Joe? He didn't come in just to play nursemaid to a new set of export rules. What's up?"

Warburg nodded at the big Barker on the counter.

"You ought to guess. Happens often enough. That's why young Eddie wouldn't back down when you tried to start something. He took you for one of the easy-money boys. Town's swarming with 'em. They follow the settlers. Grab a ripe world and squeeze it dry, quick, before the law moves in. *You* know. The town's wide open and there's been a lot of trouble already, killings, stores looted, crops damaged if the settlers won't pay protection. The usual thing. Some of us sent in a petition, and we got Major Dodd and his boys by return ship. He'll clean the place up—I suppose. Sooner or later." Warburg looked obscurely troubled.

"What do you mean?" Morgan demanded. "Rufe's

honest, isn't he? You couldn't buy Rufe with all the credits Sun-Atomic ever issued."

"No, not him, I guess." Warburg looked dubious. "But his higher-ups, maybe. All I know is, there's been too much delay. Pay-offs to political bosses have happened before now, you know. My guess is there's some routine dirty work going on, and Major Dodd's hands are tied. Or maybe he's taking a cut direct. Who knows?" Warburg slapped the Barker lightly. "One of these days we'll take things into our own hands."

"What's this 'we', Joe?" Morgan asked sharply.

Warburg shrugged. "I have a living to make."

Morgan snorted noisily. "You're soft, Joe. I never thought I'd see you with a potbelly and an apron around it. Old before your time."

"I show it," Warburg said. "You don't. I know when it's time to slow down. You're not much younger than I am, Jaime. Remember what happened to Sheml'lihhan?"

"He got careless."

"He got old. Just once, he was too slow, and the stag-bison got him. Oh no—I like it here. Times change, Jaime. We change, too. Can't help it. I'm glad of a little store like this to keep me going now. Maybe some day you'll—"

"Not me!" Morgan snorted again, an angry sound. "I'm a free man. I depend on nobody but Jaime Morgan! And a good thing, too. If I tried to depend on my friends I'd starve. Look at you—scared out of your senses by the Trade Control. I'll go on forever, getting tougher and tougher as the years go by. Just like old leather." He grinned and slapped his chest. But the grin faded.

"What's the matter with the Trade Control, Joe?" he demanded, tapping his carboy of *sehft*. "Why did they cut the price? *Why?* If the bottom's out of the *sehft* market you might as well plow up the whole planet and plant it with wheat so far as I'm concerned. *I* can't live here."

"They've synthesized *sehft,*" Warburg said stolidly.

Morgan whistled a low, angry note. Then he said, "All right, they've synthesized it. But there'll always be a market for the natural oil, won't there?"

"Maybe. But the Settlers' Council asked for an extermination order, Jaime." Warburg spoke reluctantly. "I'm sorry, but that's the way it is. You see, the *sehft*-rats are pests. They destroy crops. They've got to be wiped out, not milked of their throat-sac secretions and let go to secrete more *sehft.*"

Morgan's face went deep red under the leathery tan. He showed his teeth and swore in the hissing Martian vocables of his boyhood. A tall crate beside the counter caught his angry eye and he brought his fist down hard on its lid. The wood splintered, releasing a pungent fragrance and showing glints of bright golden fruit inside.

"Settlers!" Morgan said savagely. "So the *sehft*-rats spoil their orchards! Who was it got here first, Joe? You and me, that's who! And now you're siding with them." He kicked the crate. "Fruit orchards! Fruit orchards on Loki! Mooing livestock! Settlers stink up every world they land on!"

"I know, I know," Warburg said. "Careful of the goldenberries, Jaime. I paid hard cash for those."

"Sure you did! You'll be out there grubbing in the dirt, too, next thing you know. Joe, I don't understand it." Morgan's voice grew gentler. "Have you forgotten Deadjet Range and the time the wild Harvester bulls stampeded? Remember when young Dain and I came in with our first load of *sehft*? Joe, I passed over Chocolate Hill today, where we left Dain. The moss grows fast there, Joe, but you can still see the Martian Circle we cut for him, to mark the place."

Warburg snapped another sack open.

"I know, Jaime. I remember Dain. I land there now and then myself and cut the Circle clean again. I remember Wild Bill Hennessy, and old Jacques, and

Sheml'li-hhan as well as if they were alive today. Wild Bill's tree where he fought the red bear is standing in the middle of a cornfield now, Jaime. The farmer left it when I told him what the gouges on the trunk were. These people mean well. You've got to play along if you have a living to make. Can't turn back the clock, Jaime. You just can't do it." Sugar ran glittering into the sack.

"Settlers!" Morgan growled. "Scum! They don't belong here. This is our world, not theirs! We opened it up. We ought to run them off Loki! But I forgot. Not you—not Joe Warburg. You tie an apron around your belly and sell 'em carbon-black to warm up the soil and micrograft kits to make the goldenberries grow! Wild Bill must be turning in his grave!"

Morgan slapped the counter, making the sugar-sacks dance. The oily liquid in the carboy shivered thickly. "Fifty thousand credits!" Morgan said bitterly. "Two hours ago! Not worth the fuel to bring it in, now. That's piracy for you, Joe. I tell you, I've got more respect for those hoodlums and gamblers you're so scared of. They rob a man at gun point. They don't sneak behind his back and cry on the shoulder of the Trade Control while they pick his pockets. I think I'll find me somebody who'll pay a better price for my *sehft*. Price-juggling doesn't hurt the real value of the stuff and you know it, Joe. There must be somebody—"

"Don't you do it!" Warburg urged with sudden earnestness. "I know just what's on your mind, Jaime, and you can't get away with it. Sure, the woods are full of contraband runners, now. You go out and whistle and you'll have to comb the smugglers out of your hair. But it's dangerous business, Jaime."

Morgan laughed contemptuously. "*I* don't wear an apron," he said. "You think I'm afraid?"

"If you've got good sense, you will be. These are tough boys. And they're organized. Times have changed on Loki since you were here last, Jaime. I don't keep a Barker on the counter for nothing. You're a good man in the hills and you know the wild country inside out, but the city boys are smarter than you are, Jaime, and a whole lot trickier."

"You're a fool," Morgan said savagely. "I've got to have money, and I'll get it where I can. Nobody's tougher than Jaime Morgan. Who do I see, Joe? You know the hoods around here. Or are you too scared to tell me?"

"You think I'd do it?" Warburg asked wryly. "Even if it weren't for the danger of it, I haven't forgotten Major Dodd. He won't stand for any funny business, and he knows everything that goes on at Ancibel. He'd deport you, Jaime."

Morgan reached for the carboy.

"Somebody'll tell me," he said. "You or somebody." Cunningly he added, "If I go to the wrong dealer, I may lose my scalp. But you're too busy weighing sugar. Forget it. I'll find out."

"Jaime, if Dodd hears of this—"

Morgan hefted the carboy. "I'll ask around," he said.

Warburg sighed. "All right. Go into the Feather Road and ask for a fellow named Valley. He comes from Venus and he's smarter than you are, Jaime. Don't say I sent you."

"Thanks for nothing," Morgan snapped. He hefted the carboy to his shoulder and turned away.

"You owe me fifty credits," Warburg said stolidly. "You've spoiled half a crate of goldenberries."

Morgan said with a furious grin, "Make it an even hundred," and swung his boot. Wood crackled and a bright torrent of fruit gushed out over the smooth black floor. Morgan stamped, making the clear juice gush. His angry glare met Warburg's.

"Send me a bill to Chocolate Hill," he said. "Leave it in Dain's Circle. Or pin it on Wild Bill's tree. You'll get your money—settler!"

He went out with a heavy stride.

* * *

The fresh, cold air of morning over Ancibel Settlement was fragrant with breezes blowing over miles of orchards, rank after rank of them on the patterned hills around Ancibel.

To Morgan, it stank.

He spat in the dust of the rubberized street, took a plug of *nicca* from his belt, and bit off a chew, thinking as he did of New Moon, beyond Sirius, and the way it used to be when New Moon was a frontier world, years ago, before he came to Loki. Now settlers grew *nicca* on that dim, pearl-gray world. Waterbound Galvez II was settled in, too, now, all the mystery gone from the sliding seas. They were dotted with control islands where men grew food-crops of algae and seaweed in the watery fields.

Now they were overrunning Loki. He scowled about the single main street of Ancibel Settlement, feeling a little uneasy at the nearness of so many people. A buxom young woman in pink-striped orlon balanced a grocery-flat on her head and craned after him curiously as he passed. A man in the brown, tight uniform of the Jetborne went by, a sergeant with a weathered face, and the crowd fell silent and watched him resentfully, muttering a little, until he turned the corner and vanished.

There were three lemon-haired men from Venus lounging in the morning sun at the doorway to the Feather Road, and the townspeople gave them a wide berth. They wore Barkers conspicuously belted on over their long, fringed coats and most of their conversation was carried on in a series of rapid, fingery gestures which their opaque eyes never seemed to watch. They smelled faintly of fish.

Morgan nodded and strode between them into the big, arched, echoing room inside. It had been blown over an inflated form, like all the quickly built houses in Ancibel Settlement, and somebody had over-estimated the space the Feather Road would be needing. Or maybe they hadn't. Maybe it just hadn't got under way yet. Also, of course, this was still an early hour.

The bar looked as though it needed artificial respiration. There weren't enough customers for the Road's size and setup.

Rustling plastic curtain partitions made the room much smaller than normal—you could tell by the angles of the roof—but it still wasn't cut down enough to avoid that fatal air of desolation an interplanetary bar must shun at any cost. The customers, striking new roots, feeling lost enough as it is on an alien world. A good bar must be a convincing artificial home.

Morgan grinned sourly. A thermo roll was all the home he needed. He had taproots. All worlds were home to Morgan.

The bartender was a hawk-nosed Red Amerindian. He fixed Morgan with bright, expressionless black eyes and said, "Morning. Have one on the house, stranger."

Morgan thumped his carboy on the bar, rubbed his shoulder and said, "Sure."

The Amerindian tore the top off a fresh bottle of brandy and left it invitingly in front of Morgan, who poured himself one sparing shot and then firmly pressed the bottle's neck together, sealing it with a practiced zip of the thumbnail.

An old man with a red, bleary face hunched over the bar ten feet away, cradling a smoky glass in his hand. Beyond him were two young surveyors in swamp boots, having a quick one before they set out for the day's wet, exhausting labor. Beyond them a black-haired girl in tight, crimson orlon leaned her elbow on the bar and her chin in her hand. Her eyes were shut and she whistled a soft, dreary tune to herself.

Most of the noise in the room came from a table of heavy-shouldered young men who were playing some Ganymedan game with counters that clicked on the table top. Their voices were loud and blurred. Clearly they had been here all night. They looked to Morgan like a group of ranch hands, and he despised them.

"I'm looking for a man named Valley," he said to the bartender.

The man's black eyes appeared to grow smaller and brighter in the dark face as Morgan regarded him, waiting. The girl at the end of the bar opened her eyes briefly and stared at him, her whistle drawing out to a low note of surprise. Then she shut her eyes again and the mournful tune continued.

"Who sent you?" the bartender asked.

Morgan looked deliberately away. There was a button in front of each bar stool on the counter, and he pressed a slow forefinger upon the one beside his elbow. A section of the bar rolled aside and the hot, salty, pungent smells of a lavish free-lunch smoked up in his face. A moving belt below carried the leisurely array of thirst-making foods past.

He let a bowl of popped and buttered moss-buds go by, and a rack of pretzels, and a broad round platter of Martian soul-seeds crackling with the heat of the plate they lay on. His hand moved finally. He took up a pinwheel of blue-streaked paste, dipped it into a bowl of sullenly smoldering oil, and spinning it on its silver stick, popped the appetizer deftly into his mouth toward the back of the tongue, where the right taste buds would work on it.

When he could speak again, he said with an impatient glance at the silent and waiting bartender, "What about that man Valley?"

"I asked you a question," the Indian said.

Morgan shrugged. He slipped his hand inside the strap of the carboy on the counter and went through the motions of rising.

"I can always go somewhere else," he said.

The Indian measured him with a long, expressionless look. Neither of them spoke. Finally the Indian shrugged in turn.

"I just work here," he said. "Wait."

He ducked under the bar-flap and vanished between plastic curtains on the other side of the room. Morgan ate three mockbeaks and sat quietly on his stool, watching the illuminated mural that circled the backbar with a series of videoed dryland scenes—the Mohave on Earth, the sun-side of Mercury with every shadow etched in acid, a long shimmer of Martian desert with dustdevils dancing and the air a thin violet clearer than crystal. He allowed a certain not unpleasant quiver of nostalgia to stir in his mind at the sight.

But he caught the first shimmer of motion behind him reflected in the surface of the mural screen, and turned to face a thin, very pale Venusian in a long fawn-colored coat who was walking toward him with meticulous placement of his feet beneath fluttering fringes. The man's skin was white as dough. He had very sleek, lemon-colored hair and his eyes were round and flat and opaque.

The man bowed gravely.

"You Valley?" Morgan demanded.

"My name is Shining Valley," the pale man said. "May I buy you a drink? Bill—" He gestured toward the Amerindian, who had ducked back under the bar and was resuming his position.

Morgan said quickly, "No." He slid a hand into his pocket, fingered the few coins there in the cubical, nested currency of Loki, and pulled out one of the cubes. He shook three of the inner and smallest out onto the bar and reached for the Ferrad brandy bottle, tore off its top and poured himself another sparing shot. His thumbnail sealed the neck again.

"You talk business here, Valley?" he asked.

The flat eyes flickered at the *sehft*. "Certainly," the Venusian said, and glided forward with a flutter of fringes. He sat down on the stool next to Morgan and said crisply to the bartender, "Bill, give us a curtain."

The Indian's expression did not change, but he nodded and jerked a rope in a cluster of cords behind the bar. Morgan dodged a little, involuntarily, as something came swooping and rustling down upon them from overhead. It was another of the plastic curtains, unfurling like a sail from a semicircular rod overhead. It closed the two men neatly in, cutting off most of the noises from behind them. Morgan glanced back nervously. The curtain was moderately transparent, and he felt a little better. He looked questioningly at the Venusian.

"No one can see us from the other side," Valley said. "Nor hear. Bill, give me a gin."

Morgan wrinkled his nose as the Venusian dropped a red pill into the glass the Indian set before him. An aromatic camphor odor arose to blend with the elusive but definite fish-smell of the man from Venus.

Sipping, Valley said, "You came to the right place, Jaime Morgan. You see, I know your name. I've been hoping to make a deal with a man like—"

"Cut it, Valley," Morgan said. "Let's not be polite. I don't like Venusians. I don't like their smell."

"Then try the smell of this," Valley said, and laid a thousand-credit note on the bar's edge. Morgan lifted his eyebrows. The liquor was beginning to hit him a little; it had been months since he'd taken a drink. He realized he was going to get thirstier and thirstier from now on. As usual, it was cumulative. He ignored the note.

Valley spread out ten of his fingers in a quick, flickering gesture.

"When I flew in here today," Morgan said, "my cargo was worth fifty thousand. Do you think I'll sell it for ten?"

"The ten is only a starter. I need a man like you."

"I'm not for sale. My cargo is."

There was silence for a while. Valley sipped his camphor-smelling gin. Presently he said in a soft voice, "I think you are for sale, Morgan. You may not know it yet, but you'll learn."

"How much for the *sehft*?" Morgan demanded.

Valley exhaled softly. He made a meditative sound in

his throat, like the waters of Venus lapping with a gentle noise against his palate.

"You have forty gallons in all," he said. "Warburg won't go over five hundred for it. Major Dodd will impound your cargo and you'll get legal price—no more. I offer you more. I'm gambling, you see."

"I'm not," Morgan growled. "Make me an offer."

"Ten thousand credits."

Morgan laughed unpleasantly.

"I told you I'm gambling," Valley said in his soft, patient voice. He exhaled a smell of fish and camphor at Morgan. "The stuff's been synthesized. But one of my markets is on a planet that's passing through an H-K spectra matter cloud. They haven't got the spacecast about the price-drop. Ultra-short waves won't penetrate. A ship, of course, will. Maybe one has already. If so, the news has gone ahead of me. If not, I clean up a tidy profit by buying at a cut price and selling at the old one. That's what I mean by a gamble."

"I don't like the odds," Morgan said. "You could pay me better and still—"

"It's my price. You won't get any better offer. I'll pay you ten thousand for forty gallons." The surf-sounds of Venusian seas beat in his throat briefly. He added, *"Skalla,"* and made a rolling, interlacing gesture with his fingers, so Morgan knew that would be the top figure. When a Venusian said *skalla*, poker-bluff wouldn't work.

Still, with ten thousand— There were gambling joints in Ancibel Key now. Like most men who gamble with life and know the odds well enough to win, Morgan erroneously thought he could call the odds on other games of chance. Besides, the brandy was beginning to burn enticingly in his stomach, calling irresistibly for more of the same brand. And he couldn't buy any, not with the few coin-nest cubes in his pocket.

He reached over and took the notes from the Venusian's boneless fingers, riffling the edges to count.

There were ten. He took a key out of his pocket and dropped it on the bar.

"A locker key?" Valley inquired. "Very wise of you."

"The other two are lockered," Morgan said. "It's a deal."

"Not yet," Valley said gently, his round, flat eyes on Morgan's. "We want you to work with us. We can offer you a very good bargain on that, my friend."

Morgan got off the bar stool with a quick, smooth motion, struck impatiently at the curtain behind him. "Let me out of here," he said. "I'm no friend of yours, Valley."

"You will be," Valley murmured, gesturing. The curtain slid up with a hiss and rustle, and the noises of the bar flowed back around them.

It was noisier than it had been before. The ranch hands were stumbling up from their table, staggering a little, blinking at an angry middle-aged homesteader in the doorway.

"I'd fire you all," he was shouting as the curtain rose. "If I could, I'd do it! Outside, you loafers! Get out, before I break your necks!" His furious glare flashed around the room. "We'll clean you out yet," he roared at the bartender, who shrugged impassively. "We don't want your kind here!"

One of the ranch hands stopped quickly to drain a shot-glass on the table before he joined the rest. The homesteader crossed the floor with quick, angry strides, snatched the glass from the man's hand, pivoted and hurled it against the glass of the skylight that illumined the curtain-cubicled bar. A shower of tinkling fragments rained down upon the emptied table. The man turned and stalked noisily out, driving his reluctant help before him.

Morgan laughed shortly.

"Compared to me," he said, "he *likes* you."

"Come back when you're ready," Shining Valley said with a round, impassive look. "You'll come, Jaime Morgan. You're ready—"

Morgan spat on the floor, turned his back on Valley, and stamped out of the bar.

He needed another drink.

Painfully Morgan opened his eyes, wincing at the impact of light. For a perceptible interval he had no idea who he was, or where. Then a familiar face leaned over him and for a moment he was ten years old again, looking into the face of the ten-year-old Rufus Dodd. Rufe had been playing soldier. He was dressed up incongruously in a tight brown uniform with the Solar Ring emblem at his collar, and gold leaves on his shoulders. But outside, in the thin violet air of the Martian morning the dead sea-bottoms must be stretching, purple-shadowed under the level rays of sunrise, and in a few minutes now their mothers would be calling them both away to breakfast.

Dust-motes danced in the beam of light that struck between curtains in his eyes. He turned his head far enough to see that he lay in an unfamiliar little shack with dust thick on everything. The metal uprights of a bunk rose left and right before him. Plastic curtains discolored at the folds shut him partially in.

Bitter fumes were in his head and dead, unpleasant air was in his lungs. He squinted painfully against his headache and he saw a small black scuttling object move across the wall—man's ancient supercargo, the cockroach. He shut his eyes and grimaced. He knew now who he was.

"Hello, Rufe," he said thickly.

"Get up, Jaime," the familiar, crisp voice snapped. "You're under arrest."

Morgan sighed heavily. He rubbed his palms down the sides of his face; the harsh scratch of stubble rasped his nerves. He hated the cockroach and the discolored curtains and this whole filthy, stinking town the settlers had built upon his world, his clean, wild, lonely Loki.

"What for, Rufe?" he asked. The motion of face-rubbing had brought his wrists into view and there was a fresh knife-scratch along the edge of his forearm. He looked at it thoughtfully.

"It might be for a lot of things," Dodd said. He stepped back a pace and hooked his thumbs into his uniform belt. His face looked many times ten years old now. Time must have acted as filter between them in that first moment of waking, a filter that screened out the firm, harsh set of Rufe's jaw and the lines incised lengthwise from nose to chin, and the cool, disciplined narrowing of the eye. Rufe had never spared himself. It wasn't likely that he'd spare others.

"It might be for drunkenness, assault and battery or conduct unbecoming a human being," he told Morgan, his voice crisp. "It might be for trying to wreck a gambling joint when you lost your last credit there. But it isn't. What I'm arresting you for is selling *sehft* to a contraband runner called Shining Valley. You're a fool, Jaime."

"Sure I'm a fool." Morgan wriggled his toes in muddy socks. "Only I didn't do it, Rufe."

"Too late for lies now. You always did talk too much when you're drunk. You shoot off your mouth before a dozen settlers, Jaime, and then you hole up here like a sitting duck. Jaime, I've got orders to arrest any violators of the new *sehft*-law. I can't help myself. I don't make the laws."

"I do," Morgan said. "I make my own. You're trespassing, Rufe. Loki's *my* world."

"Sure, I know. You and a few others opened it up. But it belongs to the Trade Control now, and you've got to abide by their rules. Get up, Jaime. Put you shoes on. You're under arrest."

Morgan rose on one elbow. "What'll they do to me?"

"Deport you, probably."

"Oh no!" Morgan said. "Not me." He raised a wild and savage gaze to his old friend. "Loki's mine."

Dodd shrugged. "You should have thought of that sooner, Jaime. You've got to ride with the times."

"Nobody's going to put me off Loki," Morgan said stubbornly. "Nobody!"

"Be sensible, Jaime. There's always plenty of room—out there." He looked up; so did Morgan. "Out there" was always up, no matter how far toward the Galaxy's rim you stood. "One of the big outfits would finance you if you needed grubstaking—"

"And they'd tie me hand and foot, too," Morgan said. "When I open up a new world I do it my way, not the way of Inter-Power or Sun-Atomic. When I take a walk down Paradise Street, I go under my own power."

They were both silent for an instant, thinking of that trackless path among the stars, that road exactly as wide and exactly as narrow as a ship's bow, pointing wherever a ship's bow points and always bordered by the stars. The course on the charts is mapped by decimals and degrees, but all courses run along Paradise Street.

The explorers and the drifters and the spacehands are misfits mostly, and, therefore, men of imagination. The contrast between the rigid functionalism inside a spaceship and the immeasurable glories outside is too great not to have a name. So whenever you stand in a ship's control room and look out into the bottomless dark where the blinding planets turn and the stars swim motionless in space, you are taking a walk down Paradise Street.

"There'll always be jackpot planets left, Jaime," Dodd said, making his voice persuasive.

"I won't go," Morgan told him.

"What are your plans, Jaime?" Dodd asked ironically. "Have you looked in your pockets?"

Morgan paused halfway through a gesture to search his rumpled clothing, his inquiring gaze on Dodd. "I didn't—" he began.

"Oh yes you did. Everything. Even your guns are gone now. Those gambling joints don't let a man get away as long as there's anything negotiable on him. Go on, search your pockets if you don't believe me. You're broke, Jaime."

"Not the whole ten thousand credits!" Morgan said with anguish, beginning frantically to turn his jacket inside out.

"Ten thousand credits?" Dodd echoed. "Is that all Valley gave you? For forty gallons of the drug?"

"Drug?" Morgan said abstractedly, still searching. "What drug? I sold him *sehft*."

"*Sehft*'s a drug. Didn't you know?"

Morgan lifted a blank gaze.

"It's been kept quiet, of course," Dodd went on. "But I thought you knew. A narcotic can be synthesized from the natural raw *sehft*. Not from the synthetic stuff. It hasn't got the proteins."

Morgan looked up in bewilderment that slowly gave way to a dawning fury. "Then the stuff's worth . . . why, it'll be priceless!" he said. "If the *sehft*-rats are exterminated, what I sold Valley's worth a hundred times the penny-ante price he paid me!"

"That's what you get when you play around with city boys, Jaime," Dodd told him unsympathetically.

Morgan stared straight ahead of him at the discolored curtains and the moted sun. A vast and boiling rage was beginning to bubble up inside him. All down the line, Shining Valley had outwitted him, then. And Dodd had stepped in to take over where the Venusian left off. And Warburg sat back smugly to watch while the Trade Control put a roof over Loki and Loki's rightful dwellers. He thought for one weak and flashing moment, with a sort of bitter envy, of young Dain safe on Chocolate Hill under his Martian Circle, and of Wild Bill dead before Loki's downfall, and of Sheml'lihhan with no more problems to deal with. They'd been the lucky ones, after all.

But Morgan was no defeatist at heart. He'd think of something. Jaime Morgan would last forever, and Loki was still his world and nobody else's. He choked the fury down and turned to face Dodd.

"I can take care of myself," he said. "Kick my boot over this way, Rufe."

The major scuffled with one foot in the dust. Morgan swung his feet over the bunk's edge and stooped, grunting, to snap the clasps of his boots.

"You're wasting your time, Rufe," he said, looking up under his brows. "Why don't you get on out there and round up a few of the local hoods, if you feel so law-abiding? They're the real criminals, not me."

Dodd's face tightened. "I obey orders."

"From what I hear, the settlers are going to take things into their own hands one of these fine days," he said. "Oh well, forget it." He stretched for the farthest buckles, grunting. Then he slanted a grin up at the watching major.

"What do you hear from the cockeyed giant, Rufe?"

Dodd's stern mouth relaxed slightly. The smile was reluctant, but it came. Encouraged, Morgan made his voice warm and went on, still struggling laboriously with the boot.

"I can't reach the last snaps, Rufe," he said. "Remember that crease from a spear I got on Llap, when we stood off the Redfeet together for three days? Makes it hard for me to bend this far. Guess you don't outgrow these things once you start getting old. Damned if you're not starting to show gray yourself, Rufe."

"Maybe you aren't," Dodd said. "But your hands are shaky, Jaime."

"If you had a night like mine," Morgan grinned, "you'd be resonating ultrasonics. I'll get over it. I—" He grunted piteously, stretching in vain for the last clasp.

"I'll get it," Dodd said, and stooped.

"Thanks," Morgan said, watching his moment. When Dodd's jaw was within range Morgan narrowed his eyes, braced himself in the bunk, and let the heavy boot fly forward and upward with all his lean weight behind it.

The kick caught Dodd on the side of the jaw and lifted him a good six inches before he shot backward and struck the dusty floor, his head making a hollow thump on the rubberized plastic.

Morgan followed his foot without a second's delay. Dodd had no more than hit the dust before Morgan's knees thudded upon the floor on each side of him and Morgan's hands slapped down hard upon his throat.

It wasn't necessary. Dodd lay motionless.

"Sorry, Rufe," Morgan grinned. "Hope I didn't—" His hands explored the unconscious skull before him. "Nope, you're all right. Now I'll just borrow your gun, Rufe, and we'll see about a little unfinished business here in town. Deport me, eh? Let me give you a little good advice, Rufe. Never underestimate an old friend."

He got up, grinning tightly, slipping the stolen gun in his belt.

The hangover thudded inside his head, but he showed no outward sign of it. Moving cautiously, light and easy, he slid out of town, through the new orchards toward the woods about a mile away. Wild woods, circling down upon Ancibel Settlement in ranks unbroken for countless miles upon miles far over the curve of Loki planet.

There was a fresh-water brook coming down out of the foothills in the edge of the woods. Morgan stripped and bathed in the icy water until his head cleared and he began to feel better. Afterward he went back toward Ancibel, the gun heavy in his shirt, looking for a man named Shining Valley.

"I was waiting for you," Shining Valley said dreamily, blinking up through a rising mist of bubbles that flowed in a slow fountain from the pewter mug in his hand. He leaned his elbows on the table, moving the mug from side to side and swaying his head to and fro with it in a smooth, reptilian motion. The spray of rising bubbles bent like an airy tree in the wind. "I was waiting," he said again, only this time he sang it. All Venusians sing among themselves, but not to outsiders unless they are euphoric.

Morgan's nostrils stung with the sharp, almost painfully clear aroma of the high-C *pouilla* Valley was inhaling. He knew better than to rely on the hope that the man was drunk.

Valley made a gesture in the air, and again out of the ceiling a descending swoop and rustle sounded and a curtain closed the two of them in, this time a circle of it around the table toward the rear of the Feather Road.

Valley's opaque stare was candid and curiously limpid through the rising spray. "Now you will work with us," he sang.

"Now I'll take the rest of my credits," Morgan corrected him.

Valley's fingers caressed the pewter mug with a faintly unpleasant tangling motion.

"I paid you ten thousand. *Skalla.*"

"That was a first installment. I want the rest."

"I told you—"

Morgan inhaled, wrinkling his nose. "You told me a fish story. The stuff I sold you will be priceless as soon as Trade Control clears out the *sehft*-rats. There isn't any planet with an H-K spectra matter cloud. You'll process the *sehft* for narcotics and ask your own price. Get it, too. I want mine. Will you pay up now, or shall I blow your head off?"

Valley made the familiar sea-wave sound in his throat meditatively. Suddenly he bent his head and nuzzled his face into the spray of pin-point bubbles.

"Give me the ten thousand back," he said, "and I'll return your *sehft*. Things have been happening. Forty gallons isn't worth running a risk for, and forty's all I have."

"You're lying," Morgan told him flatly.

Shining Valley smiled through the spray. "No. I had more, yesterday. Much more. I've been collecting it for weeks now, from everyone I could buy from. But last night Major Dodd confiscated the lot. Now I have nothing but the forty gallons you sold me. You want it back?"

Morgan struck fiercely at the empty air in front of him, as if he brushed away invisible gnats. He hated this quicksand shifting underfoot. What was true? What was false? What devious double-dealing lay behind the Venusian's dreamy smile? He wasn't used to this kind of byplay. There was always one way to end it, of course. He slid his hand inside his shirt and closed it on Dodd's gun.

"I'll make you an offer, though," Shining Valley said.

Morgan tightened a little in every muscle. Here it came, he thought. They'd been maneuvering him toward some untenable spot he could yet only dimly glimpse. In a moment or two, perhaps he'd know.

"Go on," he said.

"You're in a bad position, Jaime Morgan," the man from Venus said softly. "Very bad indeed. You drunkenly squandered your money away and now you can't leave Ancibel Key. No one will sell you a liter of fuel until you pay up your old debts. I know how frontiersmen work, always one trip behind themselves, operating on credit, using this year's cargo to pay last year's bills. Without the price of the *sehft* you can't re-establish your credit. Am I right?"

Morgan bent forward, resting his chin on his hand, his elbow on the table. In this position his shirt front was covered, and he slipped Dodd's gun out and laid it on his knee, muzzle facing Shining Valley's middle under the table.

"Go on," was all he said.

"You'll be deported from Loki planet as soon as the Jetborne catch up with you," Valley went on in the same dreamy singsong. "You want to stay. But you can't stay unless you co-operate with me."

"I can work out my own problems," Morgan said. "Pay me what you owe and forget about me."

"That deal is finished. I have said *skalla* and it can't be reopened. If you offered me a ton of *sehft* now, I wouldn't give you a link for it. You have only one thing for sale I'll buy from you, Morgan—your co-operation. I'll pay you forty thousand credits if you'll do a little job for us."

Morgan moved the gun muzzle forward on his knee a little, felt the trigger with a sensitive forefinger.

"What's the job?" he asked.

"Ah." Shining Valley smiled mistily through the spray. "That *you* must tell *me*. I can only give you my problem and hope you have the answer—because you know Loki planet so well." He made a disagreeably fingery gesture toward the far end of town. "Out there stand the big ships, pointing into space," he said. "One of them is ours. We are very well organized here at Ancibel Key. Much money is behind us. But Major Dodd has grounded all the ships in port. Also, he has confiscated our treasure. What we wish to do is regain the *sehft* he stole from us, load it aboard our ship and send it off. How can we do this, Jaime Morgan?"

"You've got some idea," Morgan said impassively. "Go on."

Valley shrugged. "An idea only. Perhaps it will work. Are you afraid of the wild Harvesters, Morgan?"

"Sure I am," Morgan said. "Be a fool not to be."

"No, no, I mean, could you handle a herd of them? Guide such a herd, perhaps?"

Morgan squinted at him, letting his finger slip off the trigger a little. "You crazy?" he demanded.

"I had heard it can be done. Perhaps some frontiersman more expert than yourself—"

"It can be done, all right," Morgan interrupted. "But why should it? Where would it get you?"

"To the ship, with my cargo, if we're lucky," Valley said. "I would like you to stampede such a herd straight through Ancibel Settlement. What would happen then?"

"Blue ruin," Morgan said. "Half the population wiped out and every building in their way trampled flat. That what you want?"

Shining Valley shrugged.

"That doesn't concern me. What I want is to draw the Jetborne and the settlers away from the building where the *sehft* has been stored. I want enough confusion in Ancibel to clear the spacefield. I think what you describe would do the job nicely, don't you?"

"Yes," Morgan said dubiously. "Maybe it would."

"So you will?"

"There must be easier ways," Morgan said.

"How? Fire the town? It won't burn. Only the church and a few of the older stores are made of wood. Of course some other way might be devised, in time, but I have no time to waste. I thought of the Harvesters because one of my men reports a herd of them grazing down a valley only a few miles from here."

"The town must be protected automatically somehow," Morgan objected. "Harvesters are dangerous. There must be—"

"I believe some sort of devices have been set up. Seismographic pickups catch the vibrations of their approach and cut in automatic noisemaking devices. Harvesters I believe are very sensitive to sound? Very well. They won't react to these, because the noisemakers won't operate. My men will see to that, if you can take care of guiding the herd."

"It's too dangerous," Morgan said.

"Nobody earns forty thousand credits easily, my friend. Will you do it, or must I search for a man with less timidity for the job?"

"There isn't a man on Loki any less scared of Harvesters than I am," Morgan said practically. "I'm thinking of afterward. Do you know the only way a herd of stampeding Harvesters can be guided? Somebody's got to ride the lead bull. All right, I could do it. But I'd be pretty conspicuous up there, wouldn't I? And a lot of the settlers are bound to get hurt."

"Do you owe them anything, my friend?"

"Not a thing. I hate the sight of 'em. I'd like to throw the lot of 'em clear off Loki planet, and you and your crowd right after. Every man, woman and child in Ancibel Settlement can die for all I care, the way I feel now. But I'm not going to run my neck in a noose killing 'em. I'll be up there in plain sight, and there's bound to be survivors. If I earn that forty thousand credits, Valley, I want to live to enjoy it. I don't want a crowd of vigilantes stringing me up to a tree the minute I drop off the Harvester bull. So that's out."

"Perhaps," Valley sighed. "Perhaps. A pity, isn't it? I have the forty thousand right here."

He groped inside the sleeve of his fawn-colored robe and laid a packet of credit notes on the table. It was thick and crisp, smelling of the mint.

"This is yours," he said. "For the taking. *If* you earn it. Isn't it worth a little risk, Jaime Morgan?"

"Maybe," Morgan said. He gazed hungrily at the money. He thought of his ship lying portbound beyond Ancibel, fuelless and immobile—like himself. What did he owe the settlers, anyhow? Had they spared *him,* when they had the chance? Like most men who travel the lonely worlds, Morgan had great respect for life. He killed only by necessity, and only as much as he had to.

Still—with this much money he could get clear away. Loki was a big world, after all. He moved his fingertip caressingly on the trigger of the hidden gun.

Suddenly he grinned and his right arm moved with startling speed. The table jerked, the shining tree of spray bowed sidewise between Valley and him. When it righted again the muzzle of Morgan's gun rested on the table edge and its unwinking eye was fixed steady upon the Venusian. Valley met that round black stare, going a little cross-eyed through the bubbles. He lifted a flat, waiting gaze to Morgan.

"Well?" he said.

"I'll take the money. Now."

Valley held the flat stare for an interminable moment. Then slowly he pushed the packet of credits across the table, not shifting his eyes from Morgan's. Morgan did not look down, but his free hand found and pocketed the sheaf with a sure gesture.

The Venusian made a very small motion. Morgan gave him no time to complete it, whatever it was.

"Don't!" he advised sharply.

"You can't get away with this, Morgan," the man from Venus said. "My boys will—"

"No they won't." Morgan sounded confident. "Why should they? I'm going to earn the money."

Valley's pale brows rose. "How?"

"I'll stampede the Harvesters, all right. But not through the town. That's murder, and I won't stick my neck out that far for anybody. The Jetborne won't tolerate murder."

"What's your plan, then?"

"You know that stretch of orchards east of town? And the farmland between them and Ancibel? I could lead the Harvesters through that valley. Trample their stinking crops right back into the ground. Break their fruit trees down. Ruin a good half-year's work. It might even drive 'em clear off Loki." Morgan smacked his lips. "That ought to do the trick."

Shining Valley frowned. "I'm not so sure."

"Did you ever hear a herd of Harvesters stampeding?" Morgan demanded. "The ground shakes like a quake. Windows break for half a mile around. When the settlers feel and hear and see what's happening, they'll swarm out like wasps out of a hive. Give you all the free time you need in Ancibel. Besides, that's what I'm going to do. Nothing else. You want me to earn this money or just take it and go away?"

Shining Valley looked down at his long, boneless fingers clasping the pewter mug. He moved them intricately over and under one another, as if he were weaving a complex Venusian finger-sentence of advice to himself. After a moment he nodded and looked up, his eyes veiled by the rising spray.

"Very well," he said. "I can count on you?"

Morgan stood up, pushed back his chair.

"Sure I'll do it," he said. "My way, not yours."

Shining Valley nuzzled again among the rising bubbles. He made in his throat the noise of a Venusian sea lapping a pebbled shore.

"Your way, not mine," he agreed in the smoothest of smooth voices.

Harvesters are mindless angels of destruction. They look like kerubs, the magnificent bearded kerubs of Assyrian legend, bull-bodied, tremendous, with great lion-faces and thick, streaming Assyrian beards. Bosses of sound-sensitive antennae stud their brows and they have hair-trigger neural reactions as comprehensive as radar-sonar. Any variation from the rhythmic patterns of normality send them into terrible, annihilating flight.

A good explorer never has a dangerous adventure, Morgan remembered the old saying, and qualified it: *barring the unexpected.* New worlds have a way of being unexpected. The first water he drank on Loki registered pure by every chemical test, but gave him a fortnight's fever because of a new virus that science was able to classify—later, after he had discovered it. A virus that went through porcelain filters, withstood boiling and resisted every standard disinfectant was so far outside the normal frame of reference that extrapolation hadn't helped—not unless you extrapolated to infinity, and then you'd never dare try anything new.

Like the Harvesters. There was a way to handle them. Not many men knew the way, and fewer still had the split-second synaptic reactions that made it possible.

Morgan, waiting perfectly motionless in his ambush, scarcely breathed. He was almost as immobile as a stone. Not quite; that would have been a mistake, for he wasn't a stone, and without natural hereditary camouflage, he couldn't hope to imitate immobility. But he could perceive, with all his senses, the natural rhythm and pattern of the dark forest around him, the stars overhead, the sleeping rhythms and the waking rhythms of Loki's nighttime pattern, and slowly, gradually, sink into an absolute, dynamic emptiness in perfect tune with the world around him.

He emptied his mind. He was not even waiting. The ultrasonic gun was planted and due to go off at the right moment. He had charted the position of the grazing Harvester herd, the wind-drift, the rhythms of movement that flowed through and above this forest. The herd dozed, grazed, shifted gently down the dark forested valley toward him. Now they were motionless, drowsing perhaps under the stars. Morgan squatted in the humming quiet, letting his fingertips touch the moss and send soft vibrations toward his brain.

Once he stirred, drifting with a little scatter of dry leaves like confetti, toward a spot where the filtered starlight blended better with his own pattern. He had not realized this second spot was better until he caught the rhythm of Loki.

How many worlds he had exchanged this psychic blood-brotherhood with, this beating pulse of planetary life that opened the way for a transfusion between a living world and a living man. All Loki, it seemed to him now, slept and was unaware. Only he crouched here in perfect co-ordination with the turning world. He scarcely needed to glance at the shaded oscilloscope he had rigged to check upon his co-ordination. He knew with a deeper sense than sight how attuned he was. A shaking green line on the face of the oscilloscope translated Loki's night sounds into sight. A second line trembled across it—his own. No man could ever make those two lines completely merge, of course. At least, not while he lived.

Morgan's mind, emptied of circulating memories, let old eidetic ones swim up unbidden. *And wears the turning globe,* he remembered out of some forgotten book. A dead man, clad in the turning world. He wore Loki now, but not as the poet meant. That would come later. Some day, somewhere on some world whose name he might not even know yet, he would make that last and completest marriage with some turning globe, and then the green lines would tremble and blend.

But now he wore Loki, his world, fought for and earned. He meant to keep it. And he could. There was room. The villages would grow, and the webs of steel spin farther, but there would still be the forests and the mountains. It would be a long, long while before settlers dared explore Deadjet Range, or Great Swamp Valley, or Fever Hills.

The ground shivered. The green line on the oscilloscope wavered into a jagged dance. The Harvesters were moving.

More and more wildly the green line danced. In the moss under his fingertips Morgan felt vibrations grow strong. Scores of mighty hoofs bearing tons of tremendous bodies moved leisurely down the steep canyon valley toward him. He waited. There was no feeling of stress at all.

They were not yet in sight when the sense of movement all around him first began. Leaves rustled, tree trunks vibrated. The herd was coming near. Morgan relaxed utterly, letting the pulse of Loki carry him on its restless current.

High up among the leaves, seen dimly by starlight at a sharp angle from his crouch on the ground, Morgan was aware of a tremble of vines, a crackle and tearing, and suddenly a great, black, bearded face wreathed in torn leaves thrust forward. Vines snapped over a mighty chest and the herd leader burst majestically into sight, black and sleek and shining with blue highlights, his tight-curled mane merging with his curly beard. The antennae writhed slowly and restlessly above his round eyes, warily blinking. The breath snorted and soughed in his nostrils. The ground shook when he set his mighty hoofs upon it.

Morgan did not move, but every muscle inside him drew taut as springs, and the internal balances of his wiry body shifted for a leap. He waited his moment, and then his right hand closed hard upon the firing device that linked him with the hidden gun.

The gun was a Barker, set for its highest decibel-count of sheer noise. Morgan heard the first forerunning sound-wave of that tremendous mechanical roar, and opened his own mouth wide and shouted as loud as he could. His voice would be drowned in the noisy blast of the Barker, but he was not concerned with that. He had to balance the vibrations on both sides of his eardrums; the shout saved him from being deafened.

Upon the Harvesters the full impact of the roar fell shatteringly. All through the forest one concerted tremble and gather of mighty muscles seemed to ripple as the herd drew itself in for the spring into full stampede. Morgan had timed himself to a split second. His reactions would have to be exactly right.

It took just two fifths of a second for the Harvesters' sense-organs to drop to maximum loss of sensitivity after exposure. Very briefly indeed, the herd was deaf. It would not react with its normal supersensitivity. But in that two fifths of a second pure reflex would hurl them into headlong flight.

In that fraction of a second, Morgan sprang.

It was a tricky stunt. He timed himself to strike the bulge of the herd-leader's off foreleg with his knee in the instant before the bull surged forward. His hands seized two fists-full of curly mane and he clawed himself desperately upward in the same moment that the foreleg drove backward like a pistol, great muscles bunching to hurl Morgan upward within reach of the great black column of the neck.

He was ready and waiting when the lift came. He flung his knee over the sleek withers and fell forward flat and hard against the neck, both hands darting forward in a quick grab that had to be absolutely precise, to gather in each fist the bases of the thick antennae-clumps sprouting like horns from their twin bosses above the animal's eyes.

He felt the cool, smooth sheaf of tendrils against his

left palm, and closed his fist hard. His right hand groped—slipped—

Missed.

Missed!

It couldn't be happening. He had never missed before. He was as sure as the stars in their turning. His own body was a mechanism as faithful as the rising of the sun over Loki planet. Jaime Morgan would go on forever. How could age weaken him? It must never happen—

But he missed the right-hand boss. His own momentum carried him helplessly forward, and the fatal toss of the bull's head hurled him on over the side of the gigantic neck. He felt the strong, hard column of its throat slide by under him. He felt the sickening vibrations of the herd's thousand hoofs striking the ground in earthquaking unison. He saw the forest floor sweep by with blurring speed as he slid sidewise toward it. He remembered how a man looked after a Harvester herd had passed over him—

As he shook like a falling leaf that slid sidewise through air, his mind closed and gripped and clung furiously to one single thing—his own name.

Jaime Morgan, his mind cried frantically, tightening on that awareness and that identity which looked so close to forsaking him forever. The ground shuddered with rhythmic thunder, the Harvester's great neck pumped and tossed, the moss of the forest floor blurred by under his straining eyes.

Mixed up with Jaime Morgan was the memory of Sheml'li-hhan. *He got old. He got careless. Just once he was too slow, and the stag bison got him.* Was this how it had looked and felt to Sheml'li-hhan, in the instant before death? Morgan had never failed before—would he have a chance to fail again, ever again in this life?

Oh yes, he would.

Afterward, trying to remember exactly how he had done it, what crazy contortion had locked him into place on the bull's neck again, he found he could not remember. One instant he was swinging almost free, sliding down toward the shaking ground. The next, his knees were locked hard on both sides of that great muscular column again, and his hands frozen in the familiar grip on both the antennae-bosses, gripping and deadening the proprioceptors of the bull.

Nobody else could have saved himself, he thought, dizzy with fright and triumph. *Nobody but me.* But the words wouldn't stop there. *I missed, though. I missed. Like Sheml'il-hhan, a man gets old—*

He looked back. Behind him the Harvester herd came pouring in the strong starlight, one black, tossing waterfall of annihilation. They were magnificent, mindless angels of destruction, a host of heaven thundering down upon Ancibel Key. Tightening his fists, Morgan swung the herd leader imperceptibly toward the right side in a wide arc whose end would be the fields outside Ancibel. The leader obeyed—

Suddenly Morgan found himself roaring with laughter. Tears burned in his eyes from the wind of their passage and the pressures of his mirth. He didn't know why he laughed. He only knew that some deep, ancient fear inside him relaxed and quieted as the breath beat in his throat. Old? Not yet—not yet! Somewhere, some day—but not yet!

Lying close along the tremendous, pumping neck, his hands locked on the antennae bosses and his knees tireless in their grip upon the Harvester's withers, Morgan led the herd. Exultation boiled up in him like strong liquor, a wild intoxication of the mind. The power of the beast he rode burned through him and the rhythmic thunder of the running herd made his blood beat with the same strong rhythm. It was Loki planet itself which he was turning against the sleeping settlers, Loki rising in its anger to cast the intruders off.

Leaves whipped his face. The chill rush of wind made his eyes water. The hot, strong smell of the running bull stung in his nostrils. Then the leaves thinned suddenly and the thunder of the running beasts behind him changed in its sound as the forest fell away and open country lay before them. Morgan tightened his right hand on the bull's antennae-boss. Its perceptions dulled by the grip, it swung toward the left, toward the hillside of vines and orchards and the broad tilled fields above the town. Swinging after them came the herd, and the ground roared and trembled under their pounding hoofs.

The stars seemed to tremble, too. In the black sky nameless constellations shivered, new, foreshortened images seen from the far edge of the Galaxy and unnamed until men like Morgan came to watch by night and call them by familiar titles. He saw the Jetship sprawling its long oval above the town and the Stag-bison hurtling without motion toward the horizon. All the stars were watching along Paradise Street.

But the settlement slept. A few lights burned where saloons and gambling houses clustered at the far side of town, and out beyond, over the shielding hills, five spaceships towered against the stars. Lights from below shimmered upon their tapered sides, and stars shimmered upon their peaks. The Jetborne would be camped out there, guarding the spaceport. Morgan grinned savagely. Rufe Dodd was in for a surprise.

He leaned forward upon the tremendous neck, looking for the network of guarding wires which would warn the villagers if intruders came too close. He saw cut ends glitter and a tangle of torn netting piled aside, and he gripped the bosses harder, swinging the herd through the gap.

Now the trees loomed before them, heavy-laden with forming fruit. The orderly rows stretched downhill in ranks like soldiers. The lead bull tossed its bearded head as the strong scent of man rose before it like invisible fountains in the air. But the pressure of the herd behind it was strong, and it thundered forward among the trees.

Great shoulders crackled among the branches. The orchard's resistance seemed to madden the Harvesters. They plunged and snorted among the trees, roaring, pawing, crashing down through laden boughs. In an irresistible surging wedge driven by sheer momentum, they poured forward.

Morgan leaned forward upon the great maned neck and howled above the crashing of the herd.

"Smash 'em down!" he roared to his unhearing mount. "Smash 'em under! Flatten the last rotten, stinking fruit-tree on Loki!" He loosed his grip a little on the antennae-bosses and screamed a wild Indian falsetto to madden the bull to its utmost, as if the few weak decibels of any human voice could be heard above the bellowing and the thunder of the herd.

He was half wild himself with the drunkenness of destruction and every new row of trees that went crashing under fanned him to new heights of furious joy. It was intoxicating to think of the long labors and the endless months of effort that had gone into the planting of this orchard. He drank in the scent of crushed fruit and ruined trees, and it was like the scent of strong whiskey in his nostrils. A man could be drunk on the very thought of the destruction he was wreaking now upon his enemies.

He howled louder and drummed with his knees upon the mighty, oblivious neck.

"Smash 'em down, you juggernauts! Roll 'em under!"

Ahead of him, beyond the ruined orchards, lay the fields. Clinging tight to his terrible mount, Morgan began to measure his course. Eventually he would have to dismount. That was going to be tricky.

He couldn't go down. Not into that thundering charge. He would have to swing off the lead bull's back, and that meant something he could swing to, something higher than the Harvester.

The herd crashed through the last line of trees and

the cornfields stretched before them, silvery under the stars. Shouting, Morgan lay forward on the great neck and urged the Harvesters on. Soft ground churned under their hoofs and they plowed forward floundering and roaring until their gait adjusted to this new element of destruction. Morgan yelled with a drunken joy. He was the mightiest man alive. He wielded the thunderbolts like Jove himself, hurling his great herd down the fields.

To his right, in the town parallel with the galloping Harvesters, he saw lights begin to go on, heard shouts of alarm and presently the rhythmic clang of a bell swing wildly in the church steeple. He roared with furious laughter. Drive him off Loki, would they? Let them try! He bellowed a wordless challenge to the clanging bell.

Far ahead of him he saw a row of *serith* trees at the end of the fields. He would swing off upon one of those strong curved boughs when he reached them, for they marked the end of his journey. When the herd passed those trees, his job would be finished.

He looked back, clenching his hands hard upon the bosses he held. After him thundered the Harvesters, a terrifying melee of tossing heads, streaming beards, rippling, sleek flanks in the strong starlight. He could see the ruined orchards they had charged through, and behind them now a widening stretch of ruined fields, every blade and grain trampled into the carbon-blacked soil in a swath of total destruction. He laughed exultantly. Plow up Loki planet, would they? Plant his wild and lonely valleys with corn? Tonight he was beating those alien crops back into the soil they had invaded. The very planet shuddered under the thunder of the charge he led. He knew how the centaurs must have felt, who were half gods—

There was a furtive motion back there along the edges of the broken trees. He turned his head and saw more of it bordering the fields parallel with his course. He was leading his herd along the outskirts of the town now, and the row of *serith* trees swept closer and closer. He had no time left to concern himself with that furtive motion, because the end of the ride was almost upon him, but he didn't like it. He didn't understand it. Something was afoot he had not allowed for—

The *serith* trees, distinct in the starlight, were rushing toward him, expanding with a startling illusion of rapid growth as the herd swept nearer. He gathered his muscles taut, gauged his leap—

Between him and the trees lightning and thunder exploded with blinding suddenness. Dazed, half-stunned by it, Morgan could only clutch the antennae-bosses in a paralyzing grip and cling like death itself to the plunging neck he rode.

Under him he felt the whole enormous bulk of the bull shudder in a violent convulsion, shudder and leap and seem to turn in midair. When it struck the ground again the whole valley must have shaken with the impact. Morgan gripped hard with knees and hands, dulling the bull's perceptions as much as he could, but not enough, not enough.

The world was reeling around him, standing up edgewise upon the horizon like the world below a turning plane. It whirled upon the pivot of the Harvester's drumming hoofs, and the herd whirled with it. There was more stunning, tremendous noise, but behind them now, bursting out in crazy roarings along the edge of the trampled fields.

Barkers. Ultrasonic guns bellowing at full sonic range.

So that was it, Morgan thought, shaking his dazed head. There hadn't been lightning in the thunder at all. It was merely his shocked senses that filled the lightning in. Gripping the lead bull hard, he looked back and saw what he had half-known, all along—a row of lemon-colored heads edging the field, long pale robes flickering in the starlight, dull metal shining as the Barkers roared.

They were driving the herd, and Morgan with it. But where?

He knew before he turned. The whole simple plan was perfectly clear to him, so clear he realized what a fool he must have been not to see it all along.

Low houses flashed by the Harvester's shoulders. Morgan turned in time to see the sprawling buildings of Ancibel Key fanning out on both sides as he led the herd between them straight toward the main street of Ancibel Key.

Crazily he roared at them to halt. But his own voice was drowned in his throat by the bellow of the Barkers to their rear and the deafening thunder of hoofbeats as Harvesters and rider together swept forward into Ancibel Key in one terrible, annihilating tide.

The murderous rage of utter impotence rose strangling in Morgan's throat, rage with everything that existed. He hated the bull beneath him, and the Harvester herd they led. He hated the running settlers he could glimpse between buildings ahead. He hated the clangor of the churchbell shouting out its alarm. His mind ached with a fury of hatred for the man from Venus who had tricked him into this, and for all the men who lined the fields outside the town, lashing on the herd with roaring Barkers.

But most of all he hated Jaime Morgan, the blundering fool who rode headlong to his own destruction, and Ancibel Key's.

In the crash and crackle of ruined buildings the Harvester herd poured through Ancibel. Dust swirled blindingly as the plastic walls buckled in and the arched roofs thundered down. It was a nightmare of disaster in the dark, with rainbows of rising dust around every street-light, so that Morgan could scarcely see or breathe.

He had incoherent glimpses of running men, shouting and beckoning to one another and vanishing again into darkness. Directly before him, in a rift in the dust and the dark, he saw a settler drop to one knee, throw a rifle to his shoulder, and squint upward at the man who rode the leading bull—

Something like a red-hot wire laid itself along Morgan's shoulder. He swung himself sidewise upon the gigantic neck he rode, and the kneeling man and the alley he knelt in swept backward and away like a fragment in a dream.

When Morgan righted himself again, his knees were trembling. His grip on the antennae-bosses felt less sure. A new terror flooded through him. He could not cling to this desperately precarious perch forever, and he knew it. But his chance of swinging off the bull lay far behind, and distance lengthened between with every stride of the Harvesters.

He remembered Sheml'li-hhan again.

And still the dust swirled and the buildings along both sides of the ruined street crackled and crashed anew before the shoulders of the stampeding herd. Men's shouts and the thin, high screams of women, and deep-throated clangor of the churchbell echoed above the planet-shaking thunder of drumming hoofs.

Harvesters had been known to run for days, once the hypnotic compulsion of a stampede gripped them. They might run until they dropped. Long before that happened, Morgan's grip would slack upon the beast he rode. Thinking of it, he felt his sinews shiver anew with the effort at holding firm.

He had to swing off somehow, and he had to do it soon.

That was nonsense, of course. What was the use of prolonging by a few minutes the death that was bound to take him when the infuriated settlers reached the man who was flattening their town? Too many must have recognized him already, up here in the rider's seat upon Juggernaut. How many men and woman had gone down already under this rolling avalanche, and how many lay smashed under the ruined houses?

He took cold comfort from the thought that it was mostly business houses and gambling dens along this main street, not residences. Some had died already. Some must have died. And if one life was lost, the Jetborne would hang him whether the settlers did or not.

Stunned with the noise and the vibration that pounded through him, dazed with his own anger and dismay, blinded with the swirling dust, he looked up at last and saw rising before him above the dust and the film of reflecting lights the five tall shining towers of spaceships at the port ahead. He was near enough now to see the ladder dangling from the nearest, and a flicker of faint hope stirred anew in his mind.

The ships were one manmade thing that could withstand even a charge of maddened Harvesters. He even grinned faintly, thinking how the Jetborne would scurry in ignominious flight when this tossing avalanche pounded through the field.

The five ships poised like the fingers of a steel-gloved hand above the town, as if some gigantic figure leaned with one negligent hand upon Loki, watching a small human drama play itself out to its insignificant climax.

Up, up the hill beyond the town the Harvester herd went thundering. Now the last buildings had fallen behind, and the shouts grew thin and the lights of Ancibel fell away. Up and over the hill-crest swept Morgan's mount. He drew himself together for a final desperate effort as the ground dropped away again and the galloping bull plunged forward down the slope toward the ships.

Small figures in uniform drew up at the edge of the field, firelight flashing on leveled guns. Ultrasonics whined into the herd briefly, but it was only a gesture and Morgan knew it as well as the others did. The tremendous vitality of the Harvesters, plus their terrible momentum, made any hope of killing the beasts preposterous. Even dying, the herd would still overwhelm the Jetborne at the edge of the field.

An invisible broom seemed to catch them as the foremost bulls plowed forward. Still firing futilely, they scattered and vanished.

Now the tall ships swept toward Morgan with nightmare speed. He saw starlight glimmer on their lifted heads and firelight on the long, smooth swelling of their flanks. He saw the rope-ladder dangling from the nearest, and as the herd surged onward, dividing among the gigantic columns of steel and closing again like black water around their fins, he drew himself together, waited his moment—

And leaped.

In midair for one timeless instant his faith shook. He could not be *sure* he would make it. Sheml'li-hhan's face swam before him, every feature vivid in his mind's eye. Then his hands closed on the rope and its hard burning as it jerked through his fingers dispelled the doubt and the illusion instantly.

He held on with all his strength, feeling his arms drag at the sockets of his shoulders. At the same moment he let go with his gripping knees and felt the mighty neck of the Harvester drop away below him, felt the thunder of the herd shake the very air as he hung swaying and turning above that trampling torrent.

The weakness of exhaustion was waiting to pour like water along his muscles the instant he let them go slack. He didn't dare relax. He locked both hands on the rope, pawed the air with his feet, found a rung at last and hung there blind and deaf and shivering, while the river of the stampede surged by under him forever. He shut his eyes and held his breath and clung for dear life, never dearer than now in spite of the perils still ahead of him. A long, long lifetime went by.

The thunder was in his head, and would probably never stop again. Time took on a bewildering fluidity. He couldn't tell if it was his own blood pounding in his ears, or the pounding of the herd. It seemed to him that he heard men shouting very near by, just under him perhaps, in that twenty feet of space separating him from the galloping herd. But how could there be men down there? All initiative seemed to have drained out of him and he could only hang tight to the ropes and wait for his head to clear.

Under his hands the rope jerked violently, almost hurling him loose. Painfully he clung. Again it snapped. This time he opened his eyes and peered down stupidly past his own shoulder.

A ring of pale, upturned faces regarded him from below. It seemed to him that he still heard the Harvesters thundering by, but the beating was in his own ears, for the herd had gone. After it, upon the very heels of the last, the men from Venus came.

Starlight made their sleek, pale hair look white below him. He saw firelight glint upon the heavy carboys they carried, and on the length of rifle barrels.

Then the rope he clung to jerked violently again, and he lost one handgrip and swung in perilous midair, staring down without comprehension. What was happening? Why?

He saw two of the pale-haired men gripping the ladder's dangling ends. He saw them give the ropes another vicious shake.

They were trying to throw him off the ladder.

Morgan shook his head in a trite and futile effort to get the fog out of it. Some things, at least, were clear. Shining Valley hadn't lost a moment. In the very wake of the stampede he and his men must have looted the settlement of their treasure. Before Ancibel could pull itself together after this shattering blow, the crew from Venus would be loaded and aspace with their loot. It had all worked with machinelike precision. And they were winding up one unimportant detail now—

The ladder snapped again and the rung Morgan stood on flew out from under his groping feet. He hung by his hands, cursing helplessly. They had cheated him all down the line, then. From the very first, when they swindled him out of his precious cargo, to this moment when they seemed about to cheat him of his very life, they'd had the upper hand. It wasn't enough to drive him through Ancibel and use him as an instrument of outright murder—for he knew men had died under that juggernaut of Harvesters. Now they were going to loot him of the money he had taken and probably shut his mouth forever. Bitterly he remembered Warburg's warning. It had been true, of course. Jaime Morgan was no match for these wily and devious men.

His hands on the rope went numb. He swung dizzily. He couldn't let go to reach his gun. It took both hands to cling. Suddenly he knew without any doubt that he was old. Civilization had been too much for Jaime Morgan.

The rope jerked under his grip again and his failing hands let go. For a long moment he hurtled outward through dark air. The stars turned remotely above him, Sirius a diamond glitter in the Jetship constellation and the Stag-bison picked out in white fire upon infinity.

The ground was a good twenty feet down. He struck it hard.

He knew how to fall, of course. He'd taken worse falls than this and bounced up again ready for anything. He'd had to learn that. But this time he hit the ground stunningly and lay dazed for an interval he could not gauge at all.

Rough hands rolled him over, tore at his pockets. He felt his gun rasp out of its holster and heard the crackle of credit-notes ripped free.

"Is he dead?" somebody asked in the fluting foreign speech he understood only imperfectly.

Morgan heard his own voice say, "No!" suddenly and harshly. He levered himself to a sitting position with painful effort. He still could hear the thundering echoes in his head, and the spacefield tilted before him. He looked up into a ring of incurious faces. Behind them the hurried activity of loading went on half-heeded. He knew one face.

Shining Valley smiled down at him, pale as paper in the starlight. Morgan glowered savagely, full of fury and entirely without hope. Never before had his mind and his body failed him together in a crisis. If he couldn't outguess an opponent, he could outfight him.

Now he was helpless. He swore at Valley uselessly in middle-Martian.

"You're a hard man to kill, Jaime Morgan," Shining Valley said. "You've had good luck—until now."

Morgan cursed the man in lilting Venusian, knowing futilely that he was getting the inflections so wrong the phrases were probably innocuous.

Valley smiled. "You helped me to my goal, Morgan. I'll reward you for it. There are dead men back in Ancibel, and you'd swing for that unless I save you." He lifted a boneless hand toward the collar of his robe, where the men of his race carry their thin, straight throwing-knives. His own subtlety made him smile wider. "You shall not hang for murder," he promised.

"You will!" Morgan snarled. "The Jetborne'll get you, Valley. They'll—"

"They'll do nothing," Valley assured him. "They can't." His glance swerved to the hurried loading that went on beyond the ring that circled Morgan. "Thanks to you," he said, "their hands will be tied. We'll load the cargo you helped us get, and ship it because you cleared the field for us. The sale of it will pay our protection on Loki for as long as we choose to stay here. Your Jetborne take their orders from authority like the hirelings they are. This, however, is no concern of yours, my friend. Very little is, any longer." He gave Morgan a sweet, cold smile and touched the knife-hilt.

"Rufe Dodd will get you," Morgan promised him, hearing his own voice crack with anger that bordered on despair. "Nobody's orders will stop *him* when he finds out what—"

Shining Valley laughed abruptly. "You think not, Morgan? Then wait a moment! Perhaps you'd like a word with Dodd—while you can still speak."

Morgan regarded him fixedly, paying little attention to what the man from Venus said. It made no difference. He was wishing without hope that there was some way he could kill Valley. He formed a shapeless and not very practical plan. In the last moment before the throwing-knife was drawn, he thought he would launch himself at Valley's knees and drag him down within reach.

His own legs might not hold him, and his arms still quivered from the long strain of the ride, but with any luck at all he ought to be able to wreak some dirty work on Valley's smooth face before they killed him. He thought with reminiscent pleasure of the technique of eye-gouging, and his right thumb suddenly twisted in the dust, a small motion that meant nothing to anyone here but himself. He was grinning thinly in anticipation when Valley's shout startled him.

"Major Dodd!" the man from Venus was calling. "Major Dodd, step over here!"

Morgan went rigid on the dusty ground, not daring to turn his head. He remembered the scattering of the Jetborne before the Harvesters' charge, and knew that Rufe Dodd would not have run far— Relief for an instant made him weak. Then he knew it made no real difference whether Valley killed him with a knife or the Jetborne hanged him for murder. He was technically guilty of it and he had no defense the law would accept. Rufe wouldn't have any choice. But still—

Footsteps made the ground vibrate a little under him. Morgan did not turn, even when a familiar voice spoke just above him.

"Morgan," Rufe said with formality and in anger, "you're under arrest. Lieutenant, have him taken in charge."

Morgan regarded his own knees steadily, not looking up even when he saw brown-uniformed legs step up on both sides and felt a stranger's firm grip touch his shoulder. At the last moment Shining Valley spoke.

"Just a minute, major! You have no jurisdiction here. Stand back, you men! Morgan belongs to us."

"I'm arresting him for murder," Dodd's crisp voice said. "Lieutenant—"

"You're exceeding your authority, major," Valley interrupted smoothly. "I didn't call you over here to violate orders. You've had your instructions from headquarters, haven't you?"

Dodd's breathing was noisy in the quiet for a moment. Without looking up Morgan knew his jaw was set and his breath whistled through his nostrils. After a long pause, he spoke.

"I have, Valley."

"And what are they?"

Silence again. After another long pause Dodd said tightly, "I am not to interfere in local matters between you and civilians."

"Very well, then. I called you over chiefly to set Morgan's mind at rest." Valley smiled down at Morgan's set and averted face. "He was under the impression you might . . . ah . . . cause a disturbance if he should die as a result of an armed robbery he committed against me earlier today. He was mistaken, wasn't he, major? You couldn't interfere, could you?"

There was dead silence for a long time.

"You couldn't interfere," Valley repeated, "between me and civilians, could you, Dodd? Those are your orders? And you never violate orders, do you, major?"

Still Dodd did not speak.

Morgan, without looking up, was the one who finally broke the silence.

"Forget it, Rufe," he said. "Nothing you can do. I asked for it. Just like you to know they tricked me into that Harvester stampede. I never meant to ride 'em through the town. You heard their Barkers, didn't you? That was what—"

"All right, Morgan." Valley's voice was suddenly cold. "I haven't much time to waste here. Major, you can go now. This is a matter between me and the civilian population. You've had your orders." He lifted a tentative hand toward his knife-hilt again. Morgan gathered himself taut, one palm flat on the ground for the leap. His thumb made a small, anticipatory circle in the dust.

"Get out, Rufe," he said, not looking up. "Go on—git!"

"Be quiet, Morgan," Shining Valley said. "I give the orders on Loki now. Dodd, take your men and go." He smiled. "You might prepare to leave Loki while you're about it," he added. "Your orders will come through from headquarters as soon as this shipment gets there. Money in the right places gives very persuasive advice, major, and this is heading for the rightest possible place. In the meantime you may as well get used to taking my orders. Get out, Dodd. Get out of my sight."

Still Rufus Dodd did not speak or move. It struck Morgan suddenly how strange that was. Not like Rufe Dodd. Was something funny up? He was almost impelled to turn and look, though he had no wish to meet Rufe's eyes. He was not forgetting that he'd kicked Rufe in the face the last time they met, and he was perfectly content to look at the ground now. Rufe wouldn't have taken that too kindly.

But something about Rufe's motionless silence warned him not to turn. He had a curious notion that Rufe was listening to something he himself couldn't hear. It didn't seem likely, but he caught a faint hint of command from somewhere and wondered if Rufe had some plan in mind he wouldn't want interrupted. When you have known a man as long as Morgan had known Rufe Dodd, and shared with him spots as tight as this often before now, you can catch the vibration of a silent command when there is one in the air. Morgan sat motionless, ready for anything.

Valley's opaque eyes watched Dodd. Presently the man from Venus shrugged. "Stay if you like," he said. "I would have spared you. The impulse to meddle may be very strong, major, but you're outnumbered even if you were rash enough to disobey orders. By all means, watch if it amuses you. Morgan—" His gaze dropped. "*Skalla!*" he said.

His hand swept upward in a swift, dipping arc and flashed high with the blade in his hand already glinting red with firelight. Morgan gathered himself together against the hard ground, threw his weight forward on one knee, gauged his timing, and—

A thin, high shrilling wailed like a banshee out of the dark, and Valley's lifted hand jerked convulsively. The boneless fingers spread and the red-glinting knife fell flashing out of it. A round crimson spot the size of a quarter-credit appeared by sheer magic upon the center of the lifted wrist.

Nobody moved. Nobody breathed.

Slowly Valley turned his head to stare at his own hand. It took that long for the blood to begin pumping from his pierced wrist. The first sight of it broke the spell and everything dissolved into sudden, intensely rapid motion, most of it without purpose.

Valley snapped his wrist forward and seized it hard with his other hand, his face going gray as all color drained out of it. He chattered in incoherent Venusian to his men. There was tremendous scurry and confusion, in the midst of which Major Dodd's calm voice spoke. He had not stirred an inch, and he did not now except to say quietly:

"They're coming, Valley. Over the hill. Listen. I've been hearing them for about five minutes now. If you'll look, you'll see what I mean."

Everyone turned, as if on a single pivot. The brow of the hill between the spaceport and the town was outlined suddenly in a crown of winking lights. As they stared, the lights poured forward downhill, merged and blended and were a spreading river that jogged onward at the pace of striding men.

Under the torches light burned bright upon the dust-whitened heads and the angry, determined faces of the men from ruined Ancibel.

Shining Valley took the situation in with a quick, incredulous glance. He shouted orders in rapidly cadenced speech and the men from Venus redoubled their swarming pace around the ship they were loading. The last carboys went rapidly up the ladders and the rest of the workers began to deploy cautiously around the ship, unslinging their weapons.

Again the banshee wailed out of the darkness just beyond the reach of the firelight, and one of the riflemen under the ship reeled in a circle and fell heavily across his gun. A voice called from the darkness.

"I'll nail the next man who moves! We mean business."

Morgan breathed softly, "Joe! Joe Warburg." He knew that shooting as well as he knew the voice.

The merging river of lights streamed forward at a rapid stride. Now you could see the separate faces and the dusty, disheveled clothing of the mob. Not all of them were armed. Some carried Barkers, and some had old-fashioned projectile-rifles, and some carried the immemorial weapons of the embattled farmer on every world where farmers have been called upon to fight. Morgan saw pitchforks gleam and here and there a flash of light down the blade of an ancient, outmoded scythe, which was a wicked weapon at Flodden and Poictiers, and has not grown kindlier since.

Morgan knew some of the faces. The young settler he had quarreled with in Warburg's store strode in the front rank, his ultrasonic balanced across his heavy forearm and his flat Ganymedan face crimson with anger and firelight. A white-haired farmer walked beside him, pitchfork in hand, and on his other side the parson's eyeglass lenses caught red light. The parson's palms were raw from pulling the bellrope in the church tower, and he carried a coil of orlon rope across his arm.

When they came to the place where the banshee had wailed and the voice spoken out of darkness, a figure stood up and took familiar shape in the light. Warburg stepped out and fell into stride beside the parson, his Barker balanced lightly in his big hands, set for a killing beam.

Shining Valley spoke very rapidly in a soft, slurring voice to his men, who put their loads down and then straightened up with carefully slow motions, facing the oncoming mob. At the back, under the shadow of the ships, a few of them sank into crouches, lifting their guns and moving carefully into deeper shelter.

"Speak to them, major," Valley said. He was clutching his wrist tightly, and blood spattered the dust with light, splashing sounds. "Tell them the stampede was Morgan's fault. You saw him lead it. Speak to them—quick!"

Rufe Dodd laughed, a quick, harsh bark of sound.

"How can I interfere," Dodd asked, "between you and civilians on Loki? I have my orders, Valley!"

Shining Valley swung round toward the mob.

"Stop right there!" he shouted. "I've got men deployed around you under the ships. Stand still and nobody else will get hurt. Start something, and—"

"It's no use, Valley," Warburg said. "There's eight dead men back there in Ancibel, and two dead women. Our boys aren't in any bargaining mood. We know what happened. We saw who started this. Now get ready to finish it."

"I call on the Jetborne!" Shining Valley shouted. "We had nothing to do with that stampede! This is mob rule!"

"These are vigilantes," the young settler with the ultrasonic said. "The Jetborne's out of it. Stand by, major, if you don't want to get your men killed. We're going to string up the killers who did this, and we won't take interference." His red cheeks flushed a deeper color and his flat Ganymedan face hardened as his eyes met Morgan's.

"We'll start," the settler said in a hard voice, "with the fellow who led the herd. Stand up, mister! You rode over ten people in Ancibel tonight. If the law won't deal with you, the vigilantes will!"

Morgan got up slowly and stiffly. He did not speak a word, but his gaze sought Warburg's with a silent inquiry. Warburg shook his gray head.

"We all saw you, Jaime," he said. "We know what happened. You didn't do it alone—but you rode the herd. There's ten people dead. And the crops are ruined. There isn't a man in Ancibel who isn't ruined right along with 'em. They sank a year's work and all the money they could borrow in those crops, Jaime. The lucky guys are the dead ones—anyhow, that's the way we feel tonight. We can't bring the dead back to life, but we can sure take care of the men who killed them. You're in bad company, Jaime." His dust-streaked face was grim. "I wouldn't do a thing to stop the boys," he said, "even if I could."

Morgan nodded briefly.

"I figured you might feel that way, Joe," he said. "All right, boys. Let's go."

He stepped forward. The young settler reached for the rope the parson carried, making a long forward stride toward Morgan. Morgan braced himself, not sure what he would do next.

That was when the first shots wailed out from the shadow of the ships where Valley's men were hidden. The red-cheeked Ganymedan halted in the middle of a stride, dropped his gun, spun halfway around and grabbed futilely with both hands at his chest.

A boy jumped forward past him out of the crowd behind. It was the Mars-tanned Tim, Warburg's clerk. He seized the falling gun and went down with it, reaching expertly for the controls, his body braced and ready for the jar of his fall. The gun began to whine toward the ships in a flicker of violet fire three seconds after he hit the ground.

There was a great deal of confusion after that.

It could have but one ending, of course. The men from Venus were far outnumbered. Morgan didn't take much interest. That was because of the stunning burn across the side of the head which one faction or the other succeeded in placing on him before he prudently hit the ground a very short instant after Tim did.

He lay there curled tight against the surging of the

struggle above him, dizzy and knowing he hadn't a chance no matter who won. He was too tired to run and too dazed to fight.

He was too old.

He had some idea that the battlefield roar of Rufe Dodd's voice bellowed for a while above the tumult, demanding Jaime Morgan as his prisoner. But Rufe didn't get very far. The settlers had little patience with the Jet-borne just now. Rufe's shouting grew muffled and farther and farther away.

Somebody kicked Morgan in the head after that and he saw a burst of the stars that line Paradise Street, and relaxed into total darkness.

The next thing Morgan remembered was the reek of trampled ground and trampled growing things. Rough, moist soil was soft under him and he heard a great deal of uneasy motion and the low, purposeful rumbling sounds of determined men around him in the night. His hands seemed to be tied behind him, and he opened his eyes to discover that he was leaning against a tree. He looked up.

The tree was a *serith* and the stars regarded him through its leaves. Head-downward over the horizon the Stag-bison lurched, and blue-white Sirius at the Jet-ship's nose pointed toward Loki's pole-star. In their light he could see the ruined fields east of Ancibel, the jagged fragments of orchards black against the stars. So the men of Ancibel had brought him back to the scene of his crime to die. He whistled soundlessly through his teeth and sat up straighter to see what was going on.

This was the row of *seriths* that marked the far end of the field. It was even a little funny, he thought, that a few short hours ago he'd actually been *trying* to swing onto one of these trees.

Ten feet to the right he saw a pale figure lying bound against the bole of the nearest *serith*. Ten feet to the left lay another. Each assigned to his own gallows, Morgan thought. Was that Shining Valley at his right, fawn-colored fringes fluttering in the night breeze? He craned futilely. He thought it was, but he couldn't be sure.

Farther down the line the grim business of the vigilantes was already under way. Morgan wondered what Warburg really thought about it. It wasn't like Joe. Still, Joe had changed. Taken on settlers' ways. They were dirty ways, Morgan thought. This was no proper sort of death to inflict even on proved killers. Maybe settlers had to do it, though. No understanding how their cloddish minds worked. After all, you could hardly blame them. He'd taken his chance and lost, and when you play a stranger's game you abide by the stranger's rules. Still, it was no way to die.

They were working up the line toward him, grim, businesslike men performing their job resolutely. Somebody dropped a rope over a limb and a muttering rose like low thunder from the crowd as the loop fell over the neck of the man below.

Morgan watched critically.

He felt tired and not particularly unhappy, after all, now that the moment had almost come which he had faced and escaped so often before, on so many worlds. He whistled gently to himself and was glad he wasn't wearing a long fringed robe like the Venusian's. It fluttered so ludicrously, when a man was swinging by the neck under a *serith* tree.

The prisoner beneath the neighboring tree turned his head, catching Morgan's eye.

"Skalla," Morgan said. It *was* Shining Valley. Morgan grinned.

But then he looked away. He didn't particularly care for the thought of the company he had to keep on this final journey. It probably didn't matter. He whistled quietly to himself.

Something rustled very gently in the dark behind him. He tightened all over, listening. Then a cold touch slid like metal against his wrist and the rope that tied him gave slightly.

"Hold still, you fool," Joe Warburg's voice muttered.

* * *

Morgan picked his way carefully along the backs of Ancibel's houses, keeping to the darkest shadows. There were more people in town than he would have thought, considering the crowd out there in the fields.

He didn't feel very good. His head still buzzed from the beating he had taken, and he wasn't sure in his own mind that he'd really held that quick, muttered talk with Warburg in the shadows behind the *serith* tree while the vigilantes worked their way grimly nearer and nearer. It seemed now more like a dream a man might have, waking after a knockout blow.

"Hit for town," Warburg had urged him in the dream. "Make for the alley behind the last saloon facing the spaceport. Keep under cover. You old fool, did you really think I'd let you hang?"

Maybe it had really happened. Maybe it hadn't. Anyhow, here was the alley. Morgan flattened himself against its wall, darting quick glances up and down the street beyond. Ruined buildings, ruined pavement, a huge dead Harvester bull lying on its side, a nervous settler or two picking his way along toward the center of town. Why was Morgan here? What had Joe had in mind?

"Maybe my ship's at the port?" Morgan wondered. "Maybe old Joe filled her up? I wish I knew what—"

Then he heard the beat of marching feet, and flattened himself harder into the shadows as a detachment of the Jetborne went by, brown legs moving in unison, brown arms swinging. Morgan stood motionless, letting them pass perilously near.

Last of the Jetborne came two officers, walking side by side. One of them was Rufe Dodd.

Rufe passed just beyond the mouth of the alley. Morgan could see his shadow on the trampled street, hear his crisp voice speaking.

"You can start searching from the east edge of town," he said. "Spread out fast. He escaped only ten minutes ago. He hasn't had time to get far yet. On the double!"

The footsteps of the Jetborne went on, double-time down the street. Dodd said, more quietly, "What are you waiting for, lieutenant?"

"Your orders, sir. You said—take him alive?" The other voice was puzzled.

"Certainly. I want Morgan. He's got charges facing him."

"But he's dangerous, major. He's tasted blood now. Should I risk my men unnecess—"

"You questioning my command, lieutenant?"

There was a little silence. Dodd's shadow on the street got out a shadow-cigar and lit it leisurely, puffed smoke toward the stars. Morgan could smell the fragrance of Mars-bred tobacco. He couldn't see the other man at all. He wondered if his own heartbeats were not making very audible thunder in this narrow alley. When Dodd spoke, his voice was calm.

"Jaime Morgan won't kill anybody else tonight, lieutenant," he said. "It isn't a matter of tasting blood. It's a matter of touching pitch. Morgan got too close to civilization and he got himself fouled with it. But it'll wash off. Maybe he's learned the lesson he was bound to learn, sometime."

There was a pause.

"Sir—"

Dodd paid no attention. "Yes," he said, "when a man's young, he's always on the move. He can't stop too long on any one world. But he gets habits, and they slow him down. One day he finds he isn't ready to leave when the time comes. But he can't stop civilization moving in, the good and the bad of it. What can he do? A world gets civilized; nothing can stop it once it gets opened up. So a man like Morgan gets sucked in before he knows it. He's got to follow the rules of civilization, even when he thinks he's fighting it. You can't be neutral. Morgan didn't know that."

The shadow puffed smoke fragrantly. "Loki isn't Morgan's any more. It belongs to the settlers. But the sky's still full of stars, lieutenant. You heard about that new planet they've opened up, over by Rehoboam IV?"

The lieutenant's voice said, "That's another thing, sir. We're not guarding that freighter. If Morgan should hear about it—if he should stow away—"

"He doesn't know the *Nineveh's* taking off at dawn," Dodd said, enunciating his words with great distinctness. "He doesn't even known I've lifted the grounding orders. There's no need for a guard around the *Nineveh.* A man follows his habit patterns. Morgan will take to the woods." He chuckled. "Morgan's too old to change," he said with a certain sardonic inflection in his voice. It sounded like a challenge. "He's forgotten what other worlds are like. He doesn't remember the cockeyed giant."

"Sir?"

"Never mind, lieutenant. Get along now. Better join your men before you lose them."

"Yes, sir," the voice said, not quite convinced.

"Let's go," Dodd's voice insisted, and two pairs of footsteps moved away. Dodd's voice floated back, clear and thoughtful.

"There'll always be worlds to open, you know, and there'll always be men like Morgan to find them. There always has been. There always will be. One of the old poets wrote about Jaime. He said a man like that would always know there was—" The voice paused, then strengthened into firm command. " '*—Something lost beyond the ranges—lost and waiting for you. . . . Go.*' "

Heavy boots rang loud on the dark street, and less loud, and then mingled with the other night sounds.

Morgan stood quite still until the last rhythmic beat of footfalls was silent. Then he tipped his head back and looked westward toward the port. He saw five tall ships and the shining sky behind them.

He was feeling very sad, but much better, and hardly old at all. He stooped quickly once, and touched the ground. Good-by, Loki, he thought. Good-by, world.

Then he turned in the dark and ran soundlessly toward the west and the towering ships and the endless reaches of Paradise Street.

Promised Land

People got out of Fenton's way as he walked scowling through the palace, heading for the great steel doors that only half a dozen men in the Unit knew how to open. Fenton was one of the half dozen. The pale scar that made a zigzag like lightning across his dark cheek pulled his face awry a little as he snapped an angry command into the intercom.

A voice murmured apologetically out of it: "Sorry, he's busy right now. If you'll—"

Fenton slapped his palm with ringing fury against the metal beside the intercom. The echoing metallic boom rang like thunder down the hall behind him, where courtiers, diplomats and politicians waited their chance for an audience with the Protector of Ganymede.

"Open these doors!"

There was another pause. Then the voice murmured something again, and the great steel doors slid softly apart a few feet. Fenton stalked through, hearing them thud together behind him, shutting off the sound of whispering, angry and curious, that had begun to fill the hall.

He went through an antechamber and into a tall-columned room shaped like a well, with a dome of starry sky very far overhead. (It was day outside, on Ganymede, and thick, eternal clouds shut out the sky, but if a man is wealthy enough he can arrange to have the stars reflected into his palace if he wants them.)

In the center of the room, under the sky dome, stood the Protector's water bed where his five-hundred-pound bulk wallowed luxuriantly. Like truth, the monstrous man floated at the bottom of his well and watched the stars.

He was not looking at them now. Great billows of lax flesh stirred on his cheeks as he grinned cavernously at the newcomer.

"Patience, Ben, patience," he said in his deep rumble. "You'll inherit Ganymede in due time—when it's habitable. Be patient, even—"

Fenton's angry glance dropped to the man sitting on the raised chair beside the water bed.

"Get out," he said.

The man stood up, smiling. He stooped a little, standing or sitting, as though his big-boned frame found even the scanty weight of flesh it carried burdensome. Or maybe it was the responsibilities he carried. He had a gaunt face and his eyes, like his hair, were pale.

"Wait," the monster in the tank said. "Byrne's not finished with me yet, Ben. Sit down. Patience, son, patience!"

Fenton's right hand jerked doorward. He gave Bryne a cold glance.

"Get out," he said again.

"I'm no fool," Bryne remarked, turning away from the water bed. "Apologies, Protector, and so on. But I'd rather not be in the middle. Ben seems upset about something. Call me when it's safe." He shambled off, was lost behind the pillars. The sound of his footsteps died.

Fenton drew a deep breath to speak, his dark face flushing. Then he shrugged, sighed and said flatly: "I'm through, Torren. I'm leaving."

The Protector wallowed as he raised an enormous hand. Gasping with the effort, he let it fall back into the dense, oily liquid of his bath.

"Wait," he said, panting. "Wait."

The edge of the bath was studded with colored buttons just under the water level. Torren's gross fingers moved beneath the surface, touching buttons deftly. On a tilted screen above the tank snow fields flickered into view, a road threading them, cars sliding flatly along the road.

"You've just come from the village," Torren said. "You've talked to Kristin, I suppose. You know I lied to you. Surprised, Ben?"

Fenton shook his head impatiently.

"I'm leaving," he said. "Find yourself another heir, Torren." He turned away. "That's all."

"It isn't all." The Protector's deep voice had command in it. "Come back here, Ben. Patience is what you want, my boy. Patience. Spend thirty years in a water bed and you learn patience. So you want to walk out, do you? Nobody walks out on Torren, son. You ought to know that. Not even my inheritor walks out. I'm surprised at you. After I've taken so much trouble to change a whole world to suit your convenience." The vast cheeks wrinkled in a smile. "It isn't thoughtful of you, Ben. After all I've done for you, too."

"You've done nothing for me," Fenton told him, still in the flat voice. "You picked me out of an orphanage when I was too young to protect myself. There's nothing you can give me I want, Torren."

"Getting dainty, aren't you?" the man in the water demanded with what sounded like perfect good humor. "I'm surprised at you, Ben. So you don't want the Torren empire, eh? Ganymede wouldn't be good enough for you, even when I make it habitable, eh? Oh, Ben, come to your senses. I never thought you'd go soft on me. Not after what you've been through."

"You put me through plenty," Fenton said. "I grew

up the hard way. It wasn't worth it, Torren. You wasted your time. I tell you I'm finished."

"I suppose the light of a good woman's eyes has reformed you," Torren mocked. "Pretty little Kristin changed your mind, I suppose. A charming creature, Kristin. Only a foot taller than you, too, my boy. Only a hundred pounds heavier, I expect. But then she's young. She'll grow. Ah, what a pity I never met a really good woman when I was your age. Still, she'd have had to weigh five hundred pounds, to understand me, and such women never really appealed to my aesthetic tastes. You should have seen the charming little things in the Centrifuge, Ben. They're still there, you know—the ones who haven't died. I'm the only Centrifuge baby who got out and stayed out. I made good. I earned enough to stay out."

The monstrous head fell back and Torren opened his vast mouth and roared with laughter. The oily liquid in the bath heaved in rhythmic tides and echoes of his mirth rolled along the pillars and up the well toward the stars, rolled up the walls that had imprisoned Torren since his birth. They were walls he himself had burst apart against odds no man had ever before encountered.

"*You* grew up in a hard school," Torren laughed. "*You!*"

Fenton stood silent, looking at the monstrous being in the bath, and the anger in his eyes softened a little in spite of himself. The old respect for Torren stirred in his mind. Tyrant the man might be, ruthless autocrat—but had ever man such reason to be pitiless before? Perhaps in very ancient times when, for profit, skilled practitioners warped and broke the bodies of children to make them valuable freaks and monsters for the entertainment of royalty. Perhaps then, but not again, until the planets were opened for colonization three hundred years ago.

Fenton had seen the Threshold Planetaria, back on Earth, the fantastic conditioning units where eugenics, working through generation after generation of selected stock, bred humans who could sustain themselves in the ecology of other worlds. He knew little about these remarkable experiments in living flesh. But he did know that some of them had failed, and one such Planetarium had held Torren—thirty years ago.

"Thirteen generations," Torren said deliberately, drawing the familiar picture for him again, relentlessly as always. "Thirteen generations one after another, living and dying in a Centrifuge that increased its rotation year after year. All those treatments, all those operations, all that time under altered radiations, breathing altered air, moving against altered gravity—until they found out they simply couldn't breed men who could live on Jupiter, if they took a thousand generations. There was a point beyond which they couldn't mutate the body and keep intelligence. So they apologized." He laughed again, briefly, the water surging around him in the tank.

"They said they were sorry. And we could leave the Centrifuge any time we wanted—they'd even give us a pension. Five hundred a month. It takes a thousand a day to keep me alive outside the Centrifuge!"

He lay back, spent, the laughter dying. He moved one vast arm slowly in the fluid.

"All right," he said. "Hand me a cigarette, Ben. Thanks. Light—"

Holding the igniter for him, Fenton realized too late that Torren could have got his own cigarette. There was every possible convenience, every luxury, available to the water bed. Angrily Fenton swung away, paced to and fro beneath the screen upon which the snow fields were reflected. His fingers beat a tattoo on his thigh. Torren waited, watching him.

At the far end of the screen, without turning, Fenton said quietly: "So it was bad in the Centrifuge, Torren? How bad?"

"Not bad at first. We had something to work toward. As long as we thought our descendants could colonize

Jupiter we could stand a lot. It was only after we knew the experiment had failed that the Centrifuge was bad—a prison, just as our bodies were a prison."

"But you'd shut the Ganymedans up in place like that."

"Certainly," Torren told him. "Of course I would. I'd shut you up, or anyone else who stood in my way. I owe the Ganymedans nothing whatever. If there's any debt involved, the human race owes *me* a debt that can never be repaid. Look at me, Ben. Look!"

Fenton turned. Torren was raising his gigantic arm out of the water. It should have been an immensely powerful arm. It had the potential muscle. It had the strong, bowed bone and the muscles springing out low down along the forearm, as the Neanderthaler and the gorilla's did. And Torren had a gorilla's grip—when he did not have to fight gravity.

He fought it now. The effort of simply lifting the weight of his own arm made his breath come heavily. His face darkened. With tremendous struggle he got the arm out of the water as far as the elbow before strength failed him. The uselessly powerful arm crashed back, splashing water high. Torren lay back, panting, watching his sodden cigarette wash about, disintegrating in the tank.

Fenton stepped forward and plucked it out of the water, tossed it aside, wiped his fingers on his sleeve. His face was impassive.

"I don't know," he said. "I don't know if that debt ever can be discharged. But, by God, you're trying hard."

Torren laughed. "I need the money. I always need money. There aren't enough Ganymedans to develop the planet. That's all there is to it. With the ecology changed, normal humans can live here within ten years."

"They'll be able to live here in another hundred and fifty years anyhow, if plantings and atmospherics follow the program. By then the Ganymedans will adapt—or at least, their great-grandchildren will. That was the original plan."

"Before I got control, yes. But now *I* give the orders on Ganymede. Since Jensen isolated Jensenite out there," and he nodded toward the snowy screen, "everything's changed. We can speed up the plantings a hundred percent and the air ought to be breathable in—"

"Jensen's a Ganymedan," Fenton broke in. "Without Jensen you'd never have been able to break the original agreement about changing over. You owe the Ganymedans that much for Jensen's sake alone."

"Jensen will get paid. I'll finance him to an ambulatory asylum on any world he chooses. I owe the others nothing."

"But they're all in it together!" Fenton slapped the edge of the tank angrily. "Don't you see? Without the whole Ganymede Threshold experiment you'd never have had Jensenite. You can't scrap every Ganymedan except Jensen now! You—"

"I can do as I please," Torren declared heavily. "I intend to. Ganymede is an unimportant little satellite which happens to belong to me. I hate to mention it, son, but I might say the same thing about you. Benjamin Fenton is an unimportant young man who happens to belong to me. Without my influence you're nothing but a cipher in a very large solar system. I've invested a lot of money and effort in it and I don't intend to throw it away. Just what do you think you'd do if you left me, Ben?"

"I'm a good organizer," Fenton said carefully. "I know how to handle people. I've got fast reflexes and dependable judgment. You toughened me. You gave me some bad years. You arranged for me to kill a few people—in line of duty, naturally—and I've done your dirty jobs until I know all the ropes. I can take care of myself."

"Only as long as I let you," Torren told him with a faintly ominous ring in the deep voice. "Maybe it was a whim that made me pick you out of the asylum. But I've invested too much in you, Ben, to let you walk out on me now. What you need is work-hardening, my boy." He cupped water in his hand and let it drain out. "Who was it," he inquired, "that said no man is an island? You're looking at an island, Ben. *I'm* an island. A floating island. No one alive has any claim on me. Not even you. Don't try me too far, Ben."

"Have you ever thought I might kill you some time, Torren?" Fenton asked gently.

The colossus in the tank laughed heavily.

"I ran a risk, making you my heir," he admitted. "But you won't kill me to inherit. I made sure. I tried you. You were given chances, you know . . . no, I don't think you did know. I hardened you and toughened you and gave you some bad years, and some men might want to kill me for that. But not you. You don't hate me, Ben. And you're not afraid of me. Maybe you ought to be. Ever think of that, Ben?"

Fenton turned and walked toward the door. Between two pillars he paused and glanced back.

"I nearly killed you thirteen years ago," he said.

Torren slapped his palm downward, sending a splash of liquid high.

"You nearly killed me!" he said with sudden, furious scorn. "Do you think I'm afraid of death? When I wasn't afraid to *live*? Ben, come back here."

Fenton gave him a level look and said, "No."

"Ben, that's an order."

Fenton said, "Sorry."

"Ben, if you walk out of this room now you'll never come back. Alive or dead, Ben, you'll never come back."

Fenton turned his back and went out, through the anteroom and the great steel doors that opened at his coming.

Stooping above the open suitcase on his bed, both hands full, Fenton saw the slightest possible shadow stirring in reflection on the window before him and knew he was not alone in the room. No buzzer had warned him, though the full spy-beam system was on and it should have been impossible for anyone to pass unheralded.

He lifted his head slowly. Beyond the broad window the snowy hills of Ganymede lay undulating to the steep horizon. The clouds that blanketed the world were blue-tinged with Jupiter-light, reflecting from Jupiter's vast bright-blue seas of liquid ammonia. Between two hill-tops he could see one of the planting-valleys veiled in mist, dull turquoise warm by contrast with the snow. The reflection swam between him and the hills.

Without turning he said: "Well, Bryne?"

Behind him Bryne laughed.

"How did you know?"

Fenton straightened and turned. Bryne leaned in the open doorway, arms folded, sandy brows lifted quizzically.

"You and I," Fenton said in a deliberate voice, "are the only men who know most of the rabbit-warren secrets in this Unit. Torren knows them all. But it had to be you or Torren, obviously. You know how I knew, Bryne. Are you trying to flatter me? Isn't it a waste of time, now?"

"That depends on you," Bryne said, adding thoughtfully a moment later, "—and me, of course."

"Go on," Fenton said.

Bryne shifted his gaunt body awkwardly against the door.

"Do you know what orders Torren gave me an hour ago? No, of course you don't. I'll tell you. You're not to be admitted to him again even if you ask, which I told him you wouldn't. You're not to take anything out of the Unit except the clothes you wear, so you can stop packing. Your accounts have been stopped. All the money you're to have is what's in your pocket. This suite is out of bounds as soon as you leave it." He glanced at his wrist. "In half an hour I'm to come up here and escort you to Level Two. You eat with the repair crew and sleep in the crew dormitory until Thursday, when a frighter is due in at the spaceport. You'll sign on with the crew and work your way back to Earth." Bryne grinned. "After that, you're on your own."

Fenton touched his scarred cheek meditatively, gave Bryne a cold glance.

"I'll expect you in half an hour, then," he said. "Good-by."

Bryne stood up straighter. The grin faded.

"You don't like me," he said, on a note of sadness. "All the same, you'd better trust me. Half an hour's all we have now. After that I pass over into my official capacity as the Protector's representative, and I'll have to carry Torren's orders out. *He* thinks you need work-hardening. I may find myself finagling you into a slave-contract in the underlands."

"What do you suggest?" Fenton asked, folding another shirt.

"That's better." Bryne dropped a hand into his pocket, stepped forward, and tossed a thick packet of money onto the bed. Beside it he dropped a key and a folded ticket, bright pink for first-class.

"A ship leaves six hours from now for Earth," Bryne said. "There's a tractor car waiting in the gully at the foot of G-Corridor. That's its key. Torren keeps a close watch on all the Corridors, but the system's complex. Now and then by accident one of the wiring devices gets out of order. G-Corridor's out of order right now—not by accident. How do you like it, Fenton?"

Fenton laid the folded shirt into place, glanced at the money without expression. He was thinking rapidly, but his face showed nothing.

"What do you stand to gain, Bryne?" he asked. "Or is this one of Torren's subtler schemes?"

"It's all mine," the gaunt man assured him. "I'm looking toward the future. I'm a very honest man, Fenton. Not direct—no. You can afford to be direct. I can't. I'm only an administrator. Torren's the boss. Some day you'll be boss. I'd like to go on being an administrator then, too."

"Then this is by way of a bribe, is it?" Fenton inquired. "Waste of time, Bryne. I'm stepping out. Torren's probably rewriting his will already. When I leave Ganymede I leave for good. As if you didn't know."

"I know, all right. Naturally. I've already been notified to get out the old will. But I'll tell you, Fenton—I like administering Ganymede. I like being cupbearer to the gods. It suits me. I'm good at it. I want to go on." He paused, giving Fenton a keen glance under the sandy lashes. "How much longer do you think Torren has to live?" he inquired.

Fenton paused in his methodic packing. He looked at Bryne.

"Maybe a year," Bryne answered his own question. "Maybe less. In *his* condition he ought to be glad of it. I'm thinking about afterward. You and I understand each other, Fenton. I don't want to see the Torren holdings broken up. Suppose I keep the will that names you inheritor and tear up the new one Torren's going to make today? Would that be worth anything to you?"

Fenton looked out over the snow toward the turquoise valley where Kristin would be scattering yellow seeds into the furrows of the ploughed Ganymedan soil. He sighed. Then he stooped and picked up the money, the ticket and the key.

"You'll have to take my word for it," he said, "that it would be. But I wish I understood why you're really doing this. I thought you and Torren got along better than that."

"Oh, we do. We get along fine. But—Fenton, he scares me. I don't know what makes him tick. Funny things are happening to the human race these days, Fenton." Unexpected sincerity showed on the gaunt face in the doorway. "Torren . . . Torren isn't human. A lot of people aren't human any more. The important people aren't."

He swung a long arm toward the turquoise valley. "The Threshold people are getting the upper hand, Fenton. I don't mean here. I don't mean literally. But *they're* the inheritors of the future, not us. I guess I'm jealous." He grinned wryly. "Jealous, and a little scared. I want to feel important. You and I are human. We may not like each other much, but we understand each other. We can work together." He drew his shoulders together with a small shiver. "Torren's a monster, not a man. You know it, now. I know why you quarreled. I'm glad of it."

"I'll bet you are," Fenton said.

When it was safe, he drove the tractor car down the gorge between high banks of snow, rolling as fast as he dared toward the turquoise valley. The Ganymedan landscape framed in the square window openings all around him looked like so many television images on square screens. Probably some of it really was framed upon screens, back there in the Unit whose mile-square walls fell farther and farther behind as the tractor treads ground on.

Proabably Torren's screen, tilted above the water bath, reflected some such landscape as this. But there were often tractor cars trundling along the snowy roads. Unless Torren had reason to suspect, he was not likely to focus too sharply upon this one. Still, Fenton knew he would feel more comfortable after he had passed beyond the range of the 'visor. Not that Torren couldn't summon up a picture of any Ganymedan area he happened to feel curious about. The thing was to keep his curiosity asleep, until the time came to rouse it.

The cold hills swung by. The heavy air swirled a little as the car spun along, making eddies like paradoxic heat waves between Fenton and the road. No man could live without an insulated suit and breathing-apparatus on the surface of Ganymede—yet. But the specially bred Ganymedans from the Threshold Planetarium could.

When men first reached the planets they found their thresholds fatally different from Earth. They began to alter the planets, and to alter the men. This after one whole wasted generation in which they tried to establish colonies that could be supported from Earth and could operate from artificial shelters. It didn't work. It never worked, even on Earth, when men tried to create permanent colonies in alien lands without subsisting on the land itself.

There is more to it than the lack of bread alone. Man must establish himself as a self-sustaining unit on the land he works, or he will not work it long. Neither humans nor animals can subsist or function efficiently on alien territory. Their metabolism is geared to a different ecology, their digestive organs demand a different food, melancholia and lassitude overcome them eventually. None of the great bonanza ventures on the mineral-rich planets ever came to a successful production because agriculture could not keep up with them and they collapsed of their own weight. It had been proved true time and again on Earth, and now on the planets the old truism repeated itself.

So the Threshold Planetaria were set up and the vast experiment got under way. And they altered the planets as well as the stock that was to possess them.

Ganymede was cold. The atmosphere of heavy gases could not sustain human life. So with atomic power and technological weapons man began to alter the ecology of Ganymede. Through the years the temperature crept gradually up from the deadly level of a hundred degrees below centigrade zero. Wastefully, desperately, the frozen water was released, until a cloud-blanket began to form over Ganymede to hold in the heat.

There were many failures. There were long periods of inactivity, when the insulated domes were deserted. But as new methods, new alloys, new isotopes were developed, the process became more and more practical. When the final generation of Ganymede-slanted stock was bred, Ganymede was ready for them.

Since then, three generations had become self-sustaining on the satellite. They could breathe the air—though men could not. They could endure the cold—though men could not. They were taller than men, solider and stronger. There were several thousand of them now.

As they had driven along a genetic parabola to meet the rising parabola of an altered planetary balance, so now the Ganymedans and Ganymede together followed a new curve. In a few more generations it would circle back to meet normal humanity. By that time, Ganymede should be habitable for Earthmen, and by then Ganymedans should have altered once more, back toward the norm.

Perhaps the plan was not the best possible plan. Humanity is not perfect. They made many errors, many false guesses, when the Age of Technology began. Balance of power among the nations of Earth influenced the development of the Threshold Planetaria. Social conflicts changed and shifted as civilization found new processes and methods and power-sources.

Fenton thought of Torren. Yes, there had been many errors of judgment. The children of Torren should have walked like giants upon a free planet. Centrifuge-bred colossi. But that experiment had failed. Not even upon tiny Ganymede could Torren use the tremendous strength inherent in his helpless body to stand upright.

It was easier to work eugenically with animals. In the new Ganymedan seas, still growing, and on the frigid Ganymedan continents, were creatures bred to breathe the atmosphere—arctic and subarctic creatures, walrus and fish, snow-rabbit and moose. Trees grew on Ganymede now, mutated tundra spread across the barrens, supplemented by the photosynthesis laboratories. A world was being born.

And across the world marched the heat-giving, life-giving towers built over a hundred-year period by the Earth government, still owned by Earth, not to be touched even by Torren, who owned Ganymede. Fenton swung the tractor over the brow of the hill and paused for an instant to look west. A new tower was rising there, one of hundreds, to supplement the old towers with a new method of speeding up changes. Within ten years these snowy hills might ripple with wheat—

The road forked here. One way led toward the valley. The other lay like a long blue ribbon across the hilltops, dipping suddenly as the horizon dipped toward the spaceport and the ship that was headed for home.

Fenton touched the scar on his cheek and looked at the spaceport road. Earth, he thought. And then? He thought of Bryne's wise, gaunt face, and of Torren wallowing in his water bed that was linked like the center of a spider's web with every quarter of the mile-square Unit and every section of the little globe it stood on. No, not a spider web—an island. A floating island with no link that bound him to humanity.

Fenton spoke one furious word and wrenched violently at the wheel. The car churned up snow in a blinding haze and then leaped forward along the right-hand road, down toward the turquoise mist that hid the valley.

An hour later he came to the village called Providence.

The houses were of local stone, with moss-thatched roofs. Early experiments with buildings of metal, plastics and imported wood had been discarded, as might be expected, in favor of indigenous materials. For life on Ganymede no houses proved quite so satisfying as houses built of Ganymede stone.

The people came mostly of hardy Norse stock, with Inuit and other strains mingled for the desirable traits. The Ganymedans who came out into the snow-powdered street when Fenton stopped his car were an entirely new race. An unexpectedly handsome race, since they had certainly not been bred for beauty. Perhaps much of their good looks sprang from their excellent health, their adjustment to their lives and their world, the knowledge that the world and the work they did upon it were both good and necessary. Until now.

A big yellow-haired man in furs bent to the window of the car, his breath clouding the heavy air which no normal human could breathe.

"Any luck, Ben?" he asked, his voice vibrating through the diaphragm set in the side of the car. It was only thus that a Ganymedan could speak to an Earth-born human. Their voices had to filter to each other through carbon dioxide air and metal and rubber plates. It meant nothing. There are higher barriers than these between human minds.

"About what you expected," Fenton told him, watching the diaphragm vibrate when sound struck it. He wondered how his own voice sounded, out there in the cold air heavy-laden with gases.

Yellow heads and brown nodded recognition of what he meant. The tall people around the car seemed to sag a little, though two or three of them laughed shortly, and one big woman in a fur hood said:

"Torren's fond of you, Ben. He must be, after all. Maybe—"

"No," Fenton told her positively. "He's projected himself in my image, that's all. I can walk around. But I'm simply an extension, like an arm or a leg. Or an eye. And if Torren's eye offends him—"

He broke off abruptly, slapped the steering wheel a couple of times and looked ahead of him down the wide, clean street lined with clean, wide-windowed houses that seemed to spring from the rock they stood on. They were strong houses, built low to defy the blizzard winds of Ganymede. The clear, wide, snowy hills rolled away beyond the rooftops. It was a good world—for the Ganymedans. He tried to think of these big, long-striding people shut up in asylums while their world slowly changed outside the windows until they could no longer breathe its air.

"But, Ben," the woman said, "it isn't as if people *needed* Ganymede. I wish I could talk to him. I wish I understood—"

"Have you any idea," Fenton asked, "how much Torren spends in a year? People don't need living room on Ganymede, but Torren needs the money he could get if . . . oh, forget it. Never mind, Marta."

"We'll fight," Marta said. "Does he know we'll fight?"

Fenton shook his head. He glanced around the little crowd.

"I'd like to talk to Kristin," he said.

Marta gestured toward the slope that led down into the farmland valley.

"We'll fight," she said again, uncertainly, as the car started. Fenton heard her and lifted a hand in salute, grinning without mirth or cheerfulness. He heard the man beside her speak as the car drew away.

"Sure," the man said. "Sure. What with?"

He knew Kristin as far as he could see her. He picked her figure out of the fur-clad group dark against the snow as they stepped out of the road to let the car go by. She waved as soon as she recognized him behind the glass. He drew the car to a halt, snapped on the heating units of the insulated suit he wore, closed the mask across his face and then swung the car door open. Even inside the mask his voice sounded loud as he called across the white stillness.

"Kristin," he said. "Come over here. The rest of you, go on ahead."

They gave him curious glances, but they nodded and trudged on down the hill toward the valley. It seemed odd to watch them carrying hoes and garden baskets in the snow, but the valley was much warmer below the mist.

Kristin came toward him, very tall, moving with a swift, smooth ease that made every motion a pleasure to watch. She had warm yellow hair braided in a crown across her head. Her eyes were very blue, and her skin milk-white below the flush the cold had given it.

"Sit in here with me," Fenton said. "I'll turn off the atmosphere unit and leave the door open so you can breathe."

She stooped under the low door and got in, folding herself into the too-small seat. Fenton always felt out of proportion beside these big, friendly, quiet people. It was their world, not his. If anyone were abnormal in size here, then it was he, not the Ganymedans.

"Well, Ben?" she said, her voice coming with a faint vibration through the diaphragm in his helmet. He smiled back at her and shook his head. He did not think he was in love with Kristin. It would be preposterous. They could not speak except through metal or touch except through glass and cloth. They could not even breathe the same air. But he faced the possibility of love, and grinned ironically at it.

He told her what had happened, exactly as it took place, and his mind began to clarify a little as he talked.

"I suppose I should have waited," he said. "I can see that, now. I should have kept my mouth shut until I'd been back on Ganymede at least a month, sounding things out. I guess I lost my temper, Kristin. If I'd only known, while I was still back on Earth . . . if you could only have written—"

"Through the spaceport mail?" she asked him bitterly. "Even the incoming letters are censored now."

He nodded.

"So the planets will go on thinking we *asked* for the changeover," she said. "Thinking we failed on Ganymede and *asked* to be shut up in asylums. Oh, Ben, that's what we all hate worst of all. We're doing so wonderfully well here . . . or we were, until—" She broke off.

Fenton touched the button that started his motor and turned the car around so they could look out across the broad plain below. They faced away from the Unit, and except for blurs of turquoise mist here and there where other warm valleys breathed out moisture and the exhalation of growing things there was no break in the broad sweep of snowy hills—the towers marching in a long row across the planet.

"Does he knew we'd die in the asylums?" Kristin asked.

"Would you?"

"I think we would. Many of us would. And I think we'd never have any more children. Not even the idea of having great-great-grandchildren who might be able to walk on Ganymede again would keep the race alive. We wouldn't kill ourselves, of course. We wouldn't even commit race-suicide. We won't want to die—but we won't want to live, either—in asylums."

She twisted on the smooth car seat and looked anxiously at Fenton through the glass of his respirator.

"Ben, if the planets knew—if we could get word outside somehow—do you think they'd help? Would anyone care? I think some might. Not the Earth-bred, probably. They wouldn't really *know*. But the Thresholders would know. For their own safety, Ben, I think they might *have* to help us—if they knew. This could happen to any Threshold group on any world. Ben—"

A blue shadow gliding across the snow caught her eye and she turned her head to watch it.

Then concussion heeled the car over.

Dimly Fenton heard metal rip around him against rocks hidden under the snow they plowed through. In the echoing immobility while the vehicle hung poised, before it settled back, he tasted blood in his mouth and felt Kristin's weight heavy against his shoulder, saw the black outlines of his own hands with fingers spread, pressing the glass against the whiteness of snow.

The car smashed over the edge, jolting downward on its treads, down faster and more roughly with each jolt. The winged blue shadow wheeled back and sailed over them again.

The silhouetted hands moved fast. Fenton was aware of them turning, pulling, gripping numbly at levers they scarcely felt. The idling motor exploded into a roar and the car sprang forward, straight down the unbroken slope.

Then the second blast came.

The rear of the vehicle lifted, hurling Fenton and the girl against the cushioned panel and the thick, shatter-proof windshield, which released its safeties under the impact and vanished in a whirl of brightness somewhere outside. The treads screamed as the car ground across the bare rock and snow boiled up in a whirlwind around them. The car shot forward again to the very edge of the slope and hung tottering over a hundred-foot drop beyond.

There was a timeless interval of what felt like free fall. Fenton had time to decide that his instinct had been right. The fall was the safer choice. The car's interior was braced and shock-absorbent, and they would survive a drop better than another bomb-hit.

Then they struck the ground, whirled out, struck again, in an increasing avalanche of ice and rock and snow. The shocks changed to the thunder of bombs, and then absolute darkness and silence without echo.

Neither of them could have survived alone. It took Kristin's Ganymedan strength and vitality and the resilience that had kept her from serious injury, plus Fenton's knowledge of mechanics and his fierce, devouring anger.

Buried thirty feet under a solid, freezing mass of debris, Fenton whipped the girl with words when even her hardiness began to fail. With one arm broken, he drove himself harder still, ignoring the shattered bone, working furiously against time. Enough air was trapped in the loose snow to supply Kristin, and Fenton's respirator and suit were tough enough to survive even such treatment as this.

The mercury-vapor turbine that generated the car's power had to be repaired and started anew. It took a long time. But it was done. What Fenton wanted was the tremendous thermal energy the exhaust would give them. Very slowly, very carefully, using a part of the turbine sheath as a shield, they burned their way to the open air.

Twice settling rock nearly crushed them. Once Kristin was pinned helpless by the edge of the shield, and only Fenton's rage got them through that. But they did get through. When only a crust remained, Fenton carefully opened small view-cracks in the shadow, and waited until he was sure no hovering helicopter still waited. Then they climbed free.

There were signs in the snow where a copter had landed and men had walked to the edge of the abyss, even climbed part of the way down.

"Who was it, Ben?" Kristin asked, looking down at the footprints. When he did not answer, "Ben—your arm. How bad—"

He said abruptly, not listening to her: "Kristin, I've got to get back to the Unit. Fast."

"You think it was Torren?" she asked fearfully. "But, Ben, what could you do?"

"Torren? Maybe. Maybe Byrne. I'm not sure. I've got to *be* sure. Help me, Kristin. Let's go."

"To the village first, then," she said firmly, setting her marble-hard forearm beneath his elbow to steady him. "You'll never make it unless we patch you up first. Would Torren really do a thing like that to you, Ben? The nearest thing to a son he'll ever have? I can't believe it."

The dry snow squeaked underfoot as they climbed the hill.

"You don't know Torren," Fenton said. He was breathing unevenly, in deep gasps, partly from pain, partly from weariness, mostly because the air in the respirator was not coming fully enough to supply his increased need. But the outer air was pure poison. After awhile he went on, the words laboring a little.

"You don't know what Torren did to me, thirteen years ago," he said. "Back on Earth. I was sixteen, and

I wandered out one night in one of the old Dead Ends—the ruined cities, you know—and I got myself shanghaied. At least, that's what I thought for three years. One of the gangs who worked the ruins got me. I kept thinking Torren's men would find me and get me out. I was young and naive in those days. Well, they didn't find me. I worked with the gang. For three years I worked with them. I learned a lot. Things that came in handy afterward, on some of the jobs Torren had for me—

"When I was tough enough, I finally broke away. Killed three men and escaped. Went back to Torren. You should have heard him laugh."

Kristin looked down at him, doubtfully. "Should you be talking, Ben? You need your breath—"

"I want to talk, Kristin. Let me finish. Torren laughed. He'd engineered the whole thing. He wanted me to learn pro-survival methods right at the source. Things he couldn't teach me. So he arranged for me to learn from—experts. He felt that if I was capable I'd survive. When I knew enough, I'd escape. Then I'd be a tool he could really use. Work-hardening, he called it."

Fenton was silent, breathing hard, until he got enough breath to finish. "After that," he said, "I was Torren's right hand. His legs. His eyes. I was Torren. He'd put me into an invisible Planetarium, you see—a Centrifuge like the thing he grew up in, the thing that made him into a monster. That's why I understand him so well." He paused for a moment, swiped vainly at the face-plate as if to wipe away the sweat that ran down his forehead. "That's why I've got to get back," he said. "Fast."

Only Torren knew all the secrets of the Unit. But Fenton knew many. Enough for his purpose now.

When the rising floor inside the column of the round shaft ceased its pressure against his feet, he stood quiet for a moment, facing the curved wall, drawing a deep breath. He grimaced a little as the breath disturbed his arm, splinted and strapped across his chest under his shirt. With his right hand he drew the loaded pistol from its holster and, swinging it from the trigger guard, used his thumb to find the spring hidden in the curved wall.

The spring moved. Instantly he swung the pistol up, the grip smacking into his receiving palm, his finger touching the trigger. The hollow pillar in which he stood slid half apart, and Fenton looked straight at Torren in his water bed.

He stood still then, staring.

The colossus had managed to heave himself up to a sitting position. The huge hands gripped the edge of the tank and, as Fenton watched, the great fingers curved with desperate fury on the padded rim. Torren's eyes were squeezed shut, his teeth bared and set, and the room was full of the sound of his harsh, wheezing breath.

The blind, gargoyle face hung motionless for an instant. Then Torren exhaled with a gasp and let go. There was a tremendous wallowing splash as the Protector of Ganymede plunged back into the water bed.

Fenton's gaze lowered to the long strip of floor beside the bath where a row of tiles had been lifted to expose the intricate complex of wires leading into the banked controls by which Torren ruled his palace and his planet. The wires lay severed on the floor, tangled fringes of them ripped and cut and torn out. It was almost as much a mutilation as if Torren's actual nerve-fibres had been torn. He was as helpless as if they had been.

There was a table set up a little distance from the bath. The key wires in the flooring snaked across the tiles toward the table. Upon it a control box had been set up, and the audio and video devices which were Torren's ganglia.

At the table, his profile to Fenton, Bryne sat, his

long, thin body humped forward intently, the pale eyes fixed upon his work. He had a privacy-mute on the microphone he held to his mouth and as he murmured his fingers played lightly with a vernier. He watched the green line ripple and convulse across the face of an oscilloscope. He nodded. His hand struck down quickly at a switch, closed it, opened another.

"Bryne!" The breathless bellow from the tank echoed among the pillars, but Bryne did not even glance up. He must have heard that cry a good many times already, since this phase of his work began.

"Bryne!"

The shouted name mounted in a roar of sound up the well to the star-reflections far above and reverberated to a diminishing whisper that blended with Torren's heavy breathing. Again the huge hands slid futilely over the rim of the tank.

"Answer me, Bryne!" he roared. *"Answer me!"*

Bryne did not look up. Fenton took a step forward, onto the open floor. His eyes were hard and narrow. The blood had gone out of his face until the pale scar along his jaw was almost invisible. Torren, seeing him, gasped and was silent in the midst of another shout. The small eyes sunk in fat stared and then shut tight for an instant over a leap of strange, glancing lights.

"Why don't you answer him, Bryne?" Fenton asked in an even voice.

Bryne's hands opened with a sudden, convulsive gesture, letting the microphone fall. After a long moment he turned an expressionless face to Fenton. The pale eyes regarded the gun muzzle and returned to Fenton's face. His voice was expressionless, too.

"Glad to see you, Fenton," he said. "I can use your help."

"Ben!" Torren cried, a thick gasp of sound. "Ben, he's trying . . . that . . . that scum is trying to take over! He—"

"I suppose you realize," Bryne said in a quiet voice,

"Torren sent a helicopter to bomb you when he found you were getting away from him. I'm glad he failed, Fenton. We're going to need each other."

"Ben, I didn't!" Torren shouted. "It was Bryne—"

Bryne picked up the microphone again, smiling thinly.

"It's going to be perfectly simple, with your help, Fenton," he said, ignoring the heavy, panting gasps of the Protector in the tank. "I see now I might have taken you into my confidence even more than I did. This was what I meant when I told you Torren hadn't very much longer to rule. The chance came sooner than I expected, that's all."

"Ben!" Torren was breathing hard, but his voice was under more control now. He swallowed heavily and said: "Ben, don't listen to him. Don't trust him. He . . . he wouldn't even *answer* me! He wouldn't even pay any attention . . . as though I were a . . . a—" He gulped and did not finish. He was not willing to put any name to himself that came to his mind.

But Fenton knew what he meant. "As though I were a . . . monster. A puppet. A dead man." It was the horror of utter helplessness that had disarmed him before Bryne. For thirty years Torren had sought and claimed power by every means at his command, driven himself and others ruthlessly to combat the deepest horror he knew—the horror of helplessness. It was that which frightened him—not the fear of death.

"Don't waste your sympathy, Fenton," Bryne said, watching him. "You know Torren better than I do. You know what he planned for you. You know how he's always treated you. When he saw you escaping, he sent the 'copter to make sure you wouldn't get away. He isn't human, Fenton. He hates human beings. He hates you and me. Even now he'll play on your sympathy until he gets you to do what he wants. After that . . . well, you know what to expect."

Torren shut his eyes again, not quite soon enough to

hide the little glitter of confidence, perhaps of triumph, in them. In an almost calm voice he said: "Ben, you'd better shoot him now. He's a plausible devil."

"Just what are your plans, Bryne?" Fenton asked in a level voice.

"What you see." Bryne's gaunt shoulders moved in a shrug. "I'll pretend he's ill, at first. Too ill to see anyone but me. This is a Maskelyne vodor I've got here. I'm working out a duplicate of his voice. It's a *coup d'etat*, Fenton, nothing new. I've got everything planned thoroughly. I've done nine-tenths of the management of Ganymede for years now, anyhow. Nobody's going to wonder much. With your help, I can get the rest of the empire for us, too."

"And what about me?" Torren demanded thickly.

"You?" The pale eyes flickered toward him and away. "As long as you behave, I suppose you can go on living." It was a lie. No falser statement of intent was ever spoken. You could tell it by the flat tone of his voice.

"And the Ganymedans?" Fenton asked.

"They're yours," Bryne said, still flatly. "You're the boss."

"Torren?" Fenton turned his head. "What do *you* say about the Ganymedans?"

"No," Torren breathed. "My way stands, Ben." His voice was an organ whisper. "My way or nothing. Make your choice."

The slightest possible flicker of a smile twitched the corner of Fenton's lip. He swung his pistol higher and sent a bullet exploding straight into Bryne's face.

The gaunt man moved like lightning.

He must have had his farther hand on a gun for some seconds now, because the two explosions came almost as one. In the same instant he sent his chair clattering backward as he sprang to his feet.

He moved too fast. His aim was faulty because of his speed. The bullet whined past Fenton's ear and smacked into the pillar behind him. Fenton's shot struck Bryne an invisible blow in the shoulder that spun him half around, knocked him three-quarters off his feet. He scrambled desperately backward to regain his balance. His foot caught in a tangle of ripped-up wiring beside the water bath, and he went over backward in slow motion, his pale stare fixed with a strange illusion of calmness on Fenton's face as he fell.

For an instant he tottered on the brink of the bath. Then Torren chuckled a vast, deep, terrible chuckle and with tremendous effort lifted a hand far enough to seize Bryne by the wrist.

Still expressionless, still with that pale, intent stare fixed upon Fenton, Bryne went backward into the tank. There was a surge of heaving water. Bryne's suddenly convulsed limbs splashed a blinding spray and his hand groped out of nowhere for Torren's throat.

Fenton found himself running, without intending to or—he knew—needing to run. It was pure impulse to finish a job that needed finishing, though it was in better hands than his, now. He put his good hand on the rim of the huge tank, the revolver still gripped in it, leaning forward.

Bryne vanished under the oily, opaque surface. The incalculable weight of Torren's arm was like a millstone pressing him down, merciless, insensate as stone. After a while the thick, slow bubbles began to rise.

Fenton did not even see the motion Torren made. But when he tried to spring backward, it was too late. A vast, cold, slippery hand closed like iron over his. They wrestled unequally for several slow seconds. Then Torren's grip relaxed and Fenton stumbled back, swinging his half-crushed fingers, seeing his revolver all but swallowed up in Torren's enormous grasp.

Torren grinned at him.

Slowly, reluctantly, Fenton grinned back.

"You knew he was lying," Torren said. "About the bombs."

"Yes, I knew."

"So it's all settled, then," Torren said. "No more quarreling, eh, son? You've come back." But he still held the revolver watchfully, his eyes alert.

Fenton shook his head.

"Oh, no. I came back, yes. I don't know why. I don't owe you a thing. But when the bombs fell I knew you were in trouble. I knew he'd never dare bomb me in sight of the 'visor screens as long as you had any power on Ganymede. I had to find out what was happening. I'll go, now."

Torren hefted the revolver thoughtfully. "Back to your Ganymedans?" he asked. "Ben, my boy, I brought you up a fool. Be reasonable! What can you do for them? How can you fight me?" He rumbled with a sudden deep chuckle. "Bryne thought I was helpless! Step over there, Ben. Switch on the 'visor."

Watching him carefully, Fenton obeyed. The snowy hills outside sprang into view. Far off above them, tiny specks upon the blue-lit clouds, a formation of planes was just visible, humming nearer.

"About ten minutes more at the outside, I'd say," Torren estimated. "There are a lot of things about this set-up nobody even guesses except me. I wonder if Bryne really imagined I hadn't thought of every possibility. I allowed for this years and years ago. When my regular signals stopped going out an alarm went off—out there." The huge head nodded. "My guards would have got here in another ten minutes whether you came or not. Still, son, I'm obliged. You spared me that much time of feeling—helpless. You know how I hate it. Bryne could have killed me, but he could never have held me helpless very long. I owe you something, Ben. I don't like being obligated. Within reason, I'm willing to give you—"

"Nothing I want," Fenton cut in. "Only freedom for the Ganymedans, and that I'll have to take. You won't give it. I can take it, Torren. I think I know the way, now. I'm going back to them, Torren."

The huge hand floating at the surface of the water turned the pistol toward Fenton.

"Maybe you are, son. Maybe not. I haven't decided yet. Want to tell me just how you plan to stop me on Ganymede?"

"There's only one way." Fenton regarded the pistol with a grim smile. "I can't fight you. I haven't any money or any influence. Nobody on Ganymede has except you. But the Ganymedans can fight you, Torren. I'll teach them. I learned guerrilla warfare in a hard school. I know all there is to know about fighting against odds. Go on and put your new towers up, Torren. But—try and keep them up! We'll blow them apart as fast as you can put them together. You can bomb us, but you can't kill us all—not soon enough, you can't."

"Not soon enough—for what?" Torren demanded, the small eyes burning upon Fenton's. "Who's going to stop me, son? I've got all the time there is. Ganymede belongs to *me*!"

Fenton laughed, almost lightly.

"Oh, no it doesn't. You lease it. But Ganymede belongs to the solar system. It belongs to the worlds and the people of the worlds. It belongs to your own people, Torren—the Thresholders who are going to inherit the planets. You can't keep the news of what's happening quiet here on Ganymede. The Earth government owns the towers. When we blow them over the government will step in to find out what goes on. The scandal will get out, Torren. You can't keep it quiet!"

"Nobody will care," Torren grunted. But there was a new, strange, almost hopeful glint in his eyes. "Nobody's going to war over a little satellite like Ganymede. Nobody has any stake here but me. Don't be childish, Ben. People don't start wars over an ideal."

"It's more than an ideal with the Thresholders," Fenton said. "It's their lives. It's their future. And *they're* the people with power, Torren—not the Earth-bred men like me. The Thresholders are the future of the human race, and they know it, and Earth knows it. The new race on Mars with the three-yard chest expansions, and the new people on Venus with gills and fins may not look much like the Ganymedans, but they're the same species, Torren. *They'll* go to war for the Ganymedans if they have to. It's their own hides at stake. Ideals don't come into it. It's survival, for the Thresholders. Attack one world and you attack all worlds where Thresholders live. No man's an island, Torren—not even you."

Torren's breath came heavily in his tremendous chest.

"Not even me, Ben?"

Fenton laughed and stepped backward toward the open pillar. On the screen the planes were larger now, nearer and louder.

"Do you know why I was so sure you hadn't ordered those bombs to kill me?" he asked, reaching with his good hand for the open door. "For the same reason you won't shoot me now. You're crazy, Torren. You know you're crazy. You're two men, not one. And the other man is me. You hate society because of the debt it owes you. Half of you hates all men, and the Ganymedans most of all, because they're big like you, but they can walk like men. Their experiment worked and yours failed. So you hate them. You'll destroy them if you can."

He found the door, pushed it open wide. On the threshold he said:

"You didn't adopt me on a whim, Torren. Part of your mind knew exactly what it was doing. You brought me up the hard way. My life was spent in a symbolic Centrifuge, just like yours. I *am* you. I'm the half that doesn't hate the Ganymedans at all. I'm the half that knows they're *your* people, the children you might have had, walking a free world as yours would have walked if your experiment had come out right, like theirs. I'll fight for them, Torren. In a respirator and mask, but I'll fight. That's why you'll never kill me."

Sighing, Torren tilted the pistol. His thick finger squeezed itself inside the guard, began slowly to tighten upon the trigger. Slowly.

"Sorry, son," he said, "but I can't let you get away with it."

Fenton smiled. "I said you were crazy. You won't kill me, Torren. There's been a fight going on inside you ever since you left the Centrifuge—until now. Now it's going on outside, in the open. That's a better place. As long as I'm alive, I'm your enemy and yourself. Keep it on the outside, Torren, or you *will* go mad. As long as I'm alive I'll fight you. But as long as I'm alive, you're not an island. It's *your* battle I'm fighting. You'll do your best to defeat me, Torren, but you won't kill me. You won't dare."

He stepped back into the pillar, groping for the spring to close the door. His eyes met Torren's confidently.

Torren's teeth showed under grimacing lips.

"You know how I hate you, Ben," he said in a thick, fierce voice. "You've always known!"

"I know," Fenton said, and touched the spring. The door slid shut before him. He was gone.

Torren emptied the revolver with a sort of wild deliberation at the unmarred surface of the pillar, watching the bullets strike and richochet off it one by one until the hall was full of their whining and the loud explosions of the gun. The pillar stood blank and impervious where Fenton's face had been.

When the last echo struck the ceiling Torren dropped the gun and fell back into his enormous tank, caught his breath and laughed, tentatively at first and then with increasing volume until great billows of sound rolled up the walls and poured between the pillars toward the stars. Enormous hands flailed the water, sending spray high. The vast bulk wallowed monstrously, convulsed and helpless with its laughter.

On the screen the roar of the coming planes grew until their noise swallowed up even Torren's roaring mirth.

The Code

Through the parlor windows Dr. Bill Westerfield could see the village street, with laden branches hanging low above the blue-shadowed snow. The double tracks of tires diminished in the distance. Peter Morgan's sleek sedan was parked by the curb, and Morgan himself sat opposite Bill, scowling into his coffee cup.

Bill Westerfield watched a few flakes of snow making erratic pseudo-Brownian movements in the winter twilight. He said under his breath, *"Now is the winter of our discontent—"*

Morgan moved his heavy shoulders impatiently and drew his heavy black brows closer together. "Yours?"

"His." Both men looked up, as though their vision could pierce wood and plaster. But no sound came from upstairs, where old Rufus Westerfield lay in the big walnut bed carved with grapes and pineapples. He had slept and wakened in that same bed for seventy years, and he had expected to die in it. But it was not death that hovered above him now.

"I keep expecting Mephistopheles to pop up through a star trap and demand somebody's soul," Bill said. *"His* discontent . . . *my* discontent . . . I don't know. It's going too smoothly."

"You'd feel better if there were a price tag hanging on the bedpost, would you? 'One Soul, Prepaid.' "

Bill laughed. "Logic implies somebody has to pay. Energy must be expended to do work. That's the traditional price, isn't it? Youth restored at the cost of Faustus' soul."

"So it's really thaumaturgy after all?" Pete Morgan inquired, pulling down the corners of his heavy mouth until the lines standing deep made his face look a little Mephistophelian after all. "I've been thinking all along I was an endocrinologist."

"O.K., O.K. Maybe that was how Mephisto did it too. Anyhow, it works."

Upstairs the nurse's heels sounded briefly on bare boards, and there was a murmur of voices, one light, one flat with age but echoing now with an undertone of depth and vibration that Bill Westerfield remembered only vaguely, from his boyhood.

"It works," agreed Pete Morgan, and rattled the coffee cup in its saucer. "You don't sound too happy. Why?"

Bill got up and walked down the room without answering. At the far end he hesitated, then swung around and came back with a scowl on his thin face to match Morgan's black-browed saturninity.

"There's nothing wrong about reversing the biological time-flow—if you can," he declared. "Father hasn't got his eye on a Marguerite somewhere. He isn't doing it for selfish reasons. We aren't tampering with the Fountain of Youth because we want glory out of it, are we?"

Morgan looked at him under a thicket of black brows. "Rufus is a guinea pig," he said. "Guinea pigs are notoriously selfless. We're working for posterity ourselves, and a halo after we're dead. Is that what you want me to say? Is there something the matter with you, Bill? You've never been squeamish before."

Bill went down the room again, walking quickly as if he wanted to get to the far end before his mind changed. When he came back he was holding a framed photograph.

"All right, look here." He thrust it out roughly. Morgan put down his cup and held the frame up to the light, squinting at the pictured face. "That was Father ten years ago," Bill said. "When he was sixty."

In silence Morgan looked long and steadily at the photograph. Upstairs they could hear faintly in the stillness how the carved bed creaked as Rufus Westerfield moved upon it. He moved more easily now than he had done a month ago, in the depth of his seventy years. Time was flowing backward for old Rufus. He was nearing sixty again.

Morgan lowered the photograph and looked up at Bill.

"I see what you mean," he said deliberately. "It isn't the same man."

Biological time is a curious, delusive thing. It is no quirk of imagination that makes a year seem endless to the child and brief to the grandfather. To a child of five a year *is* long, a fifth of his whole life. To a man of fifty, it represents only a fiftieth. And the thing is not wholly a matter of the imagination. It links inescapably into the physical make-up of a man, in a sort of reverse ratio. In youth the bodily processes are demonstrably as much faster as the time-sense is slower. The fetus, during gestation, races through a million years of evolution; the adolescent in ten years' time covers an aging process that will take him another fifty years of slowing change to equal. The young heal rapidly; the old sometimes never heal. Dr. du Nouy in his *Biological Time* plunges even deeper than this into the mysteries of youth and age, speculating on the private time universe in which each of us lives alone.

Rufus Westerfield was groping his way slowly backward through his.

Another experimenter, a Dr. Francois this time, had given the clue which he was following, as Theseus followed another sort of clue through the labyrinthine ways where the Minotaur lurked in hiding. Dr. Francois trained subjects to tap a telegraph key three hundred times a minute in their normal state. Then he applied heat and cold, gently, not to distract his subjects. And heat shortened their appreciation of time. The key tapped faster. Academically speaking they were older when warmth surrounded them. In the cold, time ran slower, like the long days of youth.

It had not, of course, been as simple as all that. The cardiac and vascular systems of the human machine needed powerful stimulus; the liver had almost ceased to build red cells. For these time could not turn backward without help. And there had been hypnosis, too. Seventy years of habit-patterns took a lot of erasing, and more esoteric matters than these had to be dealt with. The awareness of time itself, flowing soundlessly past in a stream that moved faster and faster as it neared the brink.

"It isn't the same man," Morgan repeated without emotion, his eyes on Bill's face. Bill jerked his shoulders irritably.

"Of course it's the same man. It's Father at sixty, isn't it? Who else could it be?"

"Then why did you show it to me?"

Silence.

"The eyes," Bill said carefully after awhile. "They're . . . a little different. And the slope of the forehead. And the angle of the cheek isn't . . . well, not quite the same. But you can't say it isn't Rufus Westerfield."

"I'd like to compare them," Morgan said practically. "Shall we go up?"

The nurse was closing the bedroom door behind her as they reached the stair head.

"He's asleep," she mouthed silently, her glasses glittering at them. Bill nodded, stepping past her to push the door soundlessly open.

The room inside was big and bare with an almost

monastic simplicity that made the ornately carved bed incongruous. A night light glowing on a table near the door cast long humped shadows upward on walls and ceilings, like shadows cast by a fire that has burned low. The man in the bed lay quiet, his eyes closed, his thin, lined face and thin nose austere in the dimness.

They crossed the floor silently and stood looking down. Shadows softened the face upon the pillow, giving it an illusion of the youth to come. Morgan held the photograph up to catch what light there was, his lips pursed under the black mustache as he studied it. This was, of course, the same man. There could be no possibility of error. And superficially the two faces were identical. But basically—

Morgan bent his knees a little and stooped to catch the angle of forehead and cheek as the photograph showed it. He stood stooping for a full minute, looking from face to photograph. Bill watched anxiously.

Then Morgan straightened, and as he rose the old man's eyelids rose too. Rufus Westerfield lay there looking up at them without moving. The night light caught in his eyes, making them very black and very bright. They looked sardonic, all that was alive in the weary face, but young and wise and amused.

For a moment no one spoke; then the eyes crinkled in slanting enjoyment, and Rufus laughed, a thin, high laugh that was older than his years. Senility sounded in the laugh, and a man of sixty should not be senile. But after the first cracked cackle the sound deepened slightly and was no longer old. His voice was liable, at this stage, to break into senility as an adolescent's breaks into maturity. The adolescent break is normal, and perhaps Rufus' break was normal too, in a process that created its own norm because it was as yet unique in human history.

"You boys want something?" inquired Rufus.

"Feel all right?" Morgan asked.

"I feel ten years younger," Rufus grinned. "Anything wrong, son? You look—"

"No, not a thing." Bill smoothed the frown off his face. "Almost forgot your shots. Pete and I were talking—"

"Well, hurry up. I'm sleepy. I'm growing fast, you know. Need sleep." And he laughed again, no cackle in the sound this time.

Bill went out hastily. Morgan said, "You're growing, all right. And it does take energy. Have a good day?"

"Fine. You going to unlearn me any this evening?"

Morgan grinned. "Not exactly. I want you to do a little . . . thinking . . . though. After Bill's finished."

Rufus nodded. "What's that under your arm? The frame looks familiar. Anyone I know?"

Morgan glanced down automatically at the photograph he was holding, the face hidden. Bill, coming in at that moment with the nurse behind him, saw the old man's brilliant, quizzical stare, and Morgan's eyes shift away from it.

"No," said Morgan. "Nobody you'd know."

Bill's hand shook a little. The hypodermic he was carrying, point up, trembled so that the drop upon its needle spilled over and ran down the side.

"Steady," Rufus said. "You nervous about something, son?"

Carefully Bill did not meet Morgan's gaze. "Not a thing. Let's have your arm, Father."

After the nurse had gone Morgan pulled a stump of candle from his pocket and set it upon Rufus' bedside table. "Put out the night light, will you?" he said to Bill as he held a match to the wick. Yellow flame bloomed slowly in the dimness.

"Hypnosis," Rufus said, squinting at the flicker.

"Not yet, no. I'm going to talk. Look at the flame, that's all."

"That's hypnosis," Rufus insisted in an argumentative voice.

"It makes you more receptive to suggestion. Your

mind has to be liberated enough so you can . . . see . . . time."

"Mm-m."

"All right—not see it, then. Sense it, feel it. Realize it as a tangible thing."

"Which it isn't," Rufus said.

"The Mad Hatter managed."

"Sure. And look what happened to him."

Morgan chuckled. "I remember. It was always tea-time. You don't need to worry about that. We've done this before, you know."

"I know you say we have. I'm not supposed to remember." Rufus' voice imperceptibly had begun to soften. His gaze was on the flame, and its reflection wavered in miniature in his eyes.

"No. You never remember. You'll forget all about this, too. I'm talking to a level of your mind that lies beneath the surface. The work goes on down there, in the quiet, just as the shots you're getting work in secret inside your body. You're listening, Rufus?"

"Go ahead," Rufus said drowsily.

"We must shatter the temporal idols in your mind that stand between you and youth. Mental energy is powerful. The whole fabric of the universe is energy. You've been conditioned to think you grow old because of time, and this is a false philosophy. You must learn to discount it. Your belief acts upon your body, as the adrenals react to fear or anger. It's possible to set up a conditioned reflex so that the adrenals will respond under a different stimulus. And you must be conditioned to reverse time. The body and the mind react inseparably, one upon the other. Metabolism controls the mind, and the mind governs the metabolism. These are the two faces of a single coin."

Morgan's voice slowed. He was watching the flicker of the reflected light shining beneath the old man's lids. The lids were heavy.

"A single coin—" echoed Rufus' voice, very low.

"The life processes of the body," said Morgan in a

monotone, "are like a river that flows very swiftly at its source. But it slows. It runs slower and slower into age. There's another river, though, the awareness of time, and that stream runs with an opposite tempo. In youth it's so slow you don't even guess it's moving. In age, it's a Niagara. That is the stream, Rufus, that's going to carry you back. It's rushing by you now, deep and swift. But you've got to be aware of it, Rufus. Once you recognize it, nothing can stop you. You must learn to know time."

The monotone droned on.

Fifteen minutes later, downstairs, Morgan set the photograph of Rufus at sixty upon the mantelpiece and regarded it with a heavy scowl.

"All right," he said. "Let's have it."

Bill fidgeted. "What is there to say? We're doing something so new we have no precedent. Father's changing, Pete—he's changing in ways we didn't expect. It worries me. I wish we hadn't had to use him for a guinea pig."

"There was no choice, and you know it. If we'd used up ten years of testing and experiment—"

"I know. He couldn't have lasted six months when we started. He knew it was risky. He was willing to chance it. I know all that. But I wish—"

"Now be reasonable, Bill. How the devil could we experiment except on a human subject, and a man with a high I.Q. at that? You know I tried it with chimps. But we'd have had to evolve them into humans first. After all, in the last analysis it's the intelligence factor that makes the trick possible. It's lucky your father's breakdown was purely physical." He paused, looking again at the photograph. "About this, though—"

Bill spread his hands with a distracted motion. "I'd thought of every possible chance of error—except this one." He laughed wryly. "It's crazy. It isn't happening."

"The whole thing's crazy as a bedbug. I still don't believe it's working. If Rufus is really back to sixty already, then anything can happen. It wouldn't surprise me if the sun came up from California tomorrow." Morgan fished in his pocket and brought out a cigarette. "All right, then," he said, fumbling for a match, "so he doesn't look exactly as he did ten years ago. Does he act the way he did then?"

Bill shrugged. "I don't know. I wasn't taking notes in those days. How was I to guess what you and I'd be up to now?" He paused. "No, I think he doesn't," he said.

Morgan squinted at him through smoke. "What's wrong?"

"Little things. That look in his eyes when he woke awhile ago, for instance. Did you notice? A sort of sardonic brightness. He takes things less seriously. He . . . just doesn't match his face any more. That austere look . . . it used to suit him. Now when he wakes suddenly and looks at you, he's . . . well, looking out of a mask. The mask's changing . . . some. I know it's changing. The photograph proves that. But it isn't changing as fast as his mind."

Deliberately Morgan blew smoke out in a long, swirling plume. "I wouldn't worry too much," he said soothingly. "He'll never be the same man he was ten years ago, you know. We aren't erasing his memory. Maybe he mellowed more than you realize in the decade he's just retracted. At forty, at thirty, he'll still be a man who's lived seventy-odd years. It won't be the same mind or the same man that existed in the Eighties. You're just getting a case of the jitters, my boy."

"I'm not. His face has changed! His forehead angle's different! His nose is beginning to arch up a little. His cheekbones are higher than they ever were in his life. I'm not imagining that, am I?"

Morgan blew a leisurely ring.

"Don't get excited. We'll check the shots. Maybe he's getting an overdose of something. You know how that can affect the bony structure. There's no harm done, anyhow. His physical condition is good and getting better. His mind's keen. I'm more worried about you than him right now, Bill."

"About me?"

"Yeah. Something you said before we went upstairs. Something about Faust. Remember? Now, just what did you have in mind?"

Bill looked guilty. "I don't remember."

"You were talking morals. You seemed to think there might be some punishment from on high hanging over us if our motives weren't pure. How about that?"

Bill's tone was defensive, if his words were not. "You know better than to sneer at tradition just because it's smart to. You were the one who convinced me that the old boys knew more than they ever passed on. Remember how the alchemists wrote their formulas in code to sound like magical spells? 'Dragon's Blood,' for instance, meant something like sulphur. Translated, they often made very good sense. And the Fountain of Youth wasn't water by accident. That was purely symbolic. Life rose from the water—" He hesitated. "Well, the moral code may have had just as solid a basis. What I said was that energy has to be expended to accomplish anything. Mephistopheles didn't do any work; a demon has power at his birthright. Faust had to expand the energy. In the code of the formula—his soul. It all makes sense except in the terms they used."

Morgan's heavy brows met above his eyes. "Then you think someone's got to pay. Who and what?"

"How do I know? There wasn't any glossary in the back of the book to show what Marlowe meant when he put down 'soul.' All I can say is we're repeating, in effect, the same experiment Faust went through. And Faust had to pay, somehow, in some coin or other that we'll never know. Or"—he looked up suddenly with a startled face—"will we?"

Morgan showed his teeth and said something rude.

"All right, all right. Just the same, we're doing a

thing without any precedent but one, unless—" He hesitated. "Wait a minute. Maybe there was more than one. Or was it just a coincidence?"

Morgan watched him mouthing soundless phrases, and said after a moment, "*Are* you crazy?"

"Full fathoms five thy father lies," Bill recited. "How about that?

"Of his bones are coral made,
 These are pearls that were his eyes,
Nothing of him that doth fade
 But doth suffer a sea change
 Into something rich and strange—"

Morgan snorted. "Forget that and go on. What about precedent?"

"Well, say there's only been one, then. But there was that. And it won't hurt us to take as much advantage as we can of what our predecessors learned. We can't take very much. It's all hidden in legend and code. But we do know that whoever Mephistopheles and Faust really were, and whatever means they used to get where we are now, they had trouble. The experiment seemed to succeed, up to a point—and then it blew up in their faces. Legend says Faust lost his soul. What that really means I don't know. But I say our own experiment is showing the first faint symptoms of getting out of hand, and *I* say we may find out some day what that code really means. I don't want to learn at Father's expense."

"I'm sorry." Morgan ground out his half-finished cigarette. "Is it any good my saying I think you're letting your imagination run away with you? Or have you got me cast as Mephistopheles?"

Bill grinned. "I doubt if you want his soul. But you know, in the old days you'd have got into trouble. There's something a little too . . . too thaumaturgical about hypnotism. Especially about the kind of thing you put Rufus through." He sobered. "You have to send his mind out—somewhere. What does he find there, anyhow? What does time look like? How does it feel to stand face to face with it?"

"Oh, cut it out, Bill. Worry about your own mind, not Rufus'. He's all right."

"Is he, Mephisto? Are you sure? Do *you* know where his mind goes when you send it out like that?"

"How could I? Nobody knows. I doubt if Rufus knows himself, even in his dreams. But it works. That's all that matters. There's no such thing as time, except as we manufacture it."

"I know. It doesn't exist. But Rufus has seen it. Rufus knows it well. Rufus—and Faust." Bill looked up at the picture on the mantelpiece.

Spring came early that year. Rains sluiced away the last of the snow, and the long curved street outside the Westerfield windows began to vanish behind frothing green leaves. In the familiar cycle winter gave way to spring, and for the first time in recorded history a man's wintertime of life came round again to his own improbable spring.

Bill could not think of him any more as *father*. He was Rufus Westerfield now, a pleasant stranger to look at, though memory had kept pace with his retrogression and no lapse of awareness made him a stranger to talk to. He was a healthy, vigorous, handsome stranger to the eye, though. Flesh returned solidly to fill out the aesthetic, fine-drawn body that Bill remembered. It did not seem to him that his father had been so physically solid a man in his earlier youth, but he was, of course, receiving medical care now far in advance of what had been available to him then. And as Morgan pointed out, the intention had not been to recapture a facsimile of the Rufus of an earlier day, but simply to restore the old Rufus' lost strength.

The facial changes were what mystified them most. Bodily a man may change through perfectly normal causes, but the features, the angles of forehead and nose and chin, ought to remain constant. With Rufus they had not.

"We're getting a changeling in reverse," Morgan admitted.

"A few months ago," Bill pointed out, "you were denying it."

"Not at all. I was denying the interpretation you put on it. I still deny that. There are good reasons behind the changes, good solid reasons that haven't got a thing to do with thaumaturgy or adventures in hypnosis, or pacts with the devil, either. We just haven't found out yet what causes the changes."

Bill shrugged. "The strangest thing is that he doesn't seem to know."

"There's a great deal, my friend, that he doesn't seem to know."

Bill looked at him thoughtfully. "That's got to wait." He hesitated. "We can't afford to tamper much with . . . with discrepancies of the mind, when we aren't sure about the body yet. We don't want to bring anybody else in on this unless we have to. It wouldn't be easy to explain to a psychiatrist what's behind these aberrations of his."

"There are times," Morgan said, "when I wish we hadn't decided to keep quiet about all this. But I suppose we hadn't any choice. Not until we can put down Q.E.D., anyhow."

"There's plenty to be done before that. If we ever can. If the stream isn't too strong for us, Pete."

"Cold feet again? He'll stop at thirty-five, don't worry. One more series of shots, then say another month to strike a glandular balance, and he'll start back to age with the rest of us. If he weren't your father, you wouldn't jitter about the whole thing this way."

"Maybe not. Maybe I wouldn't." Bill's voice was doubtful.

They were in the living room again, on a morning in May. And as Morgan looked up to speak, the door opened and Rufus Westerfield, aged forty, came into the room.

He was handsome in the solid, sleek manner of early middle age. His hair had returned to rich dark-red, growing peaked above tilting brows. The black eyes tilted too, in shallow sockets, and there was a look in them entirely strange to any Westerfield who had ever borne the name before. The face and the thoughts behind it were equally alien to the Westerfields. But it was a subtle change. He had not noticed it himself.

He was whistling as he came into the room.

"Beautiful morning," he said happily. "Beautiful world. You youngsters can't appreciate it. Takes a man who's been old to enjoy youth again." And he put the curtains aside to look out on the new leaves and the freshness of May.

"Rufus," said Morgan abruptly, "what's that tune?"

"What tune?" Rufus slanted a surprised black glance over his shoulder.

"You're whistling it. You tell me."

Rufus frowned thoughtfully. "I dunno. An old one." He whistled another bar or two, strange, almost breathless swoops of sound. "You ought to know it—very popular in its day. The words—" He paused again, the black eyes narrow, looking into infinity as he searched his memory. "On the tip of my tongue. But I can't quite— Foreign words, though. Some light opera or other. Oh well—catchy thing." He whistled the refrain again.

"I don't think it's catchy," Bill declared flatly. "No melody. I can't follow the tune at all, if it's got one." Then he caught Morgan's eye, and was silent.

"What does it make you think of?" Morgan pursued. "I'm curious."

Rufus put his hands in his pockets and regarded the ceiling. "My young days," he said. "That what you mean? Theater parties, lights and music. A couple of other young fellows I used to see a lot. There was a girl, too. Wonder whatever became of her—probably an old woman now. Her name was—" He hesitated. "Her name was—" He shaped the name with lips, or tried to. Then an extraordinary expression crossed his face and he said, "You know, I can't remember at all. It was something outlandish, like—" He tried again to shape with his lips a word that refused to come. "I *know* the name, but I can't say it," he declared fretfully. "Is that a psychic block or something, Pete? Well, I daresay it doesn't matter. Funny, though."

"I wouldn't worry. It'll come to you. Was she pretty?"

A slightly muzzy look crossed Rufus' face. "She was lovely, lovely. All . . . spangles. I wish I could remember her name. She was the first girl I ever asked to . . . to—" He paused again, then said, "—to marry me?" in a thin, bewildered voice. "No, that's not right. That's not right at all."

"It sounds terrible," Morgan remarked dryly. Rufus shook his head violently.

"Wait. I'm all mixed up. I can't quite remember what they . . . what was—" His voice faltered and died away. He stared out the window in an agony of concentration, his lips moving again as he struggled for some reluctant memory. Morgan heard him murmur, "Neither marriage nor giving in marriage . . . no, that's not it—"

In a moment he turned back again, looking bewildered and shaking his head. There was a fine beading of sweat on his forehead, and his eyes for the first time had lost their look of sardonic confidence. "There's something wrong," he said simply.

Morgan stood up. "I wouldn't worry," he soothed. "You're still going through some important changes, remember. You'll get straightened out after awhile. When you do remember, let me know. It sounds interesting."

Rufus wiped his forehead. "That's a funny feeling—getting your memories twisted. I don't like it. The girl . . . it's all confused—"

Bill, from a far corner of the room, said:

"I thought mother was your first love, Rufus. That's the story we always heard."

Rufus gave him a dazzled look. "Mother? Mother? Oh, you mean Lydia. Why, yes, she was, I think—" He paused for a moment then shook his head again. "Thought I had it that time. Something you said about —mother, that's it. I was thinking of mine. Are those pictures you've got there, Bill? Maybe I could remember whatever it is that's bothering me if I saw—"

"Grandma's picture? It's just what I was hunting. I suddenly had an idea that you might . . . uh . . . be getting more like her side of the family as you grow younger. Don't know why I never thought of that before. Here she is." He held up a yellowed metal rectangle, a tintype framed in plush. He scowled at it. "No. She's nothing like you at all. I hoped—"

"Let me see it." Rufus held out his hand. Something very strange happened then. Bill laid the tintype in his father's palm, and Rufus lifted it and looked into the shadowy features of the picture. And almost in the same motion he cried violently, "No! No, that's ridiculous!" and hurled the thing to the floor. It bounced once, with a tinny sound, and lay face down on the bare boards.

Nobody spoke. The silence was tense for half a minute. Then Rufus said in a perfectly reasonable voice, "Now what made me do that?"

The other two relaxed just perceptibly, and Morgan said, "You tell us. What did?"

Rufus looked at him, the tilted black eyes puzzled. "It was just . . . wrong, somehow. Not what I expected. Not at *all* what I expected. But what I did expect I couldn't tell you now." He sent a distracted glance about the room. The window caught his eye and he looked out at the pattern of leaves and branches beyond the porch. "That looks wrong to me," he added helplessly. "Out there. I don't know why, but when I see it suddenly I know it isn't right. It's the first glance that does it. Afterward, I can tell it's just the way it's always been. But just for a minute—" He drew his shoulders together in a shrug of discomfort, and grimaced at the two men appealingly. "What's wrong with me, boys?"

Neither of them answered for a moment, then both spoke together.

"Nothing to worry about," Bill said, and Morgan declared in the same breath:

"Your memory hasn't caught up with your body yet, that's all. It's nothing that won't straighten out in a little while. Forget it as much as you can."

"I'll try." Rufus sent a bewildered look about the room again. For a moment he seemed not only a stranger to the house and the street outside, but a stranger to his own body. He looked so sleek and handsome, so solidly assured of his place in the world. But there was nothing but bewilderment behind the facade.

"I think I'll take a walk," he said, and turned toward the door. On the way he stooped and picked up the tintype of his mother's face, pausing for an instant to look again at the unfamiliar picture. He shook his head doubtfully and laid the tintype down again. "I don't know," he said. "I just don't know."

When the door had closed behind him, Morgan looked at Bill and whistled a long, soft note.

"Well, you'd better get the record book," he said. "We ought to put it all down before we forget it."

Bill glanced at him unhappily and went out of the room without a word. When he came back, carrying the big flat notebook in which they had been keeping, detail by detail, the record of their work, he was scowling.

"Do you realize how impossible all that was?" he asked. "Rufus wasn't remembering *his* past. He never had a past like that. Forgetting all the other aberrations, the thing isn't possible. He grew up in a Methodist minister's household. He believed theaters were houses of sin. He's often told me he never set his foot inside one until long after he was married. He couldn't have known a girl who was—all spangles. He never had any affairs—Mother was his first and last love. He's told me that often. And he was telling the truth. I'm sure he was."

"Maybe he led a double life," Morgan suggested doubtfully. "You know the proverbs about preachers' sons."

"Anybody but Rufus. It just isn't in character."

"Do you *know*?"

Bill looked at him. "Well, I've always understood that Rufus was—"

"Do you know? Or is it hearsay evidence? You weren't there, were you?"

"Naturally," Bill said with heavy irony, "I wasn't around before I was born. It's just possible that up to that time Rufus was a black magician or Jack the Ripper or Peter Pan. If you want to go nuts, you can build up a beautiful theory that the world didn't exist until I was born, and you can make it stick because nobody can disprove it. But we're not dealing with blind faith. We're dealing with logic."

"What kind of logic?" Morgan wanted to know. He looked gloomy and disturbed.

"My kind. Our kind. *Homo sapiens* logic. Or are you implying that Rufus—" He let the thought die.

Morgan picked it up. "I'm willing to imply. Suppose Rufus *was* different when he was young."

"Two heads?" Bill said flippantly. And after a pause, in a soberer voice, "No, you've got the wrong pig by the tail. I see your point. That there might be . . . some biological difference, some mutation in Rufus that ironed itself out as he grew older. But your theory breaks down. Rufus lived in this town most of his life. People would remember if he'd . . . had two heads."

"Oh. Yeah, of course. Well, then . . . it could have been subtler. Something not even Rufus knew about. Successful minor mutations aren't noticed, because they *are* successful. I mean . . . a different, more efficient metabolic rate, or better optical adjustment. A guy with slightly super vision wouldn't be apt to realize it, because he'd take it for granted everybody else had the same kind of eyes. And, naturally, he wouldn't ever need to go to an optometrist, because his eyes would be *good.*"

"But Rufus has had eye tests," Bill said. "And every other kind. We gave him a complete check-up. He was normal."

Morgan sampled his lower lip and apparently didn't like it. "He was when we ran the tests, yes. But back in the Nineties? All I'm saying is, it's not inconceivable that he started out with some slight variations from the norm which may have been adjusted even by the time he reached adolescence. But the potentialities were there, like disease germs walled off behind healthy tissue, waiting for a lowering of resistance to break out again. Maybe that happens oftener than we know. Maybe it happens to nearly everybody. We do know that for every child that's born there've been many conceptions that would have produced nonviable fetuses if they'd gone to full term. These are discarded too early to be recognized. Maybe even in normal children adjustments have to be made sometimes before the adolescent perfectly fits into our pattern. And when something as revolutionary as what we did to Rufus takes place, the weak spots in the structure—the places where adjustments were made—break down again. Or say the disease germs are turned loose and rebuild the old disease. I'm mixing my metaphors. There isn't any perfect analogy. Am I making sense at all?"

"I wish you weren't," Bill said uncomfortably. "I don't like it."

"All we can do is guess, at this stage. Guess—and wait. We can't tell without a control, and we haven't got any control. There's only Rufus. And—"

"And Rufus is changing," Bill finished for him. "He's changing into someone else."

"Don't talk like a fool," Morgan said sharply. "He's changing into Rufus, that's all. A Rufus we never knew, but perfectly genuine. My guess is that most of the adjustments took place in adolescence, and he isn't going back that far. I'm only suggesting that the stories you heard about his young days may have been—well, not entirely true. He's confused now. We'll have to wait until the changes stop and his mind clears up to find out what really happened."

"He's changing," Bill said stubbornly, as if he had not been listening. "He's going back, and we don't know where it will end."

"It's ended already. He's on his last series of shots now. You haven't any reason to think he won't stop at thirty-five, when we wind up the treatments, have you?"

Bill laid down the book and looked at it thoughtfully. "No reason," he said. "Only—the current's so strong. Biological time flows so fast when you reach the midpoint. Like the river flowing toward Niagara. I wonder if you can go too far. Maybe there's a point beyond which you can't stop. I'm an alarmist, Pete. I have a feeling we've saddled a tiger."

"Now *you're* mixing metaphors," Morgan said dryly.

In June Bill said, "He won't let me in his room any more."

Morgan sighed. "What now?"

"The decorators finished two days ago. Dark-purple hangings all around the walls. I'm sure they thought he was a little crazy, but they didn't argue. Now he's got an old clock up there he's been tinkering with, and he found a table somewhere with a chessboard top, and he's making the strangest calculations on it."

"What kind of calculations?"

Bill shrugged irritably. "How do I know? I'd thought he was getting better. Those spells of . . . of false memory haven't seemed to bother him so much lately. Or if they do, he doesn't talk about it."

"When was the last?"

Bill opened his desk drawer and flipped the notebook cover. "Ten days ago he said the view from his windows wasn't right. Also that his room was ugly and he didn't know how he'd stood it all these years. It was about then that he began to complain of these pains, too."

"Oh, the 'growing pains.' And they began to localize—when?"

"A week ago." Bill scowled. "I don't like 'em. I thought it was gastric—I still think it is. But he shouldn't be having any trouble at all. He's perfect, inside and out. Those last X-rays—"

"Taken a week ago," Morgan reminded him.

"Yes, but—"

"If he keeps having a bellyache after meals, something may have gone wrong only a few days ago. Remember, Rufus is unique."

"He's that, all right. Well, I'll start all over, if I can catch him. He's getting very skittish these days. I can't keep up with him any more."

"Is he out now? I'd like to have a look at his room."

Bill nodded. "You won't find out anything. But come on up."

Purple curtains inside clogged the door for a moment as if the room itself were trying to hold them out. Then the door came open, and a draft from the hall made the four walls billow and shiver with rich, dark-purple folds, as if things had run to hiding everywhere an instant before the two men entered. The only light come in a purple glow through curtains across the windows, until Bill crossed the room and put back the draperies that covered them. Then they could see more clearly the big carved bed, the chest of drawers, the few chairs.

At the bed's foot stood the chessboard table, chalk marks scrawled across the squares. At the back of the table stood the clock, an old-fashioned mantelpiece ornament that filled the room with a curious sort of hiccupping tick. They listened a moment, then Morgan said, "That's funny. Wonder if it's accidental. Do you hear a . . . a halfbeat between the ticks?" They listened again. *Tick-ti-tock* went the clock.

"It's old," Bill said. "Probably something wrong with it. What I want you to look at is the second hand. See?"

A long sweep-hand was moving very slowly around the broad face. It did not match the other two. The presumption was that Rugus had found it elsewhere and added it very inefficiently, for as they watched it leaped about three seconds and resumed its slow crawl. A little farther on it leaped again. Then it made almost a complete circuit, and jumped five seconds.

"I hope Rufus isn't keeping any dates by this thing," Morgan murmured. "Lucky for him he doesn't repair clocks for a living. What's the idea?"

"I wish I knew. I asked, of course, and he said he was just tinkering. It looks like it, too, in a way. But here's something funny." Bill stooped and opened the glass. "Look. It's very small. Here, and over here, see?"

Bending, Morgan made out upon the face of the clock, irregularly spaced between the numerals, a series of very tiny colored markings painted upon the dial. Red and green and brown, tiny and intricate, with curled lines like Persian writing. All around the face they went, varicolored and enigmatic. Morgan pulled his mustache and watched the erratic second-hand twitch around its path. Whenever it jumped it came to rest somewhere upon a twist of colored lines.

"That can't be accidental," he said after a moment. "But what's the idea? What does it record? Did you ask him?"

Bill gave him a long look. "No," he said finally, "I didn't."

Morgan regarded him narrowly. "Why not?"

"I'm not sure. Maybe . . . maybe I didn't want to know." He closed the glass face. "It looks crazy. But when it comes to machinery that measures time—Well, I wonder if Rufus doesn't know more than we do." He paused. "*You* turned his mind loose to explore time," he said almost accusingly.

Morgan shook his head. "You're losing your perspective, Bill."

"Maybe. Well—what do you make of the chess-board?"

They looked at it blankly. Careful scrawls had been traced almost at random within the squares, though it seemed evident that to the mind which directed that scrawling, purpose had been clear.

"He could just be working out some chess problem, couldn't he?" suggested Morgan.

"I thought of that. I asked him if he'd like to play, and he said he didn't know how and didn't want to be bothered. That was when he threw me out. I think it's got something to do with the clock, myself. You know what I think, Pete? If the clock measures hours, maybe the squares measure days. Like a calendar."

"But why?"

"I don't know. I'm not a psychiatrist. I've got one idea, though. Suppose during the hypnosis he imagined he did see something that—disturbed him. Say he *did* see something. Posthypnotic command stopped him from remembering it consciously, but his subconscious is still worried. Couldn't that emerge into a conscious, purposeless tinkering with things that have to do with time? And if it could, do you think maybe he may suddenly remember, some day, what's behind it all?"

Morgan faced him squarely across the table and the hiccupping clock.

"Listen, Bill. Listen to me. You're losing your perspective badly over this. You won't do Rufus any good if you let yourself get lost in a morass of mysticism."

Bill said abruptly, "Pete, do you know much about Faust?"

If he had expected a protest, he was surprised. Morgan grimaced, the heavy lines deepening around his mouth.

"Yeah. I looked him up. Interesting."

"Suppose for a minute that the legend's got a basis of fact. Suppose that somewhere back three hundred years there really were two men who tried this same experiment and made a record of it in code. Does that give you any ideas?"

Morgan scowled. "Nothing applicable. The legend's basis is the old medieval idea that knowledge is essentially evil. 'Thou shalt not eat of the fruit of the Tree.' Faust, like Adam, was tempted and tasted the fruit, and got punished. The moral's simply that to know too much is to disobey God and nature, and God and nature will exact a penalty."

"That's just it. Faust paid with his soul. But the point is that the experiment didn't run smoothly up to the end, and then suddenly collapse. Mephistopheles didn't really present a bill and carry off his reward. Their experiment went wrong almost from the start—like ours. Faust was an intelligent man. He wouldn't have bartered his immortal soul for a short fling on earth. It wouldn't have been worth while. The whole point was that Faust never took Mephisto seriously until it was too late. He deliberately let Mephistopheles spread out his trumpery pleasures, perfectly sure that they wouldn't give him enjoyment enough to matter any. And of course if they didn't the bargain was void. It was when he actually began to enjoy what Mephistopheles had to offer that he lost his soul, not at the end, when the bill was paid." Bill thumped the chess table emphatically. "Could a code tell you any plainer that the thing got out of hand almost at the beginning?" He looked at Morgan with narrowed eyes. "All we've got to do now is find out what the code for 'soul' means."

"Got any ideas?" Morgan inquired sardonically. "I'm worried more about you, Bill, than I am about Rufus. I'm beginning to wonder if we haven't made a mistake in our subject. You're too close to Rufus."

He was surprised at the look that came over Bill's face. He watched him frown a little, thump the table again, and then walk to the window and back without saying anything. Morgan waited. Presently:

"I'm not, really," Bill said. "Father and I never were very close emotionally. He wasn't the type. Rufus, I think, could be. Rufus has all the warmth that Father lacked. I like him. But it's more than that, Pete. There's something in the relationship between us that affects me as Rufus is affected. It's a physical thing. Rufus is my closest living relative, though he's a stranger now even in appearance. Half my chromosomes are his. If I hated him, I'd still be linked to him by that much heritage. Things are happening to him now that never happened to a human being before, so far as we know. It's as if, when you pull him out of the straight course of human behavior, you pull me too. I can't look at the thing abstractly any more." He laughed almost apologetically. "I keep dreaming about rivers. Deep, swift waters running faster and faster, with the abyss just ahead and no way on earth to escape it."

"Dream-symbolism—" began Morgan.

"Oh, I know, of course. But the river itself is a symbol. Sometimes it's Rufus on the raft, sometimes it's me. But the riptide has always caught us. We've gone too far to turn back. I wonder if—"

"Stop wondering. You've worked too hard. What you need is a rest from Rufus and everything connected with him. After you get those X-rays and figure out what's wrong with him, suppose you get away for awhile. When you come back Rufus will be thirty-five going-on-forty again and you can forget about the river and start dreaming about snakes or teeth or something like that. O.K.?"

Bill nodded doubtfully. "O.K. I'll try."

Three days later, in the Westerfield stydy, Morgan held an X-ray plate against the light and squinted at the shadowy maze of outlines. He looked a long time, and his hand was shaking when he laid the plate down carefully, scowling at Bill under brows so heavy they almost hid the expression of his eyes. It was an expression of bewilderment that verged on fear.

"You faked these!"

Bill made a futile gesture. "I wish I had."

Morgan gave him another piercing glance and turned back to the light for a second look. His hand was still shaking. He steadied it with the other and stared. Then he took up another plate and looked at that.

"It's impossible," he said. "It never happened. It couldn't."

"The . . . the simplification—" began Bill in an uncertain voice.

"The wonder is he can digest *anything*, with this set-up. Not that I believe it for a minute, of course."

"Everything's simplifying," Bill went on, as if he had not heard. "Even his bones. Even his ribs. They give like a child's ribs, half cartilage. I got to thinking, you know, after I saw that. I gave him a basal, just on a hunch, and he's plus forty. His thyroid is burning him up. But Pete, it doesn't seem to hurt him! No loss of weight, no increased appetite, sleeps like a baby—why, my nerves are twice as jumpy as his."

"But—that's impossible."

"I know."

Silence. Then, "Anything else wrong?"

Bill shrugged helplessly. "I don't know. I was afraid to run any more tests on him after that. It's the truth, Pete—I was afraid to."

Morgan put the last plate down very gently, and turned his back on the table. For the first time there was uncertainty in his motions. He was no longer a man supremely sure of himself. He said, in an indecisive voice, "Yeah. Well, we'll start tomorrow and give him a thorough going over. I . . . I think maybe we can find what's—"

"It's no use, Pete. You see that. We've started something we can't stop. He's gone too far along the river, and the current's got him. All the basic life processes that move so fast in youth are moving in him now faster than we can move. God knows where he's going—not back along any path a man ever heard of before—but he's into the current and we can't do a thing about it."

And after a moment Morgan nodded. "You were

right," he said. "You've been right all along, and I've been wrong. Now what?"

Bill made a gesture of futility. "I can't tell you. This is still your party, Pete. I'm just along for the ride. I saw the dangers first because . . . well, maybe because Rufus is my own kin and the pull was . . . tangible . . . between us. When he went off the beam I could feel it psychically. Could that explain anything?"

Morgan sat down with sudden limpness, like a man whose muscles have abruptly gone weak. But his voice, after a moment's bewilderment, began to grow firm again.

"It's up to us to find out. Let's see." He shut his eyes and rubbed the closed lids with unsteady fingers. There was another silence. Presently he looked up again and said, "He's been changing from the very first. I suppose I've been assuming that something in our treatment had shuffled his chromosomes and genes around into a new pattern of heredity, and he was beginning to throwback to some ancestor we never knew about. But now I wonder if—" He paused, and a startled look crossed his face. He stared at Bill with eyes that widened enormously. "Now I wonder—" he echoed tonelessly, as if his lips repeated something meaningless, while his mind raced ahead too fast for utterance.

After that he got up with a sudden, abrupt motion and began to pace the floor, his steps rapid. "No," he murmured, "that's crazy. But—"

Bill watched him for a moment or two longer. Then he said in a quiet voice, "I had the same idea quite awhile ago. I was afraid to say anything, though."

Morgan's head jerked up and he stared. Their eyes held in a long look, awe in Morgan's. "That they were shuffled—too much? The chromosomes could have fallen into a pattern—too different?"

"You saw the X-rays," Bill said gently.

"Let's have a drink," was all Morgan answered to that.

* * *

When they were settled again, and there was something very soothing and matter-of-fact about the tinkle of ice in their glasses, Morgan began in a voice that strained a little for the prosaic.

"There *may* be a race that looks like Rufus. Or there may once have been. No use jumping at the impossible before we exhaust normal possibilities. I've been trying to think of any race at all with just this facial characteristics, and there isn't one on earth today, but that's not saying there never has been. No race sprang full-blown into the world, you know. You and I must have had remote ancestors who lived on Atlantis, or were contemporaries of the Atlanteans anyhow. And who knows what *they* looked like?"

"You keep forgetting," Bill reminded him, still gently. "The X-rays. And this may be only the beginning. He'll move faster and faster now. Physiological time is fast—terribly fast—as it nears the source. Do you think there was ever a race like Rufus—inside?"

Morgan looked at him over the glass rim. He caught his breath to say something forcefully, then let it out in a sigh. "No. I don't think there ever was. Not here."

"All right," Bill said. "You take it from there."

"How can I?"

"Try. I'm afraid to. My ideas are too . . . too credulous. I'm curious to see if your mind follows the same track. Go on—take over."

"He's a . . . a changeling," Morgan began, groping. "There've been stories about changelings for a long time. Older than the Faustus legend. I wonder, was Faust a changeling too? Did he have the same potential trace of heredity that a time-reversal could make dominant? Changeling . . . fairy's child . . . fairies? Fragile people, invisible at will, built to another scale than ours—another dimension? Other dimensions, Bill?"

Bill shrugged. "He can't eat what we eat. If these changes go on, there won't be a food on earth he can digest. Maybe, somewhere, there is."

Morgan said abruptly, "Maybe the changes won't go on, either. We don't know they will. Are we making fools of ourselves, groping around in fairy stories for an answer we may not need?"

"I think we'll need it, Pete. Anyhow, let's go on and see what we get. Another dimension, you were saying."

"O.K., suppose there *were* changelings," Morgan said violently. "Suppose there *are* goblins and things that go bump in the night—"

" 'Good Lord, deliver us,' " Bill finished the quotation with a grin. "Use a little logic, Pete. I don't expect you to believe the pumpkin turned into a coach. But if we apply the alchemist's formula to the changeling idea, or the Faust legend, do we get anything at all?"

"Oh, that isn't so new. It's been suggested before that the supernatural beings of legend might be distorted memories of some other-dimensional visitors. But Rufus—"

"All right, Pete, say it."

With an air of deliberate sacrifice, Morgan lifted his black-mustached lip in a snarl and said, "Rufus may be—he appears to be—an hereditary throwback to some inhabitant of another world. Is that what you want?"

"It'll do."

"It explains—" Morgan suddenly glowed with an idea that justified his sacrifice. "It explains his reaction to the picture of his mother. It explains why things look wrong to him here. It even explains his impossible memories, in part."

Bill looked doubtful. "Yes—in part. There's something more, Pete. I'm not sure what—I just know this isn't all. It's not quite so easy. The clock, and the calender, if that's what the chessboard is—yes, you could say he senses a different time-scheme from ours and he's groping to recapture something familiar from some other life-experience he can't quite remember yet. But there's something more. We'll know before we're through, Pete. He's on his way back now. I'm scared. I don't want to know about it. My mind panics when I think of it. It's too close to me. But we'll know. We'll find out. We haven't got to the root of the thing yet, but when we do we'll see it isn't as easy as all this."

"The root? I wonder. There's one thing, Bill. Rufus wasn't like this during his normal growth-period. You remember what we were discussing once about the possibility of aberrations at birth that smoothed out in adolescence? He *could* be experiencing now the results of disturbing that adjustment. But you can't mutate backward. It simply isn't remotely conceivable, by any application of logic, on this or any other world. You can say he's inherited a potentiality of Martian or other-dimensional chromosomes, but that still won't explain it. Mutation is a . . . spreading out, a flowering, not a drawing in. And that *must* hold good anywhere in this—" He stopped, his heavy brows drawing together. After a while, he began again, gropingly.

"I'm wrong on that. It . . . let's see. It holds good only as long as there's the same temporal constant. And that's just what doesn't apply to Rufus."

Bill scowled. "He's going back in time, but it's all subjective, isn't it?"

"It started out that way. Could be the subjective's affecting the objective."

"That Rufus is warping *time*?"

Morgan was not listening. He had found pencil and paper in his pocket and was absorbing himself in meaningless squiggles. The heavy moments moved past. The pencil point stopped.

Morgan looked up, his eyes still puzzled. "Maybe I've got it," he said. "Maybe. Listen, Bill—"

In a railroad yard there are many tracks. Each track carries a train, moving forward relentlessly in space—and parallel.

According to the theory of parallel time, each train is a spatial universe, and the tracks are laid on the dark roadbed of time itself. Far, far back, in the black beginning, there may have been one track only, before it branched.

As it branched and branched again, the parallel roads spread out, forming in little groups—the New York Central, the Pennsylvania, the Southern Pacific and the Santa Fe. The trains—the universes—of each are roughly similar. The Penn has many cars rushing headlong through the dim mistiness of time, but they all contain recognizable variations of *homo sapiens*. The tracks branched, but the system is still a unit.

There are other units.

One thing they have in common—no, two things. They are parallel in time, and originally they came from the same unthinkable source, hidden in the mind-staggering, vast mysteries of the womb of space and time. *In the beginning*—

But you can't go back to the beginning. You can't even go back along your timetrack. Because the train is moving on, it isn't where it was twenty, fifty, eighty years before, and if you try to retrace your steps, you're walking along a strange road. It isn't quite spatial or temporal, really. It may involve—well, call it a dimension—that's so remarkably alien to us that we can't even conceive of it except as a—*difference*.

But it may be a bridge, a shortcut, this strange road the traveler finds when he tries to retrace time. It may be a tightrope stretched precariously between parallel time-tracks. The letter N expresses it. The vertical lines are the timetracks where the trains go by. The angled line is the shortcut—from the Penn to the New York Central.

Different companies. Different lines. Different—*groups*.

So you can't recapture *your* youth; you can't go home again; that home isn't there any more. It's away back along the track, lost in the dusk where the dead ashes of Tyre and Nineveh have smoldered out.

And it isn't just merely a matter of chromosomes. Not merely subjective. But going back, at an angle, into one of the parallel times where a certain equivalent of Rufus Westerfield existed.

Parallels do not imply similarity—not when the cosmic equations are involved. The basic matrix may not vary, but only a god can recognize such an ultimate basic. The mammal matrix, for example. Whales and guinea pigs are each mammalian.

So there were, perhaps, many equivalents of Rufus Westerfield, in the infinity of trains along the infinity of tracks—but he was not retracing his course along the Pennsylvania line.

The New York Central line was—parallel—but only on the Penn road were tickets sold to *homo sapiens*.

Rufus Westerfield was twenty-five. He lay at full length in the porch swing, somnolent in the hot July afternoon. One arm was behind his head and he tugged at the support-chain now and then to keep himself in lazy motion.

Laziness, indeed, was his keynote at this stage. Which seemed odd in contrast with the keen, humorous face so subtly unlike his face of forty-odd years ago, when he had once before been twenty-five. You would still have known at a glance that Rufus and Bill were closely related; the change was too subtle to alter that. But there was a sharpening of all the features now, a more than physical sharpening. And the contradictory indolence of him made Rufus look arrogant.

It was, given this outrageous setup, a normal indolence, but it went curiously with the youth of the man. At twenty-five a mind as keen and a face and body as forceful as Rufus' should have had no indolence about them. But at twenty-five the normal man is just entering upon the most productive period of his life. All through adolescence he has been building impatiently toward this fulfillment of his maturity.

But there had been nothing immature about Rufus Westerfield's immediate past. And life was not before him. The swift temporal current flowed away past him and out of sight. He moved toward the helplessness of infancy, not to the activity of his prime. And each day that went by was longer and more pellucid to him than the last. As the physical processes of his body moved faster and faster, nearing adolescence, so the temporal processes of his mind went slower. The thoughts of youth, wrote Longfellow, are long, long thoughts.

Rufus put out his free hand and deftly took up a glass from the porch floor as the swing lifted him toward it. Ice tinkled pleasantly; it was a rum collins, his fifth today. He watched the flicker of leaf-shadows on the porch roof and smiled comfortably as he sipped the sweet, strong liquid, rolling it upon his tongue. Taste was developing more and more keenly in him as the years retrogressed. The infant's whole mouth is lined with taste buds, and in Rufus' mouth, little by little, those taste buds were returning.

He had drunk a good deal in the past two months. Partly because he liked to drink, partly because alcohol was one of the few things his changing digestion could tolerate. And it helped to blur that nagging sense in him which he could not put a name to, the feeling that much he saw about him was indescribably wrong.

Rufus was an intelligent young man. Also he was tolerant. He saw no point in letting the sense of wrongness color his life unduly. He dismissed it when he could. In part this was simply an admirable adjustment to environment. It was a great pity that the man through whose changing phases Rufus moved so rapidly must remain only half known. He would have been a fascinating man, with his memories and mature wisdom accumulated over seventy years, his vigorous mind and body, and the sardonic keenness, the warmth and humor developing in him now. And with all these the enthralling subtleties of change from no source a man ever drew upon before. He was a blend, perhaps, of human and extra-human, and perhaps the best of each, but no one would ever know him wholly. The man he might have been was moving too swiftly for more than a glimpse at the life he might have lived. The stream that bore him along could not run slowly.

In part, then, it was a tolerant adjustment to life that let him accept what was happening so calmly. But it was also a form of precociousness in reverse. Because he was keenly intelligent, he would normally—at twenty-five going on twenty-six—have been in advance of his years. His brain would have fitted him to cope successfully with men many years his senior. And now, at twenty-five going on twenty-four he was still in advance of his age. But in reverse. In Rufus, it was efficiency that his mind was slowing leisurely toward the long thoughts of youth. It spared him a great deal.

The pleasant blur of drunkenness had another effect, too. It released the surface tension of his mind and let strange flotsam drift upward. Memories and fragments which he knew had no place in the past he had already lived. Knowing it, he made no effort to reconcile the paradox. More and more as time went by he approached that period when the individual questions only the superficial aspects of his world. Basically, he accepts it, turning trustfully to the protection of those around him. And in Rufus, his very intelligence forced him backward prematurely into that state of mind which belongs to childhood, because it was in that state that he could find the greatest protection from a peril his subconscious must have sensed and would not let the surface of his mind suspect.

On the surface, memories from two pasts floated and merged and sank away again, lazily, evoked by alcohol. In the beginning, memories of that other past had been thin as smokewreaths drifting transparently across the face of his clearer remembrance, indistinguishable from realities. It was a long time before he became consciously aware that two sets of memories, many of them mutually exclusive, were moving at once through his mind. By the time he was sure, he had passed beyond the stage of caring. Things beyond his control were happening with inexorable rhythms that carried him smoothly toward a goal he did not try to glimpse yet; it would come in good time, he could not miss it, he was ready.

Now the memories from that other past were superimposed over nearly all his Westerfield memories. He looked back upon Westerfield years more dimly, through a haze of obscuring events that did not seem in the least strange to him, and no more alien than his remembrances of Bill's youth, and of his long-dead wife. He could no longer distinguish at a mental glance which memory belonged to the Westerfield period and which to the other. But they had been different. Very different indeed. Individuals moved past and through his memories of Bill and Lydia, individuals whose names he knew but could not yet pronounce, beings who had played tremendous roles, perhaps, in that other past, in that other place.

But they too were veiled in this all-encompassing indifference which was his protection and his precociousness. Like the Westerfields, they belonged to an era that was moving too fast to be savored much. He had not time to spare for leisurely evocations of the past.

So he remembered, pleasantly, not questioning anything, letting the liquor release the double stream of memories and letting the memories glide by and go. Faces, colors, sensations he did not try to name, songs—like the song he was singing under his breath, now, to the slow rhythm of the swing.

Bill, coming up the steps, heard the song and tightened his lips. It was no tune at all. It was one of the nagging, impossible harmonies Rufus hummed so constantly, not really knowing that he did it. The words were not English, when he sang them in absent-minded snatches, and the melody was more alien than the cacophonies of oriental music. Bill had given up trying to understand. He had given up a great deal in the past month, since it became obvious that Rufus was going on beyond the thirty-five which was to have been his stopping point. Bill had met failure halfway and acknowledged the meeting with what equanimity he could summon. There was nothing to salvage now but sufficient grace to confess defeat.

Rufus in the swing seemed half asleep. The lids were lowered above the tilted black eyes, and the face had no expression beyond indolence. It worried Bill that although this was not a Westerfield face any more, it remained akin to his own. Again and again of late he felt with unreasoning discomfort that as Rufus changed in feature, he pulled Bill's own features awry to conform. It was not true, of course, the change was indescribably outside the mere matter of facial angles, but the effect remained disconcertingly the same.

Rufus did not open his eyes as his son's step sounded on the porch, but he said lazily, "Want a date tonight, Bill?"

"No thanks, not with one of your girls. I know when I'm well off."

Rufus laughed without lifting his lids, blind, indolent laughter that showed his white teeth. Then he stirred a little and looked up at his son, and Bill felt sudden helpless horror congealing in him. It was too abruptly inhuman a thing to face with no warning at all.

For though the lids had lifted, Rufus was not looking directly up with the black gaze that had once been sardonic and was now only lazy and amused. Something thin and blind stretched over his eyes, something that drew back slowly, with the deliberation of a cat's gaze, or an owl's. Rufus sometime in the immediate past had developed a nictitating membrane, a third eyelid.

If he knew it, he gave no evidence. He was grinning in amusement. The lid slipped back and vanished, and might never have been there. Rufus stretched and got up with a long, slow litheness, and Bill found it possible to forget for the moment what it was he had just seen.

Rufus' body had a beautiful muscular co-ordination which was in its own way tragic just now. And within it, the mechanism must differ impossibly from the norm. Bill had not checked upon the changes in the past two weeks, changes which he knew must be taking place almost while one watched. He should be fascinated, from a purely clinical viewpoint, in what took place. But he was not. He could accept the knowledge of failure, because he must, but he had in this case no urge to probe the reasons for failure. It was more than an unsolved problem. It was a matter intimately involving his own flesh and blood. As a man with an incurable disease might shun the sight of his infirmity, so Bill would not investigate any further the impossible things that were changing in this body which was half his own.

Rufus was looking at him and smiling.

"How you've aged," he murmured. "You and Pete both. I can remember when you were just youngsters, two or three months ago." He yawned.

"Have you got a date?" Bill asked. The young Rufus nodded, and for a moment his black eyes almost closed and the third lid slid drowsily forward, half veiling the irises. He looked like an aloof, contented cat. Bill could not watch him. He had become calloused enough by now to these changing paradoxes and he was not shocked out of self-possession, but he still could not look straight at this latest evidence of abnormality. He only said, "Don't look so smug," and went into the house abruptly, letting the screen slam behind him.

Rufus' eyes opened a little and the extra lid slid back, not all the way. He gazed after his son, but calmly, as incurious as a man might feel who watches a cat withdraw, disinterest in an alien species clouding his eyes.

He came in that night very late, and very drunk. Morgan had been waiting with Bill in the parlor, and they went out in silence to the taxi to bring Rufus in. His limp body was graceful even in this extremity. The driver was nearly in hysterics. He would not touch his passenger. It was impossible to make out exactly why—something that Rufus had done, or had not done, or perhaps had only said, on the way home.

"What was he *drinking*?" the driver kept demanding

in a voice that broke on the last word. "What could he have been *drinking*?"

They could not answer that, and could get no coherent reason from the man why they should. He went away as soon as Bill had paid him—he refused to accept or touch money from Rufus' wallet—driving erratically with a great clashing of gears.

"Has this happened before?" Morgan asked over Rufus' lolling, dark-red head.

Bill nodded. "Not so bad, of course. He—remembers—things when he's drunk, you know. Maybe he remembered something big this time. He always forgets again, and maybe that's just as well, too."

Between them Rufus moved a little, murmured a word, not in English, and waved both hands in an abortive gesture of expansion, rather as if vast landscapes were spread before him. He laughed clearly, not a drunken sound at all, and then collapsed entirely.

They put him to bed in the big carved bedstead upstairs, among the purple curtains. He lay as limply as a child, his familiar-strange face looking curiously like a solid mask with nothing at all behind it. They had turned to leave him, both of them tight-lipped and bewildered, and they were halfway across the room when Bill paused and sniffed the air.

"Perfume?" he asked incredulously. Morgan lifted his head and sniffed, too.

"Honeysuckle. Lots of it." The heavy fragrance was suddenly almost sickening in its sweetness. They turned. Rufus was breathing with his mouth open, and the fragrance came almost palpably from the bed. They went back slowly.

Deep waves of perfume rose to meet them as he breathed. There was no smell of liquor at all, but the honeysuckle sweetness hung so heavy that it left almost a sugary taste upon the tongue. The two men looked blankly at one another.

"It'd suffocate anyone else," Morgan said finally. "But we can't very well get him away from it, can we?"

"I'll open the windows," Bill said with restraint. "There's no way now to tell what's going to hurt him."

When they left the room the curtains were billowing gently in a breeze from the windows; the walls shuddered all around the room with the motion. In the silence Rufus' perfumed breath was the only sound except for the stutter of the clock with its long jumping hand. Just as they reached the door there came a slight change in the quality of the fragrance Rufus was exhaling. Neither pleasant nor unpleasant, an indescribable shift from odor to odor as color might shift and blend from one shade to another. But the new odor was not like anything either man had ever smelled before.

Bill paused briefly, met Morgan's eyes, then shrugged and went on out.

Downstairs in the study, Morgan said, "He's moving fast." He was silent awhile, then, "Maybe I'd better come in for awhile, Bill, until it's over."

Bill nodded. "I wish you would. It'll be soon. Awfully soon, I think. They grow so fast—you can almost *see* a child growing. And Rufus condenses years into weeks."

Biological time moved like a river, swifter and narrower as it nears the source. And temporal perception ran clearer and slower with every passing day. Rufus returned unperturbed in mind to his first childhood—or perhaps his third, by actual count, though memory of that senile past had almost vanished now. In youth, as in age, forgetfulness clouded his tranquil mind, partly because the days of his age were so far behind him now, but partly too because his brain was smoothing out into the untroubled immaturity of childhood. Borne swiftly and smoothly along that quickening stream, he moved backward toward the infinities of youth.

And now a curious urgency seemed to possess him. It was like the reasonless instinct that drives an animal to prepare the burrow for her young; the phenomenon of birth, approached from either side of the temporal current, seemed to evoke intuitive knowledge of what was to come, and what would be needed for its coming.

Rufus began to stay more and more in his room, resenting intrusion, resisting it politely. What he did was difficult to guess, though there was much chalk dust about the table with the chessboard top. And he worked on the clock, too. It had four hands now; the face was divided into concentric circles and the extra hand was a blur that spun around the painted dial. All this might have seemed the typical preoccupation of the adolescent mind with gadgetry, had there not been that urgency which no normal child needs to feel.

It was not easy any more to determine what went on in his rapidly changing body, since he resented and resisted examination, but they did discover that his metabolism had accelerated unbelievably. He exhibited none of the typical hyperthyroid traits, but the small gland in his throat was busily undoing now all the pituitaries had governed long ago, in the growth of his first childhood.

Normally a "hyperthyroid's" tremendous appetite is insufficient to keep up with the rate at which he expends energy, as his abnormally accelerated metabolism devours his very tissues in a fierce effort to keep pace with itself. In Rufus, that devouring metabolism worked inwardly upon muscle and bone. He was no longer physically a big man; he lost weight and stature steadily, from within, burning his own bulk for fuel to feed that ravenous hunger. But with Rufus it was impossibly normal. He felt no resultant weakness.

And with him, more secretly, perhaps the white corpuscles in his blood may have undergone change and multiplication, to attack his internal organs and work their changes there, much as the phagocytes of a pupa work histolysis inside the chrysalis, reducing what lies within to a plasma in which the imago to come lies already implicit in solution. But what lay implicity and hidden in the changing body of Rufus Westerfield was a secret still locked in the genes which time had so curiously disarranged.

All this was retrogression, and yet in a sense it was progress, if determined, orderly procedure toward a goal means anything. The time-stream narrowed about him, flowing backward toward its source.

"He's now, I should say, about fifteen," said Bill. "It's hard to tell—he never comes out of his room any more, even to meals, and I don't see him unless I insist on it. He's changing a good deal."

"How do you mean?"

"His features . . . I don't know. Sharper and finer, not childish at all. His bones seem quite flexible, all of them. Abnormal. And he's running a fever so high you can feel the heat without even touching him. It doesn't seem to bother him much. He just feels a little tired most of the time, like a child who's growing too fast." He paused and looked at his interlaced fingers. "Where will it end, Pete? Where *can* it end? There's no precedent. I can't believe he'll just—"

"No precedent?" interrupted Morgan. "I remember the time when you thought I was following Mephistopheles' footsteps."

Bill looked at him. "Faust—" he said vaguely. "But Faust went back to a definite age and stopped there."

"I wonder." Morgan's voice was half sardonic. "If the legend's all in code, maybe Mephisto's bill, when he presented it, had something to do with—this. Maybe what the legend coded as the loss of a soul was something like what's happening to Rufus now. Perhaps he lost his body, not his soul. Still, they were devious, those alchemists. 'Body' for 'soul' is pretty obvious."

"Too obvious. We haven't seen the end yet. Before we do, we'll know. I'm willing to admit the moral now . . . half-knowledge can be too dangerous to handle without losing . . . well, something important. But the penalty . . . we'll have to wait for that."

"Um-m," Morgan said. "You say he isn't like a child now? Remember, I haven't been in his room at all."

"No. Whatever kind of childhood he . . . *they* have, it isn't much like ours. But I haven't really seen him very clearly. He keeps it so dark in there."

"I wish I knew," Morgan said longingly. "I'd like very much to . . . suppose we couldn't just walk in and turn the lights on, Bill?"

Bill said quickly, "No! You promised, Pete. We're going to let him alone. It's the least we can do, now. He knows, you see. Reason or instinct—I can't tell which. Either way, it's no reason or instinct *our* species would understand. But he's the only one in the house who's sure of himself at this stage. We've got to let him play it his way."

Morgan nodded regretfully. "All right. I wish he weren't . . . hadn't ever been Rufus. We're handicapped. I wish he were just a specimen. I'm getting some funny ideas. About his—species. Did you ever think, Bill, how different the child is from the adult in appearance? Every proportion's abnormal, from an adult standpoint. We're so used to the sight of babies they look human to us even from birth, but someone from Mars might not recognize them as the same species at all. Has it occurred to you that if Rufus went back to . . . to infancy . . . and then reversed the process and grew up again, he'd probably grow up into something alien? Something we couldn't even recognize?"

Bill glanced up with a sudden gleam of excitement. "Do you think that might happen?"

"How can I tell? The time-stream's too uncharted for that. He might run against some current that would start him back downstream again at any moment. Or he might not. For his sake, I hope not. He couldn't live in this world. We'll never know what sort of world he belongs in. Even his memories of it, the things he said, were too distorted to mean anything. When he was willing to talk about it, he was still trying to force the alien memories into the familiar pattern of his past, and what came out was gibberish. We won't know, and neither will he. Just as well for us, too, if he doesn't grow up again. There's no criterion for guessing what shape *his* adult form would have. It might be as different from ours as . . . as the larva is from the butterfly."

"Mephistopheles knew."

"I expect that's why he was damned."

He could no longer eat anything at all. For a long while he had subsisted on a diet of milk and custards and gelatines, but as the internal changes deepened his tolerance grew less and less. Those changes must by now have gone entirely beyond imagining, for outwardly, too, he had changed a great deal.

He kept his curtains drawn, so that toward the end Bill could hardly see anything more than a small, quick shadow in the plum-colored darkness, turning a pale triangle of face from the light when the door opened. His voice was still strong, but its quality had changed almost indescribably. It was at once thinner and more vibrant, with a sort of wood-wind fluttering far back in the throat. He had developed a curious impediment of speech, not a lisp, but something that distorted certain consonants in a way Bill had never heard before.

On the last day he did not even take his tray into the room. There was no point in handling food he could not digest, and he was busy, very busy. When Bill knocked the thin, strong, vibrant voice told him pleasantly to go away.

"Important," said the voice. "Don't come in now, Bill. Mustn't come in. Very important. You'll know when—" and the voice went smoothly into some other language that made no sense. Bill could not answer. He nodded futilely, without a word, at the blank panels, and the voice within did not seem to think a reply from him necessary, for the busy sounds went on.

Muffled and intermittent, they continued all day, along with a preoccupied humming of queer, unmelodious tunes which he seemed to handle much better now, as if his throat were adjusting to the curious tonal combinations.

Toward evening, the air in the house began to grow tense in an indescribable way. The whole building was full of a sense of impending crisis. He who had been Rufus was acutely aware that the end had nearly come, and his awareness drew the very atmosphere taut with suspense. But it was an orderly, unhurried imminence that filled the house. Forces beyond any control, set in motion long ago, were moving to their appointed fulfillment behind the closed door upstairs, and the focus of this impending change went quietly about his preparations, like someone who knows himself in the hands of a power he trusts and would not alter if he could. Softly, humming to himself, he prepared in secret to meet it.

Morgan and Bill waited in chairs outside the closed door as night came on, listening to sounds within. No one could have slept in that taut air. From time to time one of them called, and the voice answered amiably but in preoccupation so deep that the answers were haphazard. Also they were becoming more muffled, difficult to understand.

Twice Morgan rose and laid a hand upon the knob, avoiding Bill's anxious eyes. But he could not bring himself to turn it. He could almost think the tension in the air would hold the door against him if he tried to push it open. But he did not try.

As the hours neared midnight, sounds from within came at longer and longer intervals. And the sense of tension mounted intolerably. It was like hurricane weather, as forces high in the upper air gathered for an onslaught.

The time came when there had been no stirring for what seemed a very long time, and Bill called, "Are you all right?"

Silence. Then, slowly and from far away, a reluctant rustling and the sound of a muffled voice, inarticulate, murmuring a syllable or two.

The two men looked at each other. Morgan

shrugged. Bill in his turn half rose and reached for the knob, but he did not touch it. The hurricane was still gathering in the upper air; they might not know when the time for action came, but they could sense, at least, when the time was not.

Silence again. When Bill could wait no longer, he called once more, and this time there was no answer. They listened. A faint, faint stirring, but no voice.

The next time he called, not even a stirring replied.

The night hours went by very slowly. Neither of the two men was aware of drowsiness—the air was too taut for that. Sometimes they talked quietly, keeping their voices low, as if whatever lay beyond the door were still within reach of sound.

Once Morgan said, "Remember, quite a while ago, I was wondering if Rufus was biologically unusual?"

"I remember."

"We decided then he wasn't. I've been thinking, Bill. Maybe I've got a glimmer of what's coming now. Rufus, say, simply switched to another time-line as he retrogressed. Any human might. Any human almost certainly would. Your ancestors wouldn't have to be abnormal or nonterrestrial, and you wouldn't have any more mutation-possibilities than anybody else. It's just that by growing young, you cut over to another circuit. Normally we'd never even know it existed. The relation between our Rufus and the . . . the Rufus of that other place must exist, but we'd never have known about it." He looked at the door without expression for a moment. Then he shook himself a little.

"That's beside the point. What I'm thinking is that the farther back he goes, the closer he's getting to the main-line track of that—other place. When he touches it—"

They knew, then, what they were waiting for. When two worlds touch, something has to happen.

Bill sat and sweated. *Has everybody got that potential?* he wondered. *Has Morgan got it? Have I? If anybody has, wouldn't I have? Inheritance. No wonder I felt Rufus was pulling me awry as he moved back along the track toward— What would I be like then? Not myself. An equivalent. Question mark.*

Equivalent. Ambiguous. Nothing I want to know about now. But maybe when I'm seventy, eighty, I won't think so. Without taste or teeth or vision, all senses dulled, I might remember the way— I might—

He was aware of a curious, secret shame, and shrugged the thought away. For a while. For a long while. For many years, perhaps.

They were silent after that. The night moved on.

And still the tension held. Held, and mounted. They smoked a great deal, but they did not leave the door. They could not begin to guess what it was they waited for, but the tension held them where they were. And the long hours of the night passed midnight and moved slowly toward dawn.

Dawn came, and they still waited. The house was tight and silent; the air seemed too taut to move through or draw into the lungs. When light began to come through the windows, Morgan got up with a great effort and said, "How about some coffee?"

"You make it. I'll wait here."

So Morgan went downstairs, moving with almost palpable difficulty that was perhaps wholly psychic, and measured water and coffee in the kitchen with hands that were all thumbs. The coffee had begun to send out its own particular fragrance, and the light was strong beyond the windows, when a sudden, perfectly indescribable *sound* rang through the house.

Morgan stood rigid, listening to that vibrating, ringing noise as it died slowly away. It came from upstairs, muffled by walls and floors between. It struck bewilderingly upon the ears and quivered into silence with perceptible receding eddies, like rings widening in water. And the tension of the air suddenly broke.

Morgan remembered sagging a little all over at that sudden release, as if it were the tautness in the atmosphere that had held him up during the long wait. He had no recollection at all of moving through the house or up the stairs. His next clear impression was of Bill, standing motionless before the opened door.

Inside it seemed quite dark. Also there appeared to be many small points of light, moving erratically, shining and fading like fireflies. But as they stared the lights began to vanish, so they may have been simply hallucinations.

But that which stood on the far side of the room, facing them, was not hallucination. Not wholly hallucination. It was—someone.

And it was a stranger. Their eyes and brains could not quite compass it, for it was not anything human. No one, confronted for one brief, stunned moment of his life with a shape so complex and so alien could hope to retain the image in his mind, even if for one evanescent instant he did wholly perceive. The perception must fade from the mind almost before the image fades from the retina, because there are no parallels in human experience by which to measure that which has been seen.

They only knew that it looked at them, and they at it. There was impossible strangeness in that *exchange* of glances, the strangeness of having exchanged looks with that which should not be looking at all. It was like having a building look back at one. But though they could not tell how it met their gaze—with what substitute for eyes, in what portion of its body—they knew it housed an individuality, an awareness. And the individuality was strange to them, as they were to it. There was no mistaking that. Surprise and unrecognition were instinct in its lines and its indescribable gaze, just as surprise and incredulity must have been instinct in theirs. Whatever housing the individual wears, it knows a stranger when it sees one. It knows—

So they knew this was not Rufus—had never been. But it was very remotely familiar, in a wrenchingly strange way. Under the complexity of its newness, in one or two basic factors, it was familiar. But an altered and modified familiarity which instinct rather than reason grasped in the moment they stood and saw it.

The moment did not last. Against the dark the impossible figure loomed for a timeless instant, its vision locked with theirs. It stood motionless, but somehow in arrested motion, as if it had halted in the midst of some rapid activity. The dark room was full of amazement and tense silence for one brief flash.

Then noise and motion swirled suddenly around it. As if a film had been halted briefly while the audience gazed, and now sprang back into life and activity again. For the fraction of a second they could see—things—in action beyond and around the figure. A flash into another world, too brief to convey any meaning. In the flash they looked back, unseeing, along the branching of the temporal track that leads from one line to another, the link between parallels along which alien universes go thundering.

The *sound* rang out again through the house. Heard from so near, it was stunning. The room shook before them, as if sound waves were visibly vibrating the air, and the four walls sprang suddenly to life as the curtains billowed straight out toward what might have been vacuum at the center of the room. The purple clouds threshed wildly, hiding whatever happened beyond them. For an instant the *sound* still quivered and rang in the air, the whipping of strained cloth audible below it, and the room boiled with stretched purple surges. And ceased.

Morgan said, "Rufus—" and took a couple of unsteady steps toward the bed.

"No," said Bill in a gentle voice. Morgan looked back at him inquiringly, but Bill only shook his head. Neither of them felt capable of further speech just then, but Morgan after a moment turned away from the bed and shrugged and managed a slightly shaken,

"Want some coffee, Bill?"

Simultaneously, as if sensation had returned without warning to their numbed faculties, they were aware of the fragrance of fresh coffee rising up the stair well. It was an incredibly soothing odor, reassuring, a link to heal this breach of possibility. It bound the past to the stunned and shaken present; it wiped out and denied the interval they had just gone through.

"Yeah. With brandy or something," Bill said. "Let's . . . let's go on down."

And so in the kitchen, over coffee and brandy, they finished the thing they had begun with such hopes six months before.

"It wasn't Rufus, you see." Bill was explaining now, Morgan the listener. And they were talking fast, as if subconsciously they knew that shock was yet to come. "Rufus was—" Bill gestured futilely. "*That* was the adult."

"Why d'you think so? You're guessing."

"No, it's perfectly logical—it's the thing that had to happen. Nothing else *could* have happened. Don't you see? There's no telling what he went back to. Embryo, egg—I don't know. Maybe something we can't imagine. But—" Bill hesitated. "But that was the mother of the egg. Time and space had to warp to bring her to this spot to coincide with the moment of birth."

There was a long silence. At last Morgan said.

"The—adult. *That*. I don't believe it." It was not quite what he had meant to say, but Bill took up the argument almost gratefully.

"It was. A baby doesn't look like an adult human, either. Or maybe . . . maybe this was a larva-pupa-butterfly relationship. How can I tell? Or maybe it's just that he changed more than we knew after we saw him last. But I know it was the adult. I know it was the . . . the mother. I know, Pete."

Across the fragrant cups Morgan squinted at him,

waiting. When Bill offered nothing further, he prompted him gently.

"How do you know, Bill?"

Bill turned a dazzled look at him. "Didn't you see? Think, Pete!"

Morgan thought. Already the image had vanished from outraged memory-centers. He could recall only that it had stood and stared at them, not with eyes, not even with a face, perhaps, as well as he could remember now. He shook his head.

"Didn't you recognize—something? Didn't it look just barely familiar to you? And so did I, to—it. Just barely. I could tell. Don't you understand, Pete? *That* was almost—very remotely almost—my own grandmother."

And Morgan could see now that it was true. That impossible familiarity had really existed, a distant and latent likeness, relationship along a many-times-removed line stretching across dimensions. He opened his mouth to speak, and again the wrong words came out.

"It didn't happen," he heard himself declaring flatly.

Bill gave a faint ghost of a laugh, quavering with a note of hysteria.

"Yes, it happened. It's happened twice at least. Once to me and once to . . . Pete, I know what the code was now!"

Morgan blinked, startled by the sudden surprise in his voice. "What code?"

"Faust's. Don't you remember? Of course that's it! But they couldn't tell the truth, or even hint it. You've got to face the thing to believe it. They were right, Pete. Faustus, Rufus—it happened to them both. They—went. They changed. They aren't . . . weren't . . . human any more. That's what the code meant, Pete."

"I don't get it."

"The code for soul." Bill laughed his ghost of hysterical mirth again. "When you aren't human, you lose your soul. That's what they meant. It *was* a code word, and it wasn't. There never was a deeper meaning hidden in a code that isn't a code. How could they have hidden it better than to tell the truth? Soul *meant* soul."

Morgan, listening to the mounting hysteria in his laughter, reached out sharply to check him before it broke the surface, and in one last fleeting instant saw again the impossible face that had looked at them through the doorway of another world. He saw it briefly, indescribably, unmistakably, in the lineaments of Bill's laughter.

Then he seized Bill's shoulder and shook him, and the laughter faded, and the likeness faded, too.

Heir Apparent

Harding stepped from the pier to the little submersible's deck and moved instantly into the shadow, black velvet on moon-white steel. He could hear nothing except water lapping softly, the distant thud and throb of machinery, and very far away, the hollow bellowing of riven air, either a jet plane passing over from Java, or a spaceship blasting off from one of the nearer islands. Phosphorescent waves rippled in the moon-track and the strong tropic stars regarded Earth dispassionately. On the deck there was no sound at all.

Harding glanced once at the white jagged dazzle that was Venus near the skyline. That diamond dot represented sixty-one thousand troubled human beings—if you could call them human—whose relations with the mother-planet had once been Edward Harding's responsibility. Or a seventh of his responsibility.

He shook his head at the bright world in the sky. He would have to get over the habit of regarding the heavens as a chart with a glittering pinhead for each planet, and so many thousand Thresholders, ex-Earth-born, bred for the ecology of alien worlds, pinned up there upon the black velvet back drop for study and control. It wasn't his problem any more. Forget the Thresholders on Mars and the Secessionists of Ganymede and the whole tangled, insoluble mess that confronted the Integration Teams. Think about this current job, which was very simple now. Harding moved quietly toward the open companionway. Either the submersible wasn't guarded at all, or Harding was expected.

He was expected.

The big man in the tiny cabin below sat back in his chair and looked up to meet Harding's gaze squarely, the china-blue eyes watchful but calm. Billy Turner was a Buddha, solidly fat, solidly placid, the heavy face turned to Harding with an oddly innocent look of surprise.

"Something?" Turner asked mildly.

"You could call it that," Harding said. "Lay off, or I'll have to kill you, Turner."

The fat man waited a minute, his gaze holding Harding's. Then he took the pipe out of his mouth, squinted at it, clucked a little and struck an old-fashioned kitchen match on the edge of the table. He sucked the flame downward into the bowl and exhaled a cloud of pungent violet smoke that smelled of the Martian deserts in full sunlight.

"Seems like I don't quite place you," he said calmly to Harding. "We met before?"

"We didn't need to," Harding said. "Wait a minute." He stood perfectly motionless by the table, listening, his eyes going unfocused with the completeness of his concentration. It was a totality almost machine-like, both more and less than human. Then he grinned a tight, confident grin and pulled out a chair, sat down across the table from Turner.

Harding was a strongly built man with an incongruously academic look about him in spite of his stained and somewhat ragged clothing. He looked younger than his real years, and he looked ageless.

"No crew aboard," he said to Turner confidently. "Just the one Kanaka up forward. No guard. But you were expecting me, Turner."

Turner blew out a cloud of aromatic smoke from a

tobacco that hadn't grown on Earth. His china-blue eyes were watchful and expectant.

"Today," Harding went on, "I was fired. Incompetence. I'm not incompetent to handle a radar fish-location unit. If I were, it wouldn't have taken the fishery a month to find it out. O.K. You assume I'll try for other jobs and lose them—through your interference. I'll end up combing beaches with a home-made Geiger counter, you figure. Then you'll buy me for whatever dirty job you have in mind. It's your usual method, they tell me. It generally works. It won't work with me, because I'm one man in the Archipelagic who could figure out a fool-proof way to kill you."

"Oh, you think so?" Turner asked, opening his blue eyes wide.

"You know what my job used to be," Harding said gently.

Turner blew out smoke, gazed thoughtfully at it.

"You were with an Integrator Team," he said.

Immediately, in the most curious way, Edward Harding's mind withdrew quietly into the middle of his head, pulling down blinds and closing doors as it went, receded along a lengthy corridor into the past that led by many closed episodes and half-forgotten things, until it came at the far end to a door. This was the door to a little square black-steel room called the Round Table. It was an entirely empty room, except for a tri-di screen, a chair and a table with a flat metal plate let into its surface.

Edward Harding in his mind's chamber sat down in the chair and put his palms flat on the plate. Instantly, as always, the tingling activation began. At first it was like wind under his hands, then water, then soft sand gently embedding his palms. He moved his fingers. Soundlessly his mind's image spoke. "Ready, boys. Come in."

Then in the chamber of memory the Composite Image moved slowly into being in the depths of the tri-di screen. Now the Round Table was open and the Integrator Team sat together at one table, no matter where the accident of their bodies placed them. Seven men made up the Team. Seven blended minds and bodies stood composite and whole in the screen of Harding's memory, as they stood perhaps at this very moment in the same screen, three thousand miles away before somebody else's watching face. Perhaps the Image spoke to somebody else as it had spoken to Edward Harding when he was . . . before he . . . well, in the old days. He wondered what the Image looked like now, with no Edward Harding in its make-up.

In the memory which Turner's careless words evoked, Edward Harding *was* in the make-up of the Composite Image. And as always, facing it anew, he looked for some trace of his own features in the blended synthesis of the seven Team-members. And as always, he failed.

Seven faces, seven minds—but you never could filter out the separate features of the men you knew so well. Always they blended into that one Image you knew even better than your own face in the mirror. The Round Table was open when you sat across the board from the Composite Image with the specialized knowledge of six other picked and long-trained Teammates literally at your fingertips, each man sitting in a chair like your own, each idly molding the test-pattern under his palms.

Doctor, lawyer, merchant, chief—biochemist, physicist, radio-astronomer—the needs of each Team met at the Round Table in the carefully chosen attributes of each member. And the needs could never have been fulfilled if all the men involved were actually in the same room, face to face. For knowledge had grown too complex. They talked a technical language made incomprehensible to one another by ultimate specialization. It took the Composite Image to integrate and co-ordinate the knowledge each member brought with the knowledge of each other member, and with the great Integrator itself.

But you could never find your own face in the Image, and you could never see the Image without your face blended into it. Harding thought of the Image as it had looked after George Mayall—left. By request. The first time the Team gathered at the Round Table with a new man in Mayall's place, how curiously flat and strange the intimate, composite features seemed with the new face incorporated. He had wondered then how Mayall felt, wherever he was, out in the cold, strange world after such a long time in the warm, intricately interlocking closeness of the Integration Team.

Well, Harding knew, now.

He thought as he had so often thought before, *What does it look like without me?* And he pictured the Composite Image cold and strange in the tri-di screen of the room no longer his, Doc Valley's face, and Joe Mall's, and the others, blending with the faces of strangers, linking with the minds of strangers, working on the old, complex, fascinating problems that weren't Edward Harding's any longer.

He slammed the door at the end of that long corridor of the mind, hauled his memory back past the shut doors and the closed episodes, and scowled into Turner's watching blue eyes.

"So let's get down to cases," Harding said harshly. "Make me an offer. I'm in a hurry. Six months from now, maybe you could pick me up off the beach and hire me for a bottle of gin. I won't wait. What are you driving at, Turner. Or would you rather I just killed you?"

Turner chuckled comfortably, his fat face quivering.

"Well, now," he said, "maybe we can arrange something. I'll tell you one thing that's been on my mind a while. I'm a busy man. I get around a lot. I got plenty of contacts. Been hearing about a fellow named George Mayall. You know him?"

Harding's hands closed on the table edge. His face went perfectly blank, like a clock's face, or a dynamo's. His eyes searched Turner's. Then he nodded.

"Mayall knows me," he said.

"I'll bet he does," Turner said, chuckling and quivering. "I'll just bet. Hates you like poison, doesn't he? He was on your Integrator Team and he got kicked off. *You* got him kicked off. Oh yes, Mayall knows you, all right. Like to get his hands on you, wouldn't he?" The chuckles broke into a thick laugh that made Turner shake like a heavy and solid jelly.

"Very funny," Harding said coldly. "What of it?"

The jelly subsided slowly.

"Thought I'd hire you to pilot me out to Akassi," Turner said, watching Harding. "Trouble is, I don't think you're ready yet."

"I'm no pilot," Harding said impatiently. "I don't know these waters."

"Ah," Turner said in a wise voice, cocking his head, "but you know the Integrator. You could get me past the barriers around Akassi. Nobody else in the world could do that."

"Barriers?"

"Acoustics, visual, UHF, scrambler," Turner said in a comfortable voice, sucking his pipe. "Playing dumb, are you? Never heard of Akassi, eh?"

"What about it?"

"Quiet place these days," Turner said. "Strong defensive system all around it. As if you hadn't heard. Ha. Nobody goes in, nobody goes out. You and I could go in and come out with more loot than this submersible would carry—or we could stay and play god, with your talents and training. Except for one little thing—George Mayall. He might not like it."

Harding's eyes dwelt steadily on the fat, calm face. He did not speak.

"Didn't know Mayall was out here?" Turner asked. "Never even heard a rumor?"

"Rumors, sure," Harding said, and thumped the table

with an impatient finger. "But not just where. Not this close. What are you getting at? What's Mayall up to?"

"In short, what's in it for you, eh?" Turner said. "Ah, that would be telling. Couldn't even guess, could you? What's likely to happen, when an Integrator man gets kicked off the Team?"

"He's given his choice of outside jobs, naturally," Harding said with some bitterness. "He doesn't stick with them." (How could a man stick with an outside job, once he had known the tight-knit interperceptivity of the Round Table? Membership in an Integrator Team is an experience which few men attain and none willingly forfeit. It is a tremendous psychic and emotional experience, the working out of a problem on the Round Table. Afterward, ordinary jobs are like watching two dimensional, gray television when you've got used to full-color tri-di images—) "A man doesn't stick," Harding said. "He drifts. He winds up in a fishery in the Archipelagic and then a trader with a lot of influence gets him fired. And won't tell a straight story afterward. Come on, Turner, let's have it."

"Don't like getting kicked out when you're on the receiving end, eh?" Turner said. "What did they throw you out for, Harding?"

Harding felt his face grow hot. He set his teeth and held his breath, trying to force the heat and the anger down. Turner watched him narrowly. After a moment he went on.

"Don't try to tell me," he said, "that it's bare coincidence brought you here, this close to Mayall. Don't say you haven't an idea what he's up to. You know more than I do, don't you, Harding?"

Harding struck the table hard.

"If you want something, say so!" he said. "If you don't, lay off and let me earn my living my own way. Coincidence? I haven't got any connection with Mayall any more. But I did once. We were picked for the same Team, and if you know what that means you won't think it's coincidence we drift the same way when we're free to drift. So we both wind up in the Archipelagic. What of it?"

"Mean to say you haven't been approached?" Turner asked keenly. "You've been out here this long and haven't heard a murmur from—anyone?"

"Murmur of what? Come to the point, Turner!"

Turner shook his head doubtfully. "Maybe they don't know about you. Maybe one Integrator man's all they needed. My good luck, anyhow. You mean the Secesh Thresholders haven't even tried to get to you?"

"Would I be here now if they had?" Harding asked reasonably. "Go on."

"Well, they got to Mayall. They set him up on Akassi with an islandful of machinery and he's feeding them all they need in Integration to organize a withdrawal from the empire. Big stuff. Now maybe you see how I could use you, if you were ready to throw in with me."

"I see," Harding remarked coldly, "how *I* could get to Akassi and take over Mayall's work and cash in on the Secessionist deal for just about as much money as an Integrator could count. But I don't see where *you* come in, Turner."

"Oh, Mayall works through me," Turner said, puffing blandly. "I've got my network spread out from the Celebes to the Solomons. The Archipelagic States couldn't hide a secret from me if their lives depended on it. Mayall needs outside contacts, and I'm the contacts." He rolled ponderously in his chair.

"Thing is," he went on, "maybe I feel it isn't enough, just being contact man. Maybe I want a bigger cut. Maybe that's why Mayall put a roof over Akassi, just in case somebody like me got my kind of ideas. I couldn't do a thing about it—without you. You know how his mind works. You know what screens he'd dope out. But without somebody like me, Harding, you'd never even find Akassi."

"I wouldn't? Don't be too sure."

"If you could, you'd have done it before now. Maybe

you haven't tried? Never mind. Mayall's no fool. He's dug humself a hole in the ocean and pulled Akassi in after him, if you want to look at it that way. The Secesh boys aren't paying him to set up an island the first stray radar beam could pick out blindfolded. Those barriers around Akassi—well, they erase Akassi, that's all. You can't see it. You can't find it. It isn't there—unless you work with Mayall and know his code. Even then you can't pass the barriers unless Mayall invites you." He puffed violet smoke and squinted through it at Harding's face.

"You ready to risk your neck yet, my boy?" he asked. "It'll take the two of us. But Mayall hates you. He'll kill you on sight. That means a risk on your part. I'll buy you higher than the bottle of gin it'd cost next January. I'd cut you in for half the take—if you get me ashore at Akassi and help me work out my scheme to take over from Mayall."

"You'll have to have something pretty good to kick Mayall out a second time," Harding said thoughtfully.

"Well now, I expect I will," the fat man agreed. He took the pipe from his mouth and narrowed his eyes at Harding. "Surprised?" he asked. "You don't look it."

"If you expect perfectly normal human reactions from me," Harding said quite gently, laying his palms flat on the table with a soft, reminiscent gesture, "you're the one who's in for a surprise. A man doesn't work ten years on an Integrator Team and stay entirely human. A gradual occupational mutation sets in. For example—" He looked up and grinned suddenly.

"For example, I know we've been under weigh for about three minutes now. There's no perceptible vibration and no roll, so how could I have guessed?"

Turner grunted, but the blue eyes gleamed.

"You tell me."

"I *am* the boat," Harding said, and laughed. There was no amusement in the laughter. "I've got a score of my own to settle—with society. All right, Turner. I'm with you. Where's the control room?"

* * *

That was the question.

From Pluto to Mercury its echoes ran. From the New Lands mankind was molding into fertile red soil out of the stuff of fire and ice, on worlds where no man could have lived before technology brought the elements of life, from all the new colonies on the new planets that question went echoing endlessly. *Where is the control room?*

The artificial Threshold Experiments that mold humanity into shapes which can live on alien worlds had done their part. Thresholders inhabited the planets and the empire of Earth spun in a tight network around its sun. Interstellar drive was on the way. Paragravity was already a little more than theoretical. The enormous complexities of science sprang in century-long leaps across time. An engineering process would drag with it a dozen allied fields frantically trying to catch up, a biological method that could enable men to survive interstellar trips shoved rivals impatiently out of its all-important path, hustled other sciences along with it.

The web from Earth had spun out, intricate and tangled, through the Solar System. Now it stretched tenuous threads toward the tremendous macrocosm of the stars, and the moment the first star was reached—Earth could fall.

It could fall as Rome fell, and for the same reason. The New Lands beyond the stratosphere grew, young and strong and integrated, but for century after century Earth had been the control room. The controls grew so complex that unification became an almost impossible task. Only by absolute unity, by a complete and bonded sense of solidarity, could the intricate socio-technological system of Earth stay below critical mass. And it couldn't stay there long.

For Earth had grown to be too small a planet. And the other planets were not ready yet to take up their burden. They brawled among themselves and they complained against Earth. They threatened secession. The isolationism of the New Lands became a menace that threatened the unity of the Solar Empire as Thresholders tugged angrily at the cords which bound them to the Earth from which they had sprung. And desperately in the meanwhile man strove for one major goal—sanity, rational thought, system, organization—integration.

This wasn't the best method, perhaps. But it was the best one they had.

The Integrators were amazing things, electronic thinking machines that could be operated efficiently only by teams of specially chosen, specially trained men who lived a specially planned life. When you lived a life like that, you were apt to mutate in unexpected ways. You didn't turn into a machine, exactly, of course. But the barrier between living, reacting man and nonliving, reacting machine broke down—a little.

Which is why Edward Harding could be the submersible boat he was guiding.

It didn't have isotopic mercury memory units, like a differential analyzer. It didn't trigger electric circuits that punched out stored information and analytical reasoning for Harding to read. But in a way it nevertheless remembered—

And Harding's instantaneous reaction-time sense made him perhaps the one pilot alive who could have guided the submersible through the strong defenses Mayall had flung out around his island.

"We through yet?" Turner asked, up on deck. Around him the blue Pacific lay glittering emptily under a flawless sky. There was a faintly unpleasant smell in the air which the trades couldn't dispel. Turner puffed strongly at his pipe, studying the empty horizon that wasn't really empty. His eyes strained to find some break, as though the sky could tear like a veil, rift from top to bottom and let the real world show through. Mayall's world, Mayall's miraculously camouflaged island, impossible to find in spite of its plain markings on the charts.

In the control room below deck, Harding sat perfectly relaxed in a cushioned chair, his arms slipped into elbow-length metal gauntlets that glistened like wet snakes. Before his eyes hung a transparent disk, shaded like a color wheel. Harding moved his head gently so that his gaze looked through this section and that of the special lens. Before him, vertical on the wall, was the cosmosphere, a great half-globe than ran and bled and fountained with shifting colors and patterns. Radar and sonar made up only part of the frequencies that were the living chart of the cosmosphere. It showed the heavens above, the waters around, the reefs below—and most of the time now, it lied.

Harding said, "We're not through yet. One more barrier—I think."

On deck, Turner puffed violet smoke at the bland blue sea.

"Afraid of Mayall?" he asked the microphone.

"Shut up a minute. Tricky here."

The false screen bled and flared, showing a clear, narrow passage through empty water. Harding moved his head around the varying shades of the lens, trying to find a frequency that checked accurately with another. Only this would keep the ship from sinking, this and the magnetic control panel.

Over the ordinary manual controls, a metal plate had been attached, corrugated and colored and marked into a pattern as dizzying as that which spun across the cosmosphere. But Harding knew it. He had used such controls with the Integrator. His gauntleted hands moved above the plate without touching it, while his glittering fingers played upon an invisible keyboard.

The varying magnetisms leaped a synapse from the ship across lines of force into the metal gauntlets, and Harding's own body-synapses snapped the messages instantly to his brain. His fingers responded as instantly on the keyless keyboard. And as his fingers moved, the ship moved, delicately, warily, perceptively, through wall after wall of frequency mirage where no ordinary compass or radar would operate sanely.

He was the ship.

"Afraid of Mayall?" he echoed Turner's question after a moment. "Maybe. I can't tell yet. I've got to find out something first. So it all depends."

"Find out something?" Turner sounded suspicious.

Harding cocked a sardonic eye at the round ear of the diaphragm. He said nothing. Presently Turner's voice came again. There was provocation in it.

"I've often wondered," he said, "why Mayall was kicked off the Team."

"Have you?" Harding asked in a noncommittal voice. He paused. After a while he said, "The important thing right now is that he blames me for it. So naturally, he hates me. He's afraid it could happen again. And it could. Oh yes, Mayall has the strongest reason in the world for hating me."

His tone grew thoughtful. "I'm a rival. I'm the heir apparent. And all he's got is Akassi. He'll be afraid of me. He'll try to kill me." Harding meditated upon this thought. "See anything up there?" he asked, after a moment.

"Nothing yet," Turner's voice came down thinly. "Sure he'll try to kill you. Wouldn't you, in his place?"

"I probably will anyhow. Try, I mean." Harding made the modification of his verb in a meticulous voice. "Akassi is—well, pretty tremendous. I hadn't actually realized it until now. These barriers are slightly phenomenal." He considered, then laughed shortly. "The defenses must be so complex that only something like this could have a chance. A direct, unexpected, outrageously simple attack. We'll have to—"

"Harding!" the diaphragm broke in with a sudden rasp. "Look! I can see the island!"

"Can you?" Harding asked dryly. There was a pause.

"It's gone," Turner said.

"Sure. And if we'd turned that way we'd be gone, too. Rocks. Wait."

The glittering gauntlets performed arpeggios in the air. "I think," Harding said, watching the cosmosphere, "I think we're through."

"We are," the voice from above said, more quietly now. "I can see the island again. Different now. I can see buildings beyond the hills there. And a spaceship, ready to take off. Take her in shore, Harding. Ground her on the beach. We've got a jet-stern, you know."

Harding had no idea what the beach looked like in a visual way, but the cosmosphere showed him all he needed to know of the strand he was approaching, the composition of the sand, what rocks lay under it, how far back the vegetation began. Under him the floor jolted upward as the ship's stern rose at a stiff slant, hesitated, grated motionless. A little shudder began in Harding's gauntleted hands and spread briefly through his body.

He took off the gauntlets.

He was no longer the ship.

He felt himself divide into two separate halves again, one flesh and blood, himself, the other mobile metal going inert as the life withdrew from it. For a rather horrible moment he wondered what it might be like some day if the machine he operated would not let him go. If the metal developed a taste for life, and the tool became the master.

"Harding?" Turner's voice called softly. "Come up. Better bring your gun."

Standing together at the rail, they scanned the peaceful, tree-fringed shore. Gentle green hills rolled upward inland a little way, and you could see rooftops over them, a high spider-web tower glittering against the sky, and farther back the unmistakable blunt, skyward pointing snout of a spaceship standing on its fins.

"It's quiet enough," Turner said, regarding a spider crab that scuttled across the sand, its eyestalks twiddling convulsively. "Have we sprung any traps yet?"

"No. I neutralized frequencies that would have

tipped Mayall off. But I doubt if we can get to the settlement without announcing ourselves."

"We may. Two men might have a chance where a small army wouldn't. Where's the best place to . . . to ring his bell?"

"Under the circumstances," Harding told him, "it's straight ahead, inland, toward those hills. Plenty of brush for cover here. The cosmosphere can't show everything, and Mayall's no fool—but spectral analysis showed that brush has had nonlethal frequencies used on it. There are microphone pickups, too, so—"

"So our trick ought to work, eh?" Turner said solemnly, tapping out his pipe over the rail. "You call out your code phrase and Mayall will hear it. Don't see how we can miss. Only, don't go getting any funny notions, my friend. You and I haven't got a chance unless we stick together. I can't help remembering you and Mayall worked together for a good many years. I keep wondering how a man feels, once he's kicked off an Integration-Team."

Harding laid his hands on the hot rail and slid the palms back and forth slowly. Then he tightened his grip so that every vibration of the boat carried up through his nerves to his responsive brain.

"A man misses it," he said dryly. "Come on. We're wasting time."

The frequency caught them in the middle of the brush field. They had been only partially prepared for this. From now on everything would have to be played out free-hand, on the spur of the moment. Turner, who had been walking ahead, flung up a warning arm. Harding felt the beginning tremor a moment before Turner did, and with desperate speed he sucked air deep into his lungs and let it out again in a shout that must have made the hidden microphones planted along the shore rattle in their clamps.

"Mayall!" he roared. *"Mayall!"* And then he added a phrase that had no meaning to Turner, a quick, glib

phrase which only an Integrator of Team Twelve-Wye-Lambda would know.

While he shouted, Harding let his muscles relax with a sort of frantic limpness, a lightning speed and control. Barely in time. The last syllables of his yell still hung in midair as he dropped into a crouch. The brush closed over his head and the vibration froze him motionless against the warm earth.

After that there was nothing but silence. The sky burned blue. The air hummed. His shouted words hung echoing in the stillness.

It seemed to Harding that he heard a sort of caught breath sough out of somewhere, hidden microphones catching the sound of it with a note of surprise. But Harding was almost instantly distracted by the urgent and immediate problem of Edward Harding, and the difficulty of staying alive.

First his eyes began to sting, because he couldn't blink. Almost immediately thereafter a frightening sensation of darkness and dizziness swept up from the brown earth and down from the clear blue sky, a shadow enfolding him from without which seemed to come hollowly and emptily from within at the same time.

He had stopped breathing.

That wasn't the worst, of course. The autonomic nervous system controls the heart, too. He hadn't anticipated this. The cosmoscope had revealed only nonlethal frequencies in this barrier field. Somehow it hadn't occurred to him that "non-lethal" is a comparative term. He felt his heart lurch heavily in his chest, aware of its nonmotion as he had never been fully aware of its beating. Doggedly for a long instant, while that caught breath of surprise from some hidden throat echoed in the microphones, and the shadow of darkness hovered, he crouched helpless under this paralyzing power.

Then out of a dozen separate little mouths, vibrating tinnily low down in the brush, a harsh, familiar voice called out.

"Harding?" it cried incredulously. "Harding, is it you? *Here?* Welcome to Akassi, Harding!" Sardonic menace sounded in the voice. It paused briefly and then rattled off a series of signal numbers that meant nothing to Harding. "I'm cutting the paralysis," Mayall's harsh voice said exultantly. "I don't want you to die—that fast."

Blood roared in Harding's ears. A sense of wide-opening distances lifted dizzily around him as the frequency-lock let go. The shadows from without and from within drew back, rose beyond the sky, sank deep into the earth, closed up like a black flower's petals and became a seed inside Harding again. Briefly and strangely he knew what death would be like, some day, Gigantic around him and tiny within him lay latent the enormous dark. Black seed within, black cloak without. When one swooped down to meet the other's swift unfolding, then the last hour would strike.

But not yet.

Someone was coming toward them through the brush. Crouched in hiding, Harding saw Turner's barrel-shaped bulk rise painfully to its full height directly between him and the approaching man. That was the plan, or part of it. He drew a deep breath, grateful anew for the air he breathed. The gun balanced delicately in his hand. He tightened his finger until it pressed cool metal hard. Then he was part of the gun. He couldn't miss.

He could still see nothing except Turner's back outlined against a clear sky, but he knew the familiar, harsh voice that spoke.

"Who are you? How did you—" There was a pause. Then, "Turner! It's Turner! I didn't send for you!"

Turner spoke quickly. "Hold on," he wheezed. "I know you didn't. Just let me get my breath back, will you? Near killed me!" He took a step sidewise and lurched heavily, rubbing his leg and swearing in a thick voice. Mayall turned automatically to face him, and now at last Harding saw his face.

It shocked him, somehow, to see that Mayall had grown a beard. He couldn't help wondering instantly, first of all, how the beard would show up in the Composite Image. If Mayall had a Team here—and he must have—would all those blended faces seem to wear it? Or would it be obliterated by the six other superimposed images?

Otherwise Mayall had not changed much. The hollow black eyes burned, under strong, meeting black brows. The gaunt body stooped forward. But Harding did not remember the eyes as quite so fiercely bright, or the mouth as quite so bitter and so violent. And the short, neatly clipped graying beard was a note of unfamiliarity that made Mayall somehow a complete stranger.

Turner muttered: "My leg's asleep," and bent to rub it, stumbling farther around so that he brought Mayall's back squarely toward the hidden Harding.

"Stand still," Mayall snapped. "You shouldn't have come. I'll have to kill you now, and I need you outside. Why did you do it, you infernal idiot?"

"Take it easy," Turner said, painfully straightening. Harding could see through the leaves the outline of the gun in his jacket pocket. From here it looked as if Mayall were quite unarmed. One hand held a microphone, the other hung empty. Mayall could order the paralysis turned on again whenever he chose, of course, but surely it would trap him in the same field if he did. Frowning, Harding waited.

"Now let me say my say before you fly off the handle," Turner was placating the bearded man. "Won't cost you anything to listen, will it? I—"

"Shut up," Mayall said, his voice sinking to a hoarse, angry whisper. "Nobody joins me. Nobody! A machine doesn't need assistants, you fool! You haven't anything to say that I want to hear. Wait."

He turned his head a little and Harding saw the thin

mouth tighten to a grimace that was half grin and half snarl of pure ferocity. Harding was aware of a sudden shock at the violence that gleamed through the smile, so near the surface of the man's mind it seemed to glare white-hot through his grimace. Mayall was not perhaps really insane—but he wasn't sane, either.

"Wait!" Mayall said, and his breath came suddenly loud in the clear, sunny silence. "You didn't come alone. I heard Harding's voice."

Turner let out his breath in a heavy sigh.

"All right, Harding," he said, keeping his eyes carefully away from the crouching man in the underbrush. "All right, let him have it. Shoot, man—shoot!"

Mayall said, "What?" and swung quickly around, raking the brush with eager glances in the wrong direction. The fat, swift hand on Turner's other side dropped toward the pocket where the gun lay.

"All right, Mayall," Turner said in a satisfied voice. "Stand still. We've got you now. Harding, shoot! Shoot!"

Harding stood up in the crackling brush, flicked his gun level and shot the revolver out of Turner's hand.

The bullet went cleanly through the fat man's wrist and whined into the brush beyond. Turner's thick fingers opened. His revolver fell spinning in the sunlight. There was an instant's total silence, broken only by the whispering sound of waves on the distant beach and the raucous scream of a bird somewhere inland, beyond the low hills. The wind brought a vagrant *thump-thump-thump* of machinery from the glitter of roofs half seen above the hill.

Slowly, slowly, Turner lifted his gaze to Harding's. He was gray-white with shock and disbelief, but as Harding met his eyes the whiteness vanished in a swift uprush of deep, angry red. Turner caught his breath and gabbled. There was no other word for it.

"Harding! Harding—I'm Turner! You've shot *me*! I hired you! What . . . why did you do it? *Why?*" His eyes darted to Mayall and back. "Is it a double cross? It can't be! You wouldn't dare! You know Mayall hates your guts!" His voice cracked. "Why, Harding, *why*?"

Mayall's laughter cut into the disorganized babble. His eyes burned like hot coals deep in the sockets of his skull. His face had the half-demented ferocity of a tiger's, grinning over bared teeth.

"Because he couldn't help it," he said. "Right, Harding? This is wonderful. I never expected this!" He glanced at the shaking Turner, gripping his bleeding wrist with the other hand and still gasping for breath in the depths of his shock.

"You chose the wrong tool, Turner. So you got tired of playing second fiddle, eh? Thought you'd hire an Integration man and take over, didn't you?" He laughed harshly. "There was one thing you didn't know. But—"

"Shoot him, Harding!" Turner cried, clutching his wrist tight and staring down at the welling blood. His hands were shaking like his voice, and a recurrent tremor ran over him so that his whole unwieldy body quivered like a large jelly. "Go on, shoot!"

Mayall laughed. "Go on, shoot!" he echoed in a mocking falsetto. "Go on, Ed. Why not shoot me?"

"You know why," Harding said.

"Why not?" Turner's voice was high with terror.

It was Mayall who answered him, with mocking politeness.

"You didn't know?" he demanded of the quivering fat man. "Hadn't you heard about the posthypnotic compulsions they jinx you with when you join an Integration Team? Didn't you know that no Team member can ever injure another Team member, no matter what his provocation is?"

Turner stared stupidly at the man. His jaw dropped a little.

"But"— he swung toward Harding— "You . . . you didn't tell me! You let me think . . . it's not true, is it, Harding? Go ahead and shoot, before he—"

"Go ahead, Harding, try!" Mayall's voice was ironic.

"Pull the trigger! Maybe you can do it. I'm not on the Team any more, remember?"

"Neither am I," Harding said gently.

A slow grin spread over Mayall's haggard face. His eyes burned.

"Kicked off too, eh?" he said, exultation in his voice. "That's good. That's wonderful! Kicked off just like me! How do you like it now, Ed? How does it feel?" The grin faded slowly. "A little bit lonely, maybe? You don't fit in anywhere?" His voice softened reminiscently. "You can't really think without an Integrator, you're an expert on an Integrator but you aren't allowed near one. You try joining lots of outfits. No good. What you want is the Team again, the chance to use your mind and your talents. You're lost without a Team."

Suddenly and harshly he laughed. "Well, I've got a Team!" he said. "My own. My own backers, my own Integrator. Everything you tried to take away from me when you got me kicked out. Now you know what it's like. Maybe you think I'll take you in. I'm not the fool you think, Harding. I know you! You have to be top dog or nothing. But you've made the last mistake of your life." He hefted the microphone and laughed his harsh, mirthless laugh.

"I've got the drop on you, even without a gun. You can't touch me, you fool. I see it in your stupid face. But I can kill you!"

Turner made an unsteady, bleating sound and swung round violently toward Harding, blood spattering from his wrist.

"It isn't true!" he said hysterically. "You can kill him if you try! Pull the trigger, Harding! This is suicide if you don't!"

Mayall showed his teeth. "That's right," he said. "But he can't do it. We were closer than brothers once. Cain and Abel." He laughed. "Any last words, Harding?" He lifted the microphone. "All I have to do is recite a series of numbers into this," he said. "It's automatic. The field reacts to the same group only once, in progressive series, so you needn't bother trying to memorize it. Then the frequency hits you both. I may let you die right now, or I may—"

"You won't do a thing," Harding said, smiling. "You can't, George. It would constitute an injury to me, and you can't do it."

Mayall flourished the mike, breathed gently into its black mouth. His eyes burned at Harding over the instrument. Everything was very still around them. Distant surf hissed upon sand, the brush rustled in a light breeze, machinery thudded like the beat of blood deep inside the arteries of the body, as if the island were alive. Three gulls sailing over on narrow wings turned curious heads sidewise to observe, yellow-eyed, the motionless men below. Beyond Mayall's bearded head the heaven-pointing muzzle of the spaceship loomed like a silver halo. Invisible above it hung Venus, blanked out by the blue dazzle of the day but swinging as if on tangible cord that linked it irrevocably to Akassi. Sixty-one thousand of the ex-Earthborn pinned high upon the chart of the heavens by a diamond pinhead waited, though they did not know it yet, the outcome of this conflict on Akassi.

"*I'm* free," Mayall said, holding the mike against his mouth. "I know when I hate a man. I can kill you whenever I choose."

"You said that before," Harding pointed out. "Go ahead."

"All I have to do is give the series into the mike," Mayall said.

"Yes. Go on. Do it."

Mayall drew an oddly unsteady breath and said into the microphone:

"Three-forty-seven-eighty . . . ah . . . eighty-two." He paused briefly. "Eighty-*five*," he corrected himself. And waited.

Nothing happened.

The brush rustled. The surf breathed against the shore. Mayall flushed angrily, gave Harding a quick, defensive glance, and said into the mike, "Cancel. Three-forty-seven-*seventy*-five—"

The breeze whispered among leaves. The distant throb beat like blood in their ears. But no shadow stooped out of the sky and no shiver in the air answered Mayall's command.

Turner laughed, a half-hysterical giggle. "So it's true" he said. "You can't!"

Mayall's face went dark with anger and a pulse began to throb heavily in his forehead. He shook the microphone, cursed the insensate macinery and stammered the numbers a third time into the diaphragm, stumbling twice as he spoke them.

For a timeless moment the three men stood motionless, waiting.

Then Turner laughed aloud and wheeled ponderously upon Harding. Ten feet of space separated them, and Harding had let his gun-hand drop—

The impact of the fat man's sudden onslaught caught him off guard and sent him staggering. The gun flew out of his hand as Turner's great, unstable bulk all but knocked him off his feet. They reeled together for an instant.

When they got their balance again Turner's huge forearm was locked across Harding's throat, blood from his wounded wrist trickled down Harding's shirt, and Turner's good hand pressed the point of a small, cold, very sharp knife against Harding's jugular.

The fat man was breathing hard.

"All right, Mayall," he said with a painful briskness, though his voice still shook. "My turn now. If this whole idea's a trick, let's find out about it! I don't know what you've got to gain by lying to me, but you can't kill me unless you kill Harding. Go ahead—turn on the paralysis again. But before you can give your signal, I can cut Harding's throat. Go on. What's stopping you?"

Mayall's face darkened terrifyingly with rage. The

grizzled beard jutted straight out with the set of his jaw, and the pulse at his temple throbbed.

"Don't tempt me, Turner!" he said in a grating whisper.

Turner laughed again. "Is it true?" he asked incredulously. "I almost think it is! I almost believe you've got to save Harding's life! All right, then." The knife-point pressed deeper. Harding felt the sharp twinge of breaking skin, and then a sticky trickling. "I'll kill him unless you do as I say."

"I wouldn't bet on it, Turner," Mayall said in a choked voice. "I—"

"I've got to bet on it," Turner wheezed past Harding's ear. "It's my one chance. I'm gambling for my life. And I'll win. You'd have turned on the paralysis by now if you dared. How do you walk through it, Mayall? No, never mind. I want to know first of all what this game is. No, Harding, don't move!"

He shook Harding a little. "I want some answers! Are you working in cahoots with Mayall? Why did you come here, if you knew you couldn't protect yourself from him? Unless you're working together, I don't see—"

Mayall made a sudden, involuntary gesture of rejection.

"You think I'd work with *him*? You think I could ever trust him again?"

"Shut up!" Turner said. "No—stop it, Mayall!" The knife-blade quivered at Harding's throat. Mayall paused rigidly, the microphone halfway to his lips, eyes on the knife as he struggled against almost unbearable compulsion.

The last thing Harding saw was Mayall's thin lips moving as he hissed into the diaphragm. Then darkness fell—total blindness, sudden and absolute.

For the second time in ten minutes Harding had a strong illusion of just having died. His first idea was that the knife at his throat had gone in, and this blindness was the first failure of the senses that presages total failure—but he could still hear. The surf still whispered on the far-off shore. Invisible gulls mewed overhead and Turner's wheezing breath caught with a gasp close to his ear.

He could still feel. Sunlight was warm on his cheek, and Turner's thick arm across his throat jerked with some sudden shock of astonishment. Turner grunted and the arm went a little slack.

Then all Harding's reactions snapped into instant alertness. Somehow Mayall had given him this one split-second chance to save himself if he could. Theoretically, he knew what had happened. Frequency juggling was a familiar trick, and phase-cancellation of vibration must have been the process Mayall's hiss into the mike set in motion. The frequencies of the visual spectrum were being cancelled now, by a broadcast of other frequencies in the right phase. But visual only, since he could feel the sun's infrared heat on his face. If Mayall had an infrared viewing apparatus handy Harding would be clearly visible now.

He worked it all out neatly in a corner of his mind while his body sprang almost of its own accord into this instant's hesitation that slowed Turner's reactions. Harding's right arm struck upward and outward inside the curve of Turner's arm as it held the knife to his throat. He felt the pressure of the blade cease, and Turner grunted heavily as Harding's elbow drove into the pit of his stomach. For an instant they struggled fiercely together in the blinding dark. Then Harding sprang free.

Brush crackled and heavy feet thudded rapidly on the ground, diminishing in distance as Turner, gasping for breath, blundered away through the dark. Harding stood still, breathing heavily, feeling sunlight warm on his face as he stared about in the intense and total blackness.

The very completeness of it told him one interesting fact—there must be a roof over the island. It was almost impossible to create darkness in the open air. In all probability some intangible dome of ionization hooded Akassi in, something that could be varied at will, used to reflect downward any frequency-beams aimed up, a simple matter of angle-of-incidence calculation you could work out in your head. Somewhere on the island a device was broadcasting a beam in the right frequency to cancel the vibrations of light blazing down from the hot, invisible tropic sky.

Mayall's voice spoke out of the darkness, after a long, reluctant pause.

"Are you all right, Ed?"

Harding laughed at the note of hope in the question. "Disappointed?" he asked.

Mayall's breath went out in a long sigh. "I hoped he'd get you. I did what I could, but I was praying for the knife to go in. At least, I can get Turner."

"Don't," Harding said with some urgency. "Let's have the light again, George. But don't kill Turner yet. I want to talk to you first. If he dies the whole espionage network he controls will fall apart, and we're going to need it. Do you hear me?"

The darkness went crimson before Harding's eyes, quivered, shredded and was gone. Day was blinding. He put up a hand to shield his eyes, seeing through his fingers Mayall's sardonic grin, the lips turned downward in a familiar inverted grimace.

"I hear you," he said. He lifted the microphone and spoke into it, his eyes still holding Harding's gaze. "Sector Twelve," he said into the mike. "Twelve? Mayall speaking. There's a fat man crossing the hills toward you. Kill him on sight." He lowered the mike and showed his teeth at Harding. "You've got maybe fifteen minutes to live," he said. "Just until I get my Team together and dope out a way to kill you. Maybe I can't beat the compulsion alone. But there are ways. I'll find one."

"You're cutting your own throat if you kill Turner."

"It's my throat," Mayall said. "I give the orders here.

He can't get away." Suddenly he laughed. "This island's a living thing, Harding. A reacting organism with sense organs of its own and an ionized skin over it. I've got surrogate sensory detectors all over the place. They can analyze anything on the island down to its metallic ions and transmit the impulses back to . . . to headquarters. I've set up an optimum norm, and any variation will put the whole island in motion. Turner's like a flea on a dog now. The island knows where he is every second."

"We're going to need him," Harding said.

"You're going to be dead. You won't be interested."

Harding laughed. "Never very practical, were you, George? You were always a bright boy, but you theorize too much. You need somebody on your Team like me. Only luck kept Turner from drilling you. Luck—and me. Look at you, standing there unarmed. What was the idea, coming out like that? The island might have been crawling with Turner's men."

Mayall grinned his wide, thin-lipped, inverted grimace.

"Ever have hallucinations, Ed?" he asked, his voice suddenly very soft. "Maybe that's the real reason they threw you off the Team. Ever hear voices out of nowhere? Look at me closely, Ed. Are you sure I'm real? Are you *sure*?"

For a moment longer the tall, gaunt, stooped figure stood there vividly outlined in the sun. Then Mayall smiled and—faded.

The trees showed through him. The silver bullet of the spaceship towered visible behind the ghost of George Mayall. The ghost went dim and vanished—

Mayall laughed softly and unpleasantly out of nowhere.

Harding was aware for a moment of a tight coldness at the pit of his stomach. It couldn't happen. It hadn't happened. He had dreamed the whole thing, or else—

"O.K., George," he said, trying to hide the sudden limpness of his relief. "I get it. Where are you, then?

Not far, I know. You can't project a tri-di image more than a hundred feet without a screen—or five hundred with relays. Let's stop playing games."

Low down in the brush Mayall laughed thinly all around him. Harding felt the hair creep on his scalp. It was not the laughter of a sane man.

"Start walking," Mayall said. "Toward the settlement over the hill. By the time you get there, I'll have a way figured out to kill you. Don't talk. I'll ask questions when I'm ready."

Harding turned in silence toward the gap in the hills.

From the hilltop he could see the settlement glinting in the sun. There was the square Integration Building with its familiar batteries of vanes on the roof, and the familiar tower thrusting a combing finger up against the sky. Long sheds lined the single street. There was a fringe of palm-leaf huts around the buildings, and farther off, over a couple of rolling green hills, the lofty tower of the spaceship balanced like a dancer on its hidden fins.

Still farther out were black rock cliffs, creaming surf and a lime-green sea with gulls wheeling over it. Brown figures briefly clad in bright colors moved here and there about the buildings, but Harding saw no sign of Mayall. Only the machinery thumping endlessly at mysterious tasks throbbed like the island's heart.

He started slowly downhill. A palm tree leaning stiffly forward over the path rustled, cleared its throat with a metallic rasp, and said:

"All right, Ed. First question. Why did they throw you off the Team?"

Harding jumped a little. "Where are you, George?"

"Where you won't find me. Never mind. Maybe I'm in my getaway ship, all set to take off for Venus. Maybe I'm right behind you. Answer my question."

"Rugged individualism," Harding said.

"That doesn't mean anything. Go on, explain yourself. And keep walking."

"I was kicked off," Harding said, "because I was so different from you. Exactly your opposite, as a matter of fact. You were the leader of the Team and you held the rest down to your level because you weren't adaptable—remember? It didn't show up because you *were* leader and set the pace. Only when a new man came in did your *status-quo* limitations show. The new man, in case you've forgotten, was I."

"I remember," the palm tree said coldly.

"You fizzled. I skyrocketed," Harding said. "I had too many boosters. They finally figured I was getting into abstract levels far beyond the Team, which is as bad as being too slow. So *I* was fired for undependable irrationality, which I prefer to think of as rugged individualism. Now you know."

Ten feet ahead a flowering shrub chuckled.

"That's very funny. *You* were the stupid, unadaptable ones—you and the rest. You couldn't realize I was simply developing along a new line, a different path toward the same goal. I wasn't lagging behind. I was forging ahead of you. Look around you. This island's the living proof. You kicked me into a pretty unpleasant gutter and I pulled myself up by myself. Not easily. I built a living island here. You can have six feet of it, and that's all."

The bush sighed. "I've dreamed of killing you," it said, rustling gently. "But I'd have left you alone if you'd stayed out of my way. I've never forgotten, though. And I'm going to get even, when the time comes—with you, and the rest of the Team, and Earth. And Earth!"

Harding whistled softly. "So that's the way it is," he said to the empty air.

The moss underfoot said bitterly: "That's the way it is. I don't care what happens to Earth now. Earth's overreached itself. Let it blow up. It and its Teams. I'll throw a shield around Venus that no power in the solar system can crack."

"Maybe that's your trouble, George," Harding told

the moss. "You think in terms of shields that can't be cracked. Sooner or later the pressure from within may force a crack. Growth can't be stopped. That was what went wrong on Team Twelve-Wye-Lambda, remember?"

The moss was silent.

"Anyhow, it checks," Harding went on, trudging downhill. "Central Integration when I . . . ah . . . left the Team, was sending out dope-sheets on an enormously complex plan under way on Venus. That would be you, George. Stuff too complex to figure out and counter without a lot of work among the Teams linked up in units. Obviously the Secessionists had themselves an Integrator at last. It didn't take a Round Table session to find out who they'd subsidized."

The moss laughed.

"It was a mistake to let me go," it said. "Do you want to know the real reason? It's the reason why no Integrator that Earth ever sets up can control Venus. The basic logic's wrong. Their key principles are based on Venus being a social satellite of Earth—and the balance has shifted. *I've* shifted it, Ed. Venus is no protectorate planet any more. That's Apollonian logic. Not a single Integrator on Earth is based on the Faustian viewpoint, which in this case is perfectly simple—Venus is the center of the new Empire!"

"You think so?" Harding murmured.

"I made it so! Every single premise the Earth Integrators base on a . . . a geocentric society has got to turn out wrong. Or multiordinal, anyhow—valid only as long as the truth of Earth's power is maintained. I stopped believing in the old truth-concepts of the Earth Empire—and they threw me off the Team.

"But right here on Akassi is the only Integrator that works from the basic assumption that Venus is the System's center."

"All right," Harding said calmly. "Maybe I agree with you."

"No," an airy whisper said above the whisper and

rustle of a red-flowering vine that hung across the path. "Not necessarily. How do I know you've really been kicked off the Team? How do I know you're not a Trojan horse?"

"There isn't much you can be sure of, is there?" Harding asked. "Your Team here can't be very efficient. You've forgotten basic psych. Why do you suppose you've dreamed of killing me?"

"Prescience," the vine said quietly.

"Displacement," Harding told it. "Who would you be wanting to kill? It couldn't be—yourself?"

Silence.

"What kind of a Team have you got, anyhow?" Harding asked after a moment. "If it can't answer a simple question like that, it can't be worth much. Maybe you need me, George, even more than I need you."

"Maybe I haven't got a Team," the vine said behind him, in a die-away voice as the distance lengthened between them.

"You'd be a maniac if you hadn't," Harding told the empty air flatly. "You've got to have a Team, if you're operating an Integrator. One man couldn't keep up with it. You need a minimum of seven to balance against a machine like that. You have a Team, all right, but an incompetent one. I'll tell you exactly what you're got—either discarded misfits or untrained men. That's all there is available. And it isn't good enough. You need me."

"You're not wanted here," a clump of bamboo said hissingly, rubbing its fronds together. "If my backers had needed another Integration man, they'd have got in touch with you. I'm all they need."

Harding laughed. "Thought of a way yet to kill me?"

The bamboo did not reply. But presently a patch of gravel hissed underfoot and said, "Go down into the village. There'll be a door open in the Integration Building." And a lizard that looked curiously down at him from the top of a flat stone appeared to add in Mayall's voice, "Maybe I've found a way—"

Harding pushed the heavy door wider and looked into the green-shadowed room. Sunlight filtering through leaves outside its broad windows made the dim air seem to flicker. Frond-shaped shadows moved restlessly upon banked controls which were the nerve-endings of the island.

In the center of the web George Mayall sat, his sunken eyes glittering, grinning above his beard at the door.

Harding stood still just inside the door and drew a long, deep breath. The smell of the room, oil and steel, the feel of it around him, the faint throb that traveled from the floor up his body and blended with the beating of his heart, made him a complete man again as he had not been for a long time now. He stood in the presence of the Integrator. He *was* the Integrator.

He closed his eyes for a moment When he opened them again he saw that Mayall's sardonic grin had widened and drawn down at the corners.

Harding nodded. "Alone?" he asked.

"What do you think?" Mayall said, and his glance flickered once toward the inner door at his elbow—the door without a knob, but a flat plate inset where the lock should be. Harding could see through the steel panels as if they were glass, because he knew so well what the little black-walled room inside looked like, with its tri-di screen and its table and its chair.

"You've been here all along?" Harding asked. *"Are you here now?"*

Mayall only grinned. Harding took out a cigarette, lit it, inhaled smoke. He strolled forward casually toward the inner door, glancing around the big room as he crossed it. A control room is seldom as spectacular as the operational devices it controls. Most of the equipment looked familiar. It was what lay out of sight that interested Harding most. For this was only the antechamber to the Integrator.

"That's far enough," Mayall said after a moment. Harding stood still, the smoke from his cigarette wreathing ahead of him toward the man behind the control desk. Mayall swung his hand edge-on, chopped through a swirl of smoke. His grin turned down farther at the corners.

"I'm real," he said. "Don't bother with smoke tests. Clever, aren't you? Stand still, Harding. Don't come any farther. I've got one more question to ask you and then—well, we'll see."

"Fire away," Harding said, looking at the door with the plate in it.

"Second question, then," Mayall said. "Second and last. Just what did you hope to accomplish by coming here?"

Harding blew smoke at him. "It could be almost anything, couldn't it?" he said. "Maybe I came to ask *you* a question. Could you guess what it is? Or would you rather I didn't speak at all?"

Mayall regarded him with narrowed eyes, burning black in hollow sockets.

"Go on," he said after a pause.

Harding nodded. "I thought you'd say that. Maybe you've been expecting somebody with—a question. Put it like this. You say all Integration has to fail that doesn't figure Venus as the center of the social system. Right?"

"I said that," Mayall agreed cautiously. "What's your question?"

"Why Venus?" Harding inquired.

"What?"

"You're not stupid. You heard me. *Why Venus?*"

Mayall licked his lips suddenly, with a quick, flickering motion, and glanced once at the big TV screen on the wall, nervously, as if the blank screen might be watching him.

"There are other Thresholders," Harding went on.

"You just pointed out that if your backers had needed another Integration man they'd have got in touch with me. Well, maybe somebody did. Not necessarily your boys, but—somebody." He blew more smoke. "Shall I go on?"

Mayall did not speak a word, but after a second he nodded jerkily.

"What you've got here is priceless," Harding said. "The group you back has a chance to win independence from Earth. So I just wondered . . . now, you take Ganymede, for instance. A flourishing little colony they've got up there. Doing a lot of exporting these days. A very rewarding business. Plenty of money in it. What would you say, George, to setting up a little problem in the Integrator to see if you could figure Ganymede as a social center?"

Mayall did not move for a long moment. Then he drew a shaken breath.

"I don't believe you," he said. "You're lying. You're trying to trick me."

Harding shrugged.

Mayall leaned forward over the control desk.

"What proof have you got?" he demanded, his voice hoarse.

Harding threw back his head and laughed. Then he took one final deep pull at his cigarette, threw it to the floor, ground it out under his toe.

"All right, Mayall," he said crisply. "You can step down now. I'm taking over."

Mayall jerked back in his chair, startled and incredulous. His tongue came out again and touched his lip lightly.

"Like hell you are," he said. "You can't throw a scare into—"

"Shut up!" Harding snapped. "Get on your feet, George. I mean it! Out of that chair and open the door for me. I've played it your way till now. But I know all I need to know. I'm a lot smarter than you ever were. I *can* take over, and I'm doing it. And you can't do a thing to stop me. You *can't* kill me! So I'm giving you one last chance—to join *me*."

"You . . . you're insane!" Mayall said, in a stunned voice. "This is *my* island. I know every nerve-center on it. My men could—"

"Could do everything but injure me," Harding said, and stepped forward briskly. "So you lose. Let's put it to the test now. I'm tired of talking. You had your fun, and you've told me enough so I know who'll win this little game."

"You're crazy!" Mayall cried, scraping his chair back. "I'll have my boys kill you! I . . . I'll send you off the island. I—"

"No you won't," Harding told him, rounding the corner of the desk. "Because you aren't sure. Maybe I've got that proof from Ganymede right here in my pocket. You want to bet I haven't? We'll call your Team together and see what—"

"Oh no you don't!" Mayall shouted, his voice shaking. "You'll never see my Team!"

"Afraid I'll get you kicked off this one, too?" Harding asked ironically. "Up! Out of that chair, George. You're going to work the trick lock on that door over there and open up your Round Table. Oh yes, you are. Then you'll call your Team together and we'll make a few trial runs. You needn't worry, George. You're perfectly safe. You and I couldn't hurt each other if our lives depended on it—and maybe they do. It doesn't make a bit of difference. Open the door."

"You'll never get that door open," Mayall said, stepping backward.

Harding snorted impatiently.

"Here, get out of my way," he said. "What kind of a code have you set it for? I haven't time to argue about it."

He ran his hand experimentally over the surface of the metal plate set where the lock should be. Between plate and palm he felt the varying pressures slide soft and rippling. There was something familiar about the pattern of the pressure. It could hardly be the old cipher, the original team-code that had opened the doors to seven Round Tables, far away in time and space. It could hardly be that, and yet—

The door swung gently open under Harding's palm.

Mayall jerked around, his breath rasping with surprise.

"Who told you my code?"

Harding fowned at him. "It's the old code. Didn't you realize that?"

"You're crazy. It can't be. I made it up, arbitrarily. Why should I have used the old code?"

"You've been fighting yourself all down the line, haven't you?" Harding said, and stepped through into the little black-steel room.

Mayall stumbled after him, stammering protests. "It can't be! You're crazy! You found it out—somehow."

Wearily Harding said over his shoulder: "You must have flunked basic psych, George. It's the old cipher, but it unlocks a different door now, no matter what your unconscious had on its mind when it set up Twelve-Wye-Lambda's key. *That* door will never open again for you. Or me. This one will have to do, and it's good enough for me. Now let's have a look at your Team. Who are they, George? Where are they?"

Mayall laughed, a high whinny of mirthlessness.

"You'll never know. I'll kill you first."

Harding snorted. "Think so? You're welcome to try."

"You can't get to my Team!" Mayall shouted. "They . . . they're all on Venus. They're—"

Harding swung round and regarded the excited man with a sudden, quickened surprise. "Don't talk like a fool, George. Of course they're not on Venus. What's the matter with you?"

"They *are* on Venus!" Mayall cried. "That's it! And if you call them together to talk about Ganymede—you know what they'll do, don't you? So you can't do it, Ed! You can't!"

Harding turned around completely and looked at Mayall with a frown between his brows.

"What's wrong with you, George? I think you really are a little crazy. Are you *jealous*, George? Is that it?" He laughed suddenly. "Maybe I've got something there. You think you *are* the Integrator, is that the trouble? Well, George, my friend, I may not be able to kill you even if my life depends on it, but—*I can dismantle your Integrator!* How would you like that?"

Mayall drew a whistling between his teeth. He stepped backward into the open doorway, leaned to grope toward his desk, his sunken eyes not moving from Harding's. Then he let the breath out in a sigh and straightened. There was sweat on his face and he was breathing hard.

"Stand back, Ed," he said grimly. "Get away from that table. Now I can do it! Now I know I can kill you!"

Harding looked down into the black eye of the pistol trained upon his middle. He lifted his gaze to meet Mayall's murderous stare.

"Go ahead," he said. "Try."

Sweat trickled down Mayall's forehead. His beard jutted. Ridges of tendon began to stand out on the back of his gun hand. But the crooked finger inside the trigger guard didn't move at all. He lowered his head, staring at the gun. Then he brought his left hand forward to grip his right in reinforcement. Both hands were shaking badly.

"Threshold reactions happen inside the body," Harding said. "What good will that do?"

Mayall's breath whistled through his teeth more sharply than before. He looked up at Harding, a white, frantic glare. Suddenly he closed his eyes, squeezing the lids shut. Panting, he tried to pull the trigger.

His gun hand quivered—quivered and began to swerve. Slowly it moved until the gun muzzle pointed beyond Harding, toward the wall.

Now the gun cracked, six times, six sharp explosions

that blended into one. Mayall's eyes stayed shut. His gun hand dropped.

"I did it," he said in a whisper. "I've killed you. I—"

Slowly he opened his eyes and looked into Harding's. Then his gaze went farther, resting upon the six silvery star-shaped holes in the black wall.

Harding shook his head gently. He turned his back upon the man in the doorway, dismissing him. He pulled out the chair that faced the tri-di screen and sank into it.

Then the chamber of memory slid softly over to superimpose upon this real chamber. The little square black-steel room was suddenly a part of Harding, as close and warm as the domed walls that shielded his living brain.

He laid his palms flat on the metal plate.

At first it was like wind under his hands, then water, then soft sand gently embedding his palms. Soundlessly he spoke. "Ready, boys," he said. "Come in."

"You can't do it, Ed," Mayall said behind him. "You can't—"

In the outer room a sudden crash sounded. A sudden voice shouted with a wheeze in it, "Mayall! Harding! Do you hear me? Turner speaking! Mayall, answer me!"

Harding twisted in his chair, glancing up with a startled face to meet Mayall's eyes. Mayall swung up his empty gun and spun too, toward the door. The antechamber was empty, but Turner's harsh breathing filled it with sound. And on the wall-screen Turner's sweating, unstable face glared blankly at the unoccupied room.

"Mayall!" the fat man shouted. "I know you're there! Step out where I can see you, or I'll blow the whole island sky-high!"

Harding said softly, with derision in his whisper, "So Turner couldn't get away, eh? Just like a flea on a dog—you know where he is every minute. Oh, sure. Now what? Is he bluffing?"

"Harding! Mayall!" Turner's voice made the antechamber echo. "I know you're there. I saw you both go into the Integration Building. I'll blow up Akassi and everything on it unless you do as I say! I mean it! I'll give you a ten-count, starting now. One. Two. Harding, do you hear me?"

"All right, Turner," Harding called, not stirring from his chair. "This is Harding. What do you want?"

The wheezing voice sighed with relief.

"Step out where I can watch you, Harding. Mayall, too. I—"

"Where are you?" Harding interrupted. "You're bluffing."

"I'm at the relay station on the hill. There's a lake south of me and I can see the village. I can see the Integration Building from here, and the door to it, Harding. I'll blow you up! I mean it!"

"You couldn't blow anybody up," Harding said, and moved his fingers urgently on the table. In a whisper he urged the tri-di screen, "Come in, boys! Come in!"

"It's no good, Harding," Mayall said, also in a whisper. "I told you. You can't work it. Nobody can but me. And I won't. You'll never see my Team!"

"Listen to me, Harding!" Turner's voice insisted from the antechamber. "Step out here and look. You'll see! I've got a UHF beam pinpointed and focused right in the middle of the fuel tanks of the spaceship. You know what ultrasonics can do, Harding?"

"I know," Harding said flatly. "If that spaceship blows, you go with it. Or do you mind?"

"How long would I live if I'm caught?" Turner asked logically. "Now do as I tell you, or—"

"It's a bluff," Harding said laconically, aloud, and bent over the table, his palms molding the test-pattern with frantic speed. *"Come in, come in, boys!"* he cried in an urgent whisper.

Mayall laughed sardonically and very softly at his shoulder.

"It's not a bluff!" Turner shouted, his voice thick.

"Look here! I broke into the relay station. I got the beam up fast through the hot frequency into UHF—so fast the fuel didn't have time to blow. Then I pinpointed it right in the middle of the tanks. I've got my hand on the lever. As long as I hold it there, O.K. But if I let go, or if I'm killed—what happens?" Triumph wheezed in the fat man's voice. "The beam runs down the scale. On the way it hits the hot frequency. In the fuel tank! I can drop it to hot as fast as I can move my hand. Now, am I bluffing?"

"You'll never do it," Harding called. "I don't believe you."

Turner was silent for a hard-breathing moment. Then he shouted suddenly:

"I've got it! You'll *have* to do as I say! Harding, are you listening? You can take the chance with your own life if you want to—*but can you take it with Mayall's*? He's in there—I saw him go in. Mayall, do you hear me? You've got to do as I say or Harding will die with everyone else on Akassi! Come out, Mayall! Harding, come out! I mean it. I'll finish the ten-count and then the whole island goes. Three . . . four—"

Harding met Mayall's eyes. He shrugged reluctantly.

"He's got us," he whispered. "Unless—" Suddenly he shoved back the chair and jumped to his feet, laughing in soft triumph. "Unless *you* call together the Team, George! Maybe I can't, but you can and you've got to . . . to save my life! Here, sit down and get at it, quick!"

For an instant longer Mayall only stared at him, blank-faced. Then—

"All right!" the bearded man snapped. "I will!" His manner changed abruptly and completely. Faced with a threat he could counter, his mental indecisiveness vanished in a breath. He flung himself into the chair and slapped both hands down hard on the plate.

"Seven . . . eight—" Turner called from the screen. "Harding, you've got about three seconds left to live. Step out here, or—"

"Go on, step out," Mayall said softly over his shoulder, his voice crisp with new decision. "I've got an idea."

"Oh, no," Harding whispered. "I want to see your Team. I'm going to—"

"You're going to die if you don't! He isn't bluffing. Listen, now! Go out and keep him quiet while I figure out an answer with my Team. You haven't any choice, Ed! *My* life depends on it, too!" He flashed a sardonic glance upward. "Look, Ed—tell him I'm dead. Tell him you killed me. Otherwise he'll insist I come out too, and I can't. Go on, quick!"

"Nine—" Turner called. "Harding, are you listening? On the count of ten the whole island blows. Mayall, do you hear? I'll—"

"Hold on, Turner," Harding said laconically, and stepped out of the door into full view. "Mayall can't hear you. He can't hear anything. I . . . I've just killed him."

Turner glared down at him from the wall. His fat face was scratched and trickling with blood from the underbrush he had run through. His clothing was torn and he had tied up his wounded wrist with a soaked rag. His good hand rested above his head on a poised lever. He was leaning heavily upon the face of the TV screen, so that he seemed to rest against empty air in the wall above Harding. Beyond him, through a window, a blue lake twinkled, and a road wound down through thickets, among trees and valley to reappear as the village street. Harding could see the image of the Integration Building clearly, with its open door. He had a moment's dreadful impulse to step to the door and wave at himself.

"Dead?" Turner repeated, and sighed gustily. "I thought . . . I thought you couldn't kill him."

"So did I," Harding said dryly, with a glance at Mayall through the inner door. "Up to the last minute. Then I had to. You can relax now, Turner. Mayall's dead.

There's just two of us now, and we'd be fools not to work together."

Turner laughed.

"I trusted you once," he said. "Come out of the Integration Building and walk north. Head for the relay station. You'll spot it when you get to the top of the hill. We'll talk a lot better when I'm pointing a gun at your belly."

"Everybody keeps pointing guns at my belly," Harding said mildly. "I'll develop a stigmatic target if this goes on. Relax. I could blow up the island too, if I felt like it. This building's the control center for the whole setup, and I know practically every gismo here. Wait a minute, Turner. I want a cigarette." He turned his back to the screen, searching upon the desk top as if for matches. "Mayall, get busy!" he whispered, rolling his eyes sidewise. "What's the delay for? Call your Team!"

"Harding," Turner said from the wall. "Turn around here. I don't trust you. Come out of that door and start walking north. I mean it!" His fat hand quivered on the lever.

"All right," Harding said. "Take it easy. Can't I light a cigarette first?" He cupped a match in his hands, and in their shelter looked anxiously at Mayall. The bearded man had taken his hands off the Round Table plate and was scribbling busily in large letters on a pad.

"No time for the Team," he whispered. "Look—read this." He held it up. Harding blew smoke and scanned the lines of writing. He nodded very slightly, turned to face Turner on the screen.

"Relax," he said. "I'm on my way. Just take it easy—we need each other now. I'll play along with you."

"Have you got any choice?" Turner demanded angrily.

"Maybe not. Any last instructions? Because after I leave this building we can't talk. I'll be beyond reach of any TV screens."

"Get going, that's all. If I don't see you before I count to—"

"Hold on!" Harding said. "I've got some . . . some stairs to climb before I reach the door. This room is two flights underground. I'll be outside in about twenty seconds. Don't be rash!"

"Twenty seconds, then," Turner said. "I'm starting to count now."

Instantly Harding turned away and stepped toward the inner door, outside the range of the screen.

Mayall moved ahead of him, on tiptoe, every gesture precise and accurate now that he had a definite job to do. But Harding didn't like the suggestion of a satisfied smirk half hidden by his beard.

"Mark time!" Mayall said urgently. *"Mark time!"*

He had swung open a section of the wall, revealing within, between parted chain mail curtains, a little cubicle hung with glittering, swinging mesh from floor to ceiling. A shove sent Harding staggering into the shining tent. The curtains closed behind him. Mayall's whisper sounded disembodied from outside.

"Mark time—but stay in the same place. Like a treadmill." A switch clicked loudly somewhere behind the curtain. "You're on. He can see your image. Start moving, Ed."

Suddenly, without having moved a step, Harding found himself facing the village street. In perfect reflection upon the swinging walls around him he saw dusty roads patterned with sun and shadow, the sheds across the way, the Integration Building looming behind him, its door swinging open. Then the street swung smoothly from right to left before him, lay out straight toward the vanishing point between two distant hills. It was exactly as if he and not the street had turned.

"Mark time, you fool!"

Harding belatedly began to walk, swinging his arms a little, moving his feet, almost taken in by the illusion of what he saw around him. It seemed strange that the breeze which made the leaves move soundlessly did not ripple his own hair.

To all intents and purposes he was actually outdoors, walking at a leisurely pace toward the hills beyond which the spaceship towered. Overhead was the clear sky and the sun. Around him, stereoscopic and in perfect perspective, lay the village. Again the images swung dizzily and he was facing in a new direction as the path turned itself under his feet, sliding backward below him at the rate of a man's normal walk.

"Don't stop for a second," Mayall's voice said from the other side of that unreal curtain which looked like the airy distances between Harding and the hills. "Keep walking, and keep in the path. Your image is being projected outside—like a mirage. Turner's watching you. It's a moving mirage. Your image is being moved forward across the island at a slow rate of speed, but you've got to keep your feet treadmilling or Turner may get suspicious. Can you see your way?"

"Just as if I were outside," Harding said, marking time. "Is it all right to talk?"

"For a few minutes, yes. You're still too far away for him to see your lips move, and I've got the sound cut. I've set the projection for straight on down the road and over the two hills to the relay station. It'll take care of itself now as long as you guide your course so you don't seem to be walking in the air or through the houses."

"Nice work," Harding said admiringly. "I've seen something like this done before, but only under restricted lab conditions. How do you do it?"

"Wouldn't you like to know?" Mayall said mockingly. "This whole island *is* a lab. Or a theater. All I need is a specially sensitized frequency beam reflected down from the ionized island roof, to serve as light-sensitive cells. I've got projecting devices, carrier and receiver, two sets of them, one for you here inside and one for the outdoor illusions. Two-way visual projection, plus a mobile unit, chiefly a series of relay zoom lenses. But the details are my business, naturally. All you need to know is that you'll keep marking time with your feet for about ten minutes before your projected image comes within clear sight of Turner, and he comes in sight of you—exactly as if you really were walking through the village. Only, this way I can keep my eye on you."

"Get busy, then," Harding urged the blue hills before him. "Make it fast. Turner *will* use that hot sonic once he finds out he's being tricked."

"I'm calling the Team now—"

Harding turned sharply toward the sound of the voice. His steps on the sliding road faltered. He glanced back at the curtains through which he had entered, meditating possible action.

"Don't you do it!" Mayall's sharp voice snapped, as if the hills had spoken. "I'm watching you. You can't do a thing but stay put and keep walking. If you step out of line, we both die. Remember, my life depends on you!" He laughed. "The Team's coming in now. Don't strain your ears. You won't hear a thing. I've got that sound cut."

"You may not need the Team," Harding said, trudging in one spot doggedly. "Why not order the spaceship to take off? Then Turner can't—"

"On no. That's my insurance. Without it, I'm immobilized. Besides, it wouldn't work—you see why, don't you?"

Harding nodded. Of course he saw. The usual slow-starting take-off would give Turner time to keep his beam focused on the fuel tanks while he exploded them, and a top-speed take-off, never used on Earth, would blast the entire village. Space flight, to be safe, was a job for boosters initially, and that inevitable, fatal slowness was the final wall of the trap in which Turner had caught them. But—

"Phase?" Harding suggested.

"That's the only out," Mayall said flatly.

* * *

"It'll take a good Team."

"I've got one."

Harding was silent, turning over possibilities in his mind, marking time briskly as the dusty way glided under his feet. Tension was tightening in him. He wanted to start running. But he was trapped in a squirrel-cage helplessness that kept him immobilized while Mayall hatched schemes with his mysterious Team in Round Table session. Who could guess what murky plans moved in that strange, unstable mind?

The visual mirage around Harding was perfect. So perfect the impulse to test the nearest tree with a questing finger was almost irresistible. Was he really indoors? Halfway he disbelieved it. Only the ghostly silence of the world he walked through attested to its unreality.

The fringes of the village slipped away behind him. Now he was climbing the first hill, remembering to bend forward a little as the ground seemed to rise steeply before him. The domed relay station where Turner waited dropped below the hilltop and vanished for a moment. Until he reached the rise of ground ahead, he would be hidden from Turner. But that did no good. If he didn't reappear on schedule at the hilltop, Turner would certainly suspect a trick. And if he did suspect, he was very likely to act. A man with a bullet through his wrist is apt to be impulsive.

The spaceship would blow, and the island with it. Or at least, a good part of the surface of the island, along with whatever life forms happened to be there at the time.

Phase. Phase was the answer. Harding kept walking automatically across the grassy rise, tilting his body forward to compensate for the slant. No, he needn't bother yet with that. Turner couldn't see him. He stopped walking. There was no need. Eerily, the landscape still moved backward around him at a walking pace. Once, a little while ago, he had crossed this island's hills and talked to its trees, hearing the leaves reply in Mayall's bitter voice. Now he glided in utter silence where sight was the least reliable of the senses.

He looked ahead, deep into the illusion, estimating the distance to the rise. The landscape flowed by around him. Tentatively he reached for the curtains upon which all this unreality unrolled itself. His hand touched woven metal, invisible in midair. He waited, listening. No sound came from Mayall. If he were really able to see into the cubicle, he was not looking now. He sat at his Round Table, facing the Composite Image of his Team.

Moving swiftly, Harding stepped backward on the gliding path and slipped out between the curtains of sunny air. The shadowy control room lurched violently underfoot as the slanting hillside seemed to give place to level floor. On the wall, visible at an angle, the TV screen from which Turner had spoken still showed a foreshortened and flattened relay chamber, and Turner's broad back leaning toward the window that opened in its far wall.

Turner's hand was on the lever. He was stretching to watch the village, the path along which Harding's illusion moved leisurely. His intentness as he stared at the hilltop was so compelling that Harding himself could not be sure his own image would not in the next moment come strolling into view.

Soundlessly, hugging the wall to stay outside the TV screen's range in case Turner should glance back, he slid toward the door of the Round Table room. It was closed. Quietly he laid his hand flat on the lock plate. The vibrations rippled softly under his palm, but he did not manipulate the code of the lock. He put his ear to the panels instead, listening. He could hear only an inarticulate murmuring from inside.

He dared not interrupt.

Absolute concentration would be necessary to work out the phase method that could counter Turner's threat. Phase. He had used it himself, getting through the barriers around the island. But this was a more precarious matter—the sending out of a frequency from another relay station that could cancel Turner's was easy enough, but timing was another matter. When the UHF started slipping down the spectrum, the other frequency would have to slip down too, at exactly the same pace, so that the phase cancellation would operate while Turner's beam passed through the dangerous hot band which would explode the ship's fuel unless the controller beam nullified it.

Only an Integration Team was capable of the enormous concentration that could ensure perfect co-ordination with Turner. It called for faster than instant perception and reactivity. And Harding thought it extremely doubtful whether many Integrator Teams could manage it. Only the best, the ones who had worked together for years, developed a Composite Image that was an absolute projection and synthesis—and what was Mayall's Team like?

Turner in the TV screen shifted his feet noisily on the floor, exhaled an impatient breath. Harding glanced up, alarmed. Clearly it was time for his projected image to come over the top of the hill. Past time, perhaps. Turner's hand was quivering on the lever already.

Harding flattened himself to the wall once more and slid back rapidly toward his cubicle. Just before he ducked inside he measured the distance between the probable inner wall of the Round Table room and the room where the metal curtains hung. They were side by side, sharing a single wall. Bullets would pierce that wall.

There was no time to waste now. Harding slipped between mesh hangings that swayed like the curtains of reality, blue sky and green grass shivering, warping space, settling again into the illusion of a solid world. The ground glided past fluidly under him. Bending forward as if against a steep slope, Harding began to mark time again as the top of the hill slid level with his feet.

He began to descend the hill. Now he could see the

domed building again, and the lake below. He thought of Turner, a white shape dimly visible at a window under the dome, letting out a loud wheeze of relief as his image came into view. The disorienting sense of doubled projections everywhere made Harding's head swim when he tried to think.

"Harding?" The blue lake seemed to speak in Mayall's voice as Harding's path carried him smoothly down toward the shore. "Everything all right?"

"So far," Harding said, moving his feet dutifully as the path skirted the water's edge. "How are you doing?"

"I think we're getting it," Mayall said, apparently out of the rushes around which soundless water lapped.

"You'd better," Harding said, thinking grimly that if they didn't, this ghost of himself might go on gliding for years to come over the desolate island, always supposing the projective equipment survived, by some miracle. Or no—no, the man himself had to stand here before the ghost could walk.

"Harding," the rushes said, half hesitantly, "we've got a few minutes. I want to talk to you. Suppose we succeed. I've got a paralysis beam set upon Turner now. The moment we cancel his hot sonic, the paralysis goes on. Turner's a dead man already, as far as his chances go. But afterward . . . Ed, what about this Ganymede deal? Have you got *proof*?"

Harding chuckled.

"Do you take me for a fool? Once Turner dies, do you think I don't know the next question you'll put to your Team? *'How can I force myself to kill Harding?'* Maybe it's set up already, just waiting until they're free. They'll give you an answer, too—if we survive. If they're good enough to cancel Turner's beam, they'll be good enough to tell you how to get rid of me. If I die, George, you'll never know the truth about Ganymede."

The rushes were silent. The whole ghostly world was silent, for the distance of a dozen paces. Harding trudged on around the edge of the phantom lake under a phantom of sunlit sky. At the top of the next rise stood the phantom of a domed building where a phantom Turner waited to recognize a phantom.

"Ed, tell me the truth," a phantom of Mayall's voice said out of air. "Are you from the Ganymedans?"

"Why not ask your Team?" Harding mocked him. "Maybe I was lying. Maybe I'm just a washed-out Team member trying to muscle in on your racket."

"Or maybe you *weren't* washed-out," Mayall said. "Maybe the Team sent you to stop me, because they couldn't stop me any other way."

"That would be a joke, wouldn't it?" Harding said, chuckling. "Building up Integrators and Teams to such a pitch of complexity they cancel each other, and we have to go right back to the old prehistoric days of man against man, unarmed—without even weapons against each other, George! Because we can't hurt each other with *any* weapons. Yes, that would be very funny—if it were true."

"Is it true?"

"Ask your Team," Harding said again cheerfully. "There's another possibility you may not have thought about. What if Venus sent me, George?"

"Venus?" Mayall echoed in a startled voice.

"They might have. They may have been waiting and watching for just such a man as me, George. They snapped you up when you were bounced off the Team. O.K. Maybe they snapped me up, too. I've never *said* I wasn't approached, have I?"

"But why?" Mayall's voice was bewildered.

"Lots of reasons. Maybe they were curious to know if you'd sell them out when a better offer came along." Harding chuckled again. "Well, they'd know the answer to that, wouldn't they, once I got in touch with *my* backers again?"

"You won't leave this island," the green hillslope said grimly. "Ever."

"One of us won't. That's sure. But maybe you'll be the boy who stays. Do you really wonder why Venus might want you kicked off this Team too, George?

Maybe for the same reason Twelve-Wye-Lambda had to. What disqualified you for one Team might disqualify you for another. Might? It would!"

"There's no reason—" Mayall sounded a little choked.

"There's every reason. Why is it Venus hasn't made any offensive moves against Earth for . . . how long has it been now? . . . six months? Eight? All Venus does is counter Earth's aggressions—successfully, but defensively. Only defensively. Things are settling down to a *status quo*—another Hundred Years' War. I wonder why?"

"Why?" Mayall asked harshly.

"Because the top brass always hates for a war to end. And you're top brass as long as Venus depends on your Integrator. Why, you've put up such defenses yourself nobody could get in to stop you, until I came along. Maybe for a long time now your backers have wanted to change things on Akassi. But how could they? They've set up a Frankenstein's monster.

"Did you pick out an incompetent Team on purpose, George? One you could boss around the way you bossed Twelve-Wye-Lambda until I came along? Or have you got 'em drugged or hypnotized? It looks like a draw between Earth and Venus, infinitely prolonged, because Earth's too vitiated to expand and reconquer, and Venus just isn't asking any questions.

"That's what wins any fight, George—asking questions. That's what progress and growth is. Not answering questions so much as asking 'em. And it's the one thing a thinking-machine can't do."

"I suppose you know all the answers, Ed," Mayall said coldly. "I suppose—"

"Nobody knows all the answers. Nobody can. The only way a machine could know them all would be to draw a circle and destroy everything outside it, everything it couldn't handle. And that's what you're doing, George. You're not *using* your Team or your Integrator or yourself. The one thing nobody wants is *status quo* right now. Only a machine's at optimum at *status quo*—and you're a *status quo* man from away back, George. It's why they threw you off our Team. It's why Venus *might* have sent me to Akassi."

The landscape unrolled silently when Harding's voice ceased. Mayall said nothing. The lake wheeled away behind and the pathway, straightening itself ahead, swung the whole island around with it until the domed station where Turner sat waiting lay directly before Harding, at the top of the nearing hill.

He grew tense as the time drew out and still Mayall did not speak. What was happening behind that illusory veil upon which the world reflected itself? Whatever was happening, it couldn't go on much longer. Already Harding could see the thick white shape of Turner leaning at the window eagerly, watching him—watching his illusion—toil up the steep hillside toward the dome.

Something was going on. In the square, small room on the other side of the wall, where Mayall sat at a table before a tri-di screen, something was certainly moving to a climax. It had to. Because in another two or three minutes Harding was going to reach the door of the relay station—no, not Harding, but Harding's phantom. Just how convincing it looked Harding had no way to guess, but sooner or later the limits of illusion would have to be reached, and then—

Then Turner would pull the lever and the whole game would be canceled on Akassi.

Now Turner was leaning over the windowsill, waving to the oncoming ghost. Harding could see his quivering, fat face with the blood streaks on it. He saw the mouth open and knew Turner must be shouting to him. But since this illusion of Akassi was silent, he didn't know what Turner was saying. It might be a command to halt. It might be an invitation to come in. It might be a question upon whose answer all the lives on Akassi depended. But he could not answer if he could not hear.

He said, "George!" in an urgent undertone, pitching

his voice low because of the irrational feeling that Turner *must* hear him if he spoke aloud. He was so near now—he was looking up at the fat man in the window from so close he could see the sweat beading the heavy face. The closed door of the relay station rose up within a hundred feet of him, and he was nearing it with every step.

When he got there, what would happen? His hand was solid and the door *looked* solid, but the width of the island lay between them, and once the unreeling illusion swept him irresistibly into contact with the door, Turner would see the truth.

"George!" Harding said again, his eyes meeting Turner's eyes.

From the other side of the illusion, he heard the hillside laugh—

It was Mayall's voice, and it did not speak a word, but the laughter was a freezing sound.

Between one step and the next, Harding knew the truth.

He stopped dead still, stunned for an instant by the knowledge of what was happening in the black steel room—what had already happened, while he plodded blind and lost through the mirage.

He should have known when Mayall first spoke a few moments ago, after the long silence of concentration upon the Composite Image and its problem. Mayall would not have broken silence *before* the problem was solved.

That meant the Team already knew its answer to the question of Turner. And that meant the Team was free to give Mayall the second answer upon which his life depended. He must already have asked that final question, and the Integrator must be answering it in this very moment. *"How can I kill Ed Harding?"*

No wonder the hillside laughed at him.

Smoothly the pathway swept backward beneath his unmoving feet. Smoothly the ghost of the domed building glided toward him. At its window Turner leaned, staring down anxiously. Harding made his feet move, striving for illusion to the last. For the fat man's hand quivered on the lever. He sensed something wrong, though he did not yet see what.

"George!" Harding said desperately, putting up a hand to hide his mouth so that Turner would not realize the ghost's lips moved soundlessly. "Look, George! I'm almost there. Are you watching?"

The hillside laughed again, the same chilling sound.

Of course Mayall would make no move—yet. There were still several seconds left, and as long as Turner stayed alive, Harding was trapped in his little treadmill of mirage. He dared not break the illusion while Turner could still be held by the last slow-running moments of it. But while Harding plodded in his trap the Integrator gave Mayall the answer that was all he needed to extinguish Harding forever.

"George!" Harding shouted suddenly and desperately. "George, look" And with frantic resolution he snatched the revolver out of its holster at his side.

The hillside gave its freezing laugh again. "You can't shoot me," Akassi said to Harding. "All I need is half a minute more, and—"

"I'm not trying to shoot you," Harding said, taking careful aim. "George, if you aren't watching we're all dead! George—I'm going to fire at Turner!"

The ghost of Turner shouted soundlessly in its window just over Harding's head. To that ghost, the man and the gun below looked desperately real. Turner lurched backward clumsily, mouthing shouts that made no sound.

The fat hand tightened on the lever.

The lever moved.

"George!"

"All right!" Mayall snarled from the other side of the hill. The air began to fill with a strange, thin singing sound too far above the threshold of hearing to impinge except as a stinging and tickling in the ears.

But Harding knew what it was. The Team and the Integrator, working as one tight-welded unit, were bending every iota of their blending efforts to cancel Turner's UHF as it slid down the spectrum toward explosion. It would take full concentration from Mayall and his Team and his Integrator—for a few seconds.

In those few seconds, Harding had to act.

He thought, *If I can ever kill him, the time is now!*

He saw through the window just above him the deadly lever dropping under Turner's hand. While the united Team rode the beam downward invisibly Harding was safe—and only that long. Then their full concentrated attention would go back to the problem of Harding's death.

The mirage was vividly real before him—but he knew it for a mirage. He knew that where open hills and a lime-green sea seemed to stretch before him in the sun there was really only a mesh curtain, and beyond that a steel wall which bullets could pierce, and beyond that—George Mayall.

He swung his gun around toward the spot on the wall where he knew Mayall would be sitting. Even if Mayall were watching him now, he couldn't move from that spot. He had to focus his full attention upon the screen and the Integrator. If Harding *could* fire, then the game was his.

If he could fire.

Until this moment he had not consciously tried to kill Mayall. He knew the strength of the compulsion that forbade him to shoot, and he had not wanted to build up defeat-patterns until he made his final effort. But it was now or never.

He thought. *I can fire a gun at nothing. And there's nothing in front of me. Nothing but empty air. The bullet will clear the corner of the relay station and go out over that hill and drop into the ocean when it's spent. There is no mesh in front of me. There is no wall. There is no George Mayall. I'm shooting into midair—*

The revolver was a part of himself, an extension of

his outstretched arm. The new synapse waited to be bridged between the crook of his finger and the smooth, cool trigger it pressed. He *was* the gun.

The gun responded as his arm responded to conditioned reflex. The gun felt pain.

Sensory hallucination is an old story. The gun had symbiotic life that was one with the gunner's, and how real is psychogenic pain? Harding knew this sharp, increasing burn was purely imaginary. But it hurt. Moving backward from the muzzle, the pain burned through the steel and the hand, up his arm, contracting the muscles until the pistol wavered. He was suddenly frightened. The symbiosis was terrifyingly complete. *Could he let go when the time came?*

He made one desperate, determined effort to squeeze the trigger. And all his muscles locked. For an instant absolute rigidity held him. And for that instant he fought hard against the frightening illusion that the awareness he had projected into the gun had been seized by the gun. The tool seized the man, merged with him, might never let him go.

Then every muscle from the shoulder down went limp. The arm dropped helpless to his side. He couldn't do it. He couldn't shoot Mayall. He was conscious at the moment only of relief.

Above him in the window he saw Turner at the lever go suddenly rigid. Paralysis had struck him motionless in the middle of a gesture as the Team moved in. He saw the back of the man's thick neck go red with congestion as the breath stopped in his frozen lungs. That meant the UHF was now dropping and the Team with it, in full, fast action. Within the next few seconds they would succeed—or fail. If they failed, probably Harding would never know it. If they succeeded, then Mayall would get his answer to that other question in a matter of minutes.

There might still be one chance for Harding. If he could hear the answer—

His rebellious arm was perfectly obedient when he sent the impulse downward to holster the gun. Rubbing the numbness from his muscles, he whirled in the illusion of the sunshine and tore the universe apart like a painted veil.

Blue air and lime-colored sea separated to let him through.

On the wall of the control room the TV screen showed Turner still rigid, back to the screen, his neck purple now. He was probably quite dead already.

Walking fast, Harding crossed the room, laid his hand on the lock plate of the inner door. He watched the door slide open.

Then he stepped into the little, dark-walled metal room, and the conflict ended as it had begun, with an image on a screen.

Mayall sat with his back to the door, leaning forward over the table, his hands flat on the plate. He was staring hard at the tri-di screen, and out of it the Composite Image of himself and his tools looked back.

It was beautiful and terrible—and the answer.

It was something Harding could not believe, and yet it came as no surprise, for given George Mayall as Harding knew him, what other answer could there have been but this?

The Integration Team was complete—seven thinking brains and the Integrator. But George Mayall was the only human being on the Team. The Composite Image glittering before him on the screen blended his outlines and theirs, merged his mind with their minds. But the six minds that met with Mayall at the Round Table on Akassi were machines. And Harding knew vividly the danger of machines.

Six mechanical brains, stored with knowledge out of human brains. But not humans themselves. Not beings who could ask questions or demand accountings from the one living human on the Team.

No one man had ever before controlled an Integrator single-handed, single-minded. No one man had ever dared try. And no sane man could do it. George Mayall had tried, and in his way succeeded. But his success was a failure more terrifying than any defeat could be.

Perhaps the most terrible thing of all was his attempt to create a Round Table with his seven mechanical storehouses of human knowledge. It would have been bad enough had he simply stored the knowledge away on tapes and drums. Even then it would be fearfully dangerous to draw upon it blind-folded, as he had to, because one man's mind can hold only so much, and it takes seven minds at least to balance an Integrator. Not seven storage drums of recorded fact, but seven human minds, alive, active, perpetually posing questions and arriving at flexible decisions as no mechanical brain has ever yet learned to do.

The mechanical brain *must* be balanced by human minds, or spin out of control. Or else it must draw a circle at the limits of arbitrary control, and destroy all growth outside the circle.

Out of the tri-di screen an Image looked back at Harding which made his mind go numb. It was the most beautiful thing he had ever seen. He hated it more than anything he had ever seen.

The Image had no face, and it had no eyes. But Mayall's burning black gaze looked out of it—somehow, impossibly—blended with the glittering masks of the machines in a synthesis so perfect no watcher could decode that total linkage. Seven component parts made up the Image. It glittered, it was smooth and shining, its fine, functional lines and perfect proportions made it a thing of unthinkable beauty. But you could not separate what of that Image was human and what was machine. The steel was one part flesh, the flesh six parts steel.

A man cannot blend and merge with machines and remain sane. Nor should the machine look back at its watcher out of human eyes, with rage and terror showing in lines of passionless steel. If it were possible for a machine to be mad from too close a contact with humanity, then these machines were as mad as the man who had forced them into the impossible unity of the Composite Image.

But the machines had their revenge. They had seized the man.

It was this Image which guided the lives and fortunes of sixty-one thousand humans upon Venus, and threatened the Solar Empire.

Out of the Composite Image George Mayall looked despairingly at Harding, trapped and desperate in his inchoate prison of steel. The man in the flesh sat three feet away from Harding, but the man in the Image was the real George Mayall. And Mayall *was* the machine.

Drowned, lost, hopeless in the steely beauty of the Image, Mayall's face looked back at Harding out of the bright, burning, multiple mask of the machines. There was helpless terror in the look, and a desperate appeal.

For Mayall had set up upon Akassi too strong a Team. He had laid out his defenses too well. And no one could break through to rescue him from the monster he had made and merged with. Mayall was the ultimate secessionist. He had seceded from the race of man.

Not now nor ever could Harding allow himself to injure a man who had once shared a Composite Image with him. But he lifted his revolver with a steady hand. It was no injury he was about to do Mayall now. Not any more. The time was long gone when death would be injury to George Mayall.

"I meant to tell you, George," Harding said to the Image in the screen, "why I'm here and who sent me. But it doesn't matter now, does it?" He centered the pistol upon the back of Mayall's head in the chair before him. *That* wasn't Mayall any more. Harding spoke only to the composite thing in the screen. "It makes no difference at all who sent me. It only matters that I'm here, and that I should win. And that you should die, George. This was what you wanted, wasn't it?"

He *was* the gun. The trigger pressed backward of its own accord.

On the screen, steel suddenly shattered outward and blood gushed over the hard, bright face of the metal Image and spread down the metal breast.

The screen began to dim. The fading face upon it was all steel now.

When the last trace of humanity melted from the metal, and the last trace of the Image from the screen, Harding put his gun back in the holster. He had been in time, then. Mayall was merely the first.

He closed his mind to that terrifying thought, that inevitable possibility. It might not happen. It might never happen, as long as men were willing to accept defeat rather than win conquests at a cost which all mankind must pay.

Man is a rational animal that can ask questions, and fail, and go on again from failure. But Mayall had come close to creating a machine which could not fail. It could maintain optimum—an eternal, functional, inhuman optimum, guarding its charmed circle with perfectly adaptive defense against all attacks from men—as long as men lasted.

No, surely it was impossible. That blinding, beautiful foreshadowing upon the screen had been a promise and a threat, but fulfillment must never happen. Now or ever. Harding would have a job of destruction to do—dismantling of the robots, so the Integrator might function normally, harnessed and guided by a human Team which he could get from . . . no, that didn't matter. All that mattered was this.

Harding lifted his hand and touched his forehead gently. There the real Integrator lay. Once, a very long time ago, premen in the days of their unreason carried under their skulls brain-mechanisms of potentially great capacity. But at first they did not use them. Not until—something unknown—happened, and the flame of reason kindled in the waiting Integrator of the human brain. *Homo sapiens*—

Machina—?

Harding shook his head angrily. He turned toward the door, but on the threshold he paused to look back once, doubtfully, at the empty screen that was like a closed door on the wall.

"Rich in character, background and incident—unusually absorbing and moving."

Publishers Weekly

"This is an exciting future-dream with real characters, a believable mythos and, what's more important, an excellent readable story."

Frank Herbert

The *"haunting, rich and tender novel"** of a unique healer and her strange ordeal.

**Robert Silverberg*

A Dell Book $2.25 (11729-1)

At your local bookstore or use this handy coupon for ordering:

Dell | **DELL BOOKS** DREAMSNAKE $2.25 (11729-1)
P.O. BOX 1000, PINEBROOK, N.J. 07058

Please send me the above title. I am enclosing $__________
(please add 35¢ per copy to cover postage and handling). Send check or money order—no cash or C.O.D.'s. Please allow up to 8 weeks for shipment.

Mr/Mrs/Miss__________

Address__________

City__________ State/Zip__________